Lorna Cook is the author of the Kindle #1 bestseller *The Forgotten Village*. It was her debut novel and the recipient of the Romantic Novelists' Association Joan Hessayon Award for New Writers. Lorna lives in coastal South East England with her husband, daughters and a Staffy named Socks. A former journalist and publicist, she owns more cookery books than one woman should, but barely gets time to cook.

Also by Lorna Cook

The Forgotten Village
The Forbidden Promise

LORNA COOK

The Girl from the Island

avon.

Published by AVON
A division of HarperCollins*Publishers* Ltd
1 London Bridge Street
London SE1 9GF

www.harpercollins.co.uk

HarperCollins*Publishers*
1st Floor, Watermarque Building, Ringsend Road
Dublin 4, Ireland

A Paperback Original 2021

1

First published in Great Britain by HarperCollins*Publishers* 2021

A catalogue copy of this book is available from the British Library.

ISBN: 978-0-00-837906-3

Typeset in Minion Pro by Palimpsest Book Production Ltd,
Falkirk, Stirlingshire
Printed and bound in UK by CPI Group (UK) Ltd, Croydon CR0 4YY

MIX
Paper from
responsible sources
FSC® C007454

This book is produced from independently certified FSC™ paper
to ensure responsible forest management.

For more information visit: www.harpercollins.co.uk/green

This book is dedicated to all Channel Islanders who endured the Nazi Occupation, to Jews who were transported, to those Islanders who bravely resisted and to those who were arrested, transported and who never returned.

And for Sarah.
Best friend, godmother extraordinaire
and chief purveyor of twists.

Prologue

Guernsey, Channel Islands
1945

There is a fine line between love and hate. She had tried not to cross that line, invisible as it was, but since the Germans came, she knew she had. She stood in the harbour of St Peter Port, and looked up at the town, the shops and hotels along the waterfront, the small houses nestled together in the distance. Only a few months after the liberation of her island, she breathed in the cool air of the place she'd always called home. It looked so different now but so much was the same, since the Nazis came. Since the Nazis left.

She passed along the harbour. The swastikas were gone, along with the occupying force that had placed them there. The street signs – crude wooden structures, made to inform the Germans where things were in their own language – had been taken down. At first glance, it was almost as if the war had never happened on this small stretch of the British Isles, almost as if the Germans had never been here. Except of course they had. And what they had left behind were the enormous concrete fortifications – grey scars on the landscape – that stark reminder that the Channel Islands had been part of Hitler's Atlantic wall, part of his island madness. But what the Nazis had left behind could never compare to what they had taken.

Passengers were disembarking from a ferryboat, tourists mostly, tentatively setting foot back in the Channel Islands; back for its famous sand, its enviable sun. She was pleased the Channel Islands once again might be seen as a glorious holiday destination, the memory of what had passed in the war bleached away with the sunshine. But that wasn't what she saw. She wondered how long it would be before she could see it that way again – how long before she would forget.

There were some things she would never forget, such as the power of a letter. Such an innocent thing, a piece of paper, but it held so much power.

Others had written similar letters; she knew that. She'd heard whispers that during the Occupation the island's post office workers had steamed open envelopes addressed to the Germans, knowing full well that what was inside would condemn someone: a note that there was a radio hidden under floorboards here, a gun stashed in an attic there.

The power a letter held, the damage it could do. No, she knew she would never forget that.

Chapter 1

Guernsey, Spring 2016

The short flight hadn't been long enough to drink the miniature bottle of warm wine bought when the drinks service had eventually reached her at the back of the plane. Lucy had only drunk half of it by the time the captain told crew to prepare the cabin for landing, so she screwed the lid back on the bottle and put it inside her bag. She'd see her older sister Clara in a matter of minutes; she might need to save the remaining half for that ordeal.

It was only an hour in the air from London, but Guernsey felt a whole lifetime away. Perhaps that's what being far from home did to you after years away – gave you a false sense of time and distance. It had been too long; she knew that. But there'd always been a valid reason why she couldn't return, and on the occasions she had it had only ever been for a night, and then she'd always had to go back to the mainland the next day. Lucy thought back. Perhaps it had been three years, maybe four, since she'd been to Guernsey. Her niece's christening – that was the last time she'd been back. And before that it was Clara's wedding a few years prior. Although she'd seen them all when they'd come across visiting her on the mainland.

Only official events that came with expectant invitations attached had the power to draw Lucy back to Guernsey. But now, the reason to return was merely logistical: a funeral to arrange for an elderly relative Lucy barely remembered and an uninhabited house to sell. No matter how hard she thought back to family events over years gone by, memories would barely surface of her elderly first cousin once removed: Dido. Of course, Dido hadn't been elderly when Lucy had been young, but she had always seemed it.

Once the upcoming funeral was over, Lucy, for once, wouldn't be leaving in less than twenty-four hours. Clara had instructed Lucy to stay and hear the will read, help Clara sort out Dido's affairs and get the house ready to go on the market on behalf of their father, Dido's nearest relation, who would inherit the bulk of the estate. Then, and only then, according to Clara, was Lucy permitted to get off the island and return to the mainland.

Lucy's mum and dad had hotfooted it to warmer climes last year, after retirement. They'd bought a house in Barbados, and kissed goodbye to the Channel Island where they'd lived their whole lives, which did rather leave Lucy and Clara to fend for themselves in this matter. When Lucy had joked to Clara that in their early thirties they weren't adult enough to plan a funeral, Clara had replied, 'Speak for yourself,' and that had been an end to it.

The plane banked and Lucy glimpsed the island's imposing, concrete fortifications on the coast before the runway came into view. To the uninitiated, the winding borders of grey concrete wall installed by Hitler's war machine all those years ago must offer a surreal first glimpse of the Guernsey coastline. To Lucy, while it hadn't always *felt* like home, especially recently, it had always *been* home.

'Have you been waiting long?' Lucy asked as Clara stepped forward to embrace her in the arrivals terminal. The sisters looked relatively alike. Brunette, brown eyes.

'No, not long,' her older sister replied, glancing down at Lucy's holdall. 'Is that all you've brought? One bag?'

'Yes. I'm not staying long, I don't think. And you've got a

4

washing machine so I can just . . .' Lucy stopped as she watched Clara's look of horror.

'Are you staying with me?' Clara asked.

Lucy paused, unsure if her sister was joking. 'Am I not staying with you then?'

'Well, you didn't ask if you could,' Clara said as they left the terminal and walked into the bright sunshine towards the car park. 'So I assumed you weren't. I assumed you'd made other arrangements. A hotel or . . . something.'

How had it become like this between them? Not too long ago Clara would have thrown open her doors for Lucy but now . . .

'I'm a freelancer, not a millionaire,' Lucy started and then: 'But it's fine honestly, I'll book into a hotel.'

'No, I'm not saying that,' Clara was quick to cut in. 'Stay for a couple of days first to spend some time with your niece and then after that it might be easier if you find somewhere.'

Lucy smiled to herself and held her tongue, silently congratulating Clara on having won a game Lucy hadn't even known they were playing.

'Molly misses you,' Clara continued in a softer tone. 'She's excited to cook you dinner. She's just learnt to make fajitas at school and we've had them three nights on the trot. Tonight will be the fourth.'

'I miss her too,' Lucy said as Clara drove the car barely five minutes through the country lanes and down into the little winding valley in the Forest parish. And then: 'Dido's house?' she asked as they passed crumbling plinths that should have held a wrought-iron gate. It was no longer on its hinges but placed upright inside the boundary. A sign that told visitors the name of the house – Deux Tourelles – was also no longer on the plinth but propped up against the front of it.

'How long has it been since you were here at the house?' Clara asked as she pulled up in the long gravel driveway, littered with weeds.

'Not for years.'

The house was part French country house, part Georgian manor. At either end were tall turrets from which the house got its name. The double-fronted bay window frames were peeling paint horribly and layers of thick green ivy had blanketed over the grey brick frontage on one side. It looked rather pretty. In autumn it would turn a russet colour and for a reason she couldn't pinpoint that comforted Lucy.

'God, I hate ivy, don't you?' Clara asked. 'It's just the worst kind of weed. I don't know what possesses people to grow it.'

Lucy smothered a laugh. 'Why are we here?'

'The undertaker needs a nice outfit in which to dress Dido.'

Lucy turned cold. 'What was she wearing when she died? Can't she just wear that?'

'She died in her sleep. She was wearing a nightie.'

'And it's not all right to bury someone in their nightie?'

Clara adopted a horrified expression. 'No, it bloody isn't,' she replied, battling with the key until the lock gave way and the door yielded to the pressure, swinging open slowly. 'Someone needs to grease these hinges,' Clara said absent-mindedly.

A strong smell of damp and dust penetrated Lucy's senses and it took her a minute or two to adjust to the smell of the old property. Inside the blinds and shutters were closed, but early evening sunshine fell through the doorway onto a circular wooden table in the middle of the hall. An oversized, empty vase cast droplets of sunlight like a prism, offering a bewitching effect. Clara switched on the overhead light and the prism was gone. The empty vase was the only ornament in the entrance hall but a stack of mail had been placed on the central table. Nosily, Lucy picked it up but there was nothing of interest as she rifled through, just circulars, bills and parish newsletters.

Glancing into the two front rooms that led off either side of the hall, Lucy saw they looked equally sparse. Where was all the stuff? Why no plethora of ornaments out on sideboards? Why no bundles of family photographs on top of the mini grand piano that sat at the far end of the sitting room? Why was she here to help clear out all the knick-knacks if there weren't that many to clear?

It really had been years since Lucy had been inside Deux Tourelles. She didn't remember the interior layout at all, barely remembered the exterior although she was sure it hadn't looked quite so ramshackle whenever it was she'd last been here.

Clara called down from the stairs she'd begun climbing. 'Are you coming up or standing there all day?'

Lucy followed her sister to the first floor. 'How do you know where you're going?'

Clara flicked the light switch at the top of the stairs and the first-floor corridor lit up in a yellow haze from an old-fashioned light bulb in a rather tatty shade. There were at least six doors, all closed, and Clara turned right and went to one of two rooms facing the front of the house and opened the door.

'I popped in to fetch things for Dido when she went into hospital but it was a bit late for all that. She'd passed away by the time I made it there.'

Lucy stepped inside the dark room while Clara busied herself switching on a table lamp and starting to look through the large mahogany wardrobe for a suitable dress. Lucy opened the thick damask curtains by the window and let the evening sunshine stream into the room, sending dust motes flying and whirling around her. She looked down the front drive towards the broken gate and then out towards the winding lanes and small field that abutted Dido's house. She could see the edge of a cottage hidden behind trees and its own track of driveway that she'd not seen from the road. She wondered who lived there, if they'd known Dido, or if it was just a little holiday cottage these days.

'You don't miss it at all, do you?' Clara said, interrupting Lucy's thoughts. It sounded kindly meant but the words had sharp edges.

Like most things Clara said in Lucy's direction, the sharp edges were meant to dig in deep, probe hard.

Lucy turned, smiled guiltily. 'Guernsey? I'm not sure that I do. Not really. I don't really think about it. Is that the wrong thing to say?'

'Not if it's the truth.'

Lucy wasn't sure how to reply so simply chose not to.

It was met with silence in return from Clara. A quiet battle; both standing their ground by avoiding discussion entirely. It was so easy to avoid Clara when Lucy was back on the mainland. But here, not so much.

Lucy changed the subject. 'So Dad gets this old place, given he was the nearest relation. Did she have any others?'

'Any other what?'

'Relations? She had no children, no siblings?'

'Not sure,' Clara said distractedly. 'Not any that are living, I don't think. There was mention of a sister, I vaguely remember, a while back.'

'A sister?' Lucy looked at the back of Clara's head as she rifled in the wardrobe, pulling hangers noisily along the metal rail, and waited for more. 'I didn't know that.'

'Mmm. She mentioned it when we were at someone's funeral a few years back. She was surprised she'd been asked to attend. She said she'd thought everyone she'd ever known had already died.'

'Macabre.' Lucy shuddered as she sat on the bed, made up tidily with a rose bedspread. 'Such a shame, being so alone.'

Lucy looked at Clara and felt grateful she had her, even if they had become more distant as the years rolled on. 'What happened to the sister?'

'I don't know.'

'Was she older or younger?' Lucy asked, glancing out towards the little cottage, watching the smoke plume from the chimney.

'I don't know,' Clara said exasperatedly.

Lucy switched her attention from the cottage to the room and

8

looked properly around. The only items in frames were floral watercolours. 'Where are all the family photographs? Her parents, sister and the like?'

'How should I know? Are you going to help?' Clara snapped.

Lucy stared at her sister's back and then walked over to the wardrobe. 'Maybe they grew apart. It's easy to drift apart when people lead such busy lives.'

'You certainly do,' Clara teased. 'I see your social media feed. How many parties can one girl go to each week? I'm exhausted just looking at it.'

Lucy opened her eyes wide in surprise. Clara never clicked 'like' on any of Lucy's posts. Not one. But she'd admitted she'd seen them. Lucy would work that one out later. 'When you live alone you need to get out and about,' Lucy justified. 'Dinner with friends or a microwave meal for one . . . I know which I prefer.'

Clara looked at her as she moved away from the wardrobe, a navy two-piece suit in her hands in which to bury the elderly woman they'd not really known. 'If you say so. How can you afford it?' Clara probed.

'I earn OK money and I've only got myself to worry about.'

'You must be up to your eyes in student debt, though?'

Lucy sighed, pulled her brown hair up into a ponytail. They'd been over this before and she couldn't do it again. 'Righto, what else do we need to get? Do we need a pair of shoes for the . . . thing?'

'The funeral director just said an outfit,' Clara replied with a tinge of horror in her voice. 'I hadn't thought about shoes.'

Lucy opened the wardrobe doors and got on hands and knees to look at the assortment of different-coloured shoeboxes piled on top of each other. 'Oh,' she exclaimed as she began lifting the lids to peek inside.

'What?' Clara asked, the outfit folded in her arms.

'These aren't all shoeboxes, or rather, they are shoeboxes but they don't all contain shoes. Some have got other things in them.' Lucy lifted lids at random.

'Such as?' Clara asked with an uninterested tone.

'Letters, newspaper clippings, photos.' Lucy rifled. 'I thought it was a bit odd there were no photos at all in the house. They're all in here.'

'Photos?' Clara sounded interested now. 'Why would they be hidden in a box?'

Lucy shrugged and held a little stash of photographs out for her sister who put the outfit down, dipped to her knees and sat beside her, flicking through the square, sepia images. They were mostly scenery from before the war, Lucy realised, the garden at Deux Tourelles in better days, the local beaches – the concrete fortifications yet to have been built when these were taken. She pulled out a sepia image of four young people laughing on a beach. Two teenage girls, wet hair falling about their shoulders and two young men, all of them in old-fashioned bathing suits and looking as if they were jostling each other good-naturedly for space in front of the lens. Lucy couldn't help but smile back at them.

She turned the photograph over and read the caption on the back. 'Persephone, Jack, Stefan and Dido. Summer 1930.'

'Persephone? What a mouthful of a name,' Clara said.

'It's Greek,' Lucy replied, turning the photograph back over and looking at the foursome on the beach. 'Persephone was queen of the underworld in ancient mythology.'

Clara looked at Lucy, amused. 'How do you know that?'

'Pub quiz. It came up once. I didn't know the answer though. I'm mostly in charge of literature and celebrity gossip.'

Her sister laughed. It was a lovely sound, and Lucy knew right then that deep down she missed Clara. She would tell her. Later.

'Now I think about it, Dido is from ancient mythology as well,' Lucy said thoughtfully. She ran her finger over the faded ink on the back of the photo. History lessons at school in Guernsey had taught her that roughly a decade after this picture was taken the

Germans invaded the Channel Islands and Hitler's obsession with Guernsey and the surrounding archipelago, nestled in between England and France, had begun in earnest. But she knew, or rather she remembered, very little about the islands' history before that time. She traced the name Persephone with her finger. 'What a beautiful name. Do you think she's the sister? She has to be the sister. Bit coincidental to have two girls with ancient Greek first names unless two sets of parents were being particularly pretentious,' Lucy mused.

'You should hear some of the ridiculous names of the kids that Molly's at school with. I can't spell half of them,' Clara said.

'She looks older than Dido,' Lucy said, examining the teenage girls in their bathing costumes, wet hair around their faces.

'She looks taller, which is not always the same thing,' Clara reasoned, looking at Lucy who was two inches taller than Clara and always had been since they were sixteen. Clara looked at her watch. 'Molly and John will probably be hopping up and down wondering where we are.'

Lucy opened the lid of another box. This one was older, sturdier, browning with age. Inside was a stash of papers, wafer thin, carbon copies as if ripped hastily from a receipt pad. Each page was filled tightly with indiscernible lines, swoops and squiggles. Lucy groaned, recognising it at once as shorthand, something she had half-heartedly toyed with learning almost a decade ago on her graduate trainee course when she'd temporarily been a journalist on a local newspaper. But she'd bunked off from most of the classes, realising she could type faster than she could compile shorthand.

Clara peered down at the papers. 'What on earth? Was someone blind drunk when they wrote this?'

'It's shorthand.' Lucy laughed. 'Strokes and loops represent words. Phonetically I mean. At first glance I can't work out any words on this page and . . .' Lucy looked at the next one. 'Maybe only one on this one. I'm so rusty.' She didn't dare tell Clara she'd skipped most of the classes.

11

'What's the one word you can make out?' Clara asked as she stood.

Lucy studied the pen marks. 'I think I'm guessing more than anything.'

'Go on . . .' Clara said.

Lucy folded the papers up gently and replaced them in the box. 'I'm not sure but . . . I think, possibly, it says "resistance".'

Chapter 2

Persephone jolted as the bedroom door was pushed opened so abruptly that it crashed into the wardrobe behind it. Her younger sister Dido ran into the room, blonde hair falling from the pins in which she usually kept it elegantly rolled, blue eyes flashing with a mix of fear and excitement.

'They're here, Persey,' Dido said. 'The Germans. They're actually bloody here.'

Persephone closed her eyes, tipping her head down, letting her brown hair fall around her face. 'We knew it would happen. I just didn't think it would be so soon.'

After the trucks laden with tomatoes had been bombed in the harbour at St Peter Port, as they waited for export to England, the Islanders had all known it was only a matter of time before the Germans walked in. When the British army had demilitarised and left the island only days before, it was as if the door had been held wide open for the Nazis.

'Do you think it's too late to leave?' Dido asked, glancing down at their mother. She had been in bed with influenza for the best part of the week and Persey was more than a little worried.

'Yes. It's too late. How would we ever get off the island now? How would we get Mother off? She's too sick to be moved. It's

13

why we never went days ago. I thought she would recover sooner. I thought we'd have time,' Persephone muttered.

'There must be a way,' Dido remonstrated with panic in her voice. 'There's always a way. If only Mother—'

'It's not her fault, Di. You could have gone without us. There've been boats leaving for England for days. You could have got on any one of them.'

'I didn't want to leave you, then.'

'But now?' Persey asked.

'Now it's different,' Dido explained. 'Now they're actually here. Planes have been landing. Troops have been seen. I could go and see if there's a boat or . . . It's the best time to go, now, before the Germans get their feet under the table, before they know what's what.' Dido sat on the end of the bed, causing a dip in the mattress and making their mother murmur in her sleep. 'What do you think, Persey? Shall I go and see?'

Persey reached out for her sister's hand and spoke softly. 'It's too late now. I wished you'd gone when I told you to.'

'So do I.' When Dido spoke next she whispered. 'Do you think it'll be awful? Do you think there'll be . . .?'

'What?' Persey asked distractedly as she dipped a cloth in water and bathed her mother's head. Her temperature raged and the fever had yet to break. Persey knew she needed to summon the doctor. She wondered if the telephone lines would be cut now the Germans were here. Not so soon, surely. If so, she would have to bicycle the few lanes to the doctor's house instead of telephone.

'Rapings?' Dido said, her blue eyes wide. 'Killings.'

'Dido! How can you ask such a thing?'

'It happens everywhere,' Dido said with offence. 'They're the invading force, remember. They aren't going to be our friends. Don't they always just kill the men and rape the women? They're going to want to show they're in charge.'

'By killing us?' Persephone asked. 'Hardly a way to run an

Occupation, is it? Killing off the inhabitants. I think they'll want us toeing the line, alive.'

'More's the pity,' Dido replied and then glanced at their mother. 'She's getting worse, isn't she?'

'Yes,' Persey said rising. 'I need to telephone the doctor. I don't think I should wait any longer.'

Dido grimaced. 'As long as he's not been rounded up and shot already.'

The doctor's wife advised Persey that her husband had just that moment left to visit a patient at La Villiaze and gave the address. If she was quick, she could cycle out and catch him there before he moved to his next appointment. Persey took little time pulling her bicycle from the garage and pedalling fast along the lanes. It hadn't occurred to her she would be going past the small airport until she approached it.

She paused long enough to stand at the periphery of the airfield and stare. She wasn't even aware she was doing it she was so captivated by the scene before her. A Guernsey policeman in his British uniform – who Persephone knew only in passing – was standing, looking grave, next to a group of men whose trousers were tucked into thick black boots and whose vibrant red arm bands contrasted with the light of the white swastikas they bore. Four or five Luftwaffe planes were parked, their tails bearing the distinctive Iron Crosses, and one flew over her to land, its engines roaring loudly in her ears. Its wheels bounced for a moment as it hit the grass runway before it turned and parked. It was a scene from a nightmare, surely.

Thank God Jack wasn't here to see all this. The housekeeper's son had lived in with the family and his mother at Persey's house since they were old enough to learn to walk, after his father had died as a result of injuries in the Great War. Jack was roughly the same age as Persey and had been the brother she and Dido had never had. Persey was grateful that he'd quit his job in the bank and left Guernsey weeks ago. He'd joined up in England ready to fight the Germans even though, as a Channel Islander, he wasn't required to do so.

The policeman caught sight of Persey and nodded his head by way of a solemn greeting. The German men he had been standing with turned to look at her with interest. In fear of being noticed, she looked away, mounted her bicycle and pedalled until she had left the airport far behind her. When she was down the lane, Persey jumped from her bicycle and threw it down onto the ground. Its wheels spun wildly from the abrupt action as she bent down at the side of the lane and was violently sick into the hedge.

Persey caught Doctor Durand as he emerged from his patient's cottage stepping towards his motorcar and he looked more than a little surprised to see her.

'Persephone, are you quite all right?' he asked. Doctor Durand was her father's friend of old. The two had known each other since school, and while her father had gone into accountancy, his friend had chosen to heal. With her father gone, the doctor had always kept a considerate eye on the remaining inhabitants of Deux Tourelles.

'The Germans are here,' Persey relayed to him.

The doctor stepped away from his vehicle and closed the door. He took in Persephone's face, which she knew must look pale. 'Yes, I saw. Over at the airport. Hard to believe, really.' There was momentary silence before he continued. 'You didn't cycle out here to tell me that, did you?'

'No. It's mother. She's getting worse. Will you come and see? After you've seen your next patient of course.'

'I'll come now. I can't get your bicycle in the motorcar though. All right if I leave you in my wake and see you there?'

Persey nodded.

'It means you'll have to ride past the airport again. Didn't get any trouble from any of the Germans, did you? Not sure whether it's a good idea you being on your own. We don't know what they're like.'

Persey also had no idea if it was a sensible idea being alone. 'I'll be fine. I'll pedal fast. Just in case.'

She watched the doctor drive away in the direction of Deux Tourelles and stood watching aircraft stream in one by one overhead, descending towards the airport. Everything had changed. In just a few short days, their island wasn't their own anymore. They had been bombed and now they were going to be . . . what, exactly? She didn't know. The reports from other nations that the Germans had already steamrollered their way into had not been good, had not been complimentary about Nazi behaviour. What kind of fate were they all to suffer? And for how long?

When Persey arrived home she felt a sense of relief at seeing the doctor's car parked in the sweep of the drive. Everything would be all right now. The Germans might be on the island in droves, her mother might be sick, but for the next half an hour or so Doctor Durand would know what to do; would administer medicine of some kind and Persey and Dido's mother would recover. And then tomorrow would be another day. Or would it be the beginning of hell? The beginning of Nazi Occupation? She paused in the garage where she propped her bicycle in its usual space against the wall near father's old Wolseley Series II motorcar. Other than Jack giving it a run around the island every now and again to keep the engine ticking over, it had been parked there ever since father's death two years earlier.

That day, her father had returned home from the golf club in time for supper, muttering something about needing to pop into his study for just five minutes before they dined. It was only when the housekeeper Mrs Grant had finally sent Persey to fetch her father before the gravy congealed that she discovered he'd passed away, slumped at his desk, chequebook on the table, pen in hand.

A stroke, Doctor Durand had said. No warning; he'd been in peak health until then, which was of very little comfort to anyone.

Persey reached out and touched the bonnet of the car before she left the garage, as if it would bring her closer to her father. But of course it never did.

From inside the entrance hall Persephone could hear the faint sound of someone weeping. She stood still and moved inside without closing the door and realised that it was two people weeping, not one. She was rooted to the spot, unable to move, unable to ascend the staircase; instead she stared up towards the wooden banisters of the upper landing.

Doctor Durand appeared at the top of the stairs and looked down towards Persephone. 'My dear,' he started. 'I am incredibly sorry . . .'

Persey's shoulders slumped. She knew what he wanted to say and she wouldn't let him. 'No.' She shook her head, holding his gaze, daring him to say it. 'No.'

The combined sounds of Dido and Mrs Grant crying drifted towards them in the silence on the staircase.

'She's not dead,' Persey started. 'My mother is not dead.'

'I am afraid so. I'm so terribly sorry.' He looked as if he wanted to say something else but closed his mouth, clearly thinking better of it.

In the shock that hit Persey she thought she knew what he'd been about to say: *Why didn't you telephone earlier?* It was a question she now asked herself. She hadn't been quick enough. Hadn't seen the signs in time, had let the fever rage for too long. And now . . . if she stayed standing here and didn't move, it wouldn't be real. If she didn't go into her mother's room and see her, in bed, no longer breathing . . . it wouldn't be real, wouldn't have actually happened.

'But . . .' Sobs prevented her speaking until she eventually uttered, 'But . . . I was only gone from the house for half an hour. An hour, at most. I think. She can't . . . in that time?'

Doctor Durand was spared answering as Dido appeared at the stairs.

'Oh, Dido,' Persey cried. Dido stumbled past Doctor Durand and down the stairs towards her sister, who was still rooted to the floor, and the two embraced.

'It's my fault. I should have . . .' Persey started.

'It's not your fault, Persey, it's not,' Dido said into Persey's hair between sobs. Persey felt her sister's tear-streaked face dampen her own.

Dido pulled back from her sister and looked past her towards the front door. But it was only when Persey caught Doctor Durand looking in the same direction that she felt compelled to turn and follow their collective gaze.

Her eyes were blurred with tears and so Persey wasn't able to make out the features of the man standing in the doorway, or those of the two other men behind him. But the uniform told her all she needed to know. That dark jacket, belted at the waist, eagle insignias embroidered onto the breast and the peaked cap that shielded the man's eyes. His head was tipped down as if . . . ashamed? No, Persey thought. But if not that, then what?

He spoke perfect English in a German accent that should have surprised Persey but didn't. He was German. Of course he was. And he was in the entrance hall of Deux Tourelles.

'I appear to have called at a difficult time,' he said.

'Yes, you bloody have,' Dido cried. 'How dare—?'

Persey grabbed her sister's hand, clutching it tightly, stopping Dido from saying anything she shouldn't in the presence of the enemy. But she herself was unable to speak, unable to save the situation. She blinked in disbelief at the past few minutes, at the sudden loss of her mother and the surprising arrival of the Germans not only on the island but also at her front door, their jackbooted feet on the welcome mat of their home.

She nodded, only able to whisper an almost silent, 'Yes. It is a dreadful time.' She gulped back tears. 'We have had a death.'

19

'Then I apologise at my poor timing.' He looked behind him at the two men who had accompanied him, his face now cast in the shadow from the peak of his cap. 'I will return tomorrow.'

Persey's eyes fogged with fresh tears. She wanted to say no and to shout, *Don't you dare come back*. But she couldn't speak anymore. She wiped her eyes and nodded as the three men turned and walked nonchalantly down the drive towards the car parked at the gate as if they hadn't a care in the world.

'What in God's name do you think they wanted?' Doctor Durand was the first to speak.

'I don't know,' Persey whispered, confusion rattling around inside her mind.

'We'll find out tomorrow,' Dido said quietly.

It was real. The Germans were here, the arrival of the enemy was upon them and Persey knew she would forever remember the day her mother died as the day the Germans arrived.

In bed later, Persey was unable to sleep, unable to cry anymore, unable to think. Visions of her mother holding her as a child, buckling her shoes for her on her first day at school, fixing her grazed knee when she'd fallen from the tree house at the end of the garden. That tree house was gone now. So was her mother.

She stared at the ceiling and then in an exhausted resignation moved to the window, lifting the tight-fitting blackout blind out of place and staring down the driveway towards the field in the distance and the single cottage that bordered their small, two-acre grounds. It had been abandoned only yesterday by the Jewish owners, who had sailed to England to escape the Nazis. If it hadn't been for the moon casting a bright light down onto the pasture she'd not have been able to see anything but she'd have known what she was looking at; the view imprinted on her memory. She'd been born in this house. She'd never known anything else, never wanted anything else.

Her mind wandered aimlessly as she placed the thick blackout frame silently on the carpet of her room. The Germans were here now; why was the blind needed? But Mrs Grant had a copy of the *Evening Press* with the horrific announcements from the occupying force littering the pages. Things were to continue in much the same way, for now. Tonight the blackout wasn't in place to prevent the Germans from bombing Guernsey – it was to prevent the British from bombing the island and driving the Germans into submission.

Unthinkable really, that the British would bomb Guernsey now. But then, prior to the last few weeks it had been unthinkable that the Germans would occupy Guernsey, yet it had happened. So why not the former?

'The world has turned upside down,' she whispered to herself. She looked towards the garage, its wide doors left open. She hadn't closed the house properly for the night and she stared as the moonlight bounced a silver light off the bonnet of her father's car, taunting her, telling her that she had let everyone down today by letting her mother die and now, her father's car was visible to any German who wanted to take it; inconsequential as it was in the grand scheme of things.

Persey pulled her dressing gown from the hook behind her door and made her way along the landing. She stopped at her mother's closed door and put her hand against it. The undertaker had been – promptly summoned by Doctor Durand – and her mother was no longer in the house but still Persey didn't know why the door had been closed. She opened it wide and looked in. The pain was too great in her chest, looking at her mother's things, items that she knew her mother would never touch again. Her hairbrush on the dressing table, her book – open and face down. Her mother had been too weak to read it for so long. How had Persey not registered that? Her mother's face flashed in her mind and, guiltily, Persey closed the door again and with it closed her own eyes, hoping it would take the pain away. But it didn't.

Doctor Durand had said there was nothing he could have done.

The influenza had taken over and her mother's lungs, weakened from when she'd caught tuberculosis as a child, had been the root cause of her demise. But still Persey blamed herself. Why hadn't she telephoned earlier? Why? There might have been something Doctor Durand could have done.

She continued downstairs towards the garage. She would shut the doors and return to bed to try and force sleep to come. But as she closed the first door she heard a noise at the back of the garage where her father's tools still hung. She stood still. It had sounded as if someone had backed into the wall and knocked one of the spades or rakes hanging from the tool hooks. The clatter of metal on brick died out as quickly as it had started, as if someone had grabbed at the implement to silence the noise.

As soon as the word 'Hello?' fell from her lips she knew it had been a mistake to speak. She turned to run away but wasn't quick enough. Her foot had barely moved an inch before she saw someone lurch towards her, grab her by her dressing gown and pull her back inside the garage. Almost as quickly, the man's other hand clamped around her mouth and the scream that came from her was silenced, heard by no one inside the house.

Chapter 3

The man kept his hand over her mouth as he stared into her eyes through the slit in his knitted balaclava. 'Don't say a word.'

Persey nodded in startled agreement and then slowly the man lifted his hand from her mouth. Immediately she reneged on her agreement not to speak and realising she was looking at the housekeeper's son cried, 'Jack! What on earth are you doing here?'

'For Christ's sake, Perse, shh.'

She was quieter when she spoke this time. 'We thought you were in England. We thought you'd joined up weeks ago.'

'I was. I have.' He spoke quietly and pulled her towards the back of the garage, as if the extra few feet of space between them and the house would make all the difference.

'How are you here then?' she asked with wide eyes.

'I've been sent back,' he said proudly. He looked at her expectantly, awaiting her reaction.

'Are you that terrible at soldiering they've returned you already?' She hadn't meant to be funny but Jack laughed.

'Don't be ridiculous. I'm only back because they needed to find someone local – someone who knows the lay of the land. And then, with any luck, I'll be gone again, bursting with information to help win the war.'

Persey stared. 'Are you a spy?' she asked blankly. 'Oh, Jack, they'll kill you. You know that, don't you? The Germans. There are so many of them. I've been past the airport and—'

'And how many of them are there?'

Persey thought. 'I don't know. Lots. And I'm sure more will be landing imminently. And then of course troops will be coming in their droves by boat from France. You shouldn't be here. It's far too dangerous.'

He looked proud. 'That's exactly why I am here. Listen, do you think you could go past the airport again and take another look? Sit tight for a while, watch how many planes come and go over the course of the week?'

'Are you asking me to spy for you?'

'No, I'm asking you to spy for Britain.'

Persephone rubbed her hand over her tired eyes. It was too much. It was all just far too much.

He waited, a determined expression fixed on his face while she looked at him.

'Jack, why are you in the garage? And . . .' She looked him up and down. 'And why are you wet?'

'I'm wet because I had to wade in once they'd dropped me from the canoe. And I'm in the garage because, given the hour, I didn't want to wake the house.'

For the first time in ages, Persephone laughed. 'Oh my word. It's not like you to be quite so polite. So you're hiding in here, soaked to the skin because you didn't want to wake us all up?' She couldn't help it, she laughed again.

'I don't wish to damage the good opinion you've formed of me but no, sorry. I don't mind waking you all up one jot but I did rather want to stay put and keep an eye on the house for a few hours. See how many Germans came and went in the morning and see if it was safe to show my face at Deux Tourelles.'

'Germans? Here?' she asked. 'Why would they be here?' Although her mind moved back to earlier that day, when the

24

young man in uniform had stood by her door. He'd never said what he'd wanted.

'They'll need somewhere to live while they're here,' Jack said simply. 'Deux Tourelles is one of the closest houses to the airport. Stands to reason they'll want to pop their heads in at some point. You might find yourself being turfed out.'

Persey's stomach tightened.

'Or even worse,' Jack continued. 'You might find yourself staying and then having one or two of them living with you.'

'Don't say that,' Persey replied.

'Well, listen,' he said, 'I'm here for a week. But I'll need somewhere to stay so I'll have my old room back, next to my mum's if a German hasn't moved himself in and if it's not full of Dido's clothes already?'

'I know we've grown up together but you really can be very forward at times,' Persey chastised.

'You want me to know my place as the housekeeper's son, is that it?' He folded his arms.

'No, I didn't mean that. I'm sorry,' Persey said. 'You know I don't think anything like that. You've only been gone a few weeks so of course your room is still yours. As if your mother would let us do anything else. She's going to be overjoyed to see you.'

'I'm not so sure about that,' Jack said darkly. 'So it's safe.' He angled his head towards the house. 'In there?'

'No Germans yet but what if one does come? We had one earlier in the day and he said he'd be back.'

'We don't tell them I've joined up. I've been here the whole time. Never left the island. As long as we all keep to that story for a week, and I stay hidden out here away from prying eyes then it's too easy.'

'Too easy . . .' Persey repeated thoughtfully. 'We should wake the house and tell them. Get you dry and into some fresh clothes.'

'Dido and your mother won't believe their eyes,' Jack said.

Persey stopped and dipped her gaze to the floor. When he asked what was wrong, fresh tears threatened as she told him about her mother's death.

'Oh dear God. That's the worst news imaginable. Oh, Persey, I'm so sorry. I don't know what to say. I can't believe it. She was fine when I left,' he said as if that would change facts. 'Your mother was always very good to me. Very kind to Mother after Father died,' Jack said quietly. 'The best sort of woman. I can't believe she's gone.'

Persey let the tears fall freely and Jack pulled her towards him, holding her close.

'You're wet,' Persey said through her tears.

'I am rather, yes, sorry. Those tears don't help.'

Persey pulled back, sniffed and wiped her eyes. 'Let's go inside.'

The shouting between Jack and his mother went on and on in the kitchen at the back of the house. Persey and Dido sat on the stairs, their heads in their hands. And then when it became clear Mrs Grant was gearing up for another yell, the girls moved into the sitting room and closed the door to drown out the Grants' argument. Persey backed against the door, tipped her chin up and closed her eyes. She wanted to block out the horrific, awful day.

Could one be classed as an orphan at the age of twenty-five? Because surely that's what she and Dido were. Orphans. She looked over at Dido, whose expression was fixed, as she hunted around for something to do or touch or divert herself with. Persey weighed up the options for her mother's funeral, in the face of Nazi Occupation – something she could hardly contemplate but which she knew would have to be thought about. Thank goodness for Doctor Durand taking charge with the undertaker. Thank goodness for Mrs Grant helping so readily with everything.

Persey had loved her mother but it was her father who she'd shared a special relationship with as the years moved on. Dido had been happy to drift between the two of them equally, finding true comfort in both parents, easy to love and easy to be loved.

Whereas Dido had always accused Persey of being too strait-laced and too tight-lipped. She wasn't tight-lipped, or especially private. Persey just never had anything to tell.

Dido pulled the stopper off the decanter and poured a brandy. 'God-awful day. The worst. Want one?'

Persephone shook her head as she moved towards the fireplace, even though it hadn't been lit that day. It was June, but no matter the time of year, the room was always cold. Wrapping her dressing gown around her she wondered what her sister was thinking. 'I can't drink. Not at this hour. I'd like some tea but I daren't go in the kitchen. I thought Mrs Grant would be pleased to see him.'

'Did you?' Dido replied. 'Really? Jack's risked his life to spy. Of course she's angry. The first war killed her husband, after a fashion. And if he's caught, this second one will take her son. It really is rather stupid of him to have come back.'

'What would you do, though, if asked?' Persey suggested. 'If you were in England and you'd joined up even though, as an Islander, you didn't have to? If you thought strongly enough about this war to actually do something about it, and then you were offered the chance to return home, do something about knocking the Nazis off your very own patch of soil . . . what would you do?'

Dido made a show of thinking, which made Persephone half smile. 'I'd tell Churchill: *Not on your nelly, Winnie.*'

'I don't think you would.'

Dido poured a measure of brandy and held it out to Persey. 'No arguments. Just drink it.'

Persey breathed in deeply and took the smallest sip of alcohol. Then the inevitable knock at the sitting room door came. Jack opened the door and looked as if the ordeal of landing back in occupied Guernsey was nothing to the verbal hammering his mother had just given him. He sat on the settee, looking pale.

'You're still in your wet things,' Persey said, handing him her glass.

'Mother thinks I shouldn't have come.'

'We could hear,' Dido said, perching on the arm of the settee opposite.

Jack smiled. 'It's only a week. I'll be picked up by the navy and then . . .'

'And then you leave us to it?' Persey questioned. 'To the fates?'

Jack looked sheepish and sipped Persey's brandy.

'Well you'd better not get caught then,' Dido said. 'Because, if you do, you'll bring us all down with you.'

Jack went to get some rest and they were to convene with him at breakfast. Dido asked to sleep in with Persey and the two pulled Persey's blankets up underneath their chins, staring at the ceiling in the darkness.

'This is a bit like when we were children,' Dido pointed out. 'When I used to have nightmares and climb in with you.'

Persey nodded. 'Yes,' she said absently.

'I feel numb. Don't you?' Dido continued.

'Yes, I suppose I do.'

'Mother's gone.'

'Yes,' Persey replied. Perhaps it was the shock of it all but Persey had run out of emotion, anaesthetised by the day's events, and could say no more on the subject.

'And now Jack,' Dido lamented.

'And now Jack,' Persey repeated. She thought about what Jack had asked her to do, spying at the airport. Would it really be so very different to cycling past, as she often did, but to pay proper attention? Count the aircraft lined up near the landing strip? Take in how many men appeared to be onsite? Perhaps see if any guns had been set up already and whereabouts? Where was the harm in just looking? As long as she didn't get caught. And why would they arrest her just for cycling past the perimeter fence? As fragments of early morning sunlight broke through the fine gap at the end of the blackout blind she'd replaced in the night, she eventually drifted off to sleep.

If she had expected to dream of anything she thought it would have been about her mother or of Jack being arrested by the Germans. But instead it was half a dream, half a memory that filtered in and out of Persey's foggy mind. There had been four of them on the cliffs, much younger than they were now, perhaps she had been fifteen or sixteen years old. Jack had challenged them all to a race on the precarious path as they walked the cliffs towards Fermain Bay, drawing a start line in the gravel with the heel of his shoe.

'We'll go in teams,' Jack had announced, looking at his watch as the four stood on the cliff path.

Persey peered over the edge while Jack spoke. Below them the waves crashed loudly against the cliffs, white horses galloping towards the rocks. Not a soul to be seen.

'I'll time us. Dido and I shall go first,' Jack continued. 'Too narrow for us all to go at once. Two minutes later, Stefan and Persey will follow on. We'll see which team gets to the bay in the fastest time. Every second counts. Stefan, let's check our wristwatches.'

Persey glanced at Stefan, blond, tall . . . taller than he had been last summer certainly. He moved toward Jack to ensure their watches were in synch. The atmosphere between the boys was jovial but there had always been that barely noticeable undercurrent of tension. Jack, the dominant surrogate older brother to the girls, was quick to laugh at Stefan if he mispronounced something. It was one of Jack's less fine qualities, although if Stefan noticed, he failed to react.

She wasn't quite sure she wanted to be alone with Stefan for two whole minutes while they waited their turn. What would they talk about? And then to have to run with him along the narrow path. At least she wouldn't be expected to speak then. She gave Jack a look that suggested she was less than happy about this. But he didn't see.

'You ready, Di?' Jack said as Stefan moved to stand beside Persephone. Stefan's shirtsleeves were rolled up and his bare forearm – warm, tanned – touched hers and she moved away. He didn't need to be that close, surely.

'Ready,' Dido announced, adjusting the laces of her shoes. At least they were flat, Persey thought, looking down mournfully at her own with their small block heel. Not at all suitable for running along a cliff path.

Jack spent an agonising time staring at his watch as Persey peered over the cliffs again.

'Be careful, Dido,' Persey said. 'For God's sake don't fall.'

'I won't,' Dido said in an annoyed tone. 'Besides, Stefan will rescue me, won't you, Stefan?'

'No,' he said without a hint of emotion. 'I will be two minutes behind you. You will be dead.'

Persey covered her mouth with her hand as a laugh attempted to escape. Had he meant to be dry? Or was he simply being German? She glanced at Dido, who was frowning, looking put out; and then Persey stole a look at Stefan. The corners of his mouth were twitching. She looked away again, now even more unsure about him.

Persey woke up. She blinked as Dido switched on the bedside lamp.

Dido looked concerned and rubbed sleep from her eyes. 'What did you say?'

Persey shook her head. 'Nothing. I think I was dreaming.'

'You were. But you said something and then you shot up and dragged all the blankets from me.'

Persey looked down. She was clutching the bedding and had pulled it all from Dido and had it in a heap on top of her. 'Sorry,' she mumbled as Dido took her half back.

Persey sat still and looked into her lap. Could her suspicions be correct?

'What were you dreaming about?' Dido asked as she lay back down and put her head against the pillow.

Persey paused a moment before speaking. 'Do you remember those summers when Mother's friend Agnes had her nephew to stay?'

'No,' Dido said sleepily. 'Is that what you were dreaming about?'

Persey nodded and then switched off the lamp and lay back down. 'Yes.' She rubbed her forefinger along her lower lip as she thought.

'Don't you remember him?'

'The nephew?' Dido said sleepily in the darkness. 'Not really. Maybe.'

'Of course you do,' Persey said. 'Think.'

'Persey, it was years ago.'

'Over ten years ago, yes. He used to spend the summers in Guernsey with Agnes and her husband and then he'd return to Germany to his studies at the end. You must remember him.'

Dido rolled over. Silence. And then, 'Johann? Was that his name?'

Persey smiled. 'Stefan.'

Dido shifted position, onto her back. 'Didn't Agnes move back to England?'

'Yes.'

'Is that why he stopped coming?' Dido asked.

'I don't know.'

'Is it important?' Dido questioned with a yawn.

'No. Only I thought . . .'

But Dido cut Persey off. 'She'll be interned in England now, won't she?'

'Who?' Persey asked as she tried to picture Stefan's face from a decade ago – wondering what he would look like now.

'Agnes. And her husband. She's English but he's German. They'll be interned, won't they? Or will it be just him? Enemy aliens and all that.'

'I suppose so, yes. How horrid,' Persey said.

'If they're German, they're the enemy,' Dido declared.

31

Persey thought about that for a long time, unsure how she felt, unsure how to respond. She wanted to ask Dido if she really thought that old friends could simply be the enemy because the government told you they were, but Dido was already breathing heavily, asleep next to her.

They had known to expect the return of the Germans to the house but none of them had realised it would happen so soon in the day. They had sat down to breakfast in the dining room, Jack waxing lyrical about the locations he needed to visit over the next week, the reconnaissance he was expected to carry out and the kind of help he might need if the girls were willing, when an efficient three-rap knock sounded at the front door.

They looked at Jack for instruction and Mrs Grant issued a startled noise.

'Don't panic,' Jack said confidently. 'Everyone knows the story . . . I've been here the whole time.'

Persey nodded, though her heart clattered in her chest.

The knocking sounded again but it was Dido who moved. 'Oh, for Christ's sake, someone should answer or it'll start to look suspicious from the off.' She was already out of the dining room door.

Persey sat still, her plate of food uneaten. Jack carried on eating as if he hadn't a care in the world, but as Persey looked closer she could see his hand shaking as he lifted his fork. She reached to still him and he put his fork down and swallowed.

There were only two men this time, led into the dining room by Dido. The men glanced around at the sage green walls and the antique furniture dotted around the room. Persey looked where they looked, an excuse not to look at the men properly, not to make eye contact.

'Excuse me for intruding,' the first said in perfect English. 'You are eating. I keep invading when you are busy.'

'Invading . . .' Dido muttered with an arched brow.

Persey looked up slowly at the man and he looked back at her.

She held her breath. She had known. Even though she had not been able to see his face fully under his hat; even though she'd had tears in her eyes, crying about her mother. She had known yesterday it was him. It was his voice.

The man looked lost for words, but eventually found his voice. 'I apologise, but we need to look at the bedrooms.'

Mrs Grant spluttered, 'I beg your pardon?'

'This property is situated close to the airport and is of a substantial size. We have men we need to accommodate on the island.'

'Here?' Persey spoke sharply.

He looked at her. Those blue eyes. 'Yes.'

'We don't have any spare,' Dido said, folding her arms.

With Jack returning to claim his room, that left only one room vacant . . . their mother's. They wouldn't be expected to house a German in Mother's room surely? Not when she'd been gone such a short amount of time. There needed to be some level of respect.

'May we take a look, please?' he asked.

Dido relented. 'We only have one. It was our mother's. Her things are . . . You might not want it.'

The German didn't speak.

Persey asked, 'Do we have a choice?'

'I am afraid not.'

Dido sighed and looked to Persey for help but she knew there was nothing they could do. Persey nodded.

'Thank you.' The man looked at Persey again and then turned to follow Dido as she moved towards the stairs.

'Should one of us go with her?' Jack asked. 'We've just left her alone with two enemy soldiers.'

'Not you,' Mrs Grant whispered to Jack. 'You keep your head down.'

Persey pushed her chair back from the table but Mrs Grant had already made her intention to follow Dido clear and had left the room.

'All right?' Jack asked Persey.

She swallowed. 'Yes, yes I think so,' she said although she wasn't fine really. Intense nerves made her voice shake. 'I should have gone with Dido. Only I can't seem to move.'

'It's actually more frightening than I anticipated,' Jack said. 'Isn't it. Seeing them here. In that awful uniform and those boots. They look just like the photographs in the newspapers.'

Persey nodded but her stomach felt hollow through nerves and lack of food. Jack reached down and took her hand from her lap and held it, giving her a look of solidarity.

The men's boots thudded dully on the stair runner and then they clunked noisily on the tiled hallway. Persey could take it no longer and although her legs felt wobbly she forced herself to follow them.

'So . . .?' she prompted as they made their way towards the front door.

The second man spoke. 'You have one bedroom suitable for an officer.'

Her heart sank. She knew as much. But so soon?

'You will need to start removing personal items—'

But the first man gave his colleague a sharp look to silence him. Why wasn't he saying who he was? It poured doubt into her mind. Was she wrong?

He spoke softly. 'My condolences to you and your sister on the passing of your mother.'

'You don't care,' Dido said under her breath from behind Persey.

'Thank you,' Persey replied a little louder than she'd meant.

She looked at him and he looked at her before he gave a small smile and turned to leave. They closed the door behind them.

Dido and Mrs Grant entered the dining room first and resumed their seats although no one touched their food now.

'They expect us to be grateful that they're here? That we're turfing Mother's things out of her room? One day after her passing?'

Persey hovered behind her chair, clutching it, unsure if she wanted to sit or stand, unsure of anything.

'And how presumptuous of him, just assuming we're sisters. I didn't tell him,' Dido said angrily.

It was this that forced Persey into movement. She had to know now. She had to be sure. She let go of the chair back and turned, walking down the corridor and throwing open the front door. The men were already at the gate. Persey had expected to see a car but the men had arrived on foot.

'Excuse me,' Persey called. They stopped and turned back to her.

The first man looked at her and then turned to his colleague and told him something in German that Persey could neither catch nor understand if she had heard. The second man walked further on and waited at a distance.

Persey continued, gravel crunching underfoot until she stopped a few feet away. She glanced back to the house, sensing rather than seeing Dido staring after her from the dining room windows.

Turning back to him, words escaped her. It could be him, it really could. She could see familiarity but she wondered if she was forcing herself to see it. The last time she'd seen Stefan had been that day at the cliffs in August 1930. It had been almost ten years ago. They'd been so young and now they were twenty-five. If it was him. He had left at the end of the summer, returned to Germany. And then . . . nothing. Stefan's annual visits had come to an abrupt end that summer. He had never come back to Guernsey despite his promises he would. Persey had often wondered why he never returned, why he never wrote to them. She had thought about it over and over and now . . . It was him. It had to be him.

She stood straight and searched his eyes. 'It is you, isn't it?'

Now she'd asked it, she felt mad and expected a rebuttal.

But the man smiled and there it was, that smile and the slight narrowing of the eyes that had always come with it.

'Hello, Persephone.'

Chapter 4

2016

The Solicitor had told Clara Dido's funeral wishes as stipulated in the will and she and Lucy had complied easily. But it had turned out to be a far more interesting affair than Lucy had expected. She couldn't think of a single time in the five funerals she'd been to where the vicar had spoken about the deceased with such warm and genuine affection, almost as if he had actually known her. She didn't know anyone who went to church anymore. She had opted out of the annual pilgrimage for Christmas carols and mulled wine at the lovely little church near her flat in Camberwell. But Dido had been a fairly regular churchgoer, arranging the flowers and compiling the parish newsletter and it had been the vicar's pleasure to offer to deliver the eulogy, quipping about Dido in her later years. Lucy had been relieved, but Clara had grumbled she felt surplus to requirements.

'But we didn't actually know her,' Lucy had hissed as the vicar finished his short speech. 'Not really.'

Clara became engaged in conversation with parishioners at the church doors at the end of the service – thanking those who had come – but Lucy extricated herself gently. To those that offered a consolatory 'sorry for your loss', Lucy mumbled words of thanks in reply but felt very false mourning someone she had hardly known. Thank goodness for nibbles and drinks at Deux Tourelles afterwards. That might help lubricate conversation a bit.

Despite asking Lucy to come back to Guernsey to help with preparations, all Clara had let Lucy organise was the wake, but she assumed it was the moral support Clara needed more than any actual help. She'd stocked up on endless bags of frozen sausage rolls and mini quiches along with other various nibbles and plenty of wine. And at Deux Tourelles, after a few minutes of passing these around, Lucy moved away, not quite knowing who to talk to or how to engage herself in conversation with parishioners who were engrossed discussing house prices, energy bills and how long it was taking them to get a doctor's appointment.

Clara was in the kitchen taking a long drink of water. She found a clean glass and poured one for Lucy and the two girls stood, backs against the kitchen cupboards, in unified silence.

Later, when everyone had left, Lucy asked, 'Do you think any of them actually knew Dido or her sister?' as she and Clara tidied up at Deux Tourelles. 'I mean, really knew them? Other than the vicar I mean.'

'Why do you ask?'

'Well when people realised I was related to Dido in a small way, they were kind about her but I couldn't get anything interesting out of them about her. They mostly knew her through church or whist and that was it,' Lucy said.

'What were you expecting?' Clara turned from cleaning a red wine stain that had appeared on the edge of the sink.

'I don't know, really. A lot of people clearly admired and liked her but I'm not sure any of them were real friends.'

'At least she got out and about,' Clara said. 'That's a lot more than some elderly people do from what I gather.'

'I suppose,' Lucy replied, putting the last of the glasses in the dishwasher.

Lucy's five-year-old niece Molly ran into the kitchen, wearing her school uniform.

'Hello, trouble,' Lucy said. 'How was school?'

'Fine.' Molly gave her aunty a hug and then descended on the leftover mini sausage rolls.

'What did you do?' Lucy prompted.

'Can't remember,' Molly said, her mouth still full.

'Awesome.' Lucy laughed and then popped a mini quiche in her own mouth.

'Are you going home now the funeral's over?' Molly asked.

'Not yet. No. I think we have things to sort. Boring grown-up things,' Lucy joked. 'So you've got me for a while longer. Did you worry I was leaving?'

Molly shrugged and reached for another sausage roll. 'I heard Mum say you'd be going to a hotel or something and she thought you'd be gone by now.'

Lucy started. 'Oh. Right then.' She glanced at Clara who was obviously pretending not to hear. She thought Clara might have changed her mind about Lucy staying. After all, she'd been there nearly a week without a grumble from her sister.

Clara's husband John entered the kitchen. 'Hiya. How'd it go?'

'Fine. For a funeral,' Lucy said and poured him a glass of red wine, remembering he disliked white.

'I'd have come if I could but I didn't have anyone to cover my class for me,' John said.

'I know. Clara told me. You don't have to defend yourself to me.'

'And then I had to pick up Molly from after-school club,' John continued.

Lucy gave him a look. 'I know,' she repeated. 'Don't worry. It's not like you missed anything.'

'Yeah, but I think Clara's a bit miffed.' John sipped his wine as Clara rolled her eyes. 'Thanks, I need this. Long day. Thank God the summer holidays are just around the corner. Year twelves were a complete bunch of—'

'Language,' Clara said from the doorway as she carried a dishcloth.

'I hadn't sworn yet,' John protested.

'I was getting in early,' Clara replied.

'Oh, come on that's not . . .' John put his wine glass on the counter a little too forcefully and red wine spilled on the side.

'Listen, guys,' Lucy said, walking towards Clara and taking the dishcloth from her. She thrust it at John with a pointed expression and he turned to wipe the wine from the counter. 'I'm thinking I should shuffle out of your way. I've been here a week and the funeral's over and you need your space again so . . .'

'Oh, you don't have to,' Clara started but Lucy cast a glance at Molly who looked back at Lucy conspiratorially.

'Yes, I do.'

'It's nearly summer. You'll pay buckets of money if you rent a cottage or a little apartment for a few weeks. And hotels are the same,' John said.

'I know, but it's all right.'

'Why don't you stay here?' Molly asked as another sausage roll made its way into her mouth.

Lucy discreetly pushed the platter back out of reach of her niece. 'Here?'

'No one lives here now, do they?' Molly asked with simple, childish logic.

'I don't think I'm allowed.'

Lucy looked at Clara, who shrugged and replied, 'The will's being read tomorrow so . . . I have no idea. If Dad's inherited as he thinks – and quite frankly I don't think Dido had any other family – then he won't mind you staying here while we put it on the market. You may as well. It's huge though. Will you be OK in a house this size all by yourself?'

'Is it haunted?' Molly asked, searching the counter for the sausage rolls.

'I bloody hope not,' Lucy replied with a shudder.

'Language,' John reminded her with a smug look.

* * *

Lucy decided she'd wait until the will had been read before packing her holdall with her few possessions and moving into Deux Tourelles for the duration of her stay. 'Just in case Dido's left it all to the local cat home and I get turfed straight back out,' she had joked.

The day had turned bright and the temperature was soaring. She'd forgotten how beautiful the island could be in the bright summer sunshine as she and Clara drove past hedgerows abundant with vibrant hydrangeas. And then, just as suddenly as they had entered the small patch of countryside, they emerged through the lanes and down the winding, tree-shaded road, the dappled light falling through the trees as the road wound into St Peter Port. The shining azure waters never failed to make her smile. How easily she'd forgotten that.

Clara parked at one of the small car parks adjacent to the water, narrowly cutting someone up in order to get one of the few remaining spaces. Lucy crouched down in her seat, shielding her eyes, ashamed of her sister's brazenness.

'Right, let's get this done and I can head back to yours and get on with a bit of work,' Lucy said, feeling neglectful of her poor client whose soft-toy brochure she was meant to be copywriting. As she watched the sun bounce from the water in the port, and she put on her sunglasses, she wasn't sure how she felt about sitting indoors and writing meaningful sentences about teddies.

'Are you still enjoying it?' Clara asked as they walked towards the office where the will would be read.

'Being here?' Lucy asked.

'No, work.'

'Yeah, it's . . . easy.'

'Easy? Lucky you. It's not exactly . . . work though, is it?' Clara said.

Lucy paused before answering cagily, 'What do you mean?'

'Using your English Literature degree to write websites for car parks or whatever that last thing was you did.'

Lucy didn't reply. She waited for Clara to finish her point. If she waited long enough, she knew there would be more.

'It's not exactly saving lives, is it?' Clara said, obviously unable to contain herself.

'No, it's not saving lives. So what?'

'Well, I thought you were made for better things.'

Lucy frowned at the backhanded compliment. 'Obviously not,' she replied.

'You don't want to do anything . . . better?' Clara persevered. 'Write about something more . . . oh, I don't know . . . just something more?'

Lucy stopped walking and steeled herself. 'Such as?'

Clara turned to her. 'I don't know. You worked so hard at university and then took all those courses and for what . . . So you could just pad through life?'

Lucy replied through teeth she realised were now gritted together, 'I'm quite happy being a copywriter. Besides, you're a florist and that's not saving lives either.'

'Yes, but I didn't spend a ridiculous amount of money going to university. And quite happy isn't very happy, is it?' Clara reasoned.

'OK.' Lucy decided to stop her there. 'What's this all about?'

'Do you even have any hobbies? Other than drinking and going out with your friends?'

'Is this about me? Or actually about you?' Lucy dared.

'What do you mean?' Clara asked, her chin tipped up pointedly.

'I don't have a problem with my job, but you obviously do. Why?'

'I just think you're made for better things. I mean usually you give up on everything so quickly and the one thing you probably should give up on is actually this.'

'No,' Lucy said.

'No what?'

'No, that's not it,' Lucy ventured. 'You're bored. You've enjoyed

41

living vicariously through me for the best part of a decade but the enthusiasm has worn off and you're pissed off now. Why?'

'How dare you!' Clara snapped, drawing the attention of an elderly couple enjoying the view of the port.

'You're angry you didn't leave when I did,' Lucy said, her voice louder than it really should have been. 'You're angry you came back after uni and couldn't find a proper job with your degree. You're pissed off that you got married young to John, who you really don't care about from what I've seen over the past week, and it's not like you even needed to get married early.'

The slap didn't exactly come from out of nowhere and so it shouldn't have shocked Lucy, but it did. It stung her cheek and made her eyes water. At first she didn't connect the startling pain with having been slapped by her sister and like an idiot – she realised later – she cast her glance about for someone else who might have lurched out and hit her. Clara held Lucy's gaze defiantly when their eyes met.

Lucy said nothing, expecting an apology. But none was forthcoming. Both sisters were as angry as each other.

'Have you quite finished?' Clara spat.

Lucy swallowed, her hand still against her face and her eyes wide. She said nothing. Neither did she nod her head. She just stared as anger turned to hurt and tears filled her eyes. How had this happened? How had they got here? Had Lucy done this – pushed her sister so far away over the years that all that was left was this? Then her anger returned just as swiftly, but not at Clara. Instead it was at herself for welling up. Clara turned away from her and looked up the gradual incline of St Peter Port, up to where the bigger offices sat at the far end of town.

Lucy slowly removed her hand from her face, wiping the tears from her eyes and wondering what on earth had happened in the last few minutes that meant the sisters were suddenly raging at each other and throwing slaps. Was it the last few minutes that had done this? Or the last few years? Her skin was red. The heat emanating from it told her that much.

'Are you coming?' Clara asked.

'No.' Lucy couldn't look at her; didn't know what to think.

'What do you mean, no?' Clara asked.

'It doesn't matter if I hear the will read or not,' Lucy said. 'It doesn't change what's on the document.'

'Fine, what will I tell them?'

'Tell them I've gone home,' Lucy announced.

'Oh, it was only a matter of time before you disappeared again, wasn't it? I had money on five days and you've lasted seven so I owe John ten pounds.'

'Oh, fuck you,' Lucy said, unable to rein it in.

'Actually, it's typical behaviour so I don't know why I'm surprised. Nothing you do surprises me. You're so predictable. Always choose the easy way out. Or give up entirely.' Clara stalked up towards the town, leaving Lucy standing rigidly.

She hadn't actually meant that she was going home to the mainland. Regardless, she couldn't stay at Clara's tonight. She just couldn't. Both girls needed to calm down and then they might be able to be civil enough to talk to each other in the morning.

Breathing deeply, she tried to push away the sudden urge to feel sorry for herself. She glanced around, intending to grab a taxi from the rank. But something caught her eye – a plaque on the wall – and she looked back and read the lettering properly.

THIS PLAQUE COMMEMORATES THE ILLEGAL
DEPORTATION BY GERMAN OCCUPYING FORCES
OF 1,003 MEN, WOMEN AND CHILDREN FROM
GUERNSEY AND SARK IN SEPTEMBER 1942 AND
FEBRUARY 1943 TO CAPTIVITY IN CIVILIAN
INTERNMENT CAMPS IN GERMANY AND FRANCE.

IT REMEMBERS THE 16 ISLANDERS WHO DIED
THERE AND WHOSE NAMES AND
AGES ARE LISTED BELOW . . .

Lucy scanned the names and ages of the men, women and even small children. The stark reality of the fate of those sixteen meant she didn't feel quite so sorry for herself and as she turned towards the cab rank she tried with a great deal of effort to remember the history of the Occupation of the Channel Islands. They'd been taught it in school, of course, but it was a long time ago for Lucy.

The things that had mattered to Lucy at sixteen were kissing boys in bus shelters and working out a game plan for eventually getting the hell off the island. She'd achieved that goal only two years later when university had beckoned on the mainland and she'd never looked back. She glanced again at the plaque and then moved on toward the taxis.

At Clara's house, Lucy asked the taxi to wait and bundled all her things into her holdall. She wrote two notes: one for Clara who barely deserved a note, telling her where she'd gone; and one for Molly, which Lucy left in her niece's bedroom. Molly's suggestion that Lucy stay at Deux Tourelles for the time being was actually a fairly sensible idea as long as Dido hadn't actually left it to a cat shelter. And while she didn't relish the idea of sleeping alone in a house that size, it beat sleeping under Clara's roof. The slap still fresh in her mind, Lucy grabbed the keys to Deux Tourelles, closed Clara's front door behind her and climbed back into the taxi.

Chapter 5

It amazed Lucy just how efficient Clara could be when she set her mind to it. Lucy scanned the kitchen cupboards and found that after the funeral her sister had cleared out every single one. Either that or Dido had been intensely frugal and had owned no canned goods whatsoever. Likewise the freezer had been emptied and Lucy looked in the fridge half-heartedly and was surprised and overjoyed to find three bottles of white wine from the funeral still inside. She grabbed one, opened it and filled a glass that had been left draining on the side, drinking half the glass before she'd even put the bottle back in the fridge.

Keys hung on hooks by the back door, which Lucy thought was a ridiculous place to put them. 'Not very burglar savvy were you, Dido?' she asked the empty kitchen. She found one marked 'Garage' and went outside, still clutching her wine glass. The evening was warm but inside the double garage it was cold and tidy. Small Perspex boxes were clearly marked with seeds and household tools, and gardening tools were hung on hooks at the back.

There was a little Renault 5, its wheel arches a little rusty, which Lucy wondered if she could borrow for the evening to get her to the shops and back. But given she was halfway through a glass of wine, drowning her sorrows after the row with Clara, she thought the old-fashioned pushbike leaning against the far wall looked more suitable; its basket big enough to hold a few essentials. She wheeled it outside and leant it against the wall of Deux Tourelles near the front door, returned to lock the garage and cursed herself for leaving her glass of wine resting on a Perspex box. She ventured back inside to retrieve it and saw the box was marked 'P'.

She cast around for a light switch but there didn't appear to be one and so she lifted the dusty box and her glass of wine and carried them back to the house, returning only to lock the garage door.

She was too hungry to sit and rifle through boxes of paperwork and so decided to first venture out through the lanes to the shops.

Was the little supermarket still on the other side of the airport? She vaguely remembered it from last time she'd been home and thought it was, and so she locked up Deux Tourelles, put her purse and keys into the basket on the front of the bike and went off to stock up on food for a few nights.

After cooking a simple supper of spaghetti and puttanesca sauce from a jar, Lucy found a record player and some old records and knelt down to flick through the collection. It included Judy Garland, Doris Day and Bing Crosby along with some classical records. Dido obviously loved her music.

'Ah-ha,' she said, pulling out a Billie Holiday record. 'That's more like it. Music to drink wine to,' she said and then laughed at herself for talking out loud. She didn't realise she was doing it at home but then, this wasn't her home and everything felt unfamiliar, even herself.

The record player told Lucy a lot about Dido. The fact Dido had owned records told Lucy the elderly lady had been reluctant to fast-forward into the twentieth century let alone the twenty-first. But it was wired up to a large, although not particularly modern set of speakers so maybe, once upon a time, Dido had been interested in pushing forward parts of her daily life rather than living in the past.

She wondered if that was true of most older people? Her elderly next-door neighbour in Camberwell was very modern in comparison, but it was only now Lucy realised that. She'd been forever Internet shopping with parcels arriving from Amazon couriers on a daily basis. And being freelance, Lucy was always the one to take delivery of them when her neighbour had been out.

Lucy cast around for a computer or laptop just out of curiosity as to whether Dido had owned one. An old radio with a dial sat on the sideboard. She twiddled it and, unable to make it play, assumed it was broken. It was only then she noticed there was no television. It seemed a lonely experience, living with no TV. Lucy rarely turned hers on at home but she at least had one for background noise or to keep up with the news. But then perhaps Dido had always preferred music and the radio.

So it was the sounds of *The Best of Billie Holiday*, cranked up as loud as the speakers would allow, that kept Lucy company as total curiosity took over and she began venturing round the house, something she hadn't been able to do thus far under Clara's watchful gaze. Was it wrong to look through a dead relation's house? Especially if you hadn't known them? Was it snooping? It was really, but she was likely going to be in charge of sorting items for charity, packing up anything and selling it on behalf of her dad, as he wasn't exactly catching a flight home soon from the Caribbean.

'Five bedrooms,' Lucy counted as she went round the immaculately made-up rooms complete with an abundance of dried flowers in vases and doilies on dressing tables, the mirrors spotted with age. The rooms were dust-free. Had Dido had a cleaner? Or did she clean the house herself? Rather too large for one person, Lucy mused. But it would make a wonderful family home. Although, who needed five bedrooms?

Lucy put her wine down on a doily and began opening chests of drawers – empty other than for a few floral-themed paper liners and bags of dried lavender that had long since lost their scent. Other rooms were the same, all traces of past lives eradicated through time, only the bulky furniture remaining.

She had already had a glimpse of Dido's belongings when choosing the dress for the funeral and the boxes in the wardrobe called out to her, although she realised in all the fuss of her arrival, Dido's funeral and then beating a hasty retreat from Clara's earlier that day that she'd taken the box to Clara's as the two sisters had meant to go through it together.

At that moment, Lucy didn't want to see her sister. That slap. What had it all meant? Would Lucy be the one to reach out to Clara or vice versa? Right now, she didn't know. They'd always had a fractious relationship. One of Lucy's friends had once listened to them both passively-aggressively arguing about a dinner reservation when Clara came over to stay, and had called them 'frenemies', but that seemed such a strange phrase to apply to siblings.

Even so, they'd never become physical with each other before. The shock of the slap was wearing off and Lucy, far from angry, was curiously puzzled. And perhaps actually, yes, a little bit angry if she really thought about it. At St Peter Port, Clara had shown no glimmer of remorse as she strode away to the solicitor's. Instead, she had looked vindicated, as if she'd been itching to slap Lucy for the best part of three decades and had finally built up to it; the culmination of years of potted resentment.

Looking in at the shoeboxes once again just to be sure she hadn't missed anything interesting, she decided the document box at Clara's wasn't going anywhere and could stay at her sister's quite happily, unlike Lucy. But before she went back to her little flat, Lucy did want to take a better look; if only to sit and translate the shorthand from some of the notes they'd found inside.

Lucy chose a cosy bedroom at the front with pretty wallpaper, peeling at the top where it met the picture rail. It wasn't Dido's.

The idea of sleeping in Dido's room felt disrespectful, and even though she hadn't actually died in there, a little too creepy.

Downstairs Billie Holiday changed track and something faster than the luxuriant melodies of before began. The fast tempo of 'What a Little Moonlight Can Do' made Lucy want to break into a Charleston so she did, only for a moment or two. Her reflection in the floor-length mirror made her laugh. She'd never been much good at dancing. The vibrations of her feet on the uneven floorboards dislodged something in the wardrobe and a loud clunk sounded from within as something fell.

Lucy stopped dancing and went to retrieve the item that had fallen and to put it back in position. It was a camera, an old-fashioned one she thought she recognised from one of her copywriting jobs for a vintage company as a Kodak Box Brownie. Given its age, Lucy wondered if she'd completely killed it or if it might still work after being bashed about like that, although the only camera she knew how to use was the one on her mobile. She turned the Brownie over in her hands, looking at the frayed strap and the catches and deciding that its name was accurate. It really did look like a little brown box.

Lucy swayed. Suddenly the music seemed too loud whereas a moment ago it hadn't. The wine, the volume Billie Holiday was emitting, the slap . . . Lucy rubbed her temples. It had been a long day and the thought of curling up in bed sounded both alluring and appalling all at once. She would go and turn the music off in a moment. Then she'd close up the house and double-check everything was locked. It was the size of the house that was unnerving her. Its rambling layout meant she knew if there was an unlikely break-in during the night she might not hear it. And then she'd be murdered in her sleep. Lucy looked at the wine accusingly, walked to the bathroom and tipped the rest of it into the old white Victoriana sink.

Night was already drawing in. Any semblance of bravery she might have felt on arrival at Dido's house had waned. She turned the little camera round, wondering how on earth one went about operating it, and if she even dared open it all up to take a peek at its inner workings – she might accidentally destroy it.

Downstairs the music stopped suddenly, halfway through the song, the needle on the record player making a horrific scratching noise that chilled Lucy. Still in the bathroom, clutching the empty wine glass in one hand and the camera in the other, she didn't dare move. Instead she stared at herself in the mirror over the sink. Her scared reflection returned her wide-eyed gaze. *Record players don't make that noise of their own accord, do they?* Something instinctively told her someone, or something, had lifted the needle roughly.

Slowly she made her way out of the bathroom and crept stealthily down the stairs, acutely aware that the steps creaked and she winced every time they did. She approached the sitting room and, holding her breath, looked round the door to see the back of a man with dark hair. He was standing by the record player and while his body was still, he appeared to be looking around the room, his head moving slowly.

She took a breath, ready to call at him to find out who he was, then paused, wondering if she should grab the empty, heavy cut-glass vase from the front hall first as some sort of weapon. Hearing her quick intake of breath he swung round and stared at her.

'Who the hell are you?' he demanded.

Lucy stared at him and stepped back a pace in the doorway. 'Who are you?' she countered. 'How did you get in?' She looked the thirty-something man up and down and her first instinct told her he wasn't there to rob the house or kill her, given he was wearing a blue and white striped apron and holding a barbeque spatula.

'I live down there,' he said angrily wielding the spatula in the direction of the window. 'In the cottage.'

'What cottage? Why are you in my house?' she asked. It wasn't her house. She wasn't sure why she'd said it. It was either that or stutter her way through a complex explanation of what she was doing there and why. She didn't owe this man a convoluted set of details.

'Your house?' he asked. 'This isn't your house.'

Lucy sighed. 'No. But I'm staying here and—'

'Who are you?' he asked again.

'It's none of your business,' Lucy said.

He looked at her, his eyes so dark she could barely see his pupils. 'I thought someone was breaking in,' he explained warily. 'Trashing the place.'

She nodded and then said, 'To the sounds of Billie Holiday?'

He became defensive. 'I don't know what people listen to when ransacking houses.'

Neither did Lucy. 'Surely they'd try to make as little noise as possible,' she reasoned.

'Which brings me on to my next point,' he said. 'The music was ridiculously loud. Why was it so loud?'

She baulked, unwilling to give him an explanation. 'Who are you?'

'I'm Will,' he said. 'I live in the cottage between Deux Tourelles and the field and up until five minutes ago I was barbequing in my garden. But the soundtrack was both far too loud and not of my own choosing and I've had enough.' He clamped his jaw shut.

The crackle from the speakers, still connected to the record player, was the only sound in the room as they stared at each other.

'Sorry,' Lucy said quietly.

He ignored her, or chose not to respond and instead asked, 'Where's Dido?' He looked around as if Dido might walk into the room any minute.

'Dido?' Lucy spluttered. 'She's . . .' She stopped, and then adopting a softer tone: 'She passed away. A few weeks ago.'

His mouth opened and he looked horrified. Slowly he said, 'She died?'

Lucy nodded. 'Yes. I'm sorry.'

51

He sat down on the sofa and looked so shocked she wondered if she should offer a drink to this man who had walked into Dido's house shouting and ranting.

'Are you all right?' Lucy asked, still standing. 'Did you know her well?'

'Shit,' was all he said, slowly.

She stood awkwardly as he looked down at the barbeque tool in his hand. He looked up at her and then stood up.

'Sorry,' he said as he walked towards the doorway. She moved back and let him pass.

'It's all right,' Lucy said when they were both in the hallway, although she wasn't sure whether he was offering condolences for Dido's passing or apologising for barging towards her.

'How?' he asked her when he reached the front door. 'How did she die?'

'She went into hospital and then died shortly after. Something to do with her lungs. Think she picked up some kind of infection during the war or after the war . . . something like that. And, well, also her age.'

He nodded and walked out the front door, then looked back at her, and in particular, the camera she was still holding.

'Is that yours?' he asked.

'No. It's Dido's. It was Dido's I mean. I just found it.'

'Do you know what it is?' he asked.

Lucy looked down at it as if it might suddenly have turned into something else. 'It's a camera.'

'It's really old,' he said. 'Be very careful with it.'

She put his patronising tone down to the shock of having found out his neighbour had just died. 'OK, I will,' she said between gritted teeth. But he had turned and gone out through the front door, which she realised now she had left unlocked when returning from the shop.

She stared after him. 'Bye then,' she called out in a sarcastic tone to his retreating figure.

But he neither called out to her by return nor waved an acknowledgement. He simply carried on walking.

Lucy spent a fitful night not sleeping, playing the day through in her mind. The argument, the slap, the man from the cottage scaring her, shouting at her and then leaving. Before bed, she'd looked out of her window to the cottage but all the lights must have been off inside because she couldn't glimpse it in the darkness.

She wasn't prone to drama but yesterday had been the most dramatic day she'd experienced in a long time. At home, she got up and went to the gym and then got down to work, met friends for dinner or trips to the theatre or cinema, planned the occasional holiday, went out for work functions, came home, slept. Rinse and repeat. There's a reason why she didn't come back here. Too much drama. Plus, she had no home in Guernsey – not after her parents sold up and left.

She only knew a few people on the island from her school days. Most, when they reached their twenties if not before, upped and left for the mainland. Some returned when they had children and wanted a more sedate pace of life, a good job, usually in finance, and to be able to finish work at five o'clock and head to the beach for a picnic. It was idyllic, now Lucy thought about it. Her childhood had been easy, all she'd known, until she'd got itchy feet and knew the rest of her life needed a little more excitement than what Clara had seemed happy to settle with.

She didn't know when she'd eventually fallen asleep but she had heard the dawn chorus at some point and that had jolted her. Her eyes stung with tiredness and she rubbed them profusely as she got ready for the day. Lucy set up her laptop in the study ready to plan her articles for upcoming issues of a medical practice's customer newsletter and to finish off the work for the plush toy company. The large desk sat in the bay window facing the room and she threw open the windows behind her, letting the cool breeze in, both airing the room and serving to keep her awake as she worked. There was no Wi-Fi in the house and so she compiled emails, saved them and made a point to visit a café, buy a coffee and send them later. She wasn't in the mood to rig up her phone data to her computer.

Every now and again, Lucy picked up her phone and checked it, but there was still nothing from Clara. She hated arguing with anyone, let alone her sister, and Lucy knew if Clara didn't make contact with her today, then she would have to make the first move; something she was loath to do.

She broke for lunch early, eating a sandwich in the kitchen, Radio 4 playing quietly on the old Roberts Radio that she'd finally managed to get working on the window ledge. The roller blind in the kitchen had been down the entire time and Lucy opened it and looked out towards the large walled back garden. With the sun shining on it, it looked beautiful and Lucy took the rest of her sandwich outside and wandered around. Rose bushes were growing a bit haphazardly but showing an abundance of small tempting curls and colourful buds. A garden bench was positioned at the far end, looking towards the house through the sweep of garden. Lucy wasn't really into gardening and knew nothing about plants, but she knew when one was pretty enough to sit and appreciate.

It distracted her for long enough to forget about checking her phone for messages from Clara, but when the sun became too bright as it lit the garden in its full glow, she went inside.

Lucy couldn't face working and she closed the laptop lid, steeled herself and messaged her sister. Had Lucy provoked Clara into slapping her in some way? Although in her tiredness she couldn't remember the exact words that had propelled Clara into violence. Lucy could be the bigger person and apologise, but surely it was Clara who owed Lucy the apology.

She paused, her fingers on the screen, ready to type but not sure quite what to put. She opted for, *'Can I collect Molly from school and spend the afternoon with her?'* Short and sweet.

Regardless of what was happening with Clara, she wanted to be able to spend time with her niece.

She barely had time to put the phone in her jeans pocket before a reply came back from Clara confirming that Molly would like that and that Clara would inform the school. It was a perfunctory reply and gave nothing away.

There were a couple of hours until Molly finished school for the day and Lucy went into the sitting room and glimpsed the Perspex box marked 'P'. She'd forgotten about it, but seeing it now reminded her about the box she'd taken to Clara's. She unclipped the lid of the Perspex box and looked at the contents. It was full of official-looking documents, newspapers and magazines and Lucy lifted them gently out to take a look. Most were from the 1940s and a few were from the 1960s, which seemed an oddly large gap of twenty years between the two dates with nothing in between.

The newspapers were yellowing and there were thin copies of *The Star* and the *Evening Press*. Some were complete newspapers, folded over, and some were just the odd scrap cut out and kept from the time of Guernsey's Occupation; acts of resistance and sabotage reported on by the newspaper staff and then, judging by the tone of voice, heavily edited by the Germans to demonstrate to all who read that these crimes would be punishable in the strictest terms and that Islanders would do best not to continue. She flicked through clippings of cables being cut, of red V for Victory signs being painted on signposts and doors, of foreign workers going missing, of prosecutions of locals for being out after curfew or for aiding those they shouldn't, of British spies being captured on the island and the condemnation of Guernsey families who'd hid them, and the arrests of those whose homes had been raided and who had been found with illicit radios hidden under floorboards after they had been expressly forbidden by the occupying force.

Lucy flicked, breathlessly, through more and more clippings of more and more 'offences' until the print swam before her already-tired eyes. She'd thought Guernsey hadn't really had a resistance, as such, but seeing these few acts of sabotage and defiance listed one after the other in the newspaper cut-outs made her think again.

At the bottom of the pile was a copy of *The Star* from July 1st 1940. Next to the masthead on the front page, presumably paid for and placed before the arrival of the Germans, were adverts for tobacconists and fertilisers. But the rest of the page was dedicated to an 'Order of the Commandant of the German Forces in Occupation of the Island of Guernsey'. The next day's newspaper held an even longer version of that published before and it was obviously a struggle to get all the orders onto one page as the second version had a smaller font and was crammed into the page.

Lucy read, entranced at things she'd learnt in passing years ago but had long since forgotten about.

The first orders related to a newly imposed curfew from eleven o'clock at night until six o'clock each morning, and a ban on motorcars for private use. Next to these, on the newspaper, was scribbled a note in elegant handwriting:

Dido, how will you get to and from the club now? We need to talk about you not singing there anymore. Persey. x

As Lucy folded the newspaper out to read the rest of the orders from the early days of the Occupation, an envelope that had been resting within the pages of the paper fell out. Lucy bent to retrieve it and looked at the address on the front:

Miss Persephone Le Roy, Deux Tourelles, Les Houards, Forest

The elaborately named Persephone had cropped up again, packed up in a box marked P. She picked up her phone and messaged her dad. He'd know a bit more, surely. Inside the envelope was a short note, written on wafer-thin paper, which Lucy read.

> Persey,
>   Condolences about your mother. I appreciate it might be a terrible inconvenience at this awful time, but can you meet me by the statue of Victor Hugo in Candie Gardens at ten o'clock this Saturday? It's important. I have something urgent I must tell you in person.
>   Lise
>   X

Chapter 6

1940

Persey read the newspaper that Mrs Grant had fetched earlier that day. The orders from the Germans were vast. She circled the ones relating to curfew strictly being imposed at eleven o'clock at night and the ban on the use of motorcars and hastily scribbled a note on the newspaper for Dido to read. Would the cabarets and clubs even be open now the Germans were here? Or if they were . . . would it just be full of German officers, watching her young, beautiful sister singing most evenings? The thought drained the colour from her face and she wondered what form their lives would take with the Nazis ruling the island. Was Dido's original prediction about rape and murder actually quite close to the truth?

She had not told Dido or Jack about Stefan's arrival on the island and found it easy to forgive them for forgetting him so readily. They had not thought about him the way she had over the years. The moment she'd had with him outside Deux Tourelles had been brief and she'd been too shocked when he'd said her name to question him further. The questions wouldn't come, and his fellow officer had coughed pointedly down by the gate and Stefan, their friend of old, had apologised, turned and left.

She had not been able to ascertain why he was here, why he'd been at Deux Tourelles, why he'd not made himself known to them . . . just stood and waited to be recognised. Was it shame? None of it made sense and what made even less sense to Persey was the fact that her kind, calm, caring friend was in a German uniform, had joined a war full of hate and malice and helped add to all of that by being a participant in it, on the side of spite and wrong.

Persey knew why she wasn't going to tell Dido and Jack just yet. If and when Stefan returned to see them, she would let him tell them why he was here.

She continued to read the notice in the paper:

All clocks and watches are to be advanced one hour . . . to accord with German time.

  No person shall enter the aerodrome at La Villiaze.

  The British National Anthem shall not be played or sung without the written permission of the German Commandant . . .

Persey baulked to read that the Reichsmark would be introduced to the island and the rate temporarily fixed at five marks to the pound and then read something that made her sit up straighter in her chair:

All British sailors, airmen and soldiers on leave in this Island must report at the police station at 9 a.m. today and must then report at the Royal Hotel.

Her hands shook and she laid the newspaper down as she thought of Jack. His story wasn't that he was on leave, which would have been quite sensible now she thought about it, especially if someone who knew he'd gone to join up saw him on the island only weeks later. Jack's story was that he hadn't left at all, although he had been adamant they wouldn't need to use that tale as he was only here for a short while and then he'd be gone with no one outside of Deux Tourelles any the wiser as to his actions if he kept a low profile. Only of course now German officers had already been inside the house, already seen him. Would the plan stay the same?

Right now, Jack was out spying. Just thinking the word made her chest tighten. He was going to attempt to lay low, down by the harbour, and watch the Germans' shipping movements, while she was expected to see how many planes landed on the island and Dido was tasked with finding out where anti-aircraft guns were being positioned.

'Oh God,' she said to herself. She was counting down the days until Jack left. Saturday. He'd be gone by Saturday. Less than a week. Once she knew he was safely off the island she might be able to relax a little more. Although then they would be in the house without a man to protect them, should they need it, which she sorely hoped they wouldn't. The important thing was for Jack to leave, safely picked up by the navy.

Persey read the final order on the paper three times to be sure she'd read it correctly.

The continuance of privileges granted to the civilian population is dependent upon good behaviour. Military necessity may from time to time require the orders to be made more stringent.

She put the newspaper down without even bothering to open the rest of it. All the news she needed was on the front page; everything else would pale in comparison.

As she was taking time off from singing in the evenings to grieve for their mother, Dido was relishing the idea of her part in Jack's mission. She had declared it the very thing to keep her mind away from thoughts of the funeral. Jack had been clear that they were to commit as much as they could to memory and not to write anything down in case they were stopped and questioned by soldiers who were busy assembling checkpoints. Dido was excited to play her part in helping Britain, 'no matter how small it is and even if they do nothing with the information,' she had said.

Persey couldn't really fathom what the British would do with the intelligence. The Channel Islands had been demilitarised, the British Expeditionary Force were hardly going to turn around and come back now, were they?

'There are over four hundred and fifty Germans here so far,' Mrs Grant surprised Persephone by saying as she walked into the kitchen with a basket of shopping.

Persey sprang up to help her, taking the heavy basket from the housekeeper's hands. There was a copy of the island's only other daily newspaper rolled up and she toyed between falling upon it eagerly for new information and ignoring it altogether. She couldn't face seeing more orders, which it would inevitably contain.

'That kind of information will please Jack. But how do you know how many soldiers there are?' Persey asked as she started unloading the fresh bread, cheese and produce into the pantry.

'I asked Mr Collins at Le Riches grocery store. He's been supplying provisions for the troops.'

Persey turned and looked at Jack's mother. 'Has he now?'

'That's the look I wanted to give him, but as someone in the queue behind me muttered, everyone's got to eat.'

'They must be expecting more soon,' Persey mused as she turned back to the shopping. 'You weren't making too much of asking were you?' Persey said, thinking how easy it would be to look too curious and thus inadvertently draw prying eyes upon Deux Tourelles and Jack.

Mrs Grant unfolded that day's newspaper. 'Everyone was asking him something,' she said defensively.

More aircraft had landed at the aerodrome since Persey last went past on the way back home after summoning the doctor. Without realising it, she'd become entrenched in her house ever since her mother had died, had not set foot outside the grounds of Deux Tourelles in two days. Today she had reason to step outside the boundary line, but found that she really didn't want to. It was easier to stay inside, ignore everything going on around her; wait for Jack to leave and pray normality resumed soon.

Condolence cards had started arriving by hand and in the post, but in the excitement of Jack's clandestine activities and the Germans' arrival, she felt people inside the house had forgotten her mother too quickly. It wouldn't have been this way if the Germans hadn't come. Persephone didn't want to forget her, but the pain of remembering her smile and thoughtfulness was too much to bear sometimes.

The undertaker had been kind enough to telephone to make most of the arrangements so far, but Persey had to visit for the final formalities that went hand in hand with a funeral. She steeled herself for that and also because she was going to try to do her bit to help Jack and take as much of a look at the airport as she could. She had done it innocently enough on the first day. So why did she feel cold whenever she thought about it? Because now it was spying – of a sort – and completely different; not at all innocent.

When she did go, she was unsure whether she should stand in plain view and make herself look less suspicious, or risk being caught hiding in the bushes. What would happen to her then? She decided to lay her bicycle down and pretend she was putting the chain back on if anyone came past, but she barely had a chance to decide whether or not to dirty her hands on the chain to give more credence to her story when a local car came past and stopped near her. Persey hadn't been expecting a man in German uniform to step out of the driver's side. In her naivety, she had assumed all Germans would be in German cars but they'd obviously already begun commandeering Guernsey vehicles.

The man walked towards her. She looked at him and was aware of her chest rising and falling before she made a concerted effort to still her breathing as much as possible.

Neither of them said anything for a moment or two but eventually they spoke at the same time.

'Persephone,' Stefan said.

But she had already started with, 'Why are you here?'

He closed his eyes and then when he opened them it was to look past her, down the lane.

'I was coming to see you,' he said. He pulled his cap off and tucked it under his arm. That blond hair, still cut the same. Self-consciously he put his cap back on.

'That's not what I mean and you know it,' she chastised.

He sighed. 'I know.'

'Well?' she said. 'Ten years, Stefan. Not a word from you. And then . . .' She gestured towards the airport laden with Luftwaffe aircraft and at him in his uniform. 'And then this,' she finished simply.

He paused before answering. 'I thought you might be pleased. Was that stupid of me?'

'Pleased?' she answered a little too loudly. 'About the Nazis being here? Have you taken complete leave of your senses?'

'No, not about that. I knew you would not be pleased about that. But about me being here. I thought you might be a little relieved to see an old friend.'

She looked away from him, towards the airport, remembering what had happened between them on the cliff. Was he remembering too? 'Ordinarily I would, Stefan. But not like this. This is—' she grasped for her words '—this is not a bit like visiting old friends.'

He nodded. 'I appreciate that,' he said. 'But I was offered the opportunity to be of use here and I am not ashamed to admit that I wanted very much to return to Guernsey—'

'To be of use?' she interjected, narrowing her eyes. 'To help do what, exactly?' She recalled the words of the orders on the front of the newspaper. 'To help enforce our good behaviour?'

'No,' he said simply. 'That is not my role here.'

'Not your role? What is your role then?'

'I'm a translator. At the moment I am carrying out different administrative tasks for the *Feldkommandantur*, involving a lot of paperwork. I am what your father would have called a pointless bureaucrat.'

They stood in silence and another car passed them. Persey watched the uniformed driver nod to Stefan and he nodded back. Something about the silent exchange disgusted her.

'Persephone, I wanted to see you all.'

'But not to tell us it was you?'

'The first time I came you were all so upset. My condolences to you again. It was not the time to say anything.'

Persey exhaled and shook her head to prevent him saying anything else on the subject of her mother's death. 'And the second time? When you came to appraise our house? You waited for me to realise it was you when you knew it was me the whole time?' she said.

'Yes, but not at first. I had never been to Deux Tourelles during those summers and when I saw you . . . I don't know why but I became . . . I am not sure nervous is the right word. The shock of seeing you all together, I felt it would be . . . inappropriate. I think I knew I had to speak to you alone first.'

She looked around to indicate there was no one else present. 'Well, here we are,' she said.

He looked at her and allowed a small smile. 'Well, here we are.' And then, 'There's too much to say now, here in this lane. Might I drive you home and perhaps we can talk there?'

'I'm not going home,' she said. 'I'm going to the undertaker.'

'May I drive you there?'

'No. You may not. I have my bicycle and besides I can't get in a car with you, Stefan. I can't be seen in a German officer's car, regardless that we used to know each other once upon a time. You must realise that? What would people say?'

He nodded, crestfallen. 'Of course. I will wait at your house for you to return.'

She stared. 'No,' she said slowly. 'No, you won't.'

'The island is only about fifteen kilometres long.' He laughed. 'We can hardly avoid each other in the foreseeable future.'

'We can if you keep away from us,' Persey declared. The words had left her mouth before she'd had a chance to think them through.

'Is that what you want?' he asked. 'Truly?'

Persey looked past him, aware whatever she said in haste now would be remembered forever. By both of them.

He cut into her thoughts. 'We can't avoid each other,' he said more sternly than he'd spoken thus far.

'Why not?' she taunted.

'Because I am to be billeted with you, Persey. I am going to be living at Deux Tourelles.'

Chapter 7

Persephone sat in the armchair and dragged her mind back to that last time she'd seen Stefan. That last time on the cliff when he'd told her he'd see them next summer, told them he'd write. Maybe he hadn't said that, now she thought about it. Maybe she'd just wanted to believe that was the case. But he hadn't returned the following summer. He hadn't written. But then, neither had she. She hadn't known what to say. Somehow she felt as if she should apologise. But for what? She had no idea. She remembered him, and what had happened between them.

She remembered Dido fiddling with her ring, which is what had started it all, and then her saying . . . 'Stefan will rescue me won't you, Stefan?'

She remembered Stefan smiling, ever so discreetly, after having stated he wouldn't be able to save a woman with a two-minute head start from falling down the cliff. She remembered every single word.

Jack and Dido had set off, Jack's hand clasping Dido's while practically dragging her behind him. Jack had always viewed Persey and Dido as surrogate sisters, but it was often Dido he protected – smaller, slighter, younger than Persey. And then they had passed a thicket of bushes and were gone, out of sight.

Stefan had looked at his watch and then at Persey. She hadn't known what to say. Two long minutes of silence had stretched out in front of them and she'd kicked at a stone absent-mindedly, watching as it flew out over the edge of the cliff and disappeared out of sight as gravity took it and it began its descent towards the sea.

He too had watched the stone disappear and then looked back towards her.

'How long?' Persey had asked.

'About a minute and forty five seconds,' Stefan had replied.

Oh, good Lord. So long. Think of something to say. Think. 'Will you . . . will you be back next summer?' she had asked.

His blue eyes looked at hers. 'I hope so, yes.'

'And . . . when do you leave this time?' she'd clawed at the threads of an awkward conversation, willing it on.

'I leave in two days.'

'Two days?' she'd said in genuine, saddened surprise. 'I thought you were here for at least another fortnight. Until the end of summer.'

'Not this year,' he'd said simply.

'Why are you going so soon?' she'd asked quietly.

'I must spend some time with my mother and father before I leave for my studies again. I would like to remain here with my aunt and uncle. And with you. With you all. But spending my last few weeks with my parents is . . . the right thing to do.'

She'd nodded, could hardly believe he had been here for almost a month and this was the first time the two of them had been alone. He had been visiting his aunt and uncle in Guernsey every summer for the past four or five years and while she had forced herself to pay very little attention to him, this year she had surprised herself by growing even more interested. He was quiet, intriguing, handsome. Had he been like that all this time or had it happened suddenly?

'It's almost our time,' he'd said, holding out his hand.

She'd looked at it but kept hers firmly at her sides.

'You do not wish me to hold your hand? To keep you safe?'

'No,' she'd cried in horror.

'Jack is holding Dido.'

'Jack is dragging Dido,' she'd clarified.

He'd laughed. 'You start and I will follow.'

'No,' she'd said, thinking of him behind her, his eyes on her as she ran. 'You start – you're faster.'

'How do you know I am faster?'

She'd opened her mouth and then closed it. And then: 'Shouldn't we be running by now?'

He'd shaken his head slowly and began running and she'd given him a slow head start that it had transpired he hadn't needed as she'd had no hope of catching up with him. He had gone, past the thicket and round the narrow cliff path as it weaved and snaked its way against the edge of the cliff. The water lashed against the rocks below even though the day hadn't been particularly windy. She'd looked over the edge. There was a sudden, terrifying beauty about the coastline. Its lines were harsh where pieces of rock had been ripped away by the weather over the centuries. It was here long before her, and would be here long after her.

Something had glinted at her from the edge. Something gold; a ring. She'd skidded to a stop, hopped forward and picked it up intending to carry on running, but her stupid block heel had got the better of her; her shoes utterly without traction. Suddenly she had been too close to the edge, gravel kicking up behind her as she'd slipped down, landing on her side with a thud. Like the stone she had kicked only moments before, gravity had held her in its clutches and she'd slid down the side of the bank, throwing her hand up to grab at something, anything.

And then Stefan had called her name and his hand had landed on her wrist, his fingers clutching at her tightly. He'd fallen to the ground, pulling her up until she was alongside him. She had barely been able to see him, blinded by fear. She had hardly been able to think. He'd stared at her, his blue eyes widened by shock as they'd lain on the ground. She'd blinked, coming to as her heart raced and she forced herself away from him, moved back from the edge and slumped into a sitting position. He'd followed on hands and knees before he was sat next to her. Both had breathed heavily, a shared silent shock at what had almost happened. She had so very nearly gone over the edge. Down, hundreds of feet onto the rocks below.

Her lips had become dry, her mouth even more so. She'd wanted to say thank you. But she hadn't been able to speak. She'd stared straight ahead out to sea as she'd tried to regain control of her senses and her breathing. Next to her, he too stared out, a hard line between his eyebrows.

She'd glanced at him, intending to look away but he'd turned to look at her with a mix of fear and anger.

'You were not behind me,' he'd muttered. 'I turned around and you were not there.'

'No, I—'

'You could have died,' he'd said. His eyes had bored into her skin, flaming her cheeks.

'Thank—' she'd started.

But she didn't get the chance to finish her sentence. His lips had been on hers, kissing her. No one had ever kissed her before and she remembered not knowing what to do, how to respond. And just as quickly he had stopped, pulled back and looked at her uncertainly.

Should she have leant forward and kissed him back or—

'There you two are,' Dido had called from the path behind them.

And then it had been Jack's turn to look put out as he'd jostled Dido out the way. 'What the hell are you doing sitting down? You should be running. You're not taking this seriously.'

'Why are you not at the finish line?' Persey had asked accusingly, unable to think of anything else to say. She'd put her fingers against her lips. She'd felt Stefan's on them still even though he had stood up, holding out his hand for her, avoiding her gaze. She'd taken his hand in hers and he'd helped pull her up and then the contact was broken. He'd walked ahead of her, past Jack and Dido, waiting.

'I lost my ring,' Dido had said. 'I came back for it. Jack says we've won by a country mile but there's no hope in hell of finding the ring but I thought we may as well try as not.'

Persey had unfurled her fingers from where she'd been grasping the ring. Wordlessly she'd shown Dido.

Her sister had trilled, 'Oh, you are too clever. Oh, well done, Persey. Well done, Stefan.'

Stefan had smiled but made no reply.

Was she cold or was it remembering that day that made her shiver now? She had walked that cliff path so many times in the intervening years, always pausing at the place Stefan had kissed her. He had left before they had the chance to talk. She hadn't had the chance to explain that his kiss had surprised her. She hadn't had the chance to say thank you for saving her. She had told no one about the fall or the kiss. That memory was not anyone else's. How awful that he'd simply gone.

And how dreadful it was that he'd now returned.

'When?' Dido asked later that day.

'He says tomorrow,' Persey replied.

'Why didn't he say anything the first time he came to the house?'

'I don't know.'

Dido's shock was evident. 'Stefan? Stefan from all those years ago is here. And you recognised him, didn't you? That's why you ran out to him. Why you asked if I remembered him the other night. Why didn't you say at the time?'

'Because I wasn't sure the first time. And I couldn't glean any further detail as to why he was here and I was astounded that it was him,' Persephone said, listing only part of the reasons she had for keeping quiet.

Dido fell into the armchair. 'Not as astounded as I am, clearly. How long is he staying?'

'I have no idea. I assume for the duration? He's an officer. Part of the administration so he's not an ordinary foot soldier, I think. But even then I don't know if that makes any difference as to how long he stays.'

'Staying for the duration? How long do we think that might be? I dread to think. Is he still nice?' Dido asked with a frown, looking out of the window. 'He was always quite sweet really. Bit dull I seem to remember, but quite sweet.'

Persephone, exasperated, replied, 'I just don't know, Dido. Really.'

'What about Jack?' Dido asked solemnly.

'I've been thinking about it all afternoon,' Persey replied. 'It's not ideal, is it? Having Stefan billeted here while Jack's here. Jack never really got on with Stefan, just sort of put up with him because he was a relation of Mother's friend, thrust upon us to be entertained. Always a tension between them. I think Jack felt a bit threatened – Stefan being taller and a better swimmer and . . . anyway. Maybe that kind of childish behaviour will be over now,' she said, then switched back to her original point: 'And then when Jack goes, Stefan will want to know where he's gone. How do we explain that?'

'I don't know. We'll have to think of something,' Dido remonstrated. 'It's bloody awful, Persey. What about getting Jack off the island? We're going to have to go in darkness, after curfew. How do we do that with a bloody German under the roof watching what we do?'

'We might be all right,' Persey said unconvincingly. 'Depends what time Jack's being picked up by the navy. If before eleven then it's before curfew and we'll be fine. If it's after . . . Are you singing Saturday night?'

Dido nodded.

'Take him with you,' Persey suggested.

'Who? Jack?'

'No, Stefan. Smile sweetly and beg a lift in that car he's taken from some poor Islander. Then keep him out as long as possible.'

'By doing what?' Dido asked.

'I don't know. Nothing you shouldn't though, Di.'

'It's Stefan,' Dido reasoned. 'If he's still as dull as he was ten years ago I imagine I'll be quite safe.'

Mrs Grant knocked and entered.

'Mrs Grant, you don't need to knock these days,' Dido said. 'The whole world's gone topsy turvy. Them and us no longer applies. Now the us and them are us Islanders and those Germans.' Dido laughed as if she'd made a wonderful joke but Mrs Grant looked put out and handed Persephone some letters.

'More condolence cards, I think,' she said and then left.

'Oh, Dido, you are tactless. Us and them?' Persey said, looking through the stash of post.

'She knows what I mean,' Dido reasoned. 'She's not offended.'

Persey raised an eyebrow. 'Let's hope not.' She gave four thick envelopes to Dido as her sister got up to fix a drink. 'You can open these. I can't read any more about Mother. It starts me off and I just can't bear more tears at the moment.'

The last piece of mail, Persey kept back. It was addressed only to her, flimsier than the rest and, on closer inspection, on cheaper paper.

Persey,

Condolences about your mother. I appreciate it might be a terrible inconvenience at this awful time, but can you meet me by the statue of Victor Hugo in Candie Gardens at ten o'clock this Saturday? It's important. I have something urgent I must tell you in person.

Lise

X

Dido looked over Persey's shoulder as she fixed them drinks. 'Who's Lise?'

'That new girl from work,' Persey replied. Working in an insurance office full of men, Persey had been overjoyed when Lise had joined as an additional clerical assistant, and not just because it meant sharing the secretarial work with another able pair of hands. 'We've become quite chummy. She's the only other girl,' she added as she sat back in the chair and accepted the glass of sherry that Dido handed her.

'Strange request.' Dido nodded towards the letter. 'Why doesn't she just wait for you to return to the office and tell you whatever it is then? When do you think you'll go back to work?' Dido asked.

'Mr Le Brost has been very good. Says I can return next week if I like. It'll be after Mother's funeral and after we've finished helping Jack. And you'll be back at the club on Saturday.'

'With our good friend the Nazi officer Stefan for company. People are going to say all sorts of things, you know, when I turn up with him. My reputation . . .' Dido took a mouthful of her sherry.

'I know. But I don't know what else to do. Just make friends when he gets here and then on Saturday evening, stick to him like glue. We just need to get Jack off the island.'

They ate dinner in silence the night Stefan arrived. To Persey's horror, the dining room had been laid out with small vases of wild flowers lining the centre of the table that ran the length of the dining room. They should have taken the middle out and shortened it because now it felt obscenely large and formal, with Persey one end and Dido the other, Jack and Stefan opposite each other in the middle. Such close proximity between the men was a concern. Persey looked down at a red wine stain from a dinner long ago on the otherwise crisp, white tablecloth; a dinner either one or both of her parents would have hosted with friends or her father's colleagues. And now it was she and her sister entertaining a German officer. Or not entertaining, as neither Dido nor Persephone had been able to say much throughout the dreary meal.

73

Mrs Grant had chosen to resume the role of 'staff', and had left her son Jack in the halfway space in between, dining with Persey, Stefan and Dido, while as housekeeper Mrs Grant had removed herself to eat in the kitchen. No one tried to stop her. It was where she said she felt most comfortable, especially with 'him' here.

Stefan had arrived in the afternoon, looking as awkward as Persephone felt. He'd unpacked upstairs in their mother's bedroom. Persey and Dido had cleared the room, emptied the wardrobe of their mother's clothes and shoes; taken her hairbrushes and jewellery box, her bottles of scent. Dido had cried and Persey had done her best to comfort her while not breaking down herself. And now Mother's things were in Persey's room, folded neatly and stacked in the corner. It would serve as an ever-present reminder of the loss of their mother.

Once he had unpacked, Stefan had ventured downstairs and then had looked unsure of himself when he had joined them in the kitchen, where Mrs Grant was folding laundry and Persey was trying to stoke the stove.

He'd stood on the threshold and coughed gently to announce his arrival in the kitchen. Mrs Grant had looked at him, as had Persey but as no one had spoken or invited him to sit he had left the room as swiftly as he had appeared.

Persey knew she'd been rude but she couldn't bring herself to invite him to join them for a pot of tea; couldn't bring herself to engage in small talk. She had breathed a sigh of deep relief when she heard the front door click shut sometime later, signalling his temporary departure from the house. It was cowardly but she just didn't know what to say to him.

'I don't like this,' Mrs Grant had said.

'Nor do I.'

'We're not the only ones to have a bloody German thrust upon us,' Mrs Grant had declared. 'I spoke to Mrs Effard this afternoon, the housekeeper at Mer Vue and she said they had two arriving imminently. Two! The field cottage has been taken over as well now the Germans have noted its emptiness. They're everywhere. We're all slowly being overrun. And it's only going to get worse.'

'I suppose we should be grateful it's just him then.' It occurred to Persey suddenly that Stefan may have had something to do with it being just him. In a house the size of Deux Tourelles, surely she and Dido could have been asked to bunk up together, or even worse, all of them evicted entirely? She wasn't sure if she should feel annoyed if he'd had a hand in it, or grateful they didn't have other soldiers thrust upon them. *Perhaps it's better the devil we know,* she thought.

'This house . . .' Mrs Grant began. 'It is yours now, isn't it?'

Persey paused as she reached for the teapot on the high shelf above the stove. She turned and looked at the housekeeper.

'As the eldest sister,' Mrs Grant continued folding laundry, 'and with your parents having no sons I just assume . . .'

Persey had swallowed. 'I hadn't thought. The solicitor knows Mummy has passed away. He says we need to visit or he can come here but he didn't let on any detail and . . . He'd have said . . . wouldn't he? He'd have said if the house had been left to someone else. The reading of the will, he hadn't said it was urgent.'

Ownership of Deux Tourelles had been the last thing Persey had thought about in all of this. They had always been well taken care of, financially; never rich but able to afford some of life's luxuries. Both girls had always been expected to earn their own money, put it away in the bank for when they might truly need it. No lazing around Deux Tourelles, day in, day out, looking forlorn and pointless, waiting for a husband. Her parents had both agreed that laziness was not what they were put on this earth for.

Deux Tourelles ran on their father's income from his job and his investments, and when her father died, his small company had naturally closed, but it had not affected their income a great deal. Her astute accountant father had always made sure to inform his wife and children about annuities and pensions, stocks and shares – when they paid out, how much could be expected. While in some of their school friends' houses money had been an ugly subject never to be discussed – at Deux Tourelles it was sometimes the starting point to family conversations and Persey knew she would forever be grateful to her parents for all their hard work and for instilling a good work ethic in her and Dido.

Later, when she sat in the dining room staring at the red wine stain, she thought about the mad state of the world that could see a man such as Hitler storm his way across Europe, get as far as the French coast and then the Channel Islands, so close to England, so close to the main prize, that absolutely nothing made any sense anymore.

While she'd been musing, a conversation had begun between Stefan and Jack that Persey had missed the beginning of. She looked up frowning and caught Dido's eye, who gave her a look of alarm. Persey began to pick up the threads as quickly as she could.

'And so you were not required to be called up?' Stefan continued.

'No. As Channel Islanders we aren't expected to. We can, of course. But conscription doesn't stretch to us here. We're only expected to fight on behalf of the Crown, if the Crown is in danger.' Jack ate a roast potato and looked nonchalant. Persey wondered if he looked too nonchalant. She hadn't eaten anything on her plate and forced herself to spear a carrot onto her fork.

'I see,' Stefan said, looking thoughtful. 'A lot of men have left the islands to fight,' he prompted.

'Yes,' was Jack's non-committal response.

Persey slowly lifted the carrot to her mouth and forced it in. Watching. Waiting.

'But not you?' Stefan asked.

'I do hope you're not suggesting cowardice?' Dido interrupted.

'No, no. Of course not,' Stefan said with a genuine look of alarm. 'I have not seen any of you in so long and I want to pick up where we left off . . . I think. To find out more about how you have been these past few years.'

The room grew silent again. How could they pick things up as if nothing had happened? As if Stefan wasn't sitting in front of them in that uniform?

'But the thing is,' Stefan continued when no one else spoke, 'I mentioned I would be staying here to the lady who cleans the Channel Islands Hotel where we are headquartered and she said she knew of you all and she seemed upset that I would be billeted with two young women. I made sure to tell her that it was proper because there was Mrs Grant and her son.' Stefan paused. Persey swallowed the carrot too soon and it scraped the entire way down her throat.

'The cleaning lady,' Stefan continued, 'said that Mrs Grant's son could not possibly be at the house because Jack Grant left for England weeks ago to be a soldier.'

Chapter 8

2016

Lucy reread the short missive addressed to Persephone Le Roy that had fallen from the pages of the newspaper. So Persephone was a Le Roy and the address on the envelope showed she had lived at Deux Tourelles. *Persey . . . can you meet me?* someone named Lise had asked. *Something urgent . . .*

She put the letter back in its envelope, then returned it to the box. She had then rifled through the mail stacked on the centre table in the entrance hall, found a letter from Dido's car insurance company and organised the odious task of adding herself as a temporary driver. The car was battered, old and rusty and only had a few months left on the MOT. After that, Lucy sensed it would cost more to MOT it than the car was worth. She'd have to let them know Dido had passed away but that was a job for later depending on who was the executor. There would be so much of this, Lucy thought. Admin.

Just before three p.m. she was in Dido's Renault and driving through the lanes to Molly's school. After confirming who she was to Molly's teacher and offering the password Clara had told her, she gathered her niece into her arms and the two squeezed each other tightly.

'What are you doing here?' Molly asked as they walked towards the car.

'I missed you,' Lucy replied as she strapped Molly into the booster seat Clara had left out for her as arranged. When Lucy had collected it from the front doorstep she wondered if Clara had actually been inside her house at the time and was just avoiding her.

'Are we going to your house?' Molly asked.

'I don't have a house,' Lucy said, wondering whether to take Molly back to Deux Tourelles. It didn't exactly hold endless possibilities of fun for a boisterous five-year-old.

'Are you homeless now Mummy's kicked you out for being rude to her?'

'Erm . . .' Lucy replied, shocked that Molly knew what had gone on between the sisters.

'I heard Mummy telling Daddy that you had been your usual self. What does that mean?' Molly continued.

Lucy blew a puff of air out of her cheeks and sighed. 'Never mind. Don't worry about it, will you? It'll all get sorted.'

'Can we go to the beach?' Molly changed tack.

'Yes,' Lucy said, pleased the awkward conversation had ended so soon.

'And have ice cream?' Molly continued.

'Yes.'

'Before dinner?' the little girl asked.

'No.'

Lucy drove to her favourite beach, Pembroke. While others favoured Cobo Bay, Pembroke was, in her opinion, the prettiest on the island. She loved Pembroke beach not only because of its wide expanse of white sand but also because it directly faced England and although she had never actually seen the mainland from the beach, even on the clearest of days, she'd always known it was there, just out of sight, just out of reach, holding the promise of a glittering career that had, actually, never quite materialised. It was the only place in Guernsey where Lucy had felt she actually had both the time and space required to breathe; to look out towards something better.

She couldn't remember the last time she'd come to the beach on one of her flying visits. There'd never seemed to be the time. But now time was something she had plenty of and until she sorted out Deux Tourelles and put an end to this horrid row with Clara she wasn't going to give her sister the satisfaction of leaving so soon and proving her right. She was going to stay until the bitter end so no further accusations of familial negligence could be fired in her direction. Even though her mum and dad were about four thousand miles away in Barbados, Lucy noted, playing no part in the events in Guernsey.

On her final days as a full-time resident of Guernsey, she and Clara had sat on this beach and drunk cheap vodka until the early morning, returning home drunk and happy before a hung-over Lucy had caught the ferry to England and then the train to university.

In the end Lucy conceded to Molly's request for ice cream before dinner and the two of them bought delicious swirls of whipped vanilla made with thick milk from Guernsey cows. It tasted exactly as Lucy had always remembered it and unlike any ice cream she'd tasted anywhere else. Nothing matched it. The two took off their shoes and socks, buried them in Lucy's deep handbag and walked along the shoreline talking about Molly's school and her friends.

When they finished their ice creams, they scooped sand with their hands, making a gully for a rudimentary sandcastle for the tide to half fill. They lined the channel with shells. Then they ran happily to and from the shoreline, jumping over the waves as they moved in and out of the shore. Lucy, jeans soaked from jumping and knees wet from kneeling on the damp sand to dig, sat a bit further back on the dry sand and watched Molly as she hitched up her school summer dress, continuing the game and giggling as she tried to avoid getting wet.

'Hello again,' a man's voice sounded next to her and Lucy turned. Oh Christ. It was the man who'd stormed into Deux Tourelles last night. At the sight of Will she felt the fun of the afternoon drain away with the pull of the tide.

'Hello,' Lucy said stiffly, hoping he'd move on now he'd said his greeting. She avoided his gaze and looked at Molly as she played.

'Your daughter?' Will asked, glancing briefly at Molly. He smiled as he listened to her screech.

'My niece.'

He nodded and Lucy waited for him to say, 'Bye then,' and move on but he did neither.

'I'm glad I caught you,' he said. 'I wanted to apologise for last night. I was a bit short.'

'A bit short?' she echoed before clamping her mouth shut. The man had walked out of Deux Tourelles without so much as a goodbye.

'All right.' He laughed. 'I was . . . surprised. Sorry.'

'It's OK,' Lucy said, looking up at him. 'So was I, actually. I wasn't expecting a man wielding a barbeque tool to be inside the house.'

'You shouldn't have left the front door open then,' he said with a shrug.

'I won't do it again, don't worry,' Lucy said and then chastised herself as she remembered he'd been particularly cut up hearing Dido had passed away. 'I'm sorry you didn't know about Dido,' she said. 'Did Clara not tell you? I thought Clara had told everyone.'

'Who's Clara?' he asked.

'My sister. I was under the impression she'd informed everyone who needed to know about Dido's passing and then about the funeral.'

Will shook his head. 'I didn't know.'

'I'm sorry,' she repeated, this time with more feeling. 'Do you want to sit?'

Will looked at his watch and then nodded as he sat on the sand next to her.

'Were you close?' Lucy asked, suddenly acutely aware how close Will was to her.

He screwed his face up into a thoughtful expression. 'No,' he said slowly. 'Not really. I'd just help her out from time to time if things needed doing in the garden or when she needed the bins putting out.'

Lucy nodded and waited for more.

'I went to introduce myself to her when I moved in at the end of last year,' Will continued. 'We had a cup of tea once a week or so. She'd bring a plate of biscuits out and make me eat pretty much all of them. Always Garibaldis. I hate Garibaldis but once they'd made an appearance three or four times I could hardly tell her that. I think she thought I was starving down there by myself.'

'Surely not.' Lucy laughed. 'With your excellent barbeque skills.'

'It was all burnt when I got back to it last night,' he said. 'I took it off the grill and onto the hot plate before coming up to confront you but alas it was charred.'

Serves you right for storming in and scaring me. Lucy chuckled inwardly and then wondered if that was a bit mean.

'I went to bed hungry,' he said, bending and picking up a handful of white sand, which he examined and then scattered down gently. 'I'd have killed for a plate of Dido's Garibaldi biscuits at that point.'

Lucy laughed and so did he. They watched Molly jump a wave and then the little girl issued Lucy a double thumbs up, which she returned.

'So how long are you staying at the house?' Will asked.

'How long is a piece of string?' she replied. 'My sister and I are tasked with cleaning it out on behalf of my dad who was Dido's next of kin. And then it's back to work for me.'

'In Guernsey?' he asked.

'No. Mainland.'

'I've just left there. Well, at the end of last year.'

'Really?'

He nodded. 'My grandfather was born here so it was a bit like coming home, even though I've never lived here before. Just the odd holiday, you know.'

'It was the other way round for me,' Lucy said. 'I was born here and then needed to get away. Permanently,' she said.

There was a natural pause in the conversation and Molly came running. 'Can we have dinner now? I'm hungry.'

'Of course,' Lucy said, checking her watch. 'Shall we go to the café up there and get burgers. I've read they're good.'

'They are,' Will said. 'Handmade. The best.'

'Who are you?' Molly asked boldly, making both Lucy and Will chuckle.

'Will. Who are you?' he asked, holding out his hand to shake.

Molly took it and gave it a hard, serious shake, coating Will's hand in wet sand.

'Molly. I'm five and a half. How old are you?'

'Thirty-one and three-quarters,' Will replied, quick as a flash and very seriously, making Lucy warm to him a bit more.

'My aunty Lucy is nearly thirty,' Molly said in a matter-of-fact voice. 'So you are much older.'

'Not much older,' Will said with a mock-serious frown. 'Just a bit older.'

'OK, Molly,' Lucy stepped in. 'Time for burgers.'

Will smiled knowingly, his dark eyes lit amber from the sun's rays. 'It was nice to meet you, properly, this time.'

'It was,' Lucy smiled thinking him quite attractive now he wasn't shouting at her while waving a barbeque tool around.

They waved goodbye and Lucy and Molly began walking.

'Listen,' he called after Lucy. 'It's a big house for one person. If you need anything, I'm only at the end of the field.'

'Thank you,' she said. 'If I need anything I'll crank the music up in order to summon you.'

He laughed, raised his hand to wave again and carried on walking towards the shoreline. Lucy resisted turning back to look at him as long as was possible but by the time she and Molly reached the café at the edge of the beach she couldn't hold out any longer. She glanced at the beach and saw him standing at the water's edge, hands thrust in his pockets and looking out across the sea.

There was tomato ketchup all over Molly's smiling face by the time they'd finished eating and Lucy had a job to wipe it off. When they were offered pudding, Molly ordered an ice cream and Lucy had the embarrassing task of asking for it to be cancelled moments later when she remembered she'd already fed her niece an ice cream on the beach. 'You can't have two. Your mum will kill me.'

Lucy's phone dinged and she looked to see a message from Clara, saying she was running late and asking if she could take Molly back to Deux Tourelles and Clara would join them there in about an hour. Underneath it, she'd missed a reply from her dad and she clicked it open to see a response to her question about who Persephone Le Roy was.

'Dido's sister,' was the simple reply; followed by: *'Playing golf today. What are you doing?'*

She smiled. She'd tell him about her girls' dinner with Molly later.

Dido's sister? It's what Lucy had assumed but to see it confirmed when, up until her arrival on the island, there'd never even been a mention of Dido's sister to her seemed odd, and other than the few bits she'd found the house held no memory of Persephone Le Roy. She wondered what was in the box at Clara's and made a point to ask her for it when she saw her shortly.

By the time Lucy had paid and arrived back at Dido's house, Clara's car was already in the driveway.

'You're early,' Lucy said brightly, trying to mask the awkwardness that might rear again. 'Coming in?'

Clara said, 'No thanks. Got to get Molly home. She's got spellings and reading to do still.' Clara smiled thinly, enveloping her daughter in a hug, while Lucy retrieved Molly's booster seat and schoolbag from the car.

'We were right. Persephone was Dido's sister,' Lucy launched in as she handed her sister the items.

Clara frowned and gave a little theatrical shake of her head. 'What?'

'Dido's sister. It was Persephone from the photograph. Can I have the box that we found back?'

'Sure,' Clara said in a bored voice. 'In the boot.'

Lucy opened Clara's boot and retrieved the box, carrying it over and placing it on the wide stone doorstep.

'You should have come to the solicitor's,' Clara said in an accusing tone.

It was clear nothing was going to get resolved today. And she had to be joking. As if Lucy was going to accompany Clara anywhere immediately after that slap.

'Well I didn't. What happened?'

'Dido's will was short and sweet. She left money to a cat's home.'

'I bloody knew it,' Lucy cut in triumphantly.

'Dad has been left a lot of stocks and shares, which apparently adds up to a substantial inheritance. And her local church has been given a sum of money and the mini grand piano, which she specified should be primarily used in the church hall, which doesn't currently have one. In particular she wanted the Sunday School children to have use of it.'

Lucy smiled. 'Oh, that's nice,' she said. 'Well, that's that then.'

'No. Not quite,' Clara said. 'Dad got the stocks and shares but he didn't get the house.'

'What?' Lucy said in disbelief. 'Who did?'

'We did.'

'What?' Lucy gawped at her sister. 'No! We inherited Deux Tourelles. How come?'

'It's one of the reasons why I asked you to come home,' Clara said. 'I just had an inkling.'

'How?'

'It was something Dido said when Dad asked me to drop off some flowers for her birthday last year. We were discussing what I was doing and what you were doing for employment; she said that the youth of today needed a serious leg up. "You girls wait 'til I die," she'd said and then gave me a huge wink. I wasn't sure if I was supposed to take it seriously. I honestly thought Dad would get the house and you and I might get some money. If we were lucky.'

'Dad's going to be a bit shocked,' Lucy said before looking back in wonder and taking in the tired-looking windowpanes, the ivy running wild and the odd slate out of place on the roof. And then she smiled slowly. 'That's incredible. I can't believe she would do that. She really left it to both of us?'

Clara nodded.

'But she didn't even know me. Not really.' Lucy shook her head in a strange, disbelieving acceptance of the situation. 'This is crazy. Kind. And . . . crazy. How sad that she had no one else to leave it to.'

'Not sad for us,' Clara said pointedly.

'No, but what do we do with it?' Lucy asked.

'We carry on as planned and sell it, I guess,' Clara said. 'I could definitely use the money and it's not like you want to come and live here.'

Lucy paused before answering. 'No . . . I guess not.'

'We get the contents as well,' Clara pointed out.

'Wow,' Lucy cried.

But Clara carried on. 'Once we've cleared it all out together, sold the antiques and got a house clearance company to come and do the rest, you can go home. I'll sort the sale of the house. That process will take a complete age so you won't want to be here for months on end.'

Clara took charge as usual and so Lucy nodded and suggested, 'I guess we should start with paperwork?'

'Is paperwork now your strength?' Clara looked amused. 'If so can I leave you to go through this?'

Lucy looked at the box. 'Of course.'

'Good. I assume you're all right here? At night I mean?'

Lucy looked up at the house. 'Yes, I'm fine, actually.'

'OK,' Clara said uncertainly. 'Don't start quoting squatter's rights at me when it comes to selling it, will you? I need the money from this place. Aren't you a bit lonely here; a bit spooked?'

'No, actually,' Lucy said after thinking about it for a minute. 'The house could be homelier but the silence while I work in the study has been quite a change. And then there's the sexy neighbour who comes running if I turn the music up too loud.'

'Sexy neighbour?' Clara tilted her head to one side, like a dog, Lucy thought, waiting for more information.

'No I didn't mean that. I don't know why I said that.' Lucy was genuinely baffled at herself for having said something she was sure she didn't actually think.

'Interesting,' Clara said at the same time Molly asked, 'What does sexy mean?'

'Never you mind,' Clara said as she ushered her daughter towards the car. 'Say goodbye and thank you to Aunty Lucy.'

Molly did as she was told, happily, and then skipped towards the car.

'Clara?' Lucy asked. They had to sort this argument out.

'Yeah?' Clara looked at her watch and adopted a hurried expression.

'Nothing. Have a good evening.'

Lucy leafed through the vinyls, found some classical music she'd not yet played and made sure to keep the volume at a respectable level. She didn't want Will to find an excuse to descend upon her. Or did she? She laughed at herself and thought back to him on the beach, looking out across the sea. She'd not got too much out of him. Was he married? Divorced? Did he have children? What did he do for a living? She was oddly intrigued by the man who lived in the cottage by the far field. She stole a glance out of the sitting room window, looked down past the drive to where the cottage was all but hidden from this angle by tall conifers. Then she turned, retrieved her cardigan from the newel post in the entrance hall, made a mug of tea and settled down to look through the box.

There were a lot of papers within and to Lucy's untrained eye it looked mainly as if they were formal documents, forms and carbon copies of receipts for payments of goods delivered to the house over the years. That reminded her of the carbon copies of shorthand she'd found before. Where had she put those? Laundry bills and household expenses from years gone by showed regular deliveries of milk from the local farm and other items that Lucy wasn't immensely interested in. As she delved deeper within the box, lifting stacks of papers and flicking through them ad hoc, she stopped and stared at an old newspaper cutting, aged and flecked, its edges torn.

The advert read:

Compensation

For United Kingdom Victims of Nazi Persecution

On July 24th 1964 applications were invited from, or on behalf of, United Kingdom nationals who were victims of Nazi persecution, that is persons who suffered detention in a concentration camp or comparable institution. This excludes imprisonment in an ordinary Civilian Internment or Prisoner-of-War Camp.

No applications can be accepted after July 31st 1965. Victims who have not yet done so should therefore apply without delay. Application forms can be obtained from The Under-Secretary of State, Foreign Office, London, S.W.1

Lucy read the poster twice, not quite understanding it. Why was this poster in the box? She looked at it line by line. She shuddered when the phrase concentration camp leapt out at her more prominently than it had on the previous read-through. She sipped her tea thoughtfully. Who on earth had gone to a concentration camp?

Chapter 9

1940

'The cleaning lady mentioned she thought you had gone to England,' Stefan repeated at the dining table when Jack failed to respond. 'To join up.'

At the other end of the table Dido dropped her knife and it clattered noisily against the bone china, chipping a piece off the plate. To Persey it seemed that the dining room then became still and a sense of dread hovered over her.

'But she must be wrong?' Stefan said before glancing briefly at Dido's chipped plate with an expression Persephone couldn't read. He returned his gaze to Jack. 'You did not enlist? You are here.' He phrased the question so innocently, so like his old self, that Persey couldn't tell if he was probing with intent or if he was genuinely curious. She looked towards Jack who licked his lips and then rubbed them dry, stalling for time.

'Well . . .' Jack started. 'I didn't. I mean, I did go and then . . .' His hand shook as he leant forward, taking another piece of roast chicken from the dish that sat on the table between him and the German officer. Stefan leaned forward, picked the dish up to help Jack when it became clear the Islander couldn't quite reach.

'And then?' Stefan asked, his eyes narrow, but a smile touched the corners of his mouth as if he was genuinely confused.

'And then I returned.'

'Oh,' Stefan replied. He looked at his own plate, cut and sliced some chicken and then chewed. 'When?'

'When it became clear I wasn't cut out to be part of it all, I'm sorry to say.'

'In what way?' Stefan glanced suddenly towards both Dido and Persephone who had both paused eating. Persey slowly speared another carrot and willed Dido to do something normal, something that showed they weren't perturbed by this line of questioning.

'I'm not well,' Jack declared.

'In what way?' Stefan asked again.

'You do ask a lot of questions, old boy.' Jack's tone was that of exasperation. 'Dicky heart, if you must know. Failed my medical, spectacularly.'

'Dicky?' Stefan questioned the word.

'Skips a beat, far too often for a doctor's liking.'

'I am sorry to hear that,' Stefan said kindly.

'Yes, me too,' Jack lied. 'But there it is.'

The German appeared to be sated, but Jack continued and Persey wanted to scream at him to stop. 'I'm not sure what's worse, now I think about it,' Jack blundered on. 'Staying on the island pretending I never went. Or being back here, medically unfit, with my tail between my legs.'

'Well . . . yes. I think I understand,' Stefan volunteered. 'It must be . . . I am very sorry you are unwell. When did you return?'

Why was Stefan pushing this? Persey wanted to ask out loud but daren't. Stefan was a Nazi officer. Of course he was pushing it.

Jack drank a mouthful of wine and then responded. 'Not long before you chaps all arrived. Snuck in on the last boat. Lucky I did or else I'd still be in Weymouth Harbour looking towards my beloved island without a cat's chance in hell of getting here.'

'But you did not want to stay?' Stefan asked.

'In England? Why on earth would I do that?' Jack replied.

'To help win the war.'

'From a desk? From the sidelines? No thank you. I can barely organise my way out of bed in the mornings, I'm not sure I should be in charge of serious administration. Plus, also, bit boring, no?'

'It's what I do,' Stefan said kindly.

Jack took a sip of his wine and replied bitterly, 'My point exactly.'

The next day Persephone and Dido walked through St Peter Port in time to witness what Persey thought was one of the most horrific things she'd ever see in her life – a brass band of German soldiers goose-stepping through the town as the girls turned the corner past Lloyds Bank.

'Good God,' Persey exclaimed as they followed the noise and the soldiers came into view. The two backed against the wall of the bank. Dido clasped Persey's hand tightly but the older sister barely noticed. The cacophony shocked other shoppers into silence. Persey stared, mouth partly open until her tongue went dry and she closed it and swallowed. The band moved down the High Street and people began speaking in hushed tones.

Persey and Dido looked at each other, neither quite sure what to say to the other until Persey squeezed Dido's hand gently and said, 'Come on.'

Around them, as they walked, German notices had been placed in prominent locations: the latest rules and orders by which Islanders had to abide. She felt as sick as she had when she'd watched Luftwaffe planes land at the airfield.

'Do you think we'll find anything suitable to wear for Mother's funeral?' Dido asked.

'Hmm?' Persey asked distractedly.

'At Creasey's,' Dido clarified.

Persey wondered if the department store would be open, if it would have sold out of items because all the German soldiers had allegedly bought so many of the available luxury goods and sent them home to their mothers, sisters, wives. 'I just don't know.'

'I should like a new hat,' Dido said as they approached the shop and looked at the window, the mannequins wearing the latest fashions in greens, yellows and taupe, thick Guernsey jumpers folded prominently in the window to herald the coming chilly season. 'Do you think we ought to stock up?'

'What for?' Persey said.

'We might not get another chance to shop. We're cut off from the mainland now.'

'But not from the European mainland,' Persey said.

'True,' Dido mused. 'We might still get some things through from Paris. Imagine that.'

'Actually, I doubt it now I think about it. All the factories there must be given over to war production. For the Germans,' Persey reminded her as they entered the shop and were confronted with a milieu of German soldiers busily shopping along with a handful of Islanders.

One soldier appraised Dido and Persey and Dido looked kindly back at him, smiled and blushed. Persey pulled her sister away. 'Dido, don't,' she chastised. 'Just don't.'

'I only smiled,' Dido replied, pulling away from her sister and moving towards the millinery department. 'Even though they're the enemy, they're very good-looking, don't you think?'

'No,' Persey said sternly. 'I don't.'

'So blond,' Dido said. 'So tall.'

The girls queued to purchase Dido a new hat although it wasn't at all as fashionable as either of the girls would have liked. On leaving Dido whispered to Persey, 'Have you managed to get to the airport for Jack?'

'Shh, for heaven's sake, not so loud.'

'Well, have you?' Dido asked.

'Only for a moment or so before Stefan arrived in his car and put paid to that.' They strolled back through the High Street to the bus stop, which was far busier than usual on the route leaving the town. 'There weren't this many people on the way in,' Persey said, worrying if they'd be able to get home easily.

'Now people aren't allowed to use their motorcars, it's bus or bicycle if they want to come all the way into town,' Dido said.

'And probably not the bus for that much longer,' Persey said.

'We've been shopping,' Dido announced to Stefan as they met him in the drive at Deux Tourelles. Dido didn't wait for Stefan to comment, she moved past him and into the house. Persey stood and waited politely for the man she hardly knew any longer to speak.

'Did you buy anything nice?' he asked.

'No. Not really.'

Stefan looked around as if for inspiration as to how to continue the conversation but finding nothing else on the subject of shopping he said, 'I need a room.'

Persephone frowned. 'What do you mean?'

'A room that I can use to work, when I am here.'

'You don't have one of those at the hotel where your lot have descended in droves to run your precious Occupation?' she asked.

Stefan stepped forward. 'You don't have to be like this.'

'Like what?' she asked, looking away.

'I am, regretfully, part of an invading force but it is you who is hostile.'

'I—' she started but was cut off.

'Would you be like this if I was just an ordinary German official?'

'You are just an ordinary German official,' she countered.

'But I am not. Not to you,' he said meaningfully. 'And neither are you just a girl on this island to me. We have known each other for too long for this kind of behaviour.'

'Behaviour?' she questioned and then moved on. 'We haven't known each other for too long,' she said with wide eyes. 'We really haven't. It's been ten years.'

'So you are so fond of stating,' Stefan said with a smile.

'You were just a boy who used to visit, who used to stay with

94

his aunt and uncle. You were just a boy who upped and left one day and never returned. You didn't mean anything to us other than within the realms of the summer holidays. But that was then and . . . and . . .' She took a deep breath as she looked at him. His face fell and then he appeared to stand taller suddenly. 'I don't think you understand,' she said.

'I understand you perfectly,' Stefan replied. It was his deflated expression that worked within Persephone to soften her. She looked away from him for a moment, across the field. The view hadn't changed but her outlook had. She knew she'd been cruel. The truth was that she was devastated. The boy she'd liked had grown into a man in a uniform she hated. What was she supposed to do, to say, to think? Did he really think nothing would have changed and that they'd welcome him with open arms? She couldn't simply trust him because she'd once known him. She was sure this would have rung true even if he hadn't been in the uniform of an invading force. 'I'm sorry,' she tried to soften the blow of her words. 'I didn't mean—'

'About the room,' he said stiffly. 'It has become clear to me that you use the room directly to the right of the front door as your primary sitting room.'

Persey took a deep breath but didn't reply.

'And so I will take the smaller one in between that and the kitchen.'

'That's Mrs Grant's sitting room.'

'I am sorry for the hardship but this is war,' Stefan replied before abruptly turning and entering the house.

Candie Gardens bloomed with such beautiful flowers that Persephone was in danger of being late to meet Lise on Saturday as she stopped to take in the sights and smells while walking past the heated glasshouses. The garden of Deux Tourelles had once been as beautiful as this, she thought, although obviously a fraction of the size. The rose garden at the house in particular, walled on three sides, had been laid out and thrived but since the gardener had left Guernsey at the end of 1939 to join the navy, no one had paid too much attention to it at home. Instead, Mrs Grant had focused on the vegetable garden outside the kitchen door, ensuring a never-ending crop of root vegetables in the winter and salad leaves in summer. Perhaps if Persey ever found the time she would venture into the rose garden with shears and cut back the dead and cultivate the living.

Persey waited for Lise at the statue of Victor Hugo, who had been exiled in Guernsey. In the sculpture he looked thoughtful, hat in hand and bent over his cane. She'd written back to her friend to confirm she could meet at the appointed time, but at ten minutes past ten, after distracting herself by looking down the sloping gardens toward the nearby islands of Herm, Sark and Jethou, she was close to giving up on her colleague. Where was Lise?

Three Germans stood and looked up at the statue before smiling kindly at Persephone. She smiled politely back; it pained her but she didn't wish to draw attention to herself by looking surly. Suddenly one announced 'Heil Hitler' at her and they moved on. Persey's smile dropped and she struggled to breathe. Someone had dared Heil Hitler at her. She grabbed at the statue for support and breathed out deeply. How long would this all last?

What was happening on those other islands she could see from here? Were the invading forces making merry as tourists there too? How many soldiers were stationed there? How many were now stationed here? She had seen planes arriving and taking off all week. The Luftwaffe movements had been frenetic – there had been a steady influx of soldiers all week – and she'd reported all she could of use to Jack. Dido had been out also, looking at gun positions and enjoying her new task, barely making it home in time for curfew. And she knew Jack had been sneaking about the island, even after he said he wouldn't and that he'd aim to lie low.

Add to that the arrival of Stefan, even though he was ensconced in his own sitting room, door firmly closed, classical music playing from the gramophone, and the house was in a silent, secret turmoil. Mrs Grant had become snappier than usual, worrying for Jack. Thank goodness Jack's extraction was scheduled for tonight.

At quarter past ten, Persey sighed and made to move off from the statue when she heard her name being called. Turning, she saw Lise scurrying towards her, hat pulled low almost hiding her eyes and her flame-red hair. Lise had begun working at the insurance company six months ago when two members of male staff had gone to England to join up and the office found itself in need of at least one replacement. Since then, Lise, who had been to secretarial college, had been teaching Persephone shorthand and the two had bonded over this and the fact they were the only two women in their workplace.

'I thought you weren't coming,' Persey said.

'I'm sorry,' Lise said, pushing her hat back a bit and revealing her brown eyes, red through crying. 'I got held up.'

'What's happened?' Persey asked, moving towards her friend. 'Have you been crying?'

'Only a bit,' Lise admitted. 'It's all just becoming a bit too much now.'

'What is?'

'All this.' Lise nodded her head discreetly towards the soldiers in the distance, taking photographs of the view towards the harbour at St Peter Port and the gardens around them.

'I know. It's dreadful, isn't it? Unimaginably dreadful. We've one living with us, would you believe?' Persey tried to push thoughts of Stefan, angry in the driveway, out of her mind.

'No!' Lise cried and then buried her face in her hands.

'Lise? What on earth? Tell me what's the matter?'

'I need your help. I've no one else to turn to,' Lise said between sobs. 'I thought you'd have been in work but the boys at the office said you were staying away because of your poor mother . . .'

Persey enveloped a distraught Lise in her arms. 'I'm due back next week.' Persey couldn't make the real pain in her chest from losing her mother go away. She'd had no time to wallow in the pain of her mother's death. Events had moved so fast around her that she knew when she eventually did allow herself to sit and grieve, that waves and waves of tears would flood from her. She forced them away now, in public.

'I know,' Lise said, crying into Persey's coat and pulling her from her thoughts. 'I'm so sorry. I shouldn't be asking you for help at this time.'

'You can ask me for help at any time, Lise. Of course you can.'

A woman walked past and looked between Lise and Persey before moving on. 'Look, come over here. We're bringing attention to ourselves,' Persey said, taking Lise by the hand and drawing her over to a bench.

As the two women sat, Lise took a deep breath. 'You know, don't you, that I wouldn't ask if I didn't really need help?'

Persey nodded and waited.

'Although,' Lise said, 'if you have a German at your house I'm not sure you can help.'

Persey narrowed her eyes and allowed a small, curious smile. 'I don't understand.'

'I need somewhere to stay,' Lise said.

'All right,' Persey said slowly, thinking. 'How long for? You could sleep in my room and I'll put a little fold-out bed in with Dido and share with her for a bit. I'm sure she won't mind. We'll be a full house what with Stefan. But I don't mind if you don't?' Although in truth, with Jack going there'd be an extra room again. But she couldn't mention that at present.

'Stefan?' Lise jolted her head suddenly. 'You're on first-name terms with one of them, already?'

'It's a long story,' Persey replied with a sigh and then put the conversation back on track. 'Have the Germans requisitioned your room at your boarding house?'

'No,' Lise said, still eyeing Persephone with suspicion. 'But I can't stay there anymore.'

98

'Why ever not?' Persey asked.

'The woman who runs it, Mrs Renouf . . . she's not very kind. I don't trust her.'

'I see,' Persey said, not understanding at all.

'I'm . . .' Lise started then stopped, much to Persey's frustration, but it was clear the other woman was choosing her words carefully. 'I came to live in Guernsey in 1938,' Lise said eventually.

Persey nodded.

'And I liked it so very much. It seemed like heaven,' Lise said, glancing round the lush gardens and the view down towards the sea. 'It was only supposed to be temporary as I nannied for a German family who spent their summers here. But they returned home to Germany just before the outbreak of war. They knew, before I did, what was going to happen. They left and I stayed here. I didn't want to return to Germany. I didn't want anything to do with what was happening there.'

'Wise,' Persey cut in. 'I didn't realise you were German,' she said warily. 'I thought you were Swiss.'

'I'm from a town on the German and Swiss border,' Lise said. 'I read the newspapers. I could see the reach the Nazis had extended across Europe. But it wasn't until Dunkirk, until the soldiers were lifted from the beaches, the British retreating from France, that I knew we really were in much more trouble in the Channel Islands than originally anticipated; much more danger.'

Persey sighed deeply. 'Yes. We left it too late to leave,' she admitted.

'As did I,' Lise said simply. 'I tried to leave for England, although I don't know if I would have been much safer there considering how fast the Nazis are progressing. It's only a matter of time before they move across the Channel and enter England.'

'Don't say that,' Persey whispered.

'But,' Lise continued, 'when I tried to leave, I was not allowed.'

'Why not?'

'Because I am German,' she stated. 'Because England was not

accepting arrivals from nations with which it was at war unless in possession of a visa, which I did not have.'

'Oh,' Persey said. 'Of course.'

'And so I am stuck here. For my own silliness in leaving it too late.'

'But being German . . . won't that stand you in good stead with . . . them. You're one of them,' Persey joked. She nodded towards the soldiers as they laughed and joked their way happily through the gardens: Guernsey, their holiday posting, their playground.

Lise looked angry and almost spat, 'I am not one of them. I will never be one of them.'

'No, I know. Don't be angry. I'm sorry, it was a very poor joke,' Persey admitted.

'So you see,' Lise continued, attempting to calm herself. 'I can't go to England and I can't stay here either, under their gaze. I'm caught. I'm trapped. And I don't know what to do. I don't know who I can trust. I think no one.'

'But why? I don't unders—'

'I need you to help me. I don't have any friends here, not really, and I need somewhere safe to go,' Lise said.

'For how long?'

'However long the Nazis are here. However long this Occupation may last.'

'But why?'

'Because,' Lise said quietly. 'I am Jewish.'

Chapter 10

Persephone sat at the miniature grand piano at the far end of the sitting room that afternoon, her fingers placed on the keys, but she couldn't bring herself to play. She had been past the airport one last time for Jack and now she watched the pendulum swing inside the glass cabinet of the wall clock as she thought about Lise. Deux Tourelles was quiet. Mrs Grant was in the kitchen, Dido and Jack were heavens knew where and Stefan was in the sitting room he'd commandeered, much to Mrs Grant's lividness. Presumably, given it was Saturday he had nowhere else to be.

She looked across the room towards the door, which she'd left open, and out into the hallway. She wondered how long they could do this for. Perhaps she was attaching too much importance to that kiss on the cliffs all those years ago. Perhaps it had meant so little then and even less now that he'd possibly forgotten it had ever happened.

He was a stranger but not a stranger. A man she knew but didn't know. What had he been doing in those intervening years? What had he studied? Where had he lived? Who had he loved? Who had he left behind in Germany to come to Guernsey?

She had no idea what had led her mind down this path. She remembered the way he'd been all those summers ago. There had always been a level of Germanic reserve about him until that final day on the cliff when all reserve had fallen away, shocking her, thrilling her.

Earlier that hot summer he had accused her of the same thing, decreeing that she had the same oddly formal characteristics. He had said it was because she was English and she had told him in no uncertain terms that she was not English and those who went around calling Channel Islanders such needed to prepare for an uncomfortable conversation. He had laughed and told her the two of them were more similar than she realised. She wondered if that was true back then. She wondered if it was still true now.

She looked at her wristwatch. Jack would be gone in a matter of hours. The British navy was scheduled to collect him tonight and Persey had volunteered to go with him down to his pick-up point, Petit Bot Bay, where he'd been dropped last time, to help keep lookout for patrols while he made the agreed signal.

'You know the risks don't you, in coming with me?' Jack had asked when she'd volunteered even after he'd fought profusely against it.

'Yes,' she'd said. 'But you'll have to go on my bicycle and then how will I ever get it back? It'll look far more suspicious if I go up to Petit Bot tomorrow morning, after you've gone, to collect it, by which point some or other German will have put his grubby little hands on it and that'll be it gone forever.'

He'd looked at her uncertainly.

'And if we go two up on it,' she continued, 'we might be able to pass as a couple. Then if we are caught after curfew—' she shuddered at the prospect '—we might be able to talk our way out of it together.' She wasn't sure if this was wishful thinking, but she couldn't let one of her oldest friends, and Mrs Grant's only child, go it alone. She had to help. She had to know he'd got away safely.

Jack had reluctantly agreed.

With no one else in the sitting room for her to talk with, Persey allowed her mind to wander. Lise needed her help, but Persey was unsure in what kind of timescale she would need to act or what

102

she would need to do. What could she do to help this woman, her friend? The Germans hadn't made their intentions clear with regard to the island's Jewish population and Persey had given it very little thought up until now. She'd been past shops in St Peter Port that she knew had previously been run by members of the Jewish community and they had been shut up, their owners departing on the boats for England weeks ago, as Lise had tried but failed to do.

Lise needed to move away from her lodgings, where her frightful landlady knew she was Jewish. If the Germans did decide to start rounding up Jews, there was the worry the landlady might inform on Lise. She needed a general state of anonymity ideally, but how could Persey achieve that for her? Lise could hardly live here, under the watchful gaze of Stefan. How would he react if she told him about all of this? She didn't know him well enough now to risk it. But maybe if she tried, tentatively, one day soon to . . .

No. She couldn't. Deux Tourelles was exactly where Lise could not be. But where could she go?

Down the hallway, the classical music stopped abruptly and the door handle turned. Persephone watched, wordlessly, as Stefan appeared unsurely in the hallway. He looked at Persephone.

'You can come in, if you like,' Persephone said, wondering if he would.

He entered and looked around the sitting room and then at the piano. 'This is a beautiful instrument,' he said, moving towards it. 'Do you play?'

'Not today,' Persey said. 'And even then I don't play very well. It's Moth—' Persey caught herself in time and said, 'It was Mother's.' She frowned and looked down at the ivory keys.

Stefan paused before responding. 'I cannot stress how sorry I am, for all of it.'

'What do you mean for all of it?'

'Us.'

'Us?' For reasons unbeknownst to her, Persephone's stomach lurched.

'The Occupation of your island. For us, being here,' he clarified.

'Oh I see,' she said quietly.

'I'm not your enemy,' he replied. 'You know that? I was never that and I am not now.'

'Why are you wearing this?' She gestured to his uniform. 'Mighty ridiculous you're wearing it on a Saturday when you've not even left the house.' Why had she resorted to unfriendly teasing so soon in the conversation? What was wrong with her?

'I'm required to wear it at all times and I did leave the house today.'

'At all times? Even while sleeping?' she added sarcastically and then closed her mouth. He'd been her friend, once.

'No.' He smiled. 'Not while sleeping.'

When he said nothing further she spoke. 'Where did you go today then?'

'I explored parts of the area I had not previously seen on my summers here. And parts that I remembered well but wanted to see again. I saw you, actually.'

Persephone's head shot up and she stared at him. 'Where?'

'Candie Gardens.'

She paused. Had he seen her with Lise? 'Why didn't you come over and say hello?' she challenged him.

'You did not look as if you wanted company. You were with a friend. She looked upset.'

Persey paused. 'She was.'

'Why?' he asked.

Because she's Jewish and frightened for her life, she thought, and the sadness dawned afresh that she could never tell Stefan that; Stefan in his uniform that he was required to wear at all times; Stefan who had once kissed her. Persephone opted for a lie. 'The man she's been stepping out with has just finished things between them.'

'I am sorry for her.'

'Yes, me too.'

'What about you?' Stefan asked. 'Has the man you've been stepping out with gone to war or . . . is he still on the island?'

'I've not got a man,' Persey said warily, holding his gaze, wondering why he'd ask such a thing.

'Did you have one, before?'

She looked up at him, unsure how to reply. She felt, in this instance, that honesty was the best option. 'No.'

'Never?' he asked disbelievingly.

'Once I had one, years ago though.'

'How many years ago?'

She narrowed her eyes. 'Years ago, all right? Too long ago for it to be significant now.' It was the truth. She'd once been faintly interested in, and had stepped out with, a young colleague of her father's until she decided after a dreadful conversation about politics that he was actually rather a buffoon. After that she'd gone off the men she'd had the misfortune to encounter, but yet had never been motivated enough to pursue anyone with gusto, like Dido often did. It all looked far too exhausting. Dido said it was because Persephone couldn't ever quite muster the energy to be what men wanted women to be. Persephone had thought about that a lot.

'What about you?' she asked, dreading the answer. 'Have you got a special someone, some sort of blonde milkmaid, pining away for you back in Germany?'

'No,' he said with a smile and then muttered, 'milkmaid,' with a laugh.

'You've never had a special someone?' she asked, annoyed with herself that she was far too interested in what his answer might be.

'Yes, I have. More than one. But not now.'

'Why not?' she asked.

'Because I am here.'

'Yes, but if you weren't here?' she pushed, unsure why she was pushing.

'I have not left anyone behind in Germany,' he said.

The pendulum clock ticked, leaving them in a quiet moment until Stefan continued. 'Things between us are not as I expected them to be.'

She looked at him but said nothing, acutely aware of a tense feeling deep in her stomach.

'You do not trust me,' he said. 'You do not like me. Because of this.' He did as she had done and gestured at his uniform.

Persey looked down at the piano keys and absent-mindedly, slowly, pushed the same key twice, three times until Stefan's hand rested gently on hers to stop her. She started and stared at his hand on hers, until he moved it, but she couldn't bring herself to look away from the place it had just been.

'I never thought I'd see you again,' she said. 'And on the occasions I did wonder what it would be like, never in my wildest dreams did I imagine it would be like this.'

'I know,' he said.

'There's going to be so much suffering,' Persey said, eventually bringing her gaze up to meet his. 'Here, on this island, there's going to be such, awful, dreadful suffering, because of . . . your kind,' she eventually finished.

'My kind?' he said woefully before nodding his head and moving away from her. He sat on the edge of the settee and sighed. 'There will be no suffering if everybody . . .'

'If everybody . . .?' Persey questioned and then finished his sentence for him, 'Behaves? Is that what you were going to say? If everyone behaves, if we cause no trouble?'

He closed his eyes and then looked rueful. 'The things I've seen as we crossed Europe,' he said. 'The devastation left in the wake. The trouble has mainly been caused because people put up resistance.'

'What do you expect?' Persey baulked. 'You want us all to accept your arrival, your rule, here? On an island that isn't yours?'

'Yes,' he said simply. 'You have no other choice.'

'There's always a choice,' Persey said. 'You had the choice not to join up. Not to wear that uniform.'

'You really think I had a choice?'

They looked at each other, neither willing to be the first to break the gaze.

When he next spoke it was softer. 'Persephone, I spend my days sitting behind a desk, looking after the administrative duties that keep the force on this island moving. I do not kill. I do not persecute. I file paper. I translate documents to present to your government.'

How could he justify his job in this awful war, while his nation swept across Europe towards England, committing God only knew what kind of awful things? *The trouble has mainly been caused because people put up resistance.* Well of course. What did he expect? And now Hitler's forces were in Guernsey. Did they expect the Islanders just to sit quietly, cause no 'trouble'? She had no idea what she could do to make life hard for the Germans but she would not sit quietly while they marched all over her island, goose-stepping their way towards England.

She thought of Jack and how tonight he would leave for England, taking with him information that the British government might be able to use to their advantage. Information that she and Dido had helped collect for him. Stefan and his horrific army thought the Islanders would all toe the line, would cause no trouble; would put up no resistance.

They were wrong.

Chapter 11

The wind and rain lashed against Persey's face as she stood, back against the sharp cliffs in the near-pitch-dark with Jack that night. The day had turned sour just as the curfew had come into place and their trek to the bay, through woodland, lanes and hedgerows towards the cliffs had been laced with the additional peril of not being able to hear a German patrol car through the noise of the beating rain. They had given up the idea of using the bicycle. It would be too risky through the uneven ground. But with such a long, wet walk, Persey's coat clung damply to her body and she was sure she'd ripped her trousers in more than one place on branches that stuck out, catching her unawares in the darkness. She blinked rain from her eyelashes as they descended the perilous cliffs, then she looked from the choppy waters of the sea to Jack for reassurance. His gaze swept the horizon through his binoculars.

'What do you see?' she asked quietly.

He shook his head and continued scanning. 'Nothing,' he whispered but she barely heard him over the crash of the waves.

'That's good though, isn't it?'

'Yes. No boats. No Germans.' He removed the binoculars from his face and looked at her. 'You should go. Thank you for helping me. But I can take it from here. You are a rock, Persey. Remember the route back in the dark?'

'Yes, of course. I know this island like the back of my hand but I'm not leaving until I know you're safely gone.'

He put his hand on her shoulder and gave it a squeeze before looking at his watch. 'It's time,' he said and then removed his torch from his pocket, aimed it out to sea and clicked it on and off a few times.

'What are you signalling?' she whispered.

'It's the letter R in Morse code,' he said and then lowered his torch, waiting.

'R?' she enquired.

'It's just what I was instructed to do.'

Nothing.

The two were still until Persey stole a look up and back towards where the Germans often patrolled. Jack knew the times they came and went from his observations over the past week and he'd made it clear he and Persey didn't have long from the moment of arrival.

He clicked his torch again, signalling the same letter as before and then waited. He took a deep breath and Persey could see he was as worried as she.

'What do we do if—' she started.

'They're coming,' he said, cutting her off. 'They're coming.'

After a moment she tried again. 'But if they don't come this time,' she said as softly as possible. 'What's the next date to try?'

'There isn't one,' he said irritably. 'It's happening now.'

He flashed the torch again and the sound of an engine, unseen, out to sea made Persey breathe an audible sigh of relief. 'Oh, thank God,' she said. 'I was beginning to get—' But Jack put his hand on hers to quiet her. 'It's not them,' he said after a moment. 'They'd have flashed a signal in return.'

His face was horror-stricken as he looked at her. 'It's not them,' he repeated. He ran his hand through his hair and clenched his fist within it, pulling on a clump of wet hair. She could see he was unable to comprehend what had happened. A sudden flood-light brightened the sea where the boat was and then swept

109

towards the beach. Jack dropped onto the wet sand, grabbing Persey by the hand and pulling her down with him. 'Stay down,' he said. The floodlight swept the beach and he dragged her behind a rock. The light continued down the beach as the patrol boat carried on past them, painfully slowly.

'Is it worth using the torch again?' Persey asked although she suspected she knew the answer.

Beside her, on the patch of wet sand, Jack sat down listlessly. 'No,' he said. 'It's not. They're not coming.'

'What do we do now?' Persey asked.

'We go home,' he said resignedly. 'There's nothing else for it. We can't sit here all night. I've signalled more times than I should already and we're sitting ducks now. That the patrol light didn't catch us was luck. I don't know what else to do. If we don't go now, our luck will run out.'

'But maybe the navy saw the patrol boat and that's why they didn't flash back. Just one more time, Jack – you have to try now the patrol's gone. It's imperative you go tonight. They can't just leave you here.'

'They can if it's more risky to attempt to rescue me.'

'One more time, Jack. Please.'

He pulled the torch from his pocket and looked around. Persey's heart raced but it was with fear that Jack would be stranded here. They had to come. They had to. She held his other hand as he clicked the torch on and off. Both scanned the horizon, but it was clear that a British navy vessel wasn't hiding behind the drizzling rain. No reply came.

Chapter 12

The rain had almost stopped by the time Persey and Jack saw the gate of Deux Tourelles ahead of them, the earth wet and sodden as they trampled disconsolately through the woodland. They neither of them spoke but walked close together, each pulling at the other's sleeve if they heard something worrying. They took the same route that avoided the airport. Through the darkness of the woods Persey could see a German patrol had now been set up in the distance, but they could easily avoid it by staying within the thicket.

The two soldiers were in long raincoats and rounded tin hats, huddled together, one lighting a cigarette from the other's, and Persey watched their relaxed, fluid movements. She swallowed down resentment for the ease with which they conducted themselves, manning a patrol to catch errant Islanders on their own island.

She kept quiet, signalling Jack to move slower, quieter than they had been, but in the end it was Persey who gave them away, catching her foot in a tree root that had slowly and steadily wound itself out of the ground over a matter of years, waiting for her to find it, scoop her foot into its path as she moved, and to fall. She cried out in shock as she hit the ground, landing badly and twisting her ankle. She stared up at a startled Jack whose eyes were wide and who looked quickly from her toward the roadblock where the two soldiers were no longer idly smoking, but making their weapons ready, pulling their torches out and shining them into the forest. Jack fell to the ground next to Persey and she struggled to hear anything other than the sound of his breathing.

'Stay still,' she told him but she could hardly hear him over the sound of blood rushing to her ears.

'Run,' Jack said, grabbing her arm. 'Run,' he repeated, pulling her to her feet. The torchlight shone directly on them as they stood and Jack ran, his fingers clasped tightly around Persey's arm as he pulled her along behind him.

The burn of her throbbing ankle seared, making her eyes water in pain as she pounded through the forest. She would have given anything to stop but the threat of the soldiers running after her and what they would do if they found her was unthinkable. And Jack, they could not encounter Jack under any circumstance. It was this that forced her to run faster, tears of pain streaming down her face as she pushed herself forward as fast as she could. They were faster than the soldiers, who didn't know the woods like she and Jack.

The house was within sight at the end of the lane. All they had to do was cross it. She pushed Jack forward and the two of them lurched out of the wood, across the lane and through the open gate of Deux Tourelles. Gasping for breath and with no idea how close behind her the soldiers were, Persey rushed over the gravel drive towards the house. As she and Jack hurtled themselves towards the front door she was met by Mrs Grant who had obviously heard the Germans shouting. She pulled the door open and stared at her son in shock.

'Why are you still here?' Mrs Grant cried out in distinct horror.

'Shut the door.' Jack spun and with them all safely inside slammed the door so hard the glass fanlight above rattled in its pane. 'Move,' Jack shouted at Persey. 'They were right behind us.'

'Who are? Why are you still here?' Mrs Grant said in panic, looking from Persey to her son.

'The Germans,' Persey said, gasping for breath, tears of pain trailing down her face. 'They saw us. In the woods. They were there.'

'Your boat didn't come,' Mrs Grant said.

'No,' Jack said. 'They didn't come. Stall the Germans,' he said to his mother.

'How?' Her tone was high, panicked.

'We need to . . .' Jack looked Persey up and down and she looked at herself. Her gardening trousers were ripped, her knees bloody from her fall, her coat smothered in wet mulch from the forest floor, her hair wet, tangled, bedecked with leaves. Jack looked better but as if he'd been running a marathon in unsuitable clothing. 'Take your clothes off and . . . hide them,' he said.

'Both of you go,' Mrs Grant said. 'Get into your beds,' she clarified. 'Pretend you've been there all night.'

The two of them ran upstairs and Mrs Grant began picking leaves and pieces of tell-tale bracken up behind them, tucking the evidence into her apron pocket.

The knock came at the door and Persey and Jack stood at the top of the stairs and stared at each other before turning with fear towards their respective bedroom doors.

Inside her room, Persey began undressing, knowing she couldn't be found by German soldiers covered in bits of the forest. They would know she had been out after curfew. She stripped her clothes off, bundled them into a ball, lifted her mattress and pushed them underneath, praying the Germans wouldn't look there. She found her nightdress under her pillow and in her haste to climb inside it, ripped a piece of the sleeve as she caught her fingers in it. She stood and waited but no sound came from within the house. Instead, from the thin pane of glass at her bedroom window she heard people speaking.

With her room in darkness, she pulled the net aside just a fraction; enough to see out, but she prayed, not to be seen in return. Blood throbbed in her ears and she watched the scene play out in the moonlit grounds below.

In the furore of thumping up the stairs and climbing out of her clothes, she had missed the return of Stefan and Dido from the club in his staff car. It must have come only a fraction after the soldiers knocked loudly and forcefully at the door and now, below, they were talking animatedly. Persey could see Dido looking from the soldiers to Stefan who was listening as the soldiers recounted in forceful tones what it was they'd seen. Dido, like Persephone, could not speak German and after a minute of listening, Persey heard her interject and ask, 'What are they saying?'

'They are saying that they have chased a woman through the woods.'

'And they've come to tell you about it? Why?'

'They haven't,' Stefan replied. 'They have chased the woman here and our arrival has coincided with it.'

'Here?' Dido cried a little too shrilly.

'Yes, so they say.'

'Well they can jolly well unsay. They're mistaken.'

'I have told them that,' Stefan said. Persey strained to hear his quiet, calm voice, unsure if she was catching all of the scant information being spoken in English. Stefan turned back to the soldiers and continued talking to them calmly, his face now angled away from her as he gestured around the property with open arms. Was he inviting them inside to search?

The foot soldiers turned to go, looking between them as if they were unsure, as if wondering whether they were doing the correct thing by leaving.

Persey found she had been holding her breath and only now allowed herself to let it out.

It was Dido who spoke first when it became clear Stefan wasn't going to. 'What did you tell them to make them leave?'

'I told them they were wrong.'

'That was brave of you.'

'Not really,' Stefan said. Persey desperately wanted to push her ear against the glass to hear better. 'They are foot soldiers and I am an officer,' he finished simply.

'But they had seemed so sure?' Dido queried.

'Yes, they were sure.'

'And yet—'

'And yet,' Stefan interrupted, 'I have just personally vouched for every member of this household. And told them that if they were chasing a woman through the woods, then they were not chasing her here. I told them they were welcome to search the house, but after enjoying a wonderful evening listening to you sing, I would be less than impressed if they chose to conduct a raid inside my lodgings at this late hour just as I intend to go to bed.'

Dido looked impressed. 'Gosh. Well done you.'

'I had a very nice time tonight, listening to you sing. Thank you for . . .' But he stopped and looked at something in the driveway.

'Thank you for . . .?' Dido prompted.

Stefan looked back at her. 'Pardon?'

'You were saying thank you for something.' She laughed.

He looked confused and then: 'Yes, thank you for making me feel so welcome again after all these years.'

Dido nodded. 'It's all right. Goodnight, Stefan. Sleep well.'

But Stefan simply nodded and remained by the car. Persey looked down at him as he stood alone in the driveway and wondered why he wasn't making a move to enter the house. Dido left the door on the latch, presumably so Stefan could enter when he was ready without having to fumble for his key. To Persey it looked as if he had waited until Dido had entered the house before he moved. He walked across the gravel four or five steps, bent down and picked something up. Persey inched her face closer to the glass, straining to see what he was looking at.

As he righted himself, he held the item out, turning it over and over in his hands before turning round to face the house. Persey looked in horror at the object in his hands. It was a torch. Her torch. She must have dropped it as she'd run back towards the house. Had she been holding it? Or had it fallen from her coat pocket? She could hardly remember.

Stefan had stopped walking towards the front door and Persey dragged her eyes from the torch in his hands to look at his face. She wanted to see his expression, wanted to see how significant he believed the torch to be. Would he know just by looking at it? Of course not, and it struck her that she should move away from the window, stay hidden, out of sight. But she was rooted to the spot, wondering what he would do, whether he would work out its significance. If she remained still he might not see her.

Slowly, he lifted his head up and looked towards her window. She held her breath. She was too late to step back. Stefan was looking directly at her.

When the knock at her door came she was ready. Persey had heard him climb the stairs slowly, painfully slowly and she counted each tread on the stair, knowing when he was at the turn, and then at the top. He had paused on the landing stairs and she assumed it was because he was deciding whether to go towards his room or towards hers. She braced herself, looking at her bed, wondering if she should climb in and pretend she'd been asleep the entire time, but he had seen her at the window. He had looked right at her, and she at him.

Whatever the outcome of the next few minutes she would face it bravely and she would not give Jack away. Stefan was an officer of the Reich. She knew where his loyalty lay.

They had only seen a woman, the soldiers had said, and she clung to this fact as the knock came gently on her door. Once,

116

twice, so softly that if she hadn't been listening for it she might have missed it entirely. And then a third time, louder now, more determined. Persey paused, took a deep breath and slowly moved towards the door to open it.

Chapter 13

'A concentration camp?' Lucy repeated quietly as she stared at the newspaper clipping from the box and reread it, bringing a feeling of cold, intense horror. Was this why no one had heard of Persephone? Had she gone to a concentration camp? Had she died in one?

Lucy sat up on her knees and started rifling through each and every piece of paper from the Perspex box, trying to discover anything that would shed further light on this strange document. But there didn't seem to be anything worth looking at in more detail. Lucy pulled at a piece of her hair and wound it round and round her forefinger for a while, and then stood at the window, looking out, down the drive as she finished her tea. It was only once she realised she was staring, again, down towards Will's cottage, half hidden behind the trees, that she pulled the thick curtains closed, turned away and began her new evening ritual of locking the house for the night.

The next day Lucy went into St Peter Port in search of some decent coffee, breakfast that was better than the factory bread she'd bought to toast, and Wi-Fi. She scanned her inbox, including the latest email: an offer of a large freelance project, copywriting all the new marketing material for a travel company she'd once worked with years ago.

118

Lucy looked at it for a few minutes, waiting for that feeling of joy at a new commission to hit, but it didn't come. Was it because she was dwelling on the strange notice about concentration camps and compensation or was it because of another reason – one she couldn't identify yet? She would work it out later. She emailed her soft toy client to check in with them and looked through her work. Her heart wasn't in it today, but as a freelancer, she knew she had to crack on. She emailed the travel company, accepting immediately and feigning delight at the prospect. What would she do for money if she didn't put her back into it, and clients began firing her?

It then occurred to her that since the revelation that she now part-owned a rather large house in Guernsey that she and Clara intended to sell, they wouldn't be as strapped for cash as usual. It was hard to get her head around that and having now slept on the idea that she was a homeowner for the first time in her life she clicked open a property website to scout out how much five-bed manor houses in Guernsey cost on the open market.

'Jesus Christ,' she cried out rather too loudly when a small selection of glossy homes showed as a list with eye-wateringly high prices attached to them. She knew it wasn't cheap to buy a house in the Channel Islands, but she'd been away from here for so long that she'd rather lost touch with how much houses went for. She thought perhaps a million at a stretch. But the houses listed of comparable size to Deux Tourelles were at least three million pounds. Lucy sat back and sipped her coffee. Three million pounds. She and Clara had just inherited a house worth three million pounds, give or take fees, tax and all the other payments that change hands as part of a house sale. But still. She couldn't make that figure sink in.

'Buying a house?' someone said next to her.

Lucy looked up to find Will standing by her table, holding a takeaway coffee.

Still stunned by the figures on the screen and Will's unexpected appearance, Lucy didn't reply but simply stared at him with a blank expression on her face.

'Will,' he said, pointing to himself as if he thought she'd forgotten who he was.

Lucy laughed. 'I know. And no, I'm not buying a house. Just looking.' She didn't want to tell this relative stranger that she'd inherited Deux Tourelles. It seemed too personal, too much information. Besides, she quite liked Will and what if she told him and then he suddenly seemed to quite like her too, perhaps a little more than he did when she hadn't been a millionaire. She laughed to herself at this. She was a millionaire. Or she would be when she and Clara sold the house. Clara would be a millionaire also. This was insane. Had Clara looked up the price of—

'You all right? You keep disappearing.' Will spoke and jogged her back to the present.

'Yes, sorry. I'm being so rude.'

'A bit,' he said with a smile. 'But it's early. I'm a bit like that before I've had coffee so don't worry about it.'

'What are you doing here?' Lucy asked, attempting to renew her ability to make decent small talk.

Will looked at his coffee cup. 'Getting coffee,' he said in confusion. 'Have you just asked me a trick question?'

'No, I mean in St Peter Port.'

'Oh right. I've got a meeting with a gallery owner who's agreed to show some of my work.'

'Are you an artist?' Lucy asked, impressed, gesturing for him to sit down.

He shook his head and pulled out the chair opposite before sitting. He was wearing battered Converse and a well-cut black jacket. He looked effortlessly cool compared to her overstuffed rucksack full of receipts and jeans with the hole in the knee that was too big because she'd once got her foot caught in it while putting it on and had ripped it even further.

'Photographer. Landscapes mostly,' he replied.

She thought back to his horrified reaction when she'd been dangling the Box Brownie camera precariously by its handle.

'What are you doing here?' he asked.

'Free Wi-Fi,' she joked at the same time the waitress walked past and rolled her eyes at the remark. 'I've got a lot of emails and a lot of work piling up so thought today I'd better crack on.'

'What do you do?' he asked.

She told him.

'Impressive,' he said genuinely.

'It's not. Not really.'

'It is to me,' Will said. 'Do you enjoy it?'

'Yeah,' she said, thinking about it. 'I did. But I think I decided about two minutes ago that I don't want to do it forever.'

Will shrugged. 'No one wants to do anything forever, surely.'

'Hmm, probably not,' Lucy said, finishing her coffee and contemplating ordering another one. 'Perhaps I'm just distracted by all this house stuff. There's suddenly a lot to organise, although actually no more than there was yesterday. And then there's all the stuff left behind to sort. I feel reluctant just to bin things because it was someone's life.'

Will nodded. 'I know. I helped my parents sort my granddad's place years ago when he passed away. A whole life in one little cottage and then bit by bit it all went to the charity shop or the skip if it was past repair. And then it was empty and that was that. Just be grateful Dido wasn't a hoarder. Have you been in the attic yet?'

'No. I forgot all about the attic actually. God, perhaps that's where all the knick-knacks are hiding, because there is barely anything in the house. And what there actually is in the house, is mostly very . . . odd.'

'Like what?' he asked.

She told him about the poster informing those who had been sent to concentration camps that they were entitled to compensation. When she'd finished summarising the document Will said, 'That is odd. Also very interesting.'

Lucy nodded.

And then Will said, 'Were your family Jewish then?'

'I didn't think so,' Lucy said. 'Dido and her sister Persephone were our first cousins once removed so I'm not completely sure. We've just organised a Christian burial for Dido so if she was Jewish, Clara and I have got a lot to answer for. Also Dido was a churchgoer so . . .'

'They might have been Jewish,' Will said, 'and pretended not to be.'

'To stay alive? During the war, do you mean?'

Will nodded. 'Stranger things have happened. Especially here. If they were Jewish and didn't register as such, they might have been able to get away with hiding it, especially by going to church.'

'But I didn't think the poster was making reference to it being a holocaust issue,' Lucy said, trying to think back to the exact wording of the poster. 'I thought it was about punishment. Oh, I don't know.' Lucy sighed. 'There were some shorthand notes my sister and I found in the house. I can't read it well, but I'm fairly sure one said the word "resistance" and so I did half wonder what had happened in the house during the war. Maybe nothing, but then why is that poster there? It's so confusing and horrific, actually.'

'It was all horrific. My knowledge of the Occupation is scant I'm afraid so I'm not really going to be of much use, but if you need a hand making sense of any of it, I'm happy to help.' Will stood up and took his finished coffee cup to the counter before stopping at Lucy's table again. 'What are you doing tomorrow night?'

'Nothing,' Lucy said and then wished she had a hobby so she could have replied with an answer that sounded a bit more interesting.

'If you're free and want to come over, I can make us some dinner and perhaps we can do some digging. See what that poster is all about.'

She suddenly felt warm and paused before answering. 'That would be lovely. Thank you very much,' she said rather too formally.

'Eight o'clock?' he said, fiddling with the zip on his jacket. 'Bring some of those things you found and we can take a look?'

When she nodded, he waved goodbye and winked. Then looked startled that he'd done it, shaking his head as he left the coffee shop.

Lucy laughed and then glanced absent-mindedly at her laptop screen, its screensaver well into its rotating inventory of scenery from around the world.

The next day Lucy sat at the desk in the study of Deux Tourelles and used her phone's data to connect her laptop to the Internet. As she typed mindlessly from the notes provided by the holiday company about a brand-new five-star hotel they were promoting for Christmas, she knew without thinking about it that she just wasn't inspired enough. Was Clara right? Was Lucy just paddling through life? She had loved it once – the freedom of all this. But also, it was easy, second nature. And wasn't that the goal? It wasn't that well paid but that was always the way now. And if Lucy jacked her clients in at any point then there were a thousand freelancers queuing up behind her to shove her out of the way and jump into her shoes.

Her cup of tea had gone cold and the study suddenly felt stuffy. Even though spring hadn't yet quite turned to summer, it was so close, Lucy could sense it. Today wasn't a hot day but it wasn't a cold one either. She pulled off her cardigan, swung the desk chair round and went to the back of the house, opening the kitchen door that led out into the garden. She stood against the doorframe and looked out thoughtfully at the overgrown mass. The grass needed cutting. Rose buds were present but tightly closed, ready to bloom in only a matter of weeks. But for now they displayed only the faintest hint of what lay inside, a shimmer of tightly furled green with tantalisingly pale edges.

Lucy had remembered Will saying he helped Dido out a little in the garden. The elderly lady had clearly not been that interested in gardening, or perhaps she'd had no one to do it for her and was too frail herself to engage in such a task. As such the garden could do with a little nip and a tuck. She'd seen tools hanging in the back of the garage and went to find some of the smaller, sharper ones along with an electric mower.

Once she'd finished mowing, it looked so much better and she inhaled the green aroma of freshly cut grass. Then she looked around at the wildness. She knew how to prune. Her mum had shown her the basics years ago and so she started snipping and neatening up the garden, lacerating her fingers on thorns in the absence of seeing any gardening gloves in the garage.

After a few hours mostly spent hacking away at a bush that had grown over something in the garden, Lucy was worn out and desperately thirsty, but knew if she stopped to go inside and get a glass of water that she'd never go back into the garden again. And she so wanted to know what it was she could see between the rose bushes and the red-brick garden wall. She pulled at the bushes, being careful not to grab hold of any thorns, snipped and cut and pulled away until she could see an ornate curved metal garden bench. It had once been painted a glorious shade of deep racing green and fragments of paint remained scattered here and there across the bench. The rest of it had given way to rust.

Odd that something could be so engulfed in bracken and weeds, left to rot as if no one cared for it. It had once been beautiful, Lucy was sure. And the aspect from this part of the garden was stunning, facing to the back of the wide house, looking up at the two turrets from which the house got its name, the exterior coated in ivy and the rest of the rose garden. From this bench you could sit and survey everything. Lucy smiled. She would make a point later of looking up how to restore it, what kind of paint and varnish she would need. It wouldn't take her long to bring it back to life again.

Life. It was what this house sorely lacked. It was a beautiful house. It needed children in it. It needed a family to fill all those bedrooms. Lucy had felt it – the overarching feeling of sadness that emanated through its walls. If she'd been a superstitious person she might have said it had a ghostly air about it. But so far, nothing had gone bump in the night. It was just loneliness; she was one woman living alone, albeit temporarily, in a five-bedroom petit-manor house, and that didn't feel right. So how had Dido done it?

She wondered about Persephone, Dido's sister: when had she left and why? Had she moved away and married? Or had something else happened to her? Lucy tried not to think about the notice about concentration camps. There was hardly any trace of Persephone in the house now and no one at Dido's funeral had mentioned her. But then, there was hardly any trace of Lucy at Clara's house.

Perhaps delving deeper was something she and Will could think about tonight. A frisson of excitement shot through her thinking about Will cooking for her. If anything it would be good to get out of Deux Tourelles for the evening. Even if it was only next door. Clara was right: Lucy really did need a hobby. Work wasn't enough. Not anymore. Or maybe it was being here, with a lot more time on her hands, that made her acknowledge that sobering fact.

And then there was still the issue of what to do about Clara. How to approach her sister again now that it was clear she wasn't going to apologise. They had to talk about it but did Clara expect Lucy to apologise first? Maybe that's what Clara was holding out for. Lucy would do it, if that's what it took to get the ball rolling on a reconciliation. Oh, what on earth had happened between them that things had descended so horrifically after Lucy had only been back here for such a short amount of time?

She caught sight of her reflection in the kitchen window as she ran the cold tap and filled a glass with water. She looked red-faced and grubby, but it was the most exercise Lucy had engaged in for weeks. Perhaps she should take up running. Actually, perhaps she should take up gardening. It had been quite enjoyable and she knew the basics. She could get the garden spruced up before the house went on the market. It sorely needed it.

Maybe she could take up house renovation as well. The house was crying out for a bit of DIY and heaps more love than Lucy had available to give it, but a start couldn't hurt, surely. And hadn't she always seen on those property shows on Channel 4 that houses sold for much more money if they were 'staged' or spruced up in some way rather than shown in their worst, slightly dilapidated light – which was how Deux Tourelles looked now?

Yes, that's the hobby Lucy would allocate herself. She was going to do the house up, paint the rooms in a delicate range of colours from Farrow & Ball, make it look a bit more appealing rather than its current drabness with the faded, flaking magnolia that currently adorned far too many walls in the property. Strip the floors, sand them down, varnish them, maybe get some new rugs. Although she wouldn't go all out. She had to remember she wasn't actually going to be living here. It was just for staging. Just to sell. And the garden: she was going to tackle the rest of the garden while she was here.

But she supposed first she needed to ring round a house clearance company or some charity shops and sort out if any wanted the oversized and ancient-looking furniture. Or was it best leaving the furniture in the house so it looked more lived-in; better for potential buyers? Yes, that's what she needed to do. She felt pleased with herself. She'd made a grown-up decision, without Clara getting involved, and it wasn't that difficult.

As night closed in and the sun began to descend in the sky, Lucy sent a quick series of messages to Clara telling her what she had planned for the house. Clara replied that she'd sorted out a visit from three estate agents who would take valuations the next day. The next day? What planet was Clara on? Why was she in such a hurry? It gave Lucy no time to paint anything, or indeed to actually go out and buy paint and fresh flowers with which to jazz up the house. But she would explain to the agent they were intending to make it look nicer in time for photographs and that should buy some time.

Before she knew it, it was nearly eight o'clock and Lucy needed to be down the lane at Will's cottage. She'd rushed through her going-out routine, showering off the grime of a day spent in the garden and putting on the only nice day dress she'd brought with her; red, short-sleeved and just above the knee. Was it too much? Will had only seen her in jeans thus far and she didn't want to give the impression she was keen. But she didn't want to give the impression she didn't care enough to at least change out of her daily uniform of jeans and a top. To counterbalance the panic she put on a pair of wedges and reasoned that it was a good halfway choice between the slightly more formal pair of heels she'd worn to Dido's funeral and her usual pair of trainers. Why was dressing so complicated, each item laced with meaning?

She arrived at Will's cottage, clutching the bundle of shorthand notes she remembered she'd put in a drawer in the bedroom for safekeeping, the poster relating to the concentration camp and a gift of a bottle of white wine she'd hastily grabbed from the fridge. Will opened the door and failed to mask his surprise at how she looked. Her hair was still a bit damp at the ends as she'd run out of time to dry it properly but she'd put on make-up; slightly more than she wore in the day, paying attention to elongate her lashes with a few sweeps of mascara and swiping a nude lipstick across her lips. He smiled but didn't speak.

'Hi,' she said first and when he just nodded she said, 'Am I . . . Have I got the right night?'

'Yes. Sorry, come in,' he said hastily.

'I was going to offer a lame joke about being late because the commute was so dreadful,' she said. 'But you've put me off now.'

He laughed. 'The old jokes are the best.'

'This is for you.' She handed him the wine. 'A thank you for dinner.'

'You've not eaten it yet. You might not thank me.'

'Well I can't really cook so whatever you're making is guaranteed to be a vast improvement on what I eat usually.'

'What have you been cooking, while you've been here?' he asked, leading her through a small but impeccable entrance hall and towards the kitchen. The cottage was small, with only two rooms downstairs, one either side of the entrance hall and staircase. Wood beams were exposed and old architectural drawings were arranged neatly in dark frames on the wall. It was tidy, but masculine; no plants on the kitchen windowsill, no scented candles, no hint of a woman's presence, which Lucy found interesting. Although now she thought about it, asking her over for dinner wasn't something any man in his right mind would have done if he did have a girlfriend, surely.

'This and that.' She didn't like to tell him she'd mostly been living off toast and Marmite and pasta with the odd glass of wine thrown in for good measure. She wondered if the jokes about grapes in wine counting as one of the five a day might actually have a bit of truth about it. God, she hoped so. 'I live on my own anyway so I'm used to cooking for one, but usually I'm out a lot for dinner with friends so this new solitude makes a nice change.'

'There's a good little kitchen garden out the back at Deux Tourelles. Have you seen?' Will asked.

'I've found a few things that look edible but the weeds have started taking over I'm afraid,' Lucy said.

'Probably. Dido wasn't really into the garden, just strangely keen that the vegetable patch should be maintained. She admitted it harked back to the war when rationing was in full force. And I've not been out there since the end of January when she let me weed it and sow some beans, carrots and onions so it's no surprise it's gone to wrack and ruin since then. The veg I sowed has probably died in the ground now with no one looking after it.'

'She "let" you plant vegetables?' Lucy frowned.

'I was quite happy having a bit of company and so I forced my services on her a bit, I think. Some elderly people are eternally grateful for any help you give them. While, as I learnt from my grandfather, others secretly want to tell you to piss off. I'm not sure which one Dido was. Either way, I was rewarded with a bit of chat and biscuits that I forced down. I hope she enjoyed the company too.'

'Did she ever talk to you about her sister?'

'No,' Will said as he moved over to the modern-looking hob and put a wok on, adding some oil. 'She asked a lot of questions about me, was intrigued why I'd upped sticks and moved here. Couldn't get her head round why a city boy like me would choose Guernsey, despite the fact she'd lived here her whole life.'

Lucy wasn't sure what to make of that. 'Didn't she like it here then?'

Will shrugged. 'Can you pass me the peppers from over there?' gesturing towards some vegetables he'd pre-cut. 'Not sure she was in love with her home. Just maybe didn't have it in her to move anywhere else,' he said.

'What are you cooking?' she asked as he put another pan on, added oil and when it warmed, threw in some diced chicken, which sizzled comfortingly. He switched the extractor on overhead.

'Fajitas. I should have asked, are you a vegetarian?'

'No, and I'm very at home with fajitas given I ate them twice last week courtesy of my niece Molly's new-found culinary skills.'

'Oh no, really? Twice?' He looked at the pan and frowned before switching his gaze to her. 'OK, my back-up plan was Chicken Pad Thai, which I can do if I throw some noodles in and whiz up a sauce.'

'If you're aiming to impress, it has worked.'

He laughed. 'No. I just can't let you eat fajitas for the third time in two weeks. Also, what if Molly's are better than mine? Being trounced by a five-year-old . . . that's just embarrassing.'

While eating the Pad Thai they talked about Molly, with Will saying how cute she was on the beach.

'Not sure about cute,' Lucy said as she put her knife and fork down and refreshed their wine glasses. 'I love her to pieces but precocious is probably a good word for her. She reminds me of Hermione from Harry Potter. Knows a bit too much.'

'Well I thought she was cute,' Will said diplomatically. 'And I'm not the broody kind.'

'No?' Lucy enquired. 'Don't want kids of your own?'

'Maybe one day. You?'

'Maybe one day,' she said, echoing him.

'Too busy having fun?' he asked.

'I'm not sure that's the case,' Lucy said. 'Just not really seeing anyone and not really dreaming of weddings and kids right now.'

'Good answer,' he said, taking a sip of his wine.

'You?'

'Not seeing anyone,' he said with a smile 'and not really dreaming of weddings and kids right now.'

Lucy smiled in return and then said, 'Good answer.'

A calm descended as they chatted and finished dinner and it was only then Lucy heard the music that had been playing the entire time from the sitting room. 'This singer's lovely. Who is it?'

'It's an Icelandic folk singer. I can't remember his name.'

'Icelandic folk? You're far too cool.'

Will grinned. 'Not really. It scrolls through a playlist automatically.'

'Dinner was lovely,' Lucy said. 'I'm impressed and also a little bit tipsy.'

'You drank more wine than me,' Will said with mock-chastisement.

'I think I ate more than you too. That was so good,' Lucy said before offering to help clear up. Will declined and told her to make herself comfortable in the sitting room. She took their drinks through to the room, which was lit by two small table lamps on either side, and she looked through his bookshelves, discovering lots of coffee table books about photography and a large black portfolio. She took a sip of her wine and put the glasses on the table before lifting the portfolio and looking through. Inside were beautiful landscape shots of the island as well as some of far-flung locations that Lucy couldn't identify.

'Did you take these?' she asked as Will entered.

He nodded and sat down next to her.

'These are amazing. You've got a real thing about beaches,' she said.

'I really do.'

She leafed through the rest of the book before going back to the start and looking at the shots of Guernsey, one in particular of the rocks at Cobo Bay drew her attention. The day was grey in the shot and the tide was far-reaching, pulled out to sea, leaving ridges of seaweed behind in the white sand. 'It really is a beautiful island. Sometimes it's easy to forget that, when your mind is on other things.'

He sat back and looked at her and she felt self-conscious under his gaze. Even though Will probably had no greater clue about the history of the residents of Deux Tourelles than she did, Lucy decided to go with the concept of two heads are better than one and launched in. 'I brought the poster up for you to look at and some of the other things I found. There wasn't much but even so, I have no idea what I'm looking at.'

He sat forward while she retrieved the items from her bag. He read the words from the notice out loud. 'Compensation For United Kingdom Victims of Nazi Persecution . . .' He trailed off. 'Nazi persecution?' he questioned, looking at Lucy. 'Hang on. Let me just read this again . . .' He scanned the document a second time. 'And there was nothing else with this? No further letter or explanation?'

Lucy shook her head. 'I was half hoping it referred to people from the Channel Islands being sent to concentration camps by

131

accident and being due compensation as a result. But I realise that's wishful thinking.'

Will blew air out of his cheeks and then said, 'I'm not sure the Nazis did much by accident. I think it's a real prison sentence. It must have been . . .' Will trailed off.

'Hell.' Lucy shivered. 'Gas chambers? And then relatives of those murdered were able to claim compensation?' Lucy asked.

'God. Don't.' Will picked up his wine glass and then put it back down. Obviously mistaking her shiver for a chill, he said, 'That sea breeze really rolls in.' He stood up and lit the fire. It roared to life and they sat quietly with only the sound of the wood catching. It was something beautiful and calming to watch while they pondered the vile nature of what they were discussing.

'What else did you bring?' he said after a minute or two.

'The shorthand documents,' Lucy said, producing the little bundle. 'I haven't had a go at translating them yet. Unless you can read shorthand in under five minutes as one of your many talents . . .?'

'No. I can't.' He leafed through the stack of carbon copies. 'But if we can find a how-to guide on the Internet—' he reached over to the little side table and pulled his laptop from it '—I'm sure we could divide and conquer this lot.'

'Now?' Lucy asked, not feeling quite sober enough.

Will grinned while his laptop flared to life. 'There's no time like the present.'

Chapter 14

The knock at Persephone's door was gentle. Once, twice. A few minutes prior to this she could physically feel the curiosity oozing from every other member of the household. Jack, in his room at the back, probably desperate to know what Persey could see at the front of the house. Dido, clever Dido, keeping away and not daring to enter Persey's room. And downstairs, Mrs Grant, who must have been using every ounce of her energy not to run upstairs, grab Jack by his collar and shake out of him the reason why he was still on the island and how he had come to be chased by soldiers. And now, instead of Stefan at her door, Persey would have given anything for it to be any one of them.

The third knock came louder – more forcefully. She smoothed down her nightdress and contemplated putting on her dressing gown, but chose against it. She may as well give the impression she'd just climbed out of bed, even if he knew better.

She feigned tiredness, yawned loudly – wondering if that was just a bit too much of an act – and opened the door. She looked Stefan up and down. Why did her stomach lurch every time she saw him? 'Yes?' she said.

Stefan looked at her, one hand in his pocket, the other clutching the torch, which Persey did her best not to look at. Neither of them spoke and the fact he didn't speak unnerved her. It was far more effective than shouting at her. Silently, she moved inside her room, leaving the door open for him.

She shivered in her thin nightdress and cast her eyes around for her dressing gown, regretting not putting it on now. Stefan softly closed the bedroom door behind him, moved to put the torch on her dressing table and, wordlessly, removed his jacket and placed it around her shoulders.

'You are shivering,' he said quietly. He scrutinised her face.

She looked at the torch on the dressing table and then glanced away. 'Thank you,' she said, pulling his jacket around her. It smelled of him and was warm from his body heat, but the eagle embroidered on the front sickened her.

'Is this yours?' Stefan said softly, looking towards the torch.

She paused, studying it hard. 'I don't think so. Possibly though. I have one fairly similar somewhere.' Her voice was strained, her chest tight. Her ribcage felt as if it was closing in on her, crushing her from within.

He nodded slowly. 'I found it outside. After curfew.'

'I must have dropped it earlier. If it is mine, that is,' she clarified.

'It was not there when I went out with your sister this evening.' His gaze bore into her.

'I nipped out to the garage for something,' she said, tipping her chin up defiantly.

'For what?'

'Is this an interrogation?' she asked with a laugh that sounded false even to her own ears.

Stefan's laugh was genuine. 'Of course not. But you went outside after curfew?'

'To the garage,' she said.

'No one is allowed outside at all after curfew.' He stepped towards her as if to illustrate the severity of his point.

134

'Both you and Dido were out after curfew,' Persey countered. 'Even though the club has adjusted its hours so you didn't need to be so late.'

She was aware of his proximity to her and the inappropriateness of his being inside her bedroom while she was in her nightdress. He was watching her silently and so she pushed on. 'You are both back far later than when the club closed.'

'We went for a drive.'

'Where to?' she asked, attempting to mask a terrible and unexpected feeling of jealousy.

He paused. A small smile. 'Now who is interrogating who?'

They stood and stared at each other, neither speaking, neither moving. Was he annoyed? Angry? She couldn't tell, he seemed so calm. It was he who looked away first and the thread between them broke. Stefan walked towards her dressing table. The black and white picture of her family, the four of them, she and Dido so much younger standing behind the bench in the garden, their parents sat in front of them. He picked it up and looked at it with a rueful smile.

'This is how I remember you,' he said. 'Looking like this. It shocked me to see you . . .'

'To see me?' she prompted after a long silence, desperate to know what he had been going to say.

But he changed tack. 'Persey, what are you doing?'

'What do you mean?'

'You know what I mean. Stop it. Whatever it is you are doing. Stop. You have been through something awful. I understand how you must feel.'

'The German presence is only temporary,' she said, folding her arms. 'You'll all be kicked off the island sooner or later.'

He put the picture of her parents back down. 'Do not let anyone else hear you say that. And you know that's not what I mean. You have lost your mother.'

It was her turn to tell him to stop.

'It cannot be easy to lose a mother,' he continued. 'Both your parents.'

'Don't,' she warned.

'I'm not your enemy.'

Tears formed in her eyes and she wiped them with the back of her hand.

He stepped towards her and pulled a handkerchief from his trouser pocket. He looked away as she wiped her eyes of fresh tears.

He turned and moved towards the window, pulling back the curtain and looking out as she had done. 'Your blackout blind should be in place.' But he made no move to lift it from its position on the floor and push it against the window.

Persey dried her tears and turned towards him, holding out his handkerchief. He glanced at her and shook his head before looking out of the window again.

'What is Jack to you?' he asked quietly.

'Jack?' She didn't understand the question.

'I thought he was just the housekeeper's son,' he stated.

'He is.'

'The two of you are not . . .?'

'No, of course not! He's an annoying older brother, in a way. And is it any concern of yours?' Persey asked.

Stefan smiled, his eyes narrowed but he wouldn't meet her gaze. Eventually he turned, leant his back against the window and folded his arms.

She looked away under his scrutiny. 'Did you have a nice time with Dido?' She hadn't meant to phrase it so accusingly. However, she was sure that was how it had sounded.

'Yes. I did. Thank you. She has a very beautiful voice.'

'She has, yes.'

'I'm surprised, with a voice like hers, she hasn't left Guernsey, sought fame and fortune in London or America.'

'She intended to leave, only she didn't make it off in time.

None of us did. We knew you were coming, of course. Just not so quickly.'

'They forge forward with intent,' he said.

'They?' she queried.

'We. We forge forward with intent.'

'Towards England?'

He nodded. 'That is the plan.'

'Think you'll be dining at The Ritz in a month's time?' she scoffed.

Stefan shrugged. 'I sincerely hope not.'

'Really?' she asked, her interest piqued. 'You're an intelligent man. Do you honestly think,' she continued, 'that no one here is going to stop you; that no one is even going to try to resist?' She was genuinely interested in what he thought. 'Do you think no one is going to break your pointless curfew law? We can do the same amount of damage at midnight as we can during the day.'

He sighed. 'It would be so stupid. Resistance, here.'

'Why do you say that?'

'The size of your island,' he said simply. 'The layout of it. Should a band of resistance fighters form, where would you hide? Where would you plan? Where would you get weapons?'

Persey didn't speak, her eyes downcast thinking of the truth in what he'd said.

'We do not anticipate resistance in the Channel Islands, on any serious level,' he continued. 'And if there is any, I am sorry to say it will be stamped out with force.'

His words made her shiver.

'Why would you resist?' he asked.

'Why wouldn't we resist?' she countered.

'I mean, what cause do you have?' he enquired. 'You are being treated well. We are, so far, existing together side by side in close proximity. There are, of course, rules to be followed as part of an Occupation but they are not unfair rules. You come, you go, and you live much as before. We do not drag you from your homes,

137

out into the street and shoot you or . . .' He looked around for inspiration. 'Or steal your children away when you are sleeping. We respect you.'

'And what about the Jews?' she asked, stopping him. 'Do you respect them?'

'I do,' he muttered almost inaudibly and then louder, 'Of course I do – they are no different to us. They are human.'

'Really?' she asked. 'But the rest of your kind don't; pushing a particular kind of anti-Semitic hatred around until it takes permanent hold; punishment for simply existing.'

Stefan raised his eyes to her. 'Be very careful who you say that to,' he said gently. 'You may think it. But you cannot say it.'

'Is that what you do?' she asked, stepping forward although not realising she had done so. 'Do you think it, but not say it?'

He glanced at the door as if someone might be on the other side, but Persey knew full well there wasn't. No one would dare leave their room now.

A vacuum of silence lay between them. Eventually he pushed himself away from the window, stepped towards her, which only served to confuse her, before gently lifting his jacket from her shoulders. She'd forgotten she was wearing it.

'I must go to bed. And so must you,' he said. He walked towards the torch on the dressing table, reached out to pick it up, thought better of it and left it where it lay. He looked at her, a look laced with meaning before he left, pulling the door closed behind him. He knew it had been her being chased. She just hoped he didn't know it had been Jack as well.

She had hardly slept since Stefan had been in her room but with the clocks adjusted to Berlin time and with her blackout blind left on the floor simply because she was feeling rebellious, her eyes stung with tiredness. She wished she'd put it back in place. She had awoken from her none too restful sleep far too early.

From the sitting room window, Persephone seethed with anger

as she watched the Germans requisition her father's beloved Wolseley Series II from the garage. Her teeth were clenched so tightly she was in danger of breaking one of them.

Dido entered the room, dressed in black for their mother's funeral and adjusting the net that drooped from her hat. In stark contrast to her outfit, her lips were painted a rich shade of crimson. The sisters hadn't had time to talk about the events of last night and Dido glanced behind her, closing the sitting room door.

'What happened?' Dido whispered fast. 'Jack's still here, I heard him in his room. And I'm sure I heard Stefan's footsteps in the hallway. Did he come to your room last night? Tell me, quickly.'

Persey explained how Jack's escape had gone so horrifically wrong, the frightening chase through the woods in which she thought she was seconds away from being shot or captured, and how Stefan had come to her room brandishing a torch as if it was evidence. 'Which of course it was, really.'

'Oh good Lord. So that's what he found. You must be more careful, Persey.'

'I'm being as careful as I can,' Persey hissed. 'Given the circumstances.'

'I know,' Dido said. 'It's all so dreadful. And now Jack's trapped. For how long?'

'I don't know. I think for the duration.'

'No. That can't be true.'

'There was no plan for a second pick-up if the first went wrong, which it did. Now he thinks he's been abandoned.'

'He has, probably. We all have.'

'Don't say that,' Persey said.

'It's true though, isn't it? Where's our help? We were told to hotfoot it or else. We've chosen "or else", much to our idiocy. And now we're regretting it.'

Persey thought of Stefan's words last night. 'It could be much worse.'

Dido kicked at the Chinese rug. 'Yes, I suppose.'

Persey put her hand on her sister's arm. 'How was the club last night? I think our resident Nazi appreciated your singing.' As she said it, she knew it was an unfair accusation. He wasn't a Nazi. He was willing to do his job but his heart didn't seem in it. His words last night had told her as much. His actions said the same. Would any other officer have simply given her a ticking off, a warning? No, he wasn't a Nazi, he was just wearing their colours.

'It's different now. So many Germans. The usual crowd are drifting away. The atmosphere has changed. The soldiers knew all the words to our songs. Imagine that. Sang along quite happily in English. Quite surprised me. Do you know,' Dido said thoughtfully, 'now you mention about him being our resident Nazi . . . I'm not sure Stefan is a Nazi. Something he said in the car as we sat looking at Les Hanois Lighthouse and the moon on the water did rather make me wonder.'

'That sounds romantic,' Persey said.

'Oh, it wasn't really,' Dido said, her tone dismissive. 'The club was monstrously busy and Stefan said afterwards he needed a bit of quiet, away from all the other officers. They weren't even that rowdy. All very polite, which shocked me. I was expecting leering and jeering and to have to beg Stefan to rescue my virtue, but actually they're all quite nice, miss their mothers, miss their wives, miss their children. Very grateful to be here and not elsewhere. Perhaps they're under orders to keep their hands off us all. No fraternisation.'

Persey had been to see Dido sing a few times when the hotel ballrooms had been open to paying tourists. She had only taken up the job two years ago when her musical performances at amateur dramatic societies had organically led to this. Mother and Father hadn't known whether to be furious, Dido accepting such a paying role, or proud of their daughter whose voice had been so universally appreciated. In the end they'd settled on a reaction somewhere in the middle as their daughter sang to respectable couples keen to dine and dance. Back then, her mother and father had accompanied her too and they'd taken a table for dinner, proudly watching Dido sing to mainlanders who were drawn to Guernsey by railway travel posters naming it the Sunshine Island. It really was.

But while the sun still shone down on the island, now it was an army and civil administration replacing tourists in the clubs and lounges.

Persey mused. 'No fraternisation,' she repeated. 'Thank goodness. What did Stefan say?' she asked too casually. 'At the lighthouse?'

'He said it was all such an awful shame, this war. That it was a hateful stampede that should never have happened.'

'Did he?' Persey asked. She wondered which would be worse: his being here on the wrong side or if he had never come at all? She didn't know which version of events she preferred.

'I wonder why he joined the war if he doesn't agree with it,' Dido mused.

'I don't know,' Persey replied. 'Why do any of us do anything?'

Dido looked thoughtful. 'Perhaps it was the right thing to do at the time. That's why I do things, because it seems like the right thing . . . then. And now, perhaps he's filled with deep regret for being part of the war, and its progress.'

'You do like to see the good in everyone, don't you?' Persey looked at her sister with nothing but love.

Dido shrugged as if she was offended by such a comment. 'I don't think so. But I do like to give people the benefit of the doubt. If I think they deserve it.'

'Hmm,' Persey half-heartedly agreed before turning back towards the window, torturously looking towards the Germans who were still admiring her father's vehicle. She had opened the garage for them, signed where appropriate, given the ticket that confirmed she'd be reimbursed for it when hostilities ended and had walked away without a further word. She knew she'd never see that money. She hoped they'd treat it kindly even if it did mean some general somewhere running around in her father's pride

141

and joy. There were rumours cars were being taken to the European mainland. She hoped that was its fate and that she'd not have to see anyone driving it around the island. 'I wish they'd just go. Awful people. Why are they still here?'

Dido moved to the window and looked out. 'I imagine that summarises how we all feel about the Germans in general. Do I look all right?' Dido asked. 'Lipstick not a bit much for a funeral, perhaps?'

'Perhaps,' Persey said.

'Shall I wipe it off?'

'Maybe,' Persey replied.

Dido adjusted the gauze on her hat that didn't sit quite right. 'Horrific day.'

Persey breathed deeply. 'Yes. And it's only just begun.'

'It'll be all right you know,' Dido encouraged. 'Once this bit's over.'

'I know,' Persey said, not quite believing it was true; not quite believing they were burying their mother either.

'You look nice,' Dido said.

Persey stepped away from the window and embraced her sister. 'Thanks,' she said, looking at Dido properly, taking time to look at her lovely sister. 'On second thoughts, leave the lipstick on. You look beautiful.'

'One tries,' Dido joked. 'Must go sparingly on the lipstick. One doesn't know where one's next stick of Yardley is coming from.'

Persey looked at her wristwatch and sighed deeply. 'I'll fetch Mrs Grant and Jack. We should leave now if we're going to make it to the church in good time. No funeral motorcar to take us now you know.'

'He's not all bad you know,' Dido said.

Persey frowned. 'Who?'

'Stefan, silly. He's just how I remembered him.'

'I didn't think you did remember him,' Persey returned.

'He's kind.'

'I know.' She couldn't think about Stefan anymore. She'd hardly known him back then and she hardly knew him now. Persey squeezed her sister's arm gently and braced herself for the day ahead.

Chapter 15

The organist began the first few bars of 'Jerusalem'. Dido had chosen that particular hymn for the funeral because it had been Mother's favourite, but Persey now saw it was a fitting choice for another reason. She hoped the mourners might appreciate the hint at patriotism in the midst of the solemnities as she sang, 'England's green and pleasant land,' louder than she might normally have done.

Next to Persey, Mrs Grant was crying into a handkerchief and at the far end of the pew Jack wasn't singing at all, simply staring through his hymnbook, his face impassive. He was now effectively a British spy trapped in enemy territory. They'd had no time to talk privately since the events of the previous night and she wanted so very much to reassure him that everything would be all right; that they needn't change their story.

Persey didn't even glimpse Stefan until the moment arrived that she had been dreading. The moment she remembered so well from her father's funeral two years earlier. The weather had become progressively colder in the short time since they had entered the church and now, standing by the graveside, she shivered.

The vicar had been reciting words for only a moment and Persey wiped her tear-stained eyes, forcing her gaze away from the awful space where her mother's coffin had just been lowered.

'We therefore commit her body to the ground; earth to earth, ashes to ashes, dust to dust; in sure and certain hope of the Resurrection to eternal life . . .'

Dido's hand found Persey's. Persey wished so desperately that she could do something to make everything better; that she could get Dido off the island so she wouldn't have to endure the rest of the Occupation and all the horrors it might bring with it; that she could get Jack to safety, although she knew that if that seemed out of the control of the British navy then in all likelihood it was out of her control too. She wished she could bring her mother back. She wished she could do something useful for Lise.

Overhead a bird swooped and fell on the rise and fall of a pocket of air. It barely needed to flap its wings. Up and down it went, up and down, lulling Persey into a daze. Dido squeezed her hand and Persey forced her attention away from the bird and its peaceful roaming of the sky. As she did so, she saw him, on the other side of the grave, behind her mother's friends from the knitting circle. He was a full head and shoulders above the women in front. He was watching her, a look of concern on his face.

Persey wasn't sure if she should smile in recognition of Stefan or be horrified he was there. Her first instinct was to be pleased he had been thoughtful enough to attend. Had he come because he felt genuinely sympathetic towards her and Dido and their loss? Or had he come out of a sense of duty and because it would be strange, living in their house, if he hadn't? Had he been inside the church the whole time or had he only just this moment arrived? There were a few interested glances from those standing beside the grave; a few nudges. Persey frowned. What did people think of him being here?

'Persey,' Dido whispered and Persephone came to and looked at her sister in confusion. 'It's your turn,' Dido said and held out a small box of soil. Persey took a handful and threw it softly onto the coffin. She wiped sudden tears from her face before passing the box on.

At the gathering at Deux Tourelles, Stefan stood awkwardly in the corner, looking smaller than his usual stature would indicate and nursing a sherry. It wouldn't be easy to get hold of spirits going forward, of that Persey was sure. But she knew their mother would have spun in her freshly dug grave if she'd thought her daughters had been considering restricting food and drink at an occasion such as this. And so, the girls and Mrs Grant had offered what they could, fruits and salads from items grown in the garden and also on the island including grapes, melon and even wedges from a large Camembert from France that the grocer had kept aside when Mrs Grant had mentioned the funeral to him.

Residents were swiftly learning not to expect too much in the way of outlandish culinary offerings since war broke out. At least they still had access to food from the European mainland, unlike those living on the British mainland, cut off and alone as they were from the rest of Europe. But access to better food was hardly a fair trade for living under Nazi rule.

This week Persey would return to work. At least it would be a return to a semblance of normality in a fortnight of utterly abnormal and abysmal events. As she shook hands and said goodbye to those who had said kind words and made their presence felt, she wondered, when she returned to work, if Lise would still be as distressed as she had been in Candie Gardens. What on earth could Persey do to help?

Doctor Durand was one of the last to leave and having said goodbye to Dido he gave Persey a sympathetic look at the front door. 'The worst has passed,' the doctor said. 'I'm no expert but now you can grieve. And then . . .'

'And then?'

'And then you can live. You know where I am if you or your sister needs anything, don't you? Anything at all. We live in strange times now. You only have to ask.'

Stefan edged past Doctor Durand, giving the doctor a polite nod and, turning to Persey, looked at her as if there was so much he wanted to say. But instead of interrupting, Stefan put on his cap and walked down the drive, turning towards the airport.

Before the doctor could say anything derogatory or otherwise about Stefan's presence at the funeral, Persey spoke. 'Actually,' she started cautiously. What she was about to ask of him might bring with it a phenomenal amount of trouble for everyone involved. Was it fair to ask this of him? Was it fair even to mention it to him? He had always been kind, forthright and, as far as she could tell, he hated the Germans with as much fervour as she did. And if she didn't risk it, what then? She didn't know who else she could trust. It had to be worth just mentioning it, surely. 'Actually, Doctor Durand,' she said bravely, 'there is something I need to ask you.'

'You haven't heard from Miss Weber, have you?' Persey's employer Edward Le Brost asked her when she'd returned to work later that week.

Persey looked up from her desk. She'd been marvelling at how much filing had been placed on her desk in her absence. Still, best to have lots to do to keep busy than far too little and so lose herself to grief.

'Lise? No,' she said, glancing at the wall clock which read half past nine. 'Sorry. Perhaps she's simply late.'

'She wasn't in towards the end of last week and now this week,' Mr Le Brost said. 'Most strange.'

Persey tried to remain calm. Perhaps she was ill, although her mind drifted to moonlight flits.

'Odd, I think. For her,' her employer continued.

'Yes,' Persey said, concerned. 'Yes, it is. You've not heard from her at all?'

He shook his head.

'Me neither, sorry,' Persey said. 'Perhaps I'd best go along to her lodgings after work and see if she's unwell.'

'Thanks. I'd intended to do the same but if you could that would be just the ticket. In the meantime, I'm rather afraid you have two people's jobs to do here,' he said, indicating the pile of papers.

'That's all right,' she said. 'It'll keep me busy.'

147

'How are you?' Mr Le Brost said, shuffling on his feet awkwardly.

'I'm well, thank you,' Persey said. 'I don't think I'm sickening for something.'

'No, I mean, after your loss.'

'I suppose as well as can be expected,' she said. 'I'm still standing at any rate.'

'Jolly good. Keep up the good work and if you hear from Miss Weber you will inform me, won't you? If she's left us and not had the good grace to tell us, I shall have to replace her.'

'Oh, I'm sure it won't come to that,' Persey said as panic for her friend filled her mind.

Walking uphill through St Peter Port after work, Persey's heart sank as she took in the plethora of new German signposts that had been put up directing soldiers to different Wehrmacht offices and to the new Feldkommandantur department that had arrived to deal with civil affairs. Was Stefan there? she wondered. Was he still just paper-pushing and translating? She hadn't wanted to know what he was doing but now she was intrigued. What on earth kept him going if – as Dido and Persey suspected – he wasn't really invested in the modus operandi of the Third Reich?

Around Persey groups of newly arrived soldiers looked excitedly in the windows of shops that were ready to close for the day. Was it cruel of her to think they were working out how much they could buy and ship home, thus depriving the Islanders of precious stocks of essentials they may not see again this side of the war ending? If it ended, Persey mused. And if the Allies won. She didn't dare admit it was a real possibility the Allies might not win.

As she turned into the botanic delights of Candie Gardens, she came face to face with a German soldier. 'Oh, I'm so sorry,' she said instinctively.

'It is all right,' the man said stiffly. He was standing far too close and so she moved back, intending to step round him politely and be on her way. But then catching sight of his face, her polite expression slipped. It was the soldier who had chased her through the woodland, the night of Jack's doomed escape, she was sure of it.

'Oh,' she said. He looked closer at her and said nothing but his eyes were narrow as if trying to place her.

Persey wondered how much of a look could he reasonably have had given it was dark and she'd been running at what she'd considered a great speed that night. 'Excuse me,' she said.

The man looked after her as she moved on, and she stole a quick glance back just to see if his reaction had changed. It hadn't. His eyes were narrowed and his frown deepening, still clearly struggling to place her.

As she passed through Candie Gardens, Persey ignored other soldiers, some of whom wolf-whistled at her. It didn't do to make a remark and, also, she was alone. She'd had enough of a brush with German soldiers to last her for the month and she didn't want any more trouble.

Soon she stood outside the door of Lise's lodging house in Brock Road, looking at the terraced two-storey cottage, gabled windows looking down onto the road and the small, gated front garden that looked in need of a good prune. She wondered if she should knock and enquire as to her friend's health or simply keep moving. Would it not cause more aggravation for Lise if she stood and had a chat with the landlady who, Lise had suggested, was likely to inform on her for being Jewish? What if Lise had left? What if Persey had waited too long? Persey had said she would enquire for her employer, but perhaps she should just fib – report back that Lise was sick and then think again in a couple of days if her friend didn't emerge.

Persey fiddled with the buttons on her summer dress and just when she had made up her mind that no, this really was a terrible idea and would only lead to further trouble for Lise, the door opened and a pinched-faced woman with a severe expression stood on the doorstep and glared at her.

149

'I saw you from the window,' the woman accused.

'Yes. I . . . was looking for . . . I have the wrong house, I see that now.'

'I've seen you before,' she said. 'You work with Miss Weber.'

'I do.' Persey wondered how the woman could know that. Persey didn't think she'd seen her before so how did she know who Persey was?

'I saw you. Leaving your office with Miss Weber after work. I was shopping in town. A few months ago. I saw you.'

Something about the woman's forceful tone cut into Persey like a knife. 'You have a very good memory,' Persey said. 'I'm afraid I don't remember you.'

'I didn't introduce myself back then but I will do now. I'm Mrs Renouf. But I expect Miss Weber may have mentioned me.'

'No, actually,' Persey dared. 'Not once.' What was it Oscar Wilde had once said? *There is only one thing in the world worse than being talked about, and that is not being talked about.*

Mrs Renouf bristled and inside Persey leapt for joy. A small win but a win nonetheless. 'You should have come over to say hello,' Persey continued. 'Always nice to meet new people.'

'Not always nice,' Mrs Renouf retorted quickly.

Persey was stumped at how to reply. The woman was such a joy.

'I take it you are here to see your friend?' Mrs Renouf said. Before Persey could respond, the woman continued, 'Well, she's not here.'

'She isn't?' Persey asked. 'Do you know where she is?'

'She's left.'

Persey raised her eyebrows. 'She's left? To go where? New lodgings?'

'How should I know? She's taken all her things. Not that she had much. And she's left owing me money, I might add.'

'Oh, that's . . .'

'She pays a month in advance, usually.'

150

'A month?' Persey queried, believing only a few weeks at a time at most was usual, perhaps even only a week. 'Is that normal?'

'On account of her being Jewish.'

Persey's mouth gaped open at the sheer awfulness of this woman. She understood Lise's concerns were not unfounded now.

'I can see you didn't know she was Jewish,' the woman said, misreading the meaning behind Persey's expression. 'They'll ask her to register soon, no doubt,' Mrs Renouf mused. 'She'll have to wear a star like we've seen in the papers. Abhorrent really.'

'What is? Her having to wear a star or her being Jewish?'

'I've nothing against her. She lived under my roof for a year,' the woman bristled.

'She was paying you,' Persey said under her breath.

'Yes, well. She's not the only one on the island who shouldn't be here,' Mrs Renouf said. It disgusted Persey that this woman was relishing gossiping about people's possible fates with a relative stranger.

'What do you mean, people who shouldn't be here?' Persey asked instinctively thinking of Jack. But the woman meant the Germans, surely.

'I happen to know there's one up at the hospital. A nurse. Already been arrested for being an enemy alien. Let her out now, though. Transpired she was a Jew.'

Good God. How many Jews were there on the island still? How had this happened? Persey's brow furrowed in confusion and concern.

'It won't end well for them. You mark my words,' Mrs Renouf said.

'No,' Persey said slowly, 'I should imagine not. I suppose the trick is not to tell the Germans they're here,' Persey said, curious as to what Lise's landlady would say to that.

'I don't want to be arrested if they find out I know something I shouldn't know. And for not doing the responsible thing about it.'

Persey's confusion must have emanated from her. 'What would the responsible thing be?'

Mrs Renouf raised an eyebrow and Persey made a move to leave, disgusted at this woman's proud anticipation over very much doing the wrong thing. Sometimes the people who mean to do the most good are those who do the most harm, Persey mused.

'Well, if Lise isn't here, I shall leave you to it. If you see her, will you tell her I was asking after her? Her employers are asking after her also.'

'What did you say your name was?' Lise's landlady asked.

There was no avoiding it. 'Persephone Le Roy.'

'Curious, isn't it?' Mrs Renouf called after Persey as she reached the garden gate.

Persey smiled thinly as she looked back at the woman. She wished firmly she hadn't gone to enquire after Lise now. She had known no good would come of it. 'What's curious?' Persey was forced to ask.

'She's not here,' the woman continued, 'she's not at work.' Unveiled delight spread across Mrs Renouf's face. 'Where could she be?'

Chapter 16

Persey was drained from another day carrying out two people's jobs, but she daren't show it to Mr Le Brost in case he took it upon himself to replace Lise before she'd had the chance to return. If she returned. Where was she? And what if it was true, what Mrs Renouf had said, that there were many more Jews still remaining on the island? She perished the thought. Concern addled her mind and she was too on edge to engage in even the minutest small talk, which she suspected suited her employer quite well.

It was after she returned from work on her bicycle, and was propping it against the wall in the garage, that she heard the crunch of gravel behind her.

'Doctor Durand, how are you?' Persey asked with genuine delight as she turned.

'Is your German here?' he asked quietly.

'He's not my German,' Persey was quick to point out. 'But I don't actually know. I've just returned from work and haven't been inside yet. What's wrong?'

'In that instance . . . best not do this here, just in case,' he said. 'Fifteen minutes? End of the lane?'

Persey nodded, intrigued. She waited for the allotted time, pretending to fiddle with the chain of her bicycle and making a great show of checking her tyres before getting back on and cycling down the lane to meet the doctor.

Doctor Durand peered into the woodland that lay beyond and deciding they were alone said, 'I've been so busy with patients I've only now found time to come to you. I didn't dare risk telephoning. Who knows who's listening these days.'

Persey looked on expectantly.

'Lise is at our house,' he said. 'We've a spare room above the waiting room. She keeps out of the way when patients call and so far, so good.'

'Oh thank God,' Persey said. 'I was so worried we'd left it too late when I found out she'd not been to work.'

'She was on her way to work when I found her,' he said. 'She took some convincing, but when I mentioned it was your idea and you suggested she had to move immediately she went into her lodging house, took all her things and left in under five minutes. Her landlady had gone into town for something or other so it was a lucky chance I arrived when I did.'

'Yes,' Persey said. 'The last thing Lise needs is that frightful woman finding out she's hiding at yours.'

'Lise has told me all about her landlady. Shockingly awful bigot. May as well be wearing a swastika herself. You did the right thing, asking me if I could find somewhere more discreet for her to live.'

'It's not permanent,' Persephone said, knowing the doctor was putting himself and his family at risk. She must find Lise a more suitable place to hide.

'Don't be silly.' Doctor Durand laughed. 'It has to be permanent. Or else, what's the point?'

Persey glanced around, just to be sure they were still alone. The trees swayed around them in the gentle breeze, but there was no other human sound. 'But what if you get a soldier billeted with you, like we have?'

'We'll cross that bridge when we come to it. I intend to keep her safe. Regardless of race and creed, keeping Lise safe when others might not is the right thing to do. I swore the Hippocratic oath. "Whatsoever I shall see or hear in the course of my profession, as well as outside my profession, if it be what should not be published abroad, I will never divulge, holding such things to be holy secrets", he quoted with a glint in his eye.

Persey smiled, impressed. 'Goodness, you were the right person to ask.'

'My wife feels the same so you can count on her discretion. Her father was gassed in the last war. Hates the Germans with a viciousness that's almost unbecoming.' He attempted a laugh.

'Is this what it's going to be like now, do you think? And how long for?'

The question was rhetorical but Doctor Durand replied regardless. 'God knows. For the foreseeable I should imagine. They're arriving in droves. There'll be more of them than there are of us soon if it carries on like this.'

'They imagine they're inching ever closer to London just because they've made it this far,' Persey said.

'Do you know one of the German doctors I met told me many young soldiers newly arrived didn't actually understand that they weren't in England. Couldn't comprehend they were closer to France than they are to the King.'

Persey shook her head in disbelief. 'And they think they're going to win the war like that?'

'Some of them seem a good sort, so far. The medical staff, I mean. That German billeted with you seems all right – Captain Keller. He and I had a few friendly words at the funeral. Think I was the only one to speak to him.'

'Were you surprised? Some of mother's friends were awfully het up about a German in their midst.'

'What possessed him to come to the funeral, do you think?' the doctor asked.

Persey breathed deeply. 'Now I think about it, I feel it was a kind thing to do. He used to know Mother and us,' Persey said, not wishing to elaborate further. She thought of that kiss on the cliffs from so long ago. 'Well, he used to know Dido and I, really. And Jack.'

'Really?' Doctor Durand said in astonishment, and Persey explained about the many summers they'd spent with Stefan. 'Well, I'd never have guessed a prior connection. I didn't see you speak to him once. And I didn't see Jack even so much as glance in his direction, I'm sure.' Doctor Durand looked interested.

Persey didn't reply. She wasn't surprised Jack didn't speak to Stefan; Jack avoided their German friend at all costs. Eager to move on, Persey was grateful when the doctor brought them back to the subject of Lise. 'I'm not sure how many more I can take feasibly, but if you hear of anyone else who needs help . . .' he said.

'Take?'

'There will be more Jews stuck here, I think.'

'Apparently so,' she replied.

'They'll be told to register soon enough.'

'Yes, I've also heard this,' Persey said regretfully.

'Who from?'

'The dreaded Mrs Renouf.'

'How does she know that?' he asked with narrowed eyes.

'I assume gossip?'

'Or perhaps she's already far too friendly with them and she's been told,' the doctor suggested.

'Don't say that,' Persey said, feeling sick at the thought of collaboration occurring so quickly.

'There'll be more like her, you know,' Doctor Durand said. 'You wait. Old scores will be settled in the most horrific of ways. We won't know who to trust soon.'

'I can count on one hand those I do trust,' Persey said, thinking of Dido, Jack and Mrs Grant, and the courageous doctor standing in front of her, willing to hide Jews from the Nazis on such a small island. But even so, she knew in order to keep Lise safe that she could never tell any of the others what they had done. It would hurt her more than anything not to tell Dido, but the risk to Lise should Dido accidentally mention it to anyone was unthinkable.

No, she trusted her sister with her own life but it wasn't fair to trust her with someone else's.

And then there was Stefan. How far could she trust him? He had gone out of his way to protect her identity when the soldier had accused her of being out after dark. 'It's all such a mess and it's only going to get worse,' she added.

'Silly question, but I don't need to tell you to keep this quiet, do I?'

'Of course not. I know how serious this is,' Persey said. 'If anyone finds out she's there . . .'

'If something happens, if they act on the attitudes they've brought with them, continue the rampage towards the Jews here, which I suspect is only a matter of time, it doesn't bear thinking about. How is it with him in your house?' Doctor Durand said returning to the subject of Stefan. He was unavoidable, even when he wasn't in her company.

'Not as awful as I thought it would be, in truth. Dido's not sure he's one of "them". I'm not sure I think he is either.'

She wasn't sure why she was telling the doctor this. Was it because she wanted, so desperately, for it to be true? Was it because she wanted Doctor Durand to agree that from their few minutes of small talk at Mother's funeral he had deduced Stefan was a good man? Did she need someone else's approval of him?

Doctor Durand looked at her as if she was stupid. 'But he is one of them, isn't he?'

Persey narrowed her eyes. 'You just said some of them were all right,' she reminded him.

'The medical staff, of course. Not their fault their calling was to save people's lives and they now find themselves wrapped up in this mess. Even then, I wouldn't even consider telling them about Lise. And although your Captain Keller also seems friendly he looks the part and wears that awful uniform. So don't even think about trusting him.'

* * *

157

The gramophone played Tommy Dorsey in the dining room as Persephone laid the table for dinner. Mrs Grant had all but banished meals involving Stefan from being held in the kitchen, so the girls were forced back to the more staid surroundings of the dining room to eat, even though they'd much rather eat in less formal an atmosphere.

Listening to 'Indian Summer', Persephone could almost imagine there was no war on outside. Just for these few, precious minutes. The summer sun had warmed the room throughout the day and she swayed slowly to the music as she neatened the cutlery and placed a jug of water on the table, setting out the crystal tumblers and throwing open the window to combat the inordinate warmth.

The smell of a rarely available, small piece of beef roasting gently in the oven was a delicious precursor to what Persey considered the main event, one of Mrs Grant's famous summer berry crumbles. Out in the countryside they were more privileged than most, with access to a large kitchen garden. Meat would be a problem – Persey knew that. Scarcity of food in general was going to be a problem. But not as much of a problem as if they had lived in town, with a postage-stamp-sized garden and strict rationing to adhere to.

Time would tell as to how awful things would get there. Even though the island was only about nine miles long it was far easier out here, surrounded by farmers, to get hold of the odd piece of illicit meat if the farmer was clever at hiding the animal from the Germans – and if Mrs Grant bartered well enough for it. And of course, they were growing their own fruit and vegetables. Mother had called the six fruit trees on the property the orchard, which had tickled Persey, Dido and their father, but now she'd have given anything for her mother to be here, reprimanding Persey jokingly for pruning them badly.

She looked at the table with its display of roses brought in from the garden. She picked up the vase and put it on the side, unsure if it was a frippery too far. She shook her head, lifted the vase up from the sideboard and replaced it on the table. She'd picked the flowers; she may as well use them to brighten the room.

'Why did you just do that?' Stefan asked from the doorway, his head tilted to one side.

How long had he been there? Had he been watching her?

'I . . . it seemed silly, to have flowers, at a time like this. And then . . . well,' she said, looking down at the vase.

'A time like this?'

'With everything going on.' She brushed past the comment. 'Dinner might be a little while yet. I'm waiting for Dido to get back.' Actually, where was Dido? She didn't say she was singing tonight. Perhaps Dido had ventured out in search of different employment now the hours she could sing in the club had been restricted by the curfew. It was mercenary to think it but now Lise would be in hiding for the duration and not returning to work, perhaps she should mention to Mr Le Brost that Dido might be interested in helping there instead? Paperwork wasn't exactly Dido's forte though.

Stefan walked towards the gramophone, which Persey realised now had finished playing. He began looking through the records. 'Do you remember,' he started, 'when we went to the youth dance at the tennis club?'

She smiled, recollecting. 'Yes,' she said slowly. 'It feels like a lifetime ago.'

She watched the back of his blond head as he selected a record. 'It was,' he said. 'We were all trying to do the Charleston and the fox trot back then.'

'I was rather good, as I recall,' Persey said looking past him.

He turned, a smile on his face. 'You were, actually. I was desperate for something slower. And when the Charleston had finished, one of Jack's friends demanded it was played again.'

'Oh yes, so they did.'

'At the time I thought, so this is what hell is like.'

Persey couldn't help but laugh. 'Oh, it wasn't that bad.'

'Your mother watched on with laughter, as I remember. Dido

stepped in to try to show me and it was the first time I'd heard the two English phrases: as red as a beetroot and two left feet.'

'Are you still that bad at dancing?' she asked, folding her arms and watching him keenly.

He shrugged and turned away, selected a record and turned back to her. 'Shall we find out?' He held out his hand to her as the comforting crackle of the track began prior to the music starting.

'Oh no, I didn't mean—' She stiffened suddenly, kept her hands down by her sides.

'Do not argue. Just dance with me.'

He took one of her hands and she inched gingerly towards him.

The slow first bars of Noël Coward's 'Where Are the Songs We Sung' struck up and he pulled her closer. All the air had been sucked from the room. It had been so long since she'd danced and never like this. He moved steadily, leading, turning them slowly in the space between the dining table and the window. She tried to think of anything other than what they were doing – anything. What on earth had possessed Dido to install a gramophone in both this room and the sitting room? It was a ridiculous extravagance. They had never needed two.

He wasn't as awkward as she. Why wasn't he? His body heat warmed her; his hand gently rested on her back. She became so acutely aware of his touch that she stumbled.

'Now who has two left feet?' he asked.

'I'll admit you've got better,' she acquiesced.

'You have got worse,' he said with a chuckle guiding her backwards, holding their intertwined hands up and indicating he wanted to spin her.

'I'm out of practice. Not much call to dance these days,' she said quietly as she turned, his hand holding hers above them.

When she faced him again, he pulled her back towards him and said softly, 'There will be call to dance again.' The comment almost made her cry. Would there? When?

160

Slowly, as he led her, she began relaxing, trying to unstiffen herself. Just as she finally let her body free into the dance, the song ended. Stefan looked down at her and smiled. 'Persephone—' he started.

A cough sounded from the doorway and Dido and Jack were standing together, their hats still on, watching. Dido began clapping.

'What is it with people lurking in doorways today?' Persey said defensively, angry both that she had allowed herself to dance with Stefan and that she had been caught doing so. She dropped Stefan's hand and moved away.

'You spin a girl very beautifully,' Dido teased Stefan.

'Thank you,' he said, not looking at Dido but still at Persephone as she moved around the room.

Persey did her best to ignore it. Confusion scattered itself throughout her mind. When she had finally begun to enjoy herself she had felt so many things she knew she shouldn't feel. Now she thought she might be tainted in some way. Was she flushed? She needed to be far away from him. 'I'll go and let Mrs Grant know you're back.'

Dido moved back from the doorway in order to let Persey pass but Jack stood his ground, forcing Persey to squeeze through a gap that wasn't really there.

'What the hell are you doing?' he hissed at her.

She ignored him and carried on towards the kitchen. As she rounded the corner and dipped out of view she leant against the kitchen doorframe waiting for the beat in her heart to still itself.

'There you are,' Mrs Grant said. 'Now everyone's back you can take this in.' She gestured towards a plate of very thinly carved beef, which would just about go round.

'Where did you get this?' Persey asked in order to distract herself.

'I have my ways,' Mrs Grant replied knowingly. 'The German says he doesn't much like English mustard, so of course, I've slathered it all over.'

As Mrs Grant turned away, Persey sighed and closed her eyes for a few moments before heading back towards the dining room.

It baffled Persey as to why Stefan wanted to dine with them every now and again when Jack was sullen throughout every meal Stefan attended. And this one was no exception. Mrs Grant had begrudgingly admitted Stefan had been bringing small gifts of tinned goods and fish recently so it was fair that he got to eat some of it. But it confused Persey even more why Jack insisted on being so petulant in front of the officer when it would be less conspicuous to at least pretend to be happy. Persey wanted to kick him, tell him to buck up and smile at least once, but she couldn't get Jack's attention and Stefan spent the majority of the meal glancing in her direction. She would talk to Jack about it later.

Dido was making a good show of small talk but strangely not about where she'd been today, which prompted Persey to enquire. Both Dido and Jack looked up sharply.

'Nowhere special,' she said. 'Just a nice long walk.'

'Jack, what will you do for work now you have been excused from the war?' Stefan asked.

Persey thought she could have heard a pin drop.

'Excused?' Jack asked eventually.

'From the war effort because of your heart,' Stefan clarified.

'Oh yes, well nothing strenuous of course, because of my heart. A man like me isn't meant for heavy lifting, it would appear. May see if one of the shops in town needs a man with a keen eye for adding up and handing over change to old ladies doing their shopping,' Jack said bitterly, and Persey felt he actually meant it. Jack prodded his beef. 'Mother's chucked a lot of mustard on this. Why's she not let us add our own today, I wonder?' He became occupied with scraping off the yellow tinge. 'Ruined a perfectly good piece of meat.'

Stefan looked at his plate curiously. 'I think I know why,' he said quietly and began scraping his own beef. 'I have been thinking, Jack,' Stefan began a new subject, 'about your friend.'

'Which one?' Jack asked.

'The one who brought you back here.'

'God, not this again,' Jack said under his breath.

'Did he stay on the island?'

Jack laughed. 'Not likely,' he said as if Stefan was stupid. 'Bit close to France. Bit close to you lot. Turns out he was right. Here you all are.'

'I looked at the lists of boats coming and going,' Stefan said, ignoring him.

'Why?' Persey interjected.

'It's my job,' Stefan explained.

'I thought you were a translator?' she said.

'Among other things,' he said kindly.

'What other things?' Persey demanded.

'Other things,' Stefan said, laying his knife and fork down. 'I have been looking at the harbour, the comings and goings of the fishing vessels, incoming and outgoing passenger lists from before the Occupation began and I do not see a boat delivering Jack. I do not see any name or Jack's name actually.'

'Why?' Persey demanded again.

She still couldn't tell which way his loyalties lay, especially when he probed so deeply about Jack.

'That is what I am attempting to find out,' Stefan said with a hint of irritation in his voice.

Dido tried to calm the waters. 'I think she means, why are you enquiring?'

Persey spoke again. 'And if you reply with it's my job again, I swear . . .'

Stefan laughed. 'What is the problem?'

'There's no problem,' Persey said with a small laugh that sounded utterly false. 'I just want to know, why you want to know.'

Stefan was silent and looked at her for what Persey considered to be far too long. She was angry with herself that she was the first to look away.

'You are not registered anywhere,' he said to Jack.

'What does that mean?' Jack asked warily.

'You have a bad heart, but there is no new note of this at the hospital. You have not been to see a doctor to report this, to pass on the medical diagnosis of the doctor who saw you in England?'

'No,' Jack said. 'I haven't.'

'Hmm,' Stefan said.

'Shall I put some music on?' Dido asked, rising, but she was ignored.

'And your friend came all this way and then just returned, without notifying the harbourmaster? Without disembarking his boat? That seems very—'

But Jack had had enough. 'You've not changed, Stefan. You used to be just like this. You love a rule, don't you? It's boring. But in the last ten years since I had the misfortune to see you, that stick has just got even further up your—'

'Jack!' Persey cried.

'Sorry,' Jack said, standing. 'Ladies present. Excuse me.' He stalked from the room.

An uncomfortable silence descended.

'What's wrong?' Dido asked Stefan as she slowly sat down again.

Stefan looked at Dido kindly and then directed his gaze at Persey. 'I do not like being lied to.'

'What makes you think you're being lied to?' Persey dared.

'Everything. Everything makes me think I am being lied to.'

Dido stood up again. 'I'm going to see if Jack's all right. Excuse me.'

When Dido had left, Persey didn't dare ask him outright what he suspected Jack of doing. She couldn't. She tried to eat but couldn't do that either and instead she breathed out audibly.

'I can see the distrust you all have of me,' Stefan said solemnly. 'And I want you to know,' he continued, 'that your doubts about

164

me are unfounded.' She had wanted so much to trust him. But Doctor Durand's words that she should trust no one were still ringing in her mind. Often she felt she knew her own mind but . . . not in this. It had been so long. It had been too long. She didn't know Stefan now. As much as she wanted to, she didn't. She hadn't known him then, not really.

Persey watched him warily and he appeared to struggle with his words, trying again to say the same thing differently. 'I want you to know that I am on your side; that I want this war no more than you do, that I have no hidden agenda.'

'Really?' she asked.

'Really,' Stefan said.

'Why have you got a bee in your bonnet about Jack?' she asked.

He smiled at her phrase and then looked at her seriously. 'If there is a reason for someone to question Jack – not me, I am grateful interrogation is not my role – but one of my superiors or someone worse. Someone . . . with different methods—'

'Different methods?' she questioned. 'Do you mean the Gestapo? The Gestapo is in Guernsey?' She looked at her plate but she wasn't really seeing it. She'd heard terrifying rumours of what men in the Gestapo did to extract information in other occupied countries. Inhumane, terrible things.

'Do you think,' he continued, not quite answering her question, 'they will do what I have just done? Or do you think they will put Jack through the worst experience of his life? Do you think they will make him a cup of tea, or do you think they will make him cry for his mother?'

'Good God, Stefan,' Persey cried out in horror.

'You need to trust me. I cannot protect you, any of you, if I do not know the truth.'

'It's not your job to protect us.'

'I know, but I want to. We were once friends. I want it to be as it once was between all of us. All those summers we had together. The ones we've missed since.'

Was it safe to trust Stefan? She wanted to so badly. But Jack's life was at stake if she did.

'If it hadn't been so long,' she replied simply.

Stefan pushed his chair back and moved towards her, kneeling next to her chair. 'I am not a Nazi,' he said. 'Do you need me to keep saying it to you?'

Persey could feel the tears in her eyes and hated herself for it. 'No. But why did you join up?'

'Because the pay was good. Because my father and mother wanted me to. Because it made them proud to see me in a uniform, to see me employed. To see me rise through the ranks because I am a fast learner and speak six languages.'

'Six?' Persey found it hard not to be distracted by this. They were both quiet for a moment. 'You're on the wrong side,' she said.

'Yes,' he agreed.

'Yes?' She moved back in her chair to look down at him. 'Do you mean that?'

He nodded and looked tired suddenly, rose and walked towards the window.

'I didn't think it would be like this,' he said. 'War.'

'What did you think it would be like?' she asked softly.

He looked back at her. 'Not like this. Trampling on nations to such an extent. Germany's rise to greatness after all these years – it is coming at a cost.'

She had nothing to say to that. She had not seen what he had seen, but she had read enough about how so many lives were being lost, so many men sent to fight, so many countries forced to surrender in the end as Hitler's dominance over Europe continued. And now the Jews were being persecuted in even greater number throughout the rest of mainland Europe, driven out of towns, out of their homes and jobs, segregated. How far would it go?

'Can you understand why I want to be here? Why I want to be with old friends who find themselves in such a place at such a time? The closer the army advanced to the British mainland, the more I worried for you all. And then, the army was here. And so was I.'

Persey's stomach twisted at his words. She nodded. 'I can understand,' she whispered. 'Thank you.'

'Did you realise?' he asked.

'Did I realise what?' she asked, looking at him.

'Did you realise how I felt about you then? Through all those summers.'

She stopped breathing; didn't know what to say, how to react.

'When I left that last time, I did not know it would be the last time,' he continued. 'If I had, I would have said something, anything to find out how you felt; to see if you felt the same about me as I did about you. But after that moment on the cliff, you said nothing. You did not say a word. You did not even react.'

Persephone's stomach knotted together so tight it hurt. She didn't know what to say. What was the point of rehashing something that had never quite been? She blinked to banish this train of thought. How did he feel now? That was more important. He hadn't said. Why did she want him to so badly and what would she do if he did? How did she feel now? That was a question she hadn't even dared ask herself.

It took her a few seconds to reply. 'Nothing could have come of it then.'

'No,' he replied softly. 'We were too young. I was leaving. I should not have done it. It was unfair to both of us and I apologise.'

'Oh,' she said in genuine surprise.

'It was not the right time,' he finished. 'And we find ourselves here, now. All these years later.'

'Don't,' she whispered. If it had been the wrong time then, it was certainly the wrong time now. Nothing about this was right. The situation, it was wrong, all wrong. The absolute worst. Even worse than before. Nothing had flourished between them then, and nothing could now.

'You did not like me then?' he pushed, his blue eyes intensely looking towards hers. She could feel his gaze and she did her very best to avoid it.

'I . . . God, I don't know how I felt then.' She laughed but it was false. She knew. Of course she knew.

She had been too young, she thought, to call it love and so she had ignored it. But when Stefan had left that final summer she had stared at the walls blankly every evening after supper for the remainder of the season and wondered what on earth had happened to her heart.

He moved towards her now and she panicked, stood up from her chair, moved away from the table, away from him. He stopped and for that she was grateful.

'And now?' he said, his eyes wide with something resembling hope.

She clutched the back of the dining chair nearest the door. 'Please stop. You have to stop.' She pulled herself up straighter, taller. 'Do you not understand?' she continued. 'This . . . whatever this might be . . . it can't be. It's utterly abnormal. You, in your uniform, on this island. You want me to pretend it's normal. I can't,' she said with determination.

Dido entered the room bearing a large dish with the summer berry crumble. 'Pudding's served,' she announced. 'I can't convince Jack to come back inside I'm afraid. He's pacing the rose garden with the last of his good cigarettes and the evening newspaper.'

Persey looked away from Stefan, who was clearly crestfallen. 'I can't possibly eat anything,' Persey said, fighting back tears of anger and worry, and with her heart in her mouth and her nerves in tatters, she left the room to be confronted with Jack as she went towards the stairs. She tried to push past him but he grabbed her wrist to stop her. He looked angry, worried, colourless.

'Are you still angry about the dancing?' Persey asked Jack. 'I know you think it's some kind of brotherly duty to be protective of Dido and I but honestly, Jack, with Stefan I don't think you need—'

'I'm not worried about you dancing with him. I've got more important things to worry about.' He showed her the evening paper. 'Have you seen this?' he asked.

She had been so used to the real news having been replaced with Nazi propaganda that she had quickly decided to no longer pay any attention to the newspaper.

Jack's face had turned white and the hand that he was using to hold the paper shook so violently she could barely see the headline.

He pulled her up the stairs and into his bedroom.

'What's wrong?' she demanded.

'I don't know what to do,' he said. 'What do I do, Persey? Help me. Tell me.' He thrust the newspaper at her and she read the article he was shakily pointing at.

She read. 'Members of the British Armed forces in the island in hiding, and those sheltering them, have three days to give themselves up. If they do so, the soldiers will be treated as POWs and no action will be taken against those who assist them.'

'Oh my God, Jack.' She looked up at him. 'How do they know?'

'All that downstairs, from him . . .' Jack spat, pointing frantically at his closed bedroom door. 'I know why he was doing it. He must be laughing down there right now. He knows. The Germans know. They know why I'm here.'

Chapter 17

Lucy sat with her legs tucked underneath her on Will's sofa and translated the final page in her bundle of shorthand papers. She glanced over at Will who looked intent. It was a strange task but it was something she was enjoying far more than her day job. Perhaps because it was a novelty.

She looked down at the final page. It started the same as all the others: with a date. This one was marked September 8th 1943 and started:

Italy Surrenders.
Five days ago, Italy surrendered to the Allies and . . .

Lucy read through the report she'd painstakingly translated from shorthand into longhand one more time. She'd got the hang of shorthand now. It had taken all evening and now as she reached her final set of pages, she was barely looking at the shorthand guide for confirmation. Understanding the sweeps and strokes of certain letters not because someone was telling her in a class, but because she was genuinely interested in the sheets of wafer-thin paper in front of her, crumbling at the edges, and the secret words they contained. It was enthralling, reading through them, each one a document of key events from the Second World War outside the Channel Islands.

Beside her, Will was still going, his back hunched, head bent over the coffee table. His notepad filled with writing that Lucy could decipher less than the shorthand she'd now mastered.

'Your handwriting's awful,' she said.

'Hmm?' He looked up and blinked at her. He'd been far away, lost inside the loops and swirls of the pages in front of him. 'Yeah, I know.' He grinned. 'My mum says I should have been a doctor with handwriting like this.' And with that he was done with the conversation, dipping his head and clicking his pen as he worked his way through the alphabet, trying to piece together the last of his document.

Lucy waited and went through her set of pages. Facts and figures littered the pages of Allied wins and Axis losses, mentions of overseas resistance and British naval conquests. Her stack held mostly events from 1943. *May 12th 1943: Axis Surrender in North Africa. July 1943: Allies Invade Sicily* . . . and so on.

She looked over at Will's pages. The date on the top sheet he'd transcribed was 1942. She didn't lift it up, didn't want to break his intense concentration again, so she waited until he'd finished.

November 10th 1942: In violation of 1940 Armistice, Germany Invades Vichy France.

'That's interesting,' she whispered, looking up to find Will had finished and put down his pen to shake his hand out. They'd been translating for hours.

'Someone was writing out the news reports,' Will said.

Lucy nodded. 'Yeah, I got that,' she said with a laugh.

'Sorry.' Will rubbed his hand across his tired eyes and yawned. 'That was a really obvious thing to say. I suppose the question is, why?'

Lucy sat and stared at the sheets. 'Swap?'

'Mmm, go on,' Will said, passing her his sheets and reaching over to take hers.

Lucy skimmed the headlines.

November 13th 1942: British Eighth Army recaptures Tobruk.

November 18th 1942: Heavy British RAF raid on Berlin with few losses.

'What's the first date?' Lucy asked.

Will flicked. 'November 10th of '42. What's the last date?'

It was Lucy's turn to rifle through their notes. 'September 8th 1943. That's ten months in total from start to finish in this bundle.'

They were silent as they read each other's notes. 'Why would someone do this for nearly a year? And then stash carbon copies away?'

Lucy recalled her history lessons from school on the island. 'Radio sets were taken away at some point in the war. Can't remember when though.'

Will opened his laptop and searched on the Internet, calling up an image of the *Evening Press* from June 1942. He angled the laptop to show her the article about the removal of wireless sets.

'They confiscated all the radios twice. The first time was only for a matter of weeks quite early on in the Occupation. Some kind of reprisal for there being a spy harboured on the island, I think. And when he'd been found and everyone suitably punished, the reprisal ended.'

'Then they were given back?' Will asked doubtfully. 'Really?'

'Yes, I remembered that from school because I remembered thinking it was so strange. Strange to let them keep the radios in the first place when plenty of other nations the Nazis had stormed had them removed. But not in the Channel Islands. They took them. Then they gave them back. Then they took them again.'

'Bit mad,' Will said. 'But,' he reasoned, 'definitely not the maddest thing the Nazis did.'

'No,' Lucy agreed.

'But in summer 1942 it was permanent,' he said, reading the article.

The fire was dying and Lucy wondered if that was a sign she

should leave, but Will looked in the direction of the fire, stood up and threw on two more logs. Lucy watched them flare and crackle as the flames licked.

'So,' Will said. 'Let me get my head around this. The Nazis took away radios a few months before our bundle of news transcripts start. And the transcripts end less than a year later. Why?'

'Why what?' Lucy said, not quite understanding what he was driving at.

'Why do they end? What happens in—' he looked at the notes '—September 1943 to make whoever's doing this stop? The war didn't end until '45 and the Germans were here until the bitter end.'

Lucy stretched and stifled a yawn. 'No idea. Maybe they didn't stop. Maybe they just didn't keep the bits of paper. Or they put them somewhere else?'

'Maybe,' Will agreed, his eyes narrowed. 'I'd love to know who did this.'

'So would I. Dido? Her sister? Both of them?'

'And why?' Will continued. 'I don't think I know enough about the Occupation to understand the significance of all this. Someone's listening to an illegal radio, writing it all down and then doing something with it, presumably. But what?'

'Telling their friends?' Lucy suggested. 'Those without radios?'

'Maybe,' he said for the second time. 'Very brave.'

Lucy stifled a yawn. 'Sorry.'

'All this excitement keeping you up?'

'A bit, yes.'

'Listen,' Will said. 'There's an Occupation museum close by. I've not been yet but I keep meaning to. Do you fancy taking a look? See if it sheds any light?'

'Sure,' she said. 'I'm sure I went there on a school trip once. Don't really remember it though.'

'Tomorrow?' Will said and then looked at his watch, which showed well past midnight. 'Actually, later today?' he said with a grin.

Lucy hesitated. 'Can I let you know later on? Clara's organised for some estate agents to come and offer valuations. She has to work so I've volunteered to meet and greet, ply them with tea and hope they all pick ludicrously high figures out of thin air.'

'Is that how you think estate agency works?' Will laughed.

'Isn't it?'

'Probably, actually,' he agreed.

Will helped her bundle the documents up and while she was putting her shoes on, he put his on also.

'Are you going out? Now?' she asked.

'No.' He looked confused. 'I'm seeing you home.'

'But I only live next door.'

'It's a long way . . . next door, and it's the middle of the night. You're not walking down the lane on your own.'

'Oh,' she said quietly, secretly pleased. 'Thanks.'

They walked the short distance out of Will's front gate and down the lane, the trees gathering overhead to form a tunnel, the moonlight full and bright but barely visible under the canopy of foliage. They turned through the broken gate to Deux Tourelles. 'Want me to fix that tomorrow?' he asked. 'Make a good impression on the estate agents?'

'Can you fix it?' she asked dubiously.

He looked at it in the dark. 'Yes, I'll just get a new hinge and replace a section of wood for now and repaint the whole gate later. It'll look more inviting then. I offered to do it for Dido months ago but she politely declined.'

'OK,' she said, feeling warm all over. 'Thank you.' They walked up the drive and towards the house. Lucy had left the lamps on in each of the front bay windows and the house emanated a warm glow. 'It looks lovely like this,' she said. 'In the dark but not quite dark.'

'Not as spooked by it as you first were?' he asked softly.

'Not now strange neighbours don't burst in on me and shout at me for playing music really loudly.'

He put his hands in his pockets and looked sheepish. 'Yeah, sorry about that.'

'You're forgiven,' she said somewhat more coyly than she'd intended.

Will kicked at a little bit of the gravel drive, his hands resolutely in his pockets. He seemed to be looking anywhere but at her. 'Well . . . goodnight,' he said.

'Goodnight,' she replied and turned towards the door. 'Thank you for a lovely evening.'

He lifted a hand from his pocket and waved as she entered the house. The moment she closed the door she counted to five and then moved to the front bay sitting room window. She watched Will turn at the gate, look back towards the house and then continue towards his cottage.

The wine and the late hour at which she'd finally gone to bed had done damage to her beauty sleep and she awoke later than planned, tired and in desperate need of a glass of water and some coffee. After she'd spent a painstaking hour hand-picking dandelions out of the front drive, she stood in the kitchen, the old flagstone flooring cold under her thick socks. The clear sky from last night had lasted well into the day and the garden was now bathed in sunlight. Her efforts in the garden had paid off, she could see that now, and she padded across the newly mown lawn, down towards the old garden bench to enjoy the fruits of her labour.

Sipping her coffee she heard her phone ring in her back pocket. It was her sister. Peace, hard to find, was so easily interrupted.

'Hey,' she said to Clara and then was cut off before she could utter anything else while Clara ran through the day's itinerary for her. It was a perfunctory conversation. Lucy half listened, inwardly wondering if it was because Clara felt some sort of resentment towards Lucy that she treated her like this? It was so hard to pinpoint why Clara ran so hot and then so cold moments later.

Three estate agents were scheduled at various times throughout the day. If only they could have been grouped a bit closer together, then Lucy could have visited the museum with Will. When she hung up after having received her orders, she composed a message to him.

Thank you for the lovely evening last night. Sorry, I can't make the museum with you today. Another time?

She wondered if he'd reply instantly and held the phone in her hand, forcing herself to drag her eyes away and look around the garden. Ideally she'd have loved to sit here, on the bench, all morning. Perhaps this visit to Guernsey was what she'd needed all along, rest and recuperation.

She looked at the lawn. Maybe her time would be better spent outside, rather than inside. No, she knew that wasn't true. What she wanted wasn't necessarily what was best for the house. This house needed love and to be a family home again. And also, being pragmatic, she didn't want to scupper their chance to get the best possible price. No, inside was where the real work was needed. Outside would be the fun project she had to save for later. Although, she thought, the lawn did need a clip around the edges. Maybe she could fit that in before the estate agents arrived.

After a few minutes, Will replied.

I had a nice time last night. Let me know when you're next free. See you soon. Will. x

Lucy spent far too long smiling at the 'x' before she put her phone in her back pocket, stood up and went inside the house for some last-minute tidying.

'Oh my God, you're joking,' Lucy spluttered when the final estate agent, Simon, gave her what he called his 'ballpark valuation'. His was by far the highest yet and by quite a phenomenal difference to the other two who had visited earlier in the day. Clara had instructed Lucy to play it cool when the agents gave her their valuations and so far Lucy had done as instructed. But not now.

The estate agent smiled. If Lucy hadn't been quite so entranced by the number he'd just given her, she might instead have been entranced by his smile.

He'd also stayed the longest of all of them, quizzing her on what she was doing with the house to improve it and how long she was planning to stay on the island – a fact Lucy hadn't yet worked out herself. He was in his thirties, quite handsome, and when he asked her out for a drink later that evening – 'If you're not busy . . .?' – it had shocked her so much that she'd replied that she'd 'love to' without actually processing what he'd just asked her.

'I know this great little bar in St Peter Port,' Simon said. 'I need to head back to the office but if you like, I'll pick you up at seven?'

Lucy agreed, spellbound by the speed at which he had confidently secured a date. As he left she looked down at her daily uniform of jeans and T-shirt and wondered if she should get changed. In the end she decided just to add a pair of heels to what she was already wearing so it didn't look like she was making too much of an effort. She was doing what Clara had suggested and was actually not going to take the easy way out of something. She was going to see something through now she'd agreed to do it. But there was something rather exhausting about the idea of drinks with this estate agent. Regardless, turning him down now felt like rather bad form and so she'd go along with it, have a couple of drinks and come home to bed.

An hour into the date, Lucy was regretting not crying off. She was right, it was exhausting, but not for the reasons she'd thought. She hadn't had to rack her brains for endless small talk to keep the conversation going and neither had she had to think of witty things to say. She'd had almost no chance to say anything at all. The man on the date with her at the bar was a completely different person to the man who'd appraised Deux Tourelles earlier that day. His chattiness at the house had been because he had a genuine interest in property, so when she'd asked if he enjoyed his job, he'd reeled off dozens of examples as to why being an estate agent was the dream job.

'I get to look in people's houses all day. And then I sell them and make money,' was Lucy's particular favourite. But when he'd continued for a full half an hour, barely pausing for breath, Lucy knew she'd made a mistake.

'The best thing is when I sell a house to someone and then a couple of years later I sell it again. It's great. Like coming full circle.'

'Mmm,' Lucy agreed half-heartedly and picked up her wine glass, groaning inwardly when she noticed it was empty. 'Actually,' Lucy said, grasping around for something to say that would cut the date short. 'I've got an early start and—'

'I thought we could grab some dinner,' Simon said, looking disappointed.

'Oh, right. I probably should . . . um . . .'

'They do tapas here. We could just grab a quick bite.'

As if in answer, Lucy's stomach groaned. Two glasses of wine and no dinner wasn't wise. 'Yes, let's,' she said, reaching for two tapas menus and hoping for the best. She couldn't spend the next hour or so listening to any more property chitchat and so tried a different tack.

'Have you lived here your whole life?'

'Yeah,' Simon said when they'd ordered food and drink.

'Do you know much about the Occupation?'

Simon looked taken aback. 'Not really. I mean, enough, you know. Do you know, I've been waiting for Deux Tourelles to come up for sale for years. One of those elusive properties. Do you know the last time it was up for sale was in 1911. Been in the same family ever since.'

'Imagine that,' Lucy said.

'And now it's on the market for the first time in three generations. Three!' Simon enthused.

'Yes, I suppose that is quite interesting,' Lucy said half-heartedly.

'A shame you haven't got sea views,' Simon mused and then
quoted an asking price that may have been fetched if Deux
Tourelles had been a coastal property.

'Yes, sorry about that.' Lucy laughed.

'Last month I sold a house fairly similar to yours that had sea
views and . . .'

Lucy zoned out as their food and drink arrived, eating her
dinner in relative silence for the next twenty minutes and when
Simon eventually took a breath she cut in quickly. 'I've had a lovely
night,' she fibbed. 'Thank you so much.' She gestured for the bill
to the waitress who had been listening in to the one-sided conversation with barely suppressed mirth.

When the bill arrived, Simon suggested they split it and, ever
a modern girl, Lucy agreed. Would Will have suggested they go
Dutch? she wondered and then wasn't sure why she was thinking
about Will all of a sudden.

'Your place or mine?' Simon said when they'd paid.

'Oh.' Lucy couldn't mask her surprise. 'I wasn't . . . I thought . . .'
she said finally. They had no chemistry. He could see that, surely?
And now he was suggesting what, exactly? That they sleep
together? On an awful first date? Surely not.

'I need to run you home anyway,' he said, pointing out that
he'd picked her up. 'Coffee at yours?' he suggested.

Her relief must have been obvious. 'Coffee,' she said, drawing
out the word. 'Yes, what a good idea. Although I've only got instant
I'm afraid. No Nespresso machine at Deux Tourelles.'

He nodded his agreement as they walked towards his car. The
journey was mute, much to Lucy's contentment. When they drove
past Will's cottage, she could see the lights on. She wondered what
he was doing now. Was he working? Editing photos or whatever
it was photographers did when not out actually taking pictures?

Or did he have his feet up, watching TV? She wondered what he watched. He looked like a crime drama kind of man, or maybe he preferred nature documentaries.

After they arrived at the house, Simon waited in the sitting room while she made coffee and he looked up when she entered carrying two cups. 'Fabulous cornicing,' he said, gesturing to the ceiling.

'What kind of programmes do you watch?' she asked, aware it was an awfully dull question, but desperate to engage him in something else.

'I don't really watch much telly,' he said. 'Channel 4 does some good property programmes these days.'

'Christ,' she whispered into her coffee. And then: 'I really should get to bed soon. We'll have to call this a night, I think.'

'So,' he said, inching closer towards her on the settee.

She backed away and said for the second time that evening, 'I've had a lovely night.' She hoped that both the words and her body language combined were pointed enough that he took the hint.

Her phone dinged and she saw it was a message from Will. 'Excuse me for a second?'

'Sure,' Simon said, kicking off his shoes and pushing them under the coffee table with his feet. What was he doing? Why was he settling in?

'How'd it go with the estate agents today?' Will's message asked.

She typed a fast reply as she walked into the hallway. *'I'm on the world's worst date with one of them. He's just run me home and now he won't leave.'*

'Seriously?' Will replied.

'Yes, he's a bit creepy. He's just taken his shoes off!'

She waited for three dots to appear indicating Will was composing a reply. But there was nothing. He'd gone. Had she offended him? Had she bored him? She stood in the hallway and looked at the phone for so long, waiting, that the backlight switched off and the phone locked itself. And then the doorknocker sounded loudly.

Lucy reached out and opened the door to find Will standing on the doorstep, and before Lucy had a chance to say anything, he said, 'How creepy are we talking?'

Lucy smiled with relief that he was here. 'Mid-level creepy.'

'Everything all right?' Simon called from the sitting room. 'You coming back, Lucy?'

Will made a face. 'Want rescuing?'

Lucy toyed with saying no thanks, I can rescue myself. But she'd done a terrible job so far and so she opted for, 'Yes please.'

Will rolled up the sleeves of his jersey.

'You're not going to hit him, are you?' Lucy asked in horror.

'Of course not.'

'What are you going to say?'

'I don't know yet.' He walked into the sitting room and stretched out his hand. 'Hello, mate, I'm Will.'

Simon stood and awkwardly shook his hand. 'Er, I'm Simon.'

'Great. Good to meet you. You the estate agent?' Will asked.

Simon looked at Lucy, still standing in the hallway. She moved into the room in a bid not to be cowardly.

'Yeah,' Simon said, looking back to Will. 'Are you . . .? Wait, who are you?'

'I'm Will. I'm her husband. Lucy's too nice to say but I think it's a bit past our bedtime now. Do you mind if we give you a ring tomorrow about the house and . . . well, the house mainly,' Will said.

Confusion passed over Simon's face and Lucy wanted to close her eyes and die of embarrassment. 'She didn't mention—' Simon started.

'Good man,' Will said. 'Bit nippy out there. You'll need your shoes.'

Lucy cringed as Simon looked at his shoes and then sat on the settee, putting them on in silence.

Eventually Simon said, 'Right. Well, yeah. I'll be in touch about . . .' His sentence trailed off and he looked around the house and gestured. 'About the house and . . . yeah . . .'

'Great, I'll show you out,' Will said and waited for Simon to walk in front of him.

Lucy stood mutely, her eyes wide. She gave Simon a nervous smile as he said, 'Goodnight,' and walked past her.

'Night,' she muttered, embarrassment rendering her unable to say anything else.

'Night, Simon,' Will called from the front door. 'Drive safe.' Will closed the front door and turned back to Lucy.

Lucy closed her mouth to stop herself from laughing. Then she raised her hand to her mouth to cover it as her shoulders started shaking and she couldn't stop.

Will stood with his back against the closed front door as they listened to Simon start his car and the crunch of gravel as it left the drive. 'And that's how it's done.'

'Oh my God, you made me look unhinged,' she said through big gasps of laughter.

'I couldn't think of anything else to say,' Will confessed. 'Worked though. The quickest methods are often the kindest.'

'Husband?' Lucy questioned, wiping tears of laughter from her face. 'I just spent the entire evening with him and . . .'

'Exactly. He's probably driving in stunned silence, wondering how on earth he missed it,' Will suggested.

Lucy shook her head in disbelief. 'I should say thank you.'

'You should,' Will said with a glint in his eye. 'Who knows what horrors I just saved you from?'

'I feel so bad for him,' she said as they moved back into the sitting room. 'He looked so confused. But he really was so incredibly dull and just wouldn't get the hint that I wasn't interested.'

'In that case, I'll try not to be offended that you chose to spend time with him rather than come out with me this afternoon,' Will said, looking anything but serious.

'I would much rather have been with you,' she said, 'but alas, I had to spend a few hours listening to property facts. Did you know that the average house price in Guernsey now is nearly £450,000?' she asked with mock excitement.

'I did not,' Will said, resting his head against the settee and looking towards her. 'That is a sexy fact. Tell me more.'

Lucy laughed, turning her body towards him while she thought. 'Some houses in the west of the island have special granite stones sticking out for witches to sit on rather than continue to cause havoc inside the house.'

'Really?' He angled his head up. 'That is actually quite interesting.'

'Don't you start,' she replied.

They sat in silence looking at each other before Will smiled. 'I should go. It's late.'

Lucy nodded but felt as if her evening had been cut short just when it had finally picked up. 'Thank you,' she said as Will rose.

'No problem. Any more bad dates, you know where I am.'

'I'm not going on any more dates,' Lucy was quick to point out. 'I'm not even sure why I went on that one.'

As Will opened the front door he said, 'Night, Lucy.'

'Goodnight,' she said as she watched him walk back towards his house. At the gate, he didn't turn back to wave as she'd thought he might and disappointment filled her. Instead, he kept walking and she waited until he passed through the gate and into the lane before she closed the door. She opened the door again and looked at the gate curiously. It was hanging back in place and she smiled, thinking of Will repairing it earlier in the day and not having said. Lucy hugged herself before closing the door, locking up for the night and collapsing into bed.

Chapter 18

'You did what?' Clara asked the next morning when she summoned Lucy to St Peter Port for a quick catch-up over coffee. 'You went on a date? With one of the estate agents? Really?'

Lucy groaned, waiting for the fallout. She wished she'd not shared this information now.

Clara sipped her coffee but looked disapproving. 'Was it good?'

'No, it was terrible,' Lucy confessed. She wished it had been a fantastic date just so she had something positive to report.

'I hate the idea of first dates.' Clara shuddered. 'If John ever dumps me, I'm finished. I don't want to go back out there again. It's terrifying.'

'Yes, well. Some of us are suffering this fate so others—' she pointed at her sister '—don't have to.'

'The sisterhood salutes you,' Clara said as their coffee arrived.

This was nice, exactly what Lucy had been missing, although she hadn't realised it until now. When she and Clara got on it was peaceful, joyous, exactly how she envisioned a relationship with her sister ought to be.

'I've got twenty minutes then I have to get to work,' Clara said. 'Tell me what happened with the other estate agents . . . the normal ones.'

Lucy filled Clara in and watched with readiness for her reaction on finding out that boring Simon was the agent who had valued the house the highest and then the dreadful way she'd roped Will into evicting Simon from the house.

'Oh Lucy!' Clara put her head in her hands. 'Why did you have to have a terrible date with the one offering the most money? I don't want to scrap him from the list. I'll have to instruct one of his colleagues, I guess. That'll be an awkward conversation.'

'Do you want me to—'

'No. I do not want you to make that phone call. Without being rude, you've done quite enough.'

'It is actually quite rude. I only went on a date.'

'Yes, well, anyway,' Clara said. And then, clearly remembering something Lucy had said moments ago. 'Hang on – Will helped get rid of him? Shouty neighbour Will?'

Lucy nodded with wide eyes. 'I know. He's turning into a bit of an asset. Fixes gates, gets rid of strange men I really shouldn't have brought back to the house.' Lucy wasn't sure what kind of reaction that was going to receive and braced herself.

But Clara became quiet and then said, 'Is he good-looking?'

Lucy looked away from her sister. 'Um, yes, I suppose.'

'How are you getting on at the house?' Clara said, abruptly changing direction – thank God.

'Today I'm going to buy paint. And then later I'll start on the house. May rip up some of the old carpets, expose some of the original wood flooring, especially in the bedrooms. Then it will look so much more attractive for when the estate agent sends the photographer.'

'Look,' Clara said, putting her cup down and eyeing Lucy with concern. 'You being here is helping no end. All the little odds and ends that need sorting at the house. But do you think all this is to put off something?'

'Put off what?' Lucy asked with genuine confusion.

Clara shrugged. 'A real job? One you love. Or settling down? You tell me.'

'I don't think so,' Lucy said but now she didn't know. Clara was making her feel unsure of herself.

'Well, first you didn't want to be here and now you don't seem too eager to leave. Why is that?'

'I'm not, actually, desperate to leave,' she said, although she hadn't realised it until this point.

'Why?'

'I don't know,' she said. 'It's a holiday, isn't it, all this? At the end, I'll pack up and go home.'

'But eventually, once Deux Tourelles sells, you'll actually have ... dare I admit this ... quite a lot of money,' Clara said.

'It might not sell for ages. These house sales take on a life of their own in the end,' Lucy reasoned. This conversation had changed direction into a more positive space and so Lucy steeled herself. They had to talk about the slap. She took a deep breath. It was going to have to be Lucy who started.

'Have you thought about what you might want to do, after?' Clara continued.

Deflated, Lucy answered. 'The same as now.' She knew it wasn't quite true. Why wasn't it quite true? What had actually changed – perspective perhaps?

'Really? OK,' Clara conceded. 'We'll leave it there.'

'Are you attempting to give me some quick-fire therapy?'

'No,' Clara said. 'As long as you're happy.'

'I am ... I mean ... well ... I am.'

'All right. I'll ring and sort the estate agent out,' Clara said, changing the subject back to safer ground. 'And I'll buzz you later and see if you need help painting, if you're in.'

'Why wouldn't I be in?'

'Seeing Will at all today?' Clara suggested, seemingly out of nowhere.

Lucy felt herself blush, which wasn't her style at all usually. 'Well, he did suggest we go to a museum together.'

186

'Did he?' Clara sipped her coffee and looked at Lucy with a knowing expression.

'Don't you have to go to work?' Lucy said pointedly. She wasn't in the mood to discuss anything else now.

'I do, yes.' Clara pulled out her purse and left money for her share of the bill then kissed Lucy awkwardly on the cheek. The same cheek she'd slapped her on, Lucy noticed, and then realised that was an unhelpful way of thinking.

Lucy pulled her phone out and searched for a DIY shop nearby. There was one in the town only a few streets away and so she ignored the stream of emails that had arrived on her phone during coffee, put her phone in her pocket and went out into the High Street, through the hustle and bustle of St Peter Port's main shopping street. She spent far too long choosing paint colours, wishing she'd actually looked at colour charts before going shopping. She eventually ordered all the paints for each of the rooms and all the fripperies that went with it including sheets to cover floors and furniture that it hadn't even occurred to her that she might need until pointed out by the shop assistant.

This was one of the most grown-up things she'd sorted in such a long time. She wasn't allowed to paint her rented flat so, she realised, this would actually be the first time she'd ever painted a wall. It was the first time she'd been inside a DIY shop, come to think of it. Homeownership was odd and strangely detailed.

After ordering the items, which the assistant said he'd deliver this afternoon and leave tucked by the side of the garage, Lucy stood in the sunshine, dug her sunglasses out of her bag and sent Will a message.

I'm ready for this museum now. If you still want to go, that is.

She wondered if he did still want to go with her. Yesterday, when he'd come to her rescue he'd said goodbye in such a strange, stilted way that it half crossed her mind he was a little bit annoyed with her. He'd been ready enough to jump to her defence and had handled removing Simon from the house masterfully, but Lucy had come out of it looking more than a little deranged. She should have been braver. She should have said, *Actually Simon, I find you terribly dull and repugnant and do not want to sleep with you. Please leave.* She imagined herself doing this in an imperious way and she laughed out loud in the street. The woman walking in front of her turned, and gave Lucy a look that left her in no doubt she thought she was not quite all there.

'Maybe I am deranged,' Lucy said to herself as she went to find a café and caught up on some work. And then as time ticked by with still no word from Will, Lucy ordered herself some lunch. The chat on the sofa with Will had been nice. It had been more than nice. It had been everything the evening with Simon had categorically not been. The evening with Simon had only served to highlight that she and Will had something . . . a spark of something. Was she imagining it? She glanced down at her phone, but there was nothing from Will. Not everyone replied within five minutes, she reminded herself. After she left the café, Lucy spied a bookshop and decided to pop in and find a book about gardening.

After half an hour of neither Will replying nor finding a book that she resonated with, the shop assistant asked if Lucy required help, which she obviously did.

'I know the difference between a weed and a flower,' Lucy said to the woman. 'I think. But I need something easy to follow; some instructions, someone to tell me what to prune, when to do it and how to do it. Gardening for idiots, something like that.'

The shop assistant reached down and found a beginner's guide to gardening, which looked colourful and more importantly, small. 'Idiot proof,' the assistant said.

'Perfect,' Lucy replied, flicking through the illustrations and photographs. Out of it fell a leaflet about distance-learning gardening courses to be studied mostly online. She glanced at it briefly and then thought of something else. 'Do you have a local section?'

'Local authors?' the assistant clarified.

'No, but I'll take a look at that too. I meant, local history, local . . . er . . . books,' Lucy said uncertainly.

The assistant nodded and led Lucy to the other side of the shop where there were more books than she knew what to do with. The assistant clearly sensed Lucy's confusion. 'What can I help you find?'

'Local history, the war, in particular, something with lots of pictures,' Lucy joked, although now she thought about it, pictures were actually the most interesting bits of history books.

The woman pointed her in the right direction and Lucy looked at her phone when she'd been left alone to peruse the section. Still no reply from Will. Maybe she'd go to this museum on her own then. No, that wasn't very kind. She wanted to go. But more than that, she wanted to go with him.

She found a lovely hardcopy book of Channel Islands photography and flicked through. Dramatic coastlines and windswept beaches met her gaze. Dark high waves crashing against the lighthouse, the wartime fortifications, the rise and fall of gulls above bunkers, the Little Chapel in Les Vauxbelets adorned with pebbles and pieces of china, a mosaic of beauty. Looking through this book again it was easy to fall back in love with the island she'd once called home. But now, to Lucy it was neither home nor holiday; Guernsey inhabited a halfway space in her mind. Why was that? Why could Will come here and call it home, and she had returned and couldn't? She wondered if Will might like the book.

'Oh, for God's sake,' she said. Why was she thinking about him quite so much? She chose one of the history books and took it to the counter with the island photography book and paid.

As she was leaving, Will replied.

Ready whenever you are. Now?

* * *

189

Lucy parked the car near the museum and climbed out. 'Hello.'

'Hello, yourself,' he said. Why did he always look so neat and presentable? There was something about a toned man in a tight V-neck tee. She should have bought some better clothes while in St Peter Port. She needed to up her fashion game. Breton tees paired with jeans and summer dresses – on the odd occasion the weather held up – were about the full extent of her wardrobe. She felt like a slob suddenly in her stripy top and jeans but his wide smile indicated he'd not noticed.

He walked towards her and she wondered if he was going to lean forward, kiss her on the cheek in greeting. But no. If she did it now, after this long a pause it would look false, awkward.

She grabbed the shopping bag from the back of the Renault. 'I've been shopping. I have a thank you present for your gallantry last night. I hope you like it. I hope you don't already have it.' She handed him the photography book and smiled, becoming quiet as he opened it and flicked slowly through the pages.

'This is lovely,' he said. 'Thank you. I don't remember the last time anyone bought me a present when it wasn't either Christmas or my birthday.'

'I felt you deserved it,' she said. 'Last night, you were . . . terrific. I was impressed. Slightly pissed off I came out of it looking like a lunatic, but impressed nonetheless.'

He chuckled. 'You're welcome. I think.'

'I don't make a habit of going on terrible dates.'

He shrugged. 'You won't know they're terrible if you don't go on them in the first place.'

'You know what I mean. I don't go on dates, well, not many.'

'Why not?'

'I don't know. No time. I work a lot. Don't meet that many new people I guess. And if I do go to friends' parties, they're mostly frequented by the kind of people I wouldn't want to date.'

'People like Simon?' Will teased.

'Not even close. Simon looks like a god compared to some of the idiots I meet.'

Will didn't reply, simply smiled. Was she digging herself into some kind of strange hole? This was the perfect time for him to admit that he, too, didn't date all that often. Maybe he did. Maybe he spent his evenings, not in front of the latest crime drama, but on his phone, manically swiping right on Tinder.

'Shall we?' Will asked with a smile as he walked towards the museum.

Inside they paid and the museum, narrow at the start, opened up like a Tardis with rooms spanning off from rooms and small nooks and crannies dotted around.

The museum was a treasure trove of wartime memorabilia, rooms laid out as they would have looked inside individual houses, complete with illicit wireless sets and mannequins looking out of curtained windows to check no one was coming. A whole street scene with shops was laid out and Will and Lucy walked down the indoor street, marvelling at the old-fashioned wares available for 'sale' inside each of the shop windows. Anti-aircraft guns and mannequins in German uniforms made Lucy swallow down an eerie feeling. And then there were display cases in small rooms that led off other small rooms in the winding and fascinating museum.

A Box Brownie camera sat in one of the display cases, its owner identified as a German soldier who'd left it behind at the end of the Occupation when the islands had been liberated and the Germans taken off the island by British forces with only what they could carry.

'What have you done with your Box Brownie, by the way?' Will asked.

'It's still in the house. What do you think I should do with it?'

'You could sell it if you don't want to keep it. Collectors will buy it. You could see if there's a specialist or antique shop while you're here, to sell it. Or there's always eBay.' He shuddered. 'I'll help if you like? I know a thing or two about cameras,' he said. 'Although admittedly more about the modern ones.'

She replied with thanks as they looked at the black and white photographs of Germans languishing on Guernsey's beaches, local girls who had been photographed looking coy, embarrassed or far too happy in the arms of a German soldier.

'This one's a bit brave, isn't it?' Will said, pointing to a picture of a Luftwaffe officer, his mouth firmly pressed against that of a civilian woman.

'I think there was a lot of that going on, I'm afraid,' Lucy said.

'I'm surprised. Island men off fighting and some of the women in the arms of the enemy.'

Lucy nodded. 'People do strange things in times of war. It's not really for us to judge now from a modern perspective, is it?'

Will looked unsure.

'Plus,' Lucy said, unsure quite why she was springing to this woman's defence. 'You try resisting the advances of a six-foot-tall blond pilot and then we'll talk.'

Will laughed. 'The heart wants what the heart wants, I suppose. But it does just seem to me that a lot of this was excitement-based.'

'Excitement-based?' Lucy mocked. 'Is that a technical term? You're not a romantic?'

'I thought I was. But even I can't get past this . . .' He gestured towards the photo. 'Sleeping with the enemy. However you look at it, even over seventy years after the event, it's wrong then and it's wrong now.'

'But you can't know what it was like for them, these women. You can't know how lonely they were. You can't know how much they wanted someone to love and someone to love them in return. The Germans were here for five years. That's a long time to be lonely, a long time to resist the charms of good-looking men in uniform.'

'I've been single for five long years,' Will said. 'It's not that bad.'

'Have you?' Her voice, when she asked, was far too shrill. 'Why? What's wrong with you?'

192

'I've dated,' he clarified.

But that wasn't an answer and Lucy stayed quiet, waiting for him to fill the silence.

'I keep dating unsuitable women.'

Lucy raised an eyebrow and pointed to the photograph. 'Pot, kettle, black.'

'Point taken,' he said.

'How unsuitable?' Lucy queried as they moved on to the next display.

He thought for a moment. 'Just women who weren't for me. But like you and Simon—' Lucy thumped him playfully at the mention of the estate agent '—sometimes you have to spend time in someone's company, as friends for a bit, before you realise it's not worth your time any longer.'

She nodded as he moved on and then . . . wait . . . what did that mean? Was he talking about her? Was she not worth dating? Was he assessing if she was? Or were they genuinely just becoming friends? Lucy pondered this as they walked round the museum.

'Look at this,' he said after a while.

He was pointing to a small display of framed newspapers, old and yellowing, the edges crumbling and some of the centres frayed in horizontal lines where they'd been folded over, presumably for decades, and unfolded again for the purpose of framing here. But instead of looking at the *Star* or *Evening Press*, the island's two main newspapers, they were looking at copies of something called *GUNS*. Will read out the blurb on the information sheet, stuck underneath the frames.

'"Guernsey's Underground News Service" was created in secret retaliation to the German order in June 1942 confiscating all radios. Although many Islanders secretly hid some radio sets, if the Germans discovered these, the punishment was severe – imprisonment in mainland occupied Europe.

GUNS *was typed up and printed at the* Star *newspaper, as well as in other locations. Its owner, Charles Machon, recruited a number of Islanders to help him at different times and in different roles, including listening and transcribing news reports in shorthand and distribution of the newspaper in secret around the island. After an inside informer betrayed them, those involved with GUNS were arrested and deported to Nazi prisons.'*

The article went on to list those involved and the locations overseas where some had died.

It sobered Lucy. A small act of defiance that the Nazis took very badly, so badly that they deported many, leading to their deaths.

'An informer,' Will mused but said nothing further.

'How awful,' Lucy said quietly.

'What possesses people to inform on each other, do you think?' he asked.

'Lots of things, I suppose.'

'Islander against Islander.' Will grimaced. 'At a time of war, when it should have been Islander against Nazi. It's the wrong way round. I just can't get my head around this.'

'Sadly it was all too common,' Lucy admitted, gesturing to the wall on the other side of the museum where a range of letters had been displayed. The wall was covered in copies of letters.

'Don't tell me they're all letters from Islanders informing on each other to the Nazis?'

Lucy had glimpsed the wall when she'd entered the room and now she moved over to take a closer look. It was one of the most unpleasant displays in the museum. 'One of our island's least patriotic moments. How petty grievances can be played out like this.'

'Petty grievances?' Will asked.

Lucy nodded. 'Let's pretend five years ago you moved your fence ten inches over my garden. We've argued, you've refused to put it back and I've not got enough money to go to a solicitor to fight for my bit of garden back. How do I get my own back? *Voilà,*' she said, gesturing to the wall.

'I've just gone cold,' Will said, looking at the wall. 'Do you think . . .?' he started and then stopped.

'What?' Lucy asked.

'It now seems very obvious what that bundle was we translated.'

Lucy nodded as realisation dawned. 'It does, doesn't it. Someone was translating the news, as we thought, and now we know why.'

'For the secret newspaper,' Will said. 'Brave.'

'Do you think they were deported? Is that why the bundle ends in '43?'

'It says the newspaper ran until they were exposed in early '44.'

Lucy was none the wiser in that case. There must have been another reason why the news reports inside the wardrobe at Deux Tourelles stopped in 1943.

'Maybe they gave up, decided it was too risky. It's a long time to defy the Nazis and not get cold feet eventually,' Will volunteered.

Lucy nodded, unsure, but deciding to stick a pin in that particular line of questioning for now. She looked closely at the horrific letters on the wall. It was clear that Islanders who were informing on each other had no idea who to address their hateful mail to. Some were addressed to the Geheime Feldpolizei, the secret police, at Grange Lodge. Some were, more chillingly, addressed directly to the Gestapo and some more generally labelled, 'For the attention of the Nazis'.

'This is disgusting,' Will said. 'I had no idea about any of this.'

Sadly Lucy did know, having learnt about it at school, albeit in brief. Perhaps that's why she wasn't as shocked as he was. She put her hand out and rubbed his arm consolingly and then began reading the letters in more detail.

To the Gestapo, my neighbour has a wireless. I hear it through the wall. Search under the floorboards at . . .

To the Nazis, my neighbour Dorothy Paquin frequently
stays out after curfew. You should look into it.

For the Guernsey Kommandant, the grocer Mr Lagarde in
Albecq operates a black market service. Keeps items under
the counter for his friends.

To the Secret Police, I've seen some of those foreign slave
workers going in and out of Adele Caron's house after dark.
She volunteers for the St John Ambulance and has been
dressing their wounds and giving them her rations.

'This makes me hate humans,' Will said, his jaw clenched.

'It's not easy reading,' Lucy agreed, wondering about the fate of Dorothy Paquin, Adele Caron and the others named and shamed in the letters on the wall. Hundreds and hundreds of Guernsey men and women, their 'crimes' laid out for the Germans to act upon. And that was only what was shown here.

'This is self-righteousness,' Will said, a hateful tone in his voice. 'But why the anonymity?' he asked, pointing to more than one that was ambiguously signed, 'A Friend'. 'Why not reveal yourself? After all, you're grassing up your friend, your neighbour: why not tell the Nazis who you are to further yourself in their eyes? Why hide yourself? It's not even maliciousness for self-improvement. It's maliciousness for the sake of it.' He was raging and Lucy was wondering if he regretted coming here now. She was starting to regret it.

Will had moved away. At the final row of letters covering the wall he had stopped. Lucy was done. She couldn't read any more now. It was too much. She had no idea how Will was still reading given how much he clearly hated reading them.

How many of these people had been informed on, arrested, imprisoned, died? Did these people know what would happen to those they'd informed on? Did they know it would lead to arrests?

Did they know it would lead to deportations and imprisonments? And if they did know, is that why they did it? Lucy gulped. How many were mothers of small children? How many were being lied about in these letters? How many—

'Lucy!' Will called. 'Come here.' His eyes were wide with shock and he raised his hand and pointed at a particular letter on the wall.

Lucy moved over and followed his finger. She read the letter Will pointed out to her in disbelief. 'No,' she said simply, her brain refusing to process what her eyes had just read once, and then again to be sure. 'No,' she repeated, horrified as she read the words '. . . *at Deux Tourelles*,' written on an informant letter.

Chapter 19

1940

Tensions were running high at Deux Tourelles since the announcement that the Nazis knew spies had landed on Guernsey. There was no hiding the announcement in the newspaper. The whole island was talking about it and so in the end they had been forced to tell Mrs Grant, who had cried uncontrollably. The orders had struck fear into all inside the house.

> *In accordance with German military law and in agreement with the Hague Convention the penalties provided for are the following:*
> * *Espionage – Death penalty.*
> * *High treason – Death penalty or penal servitude for life.*
> * *Assistance to espionage – Penal servitude: up to fifteen years.*

Jack had three days to give himself up or the hunt would begin and punishments would be enforced. Jack would be executed, and for assisting him, Persey, Dido and Mrs Grant faced imprisonment for a very long time. How old would Persey be in fifteen years? Forty. And Dido thirty-nine years old when they were released. If they survived. Mrs Grant . . . would she survive?

They watched Jack with alarm over the following two days as his state of mind disintegrated. He spent the majority of meals staring blankly at his plate, not hearing anyone who spoke to him, and every time a German staff car pulled up he stared wide-eyed at the doorway of whatever room he was in, expecting to be grabbed, arrested, interrogated. But each time it was only Stefan returning to the house.

Persey, Dido and Mrs Grant had decided not to give Jack up. Doing so was their duty, and they had no idea if they could trust the Nazis to keep their word that Jack would be treated as a POW and interned somewhere safe for the duration of the war if he handed himself in before the deadline, or whether he would be taken and shot as a spy. But whether he gave himself up would have to be his decision.

'You can't trust a Nazi to keep their word,' Jack had spat, fear in his eyes. 'I wish I'd never come back now. I could have been back in England, sitting tight now the British Expeditionary Force has been turfed out of France. I could have been safe and I wouldn't have put you in this position.' He opened his cigarette case and, finding it empty, threw it onto the kitchen floor.

Persey wanted to tell him he was safe here, but it would have been such an incredible lie that she simply couldn't bring herself to say anything soothing at all. What would happen to her and Dido when the Germans realised the spy they were looking for was Jack and that they had harboured him all this time? Perhaps she could say they had no idea? Would any of them believe that? And what kind of interrogation tactics would they use on her, on Mrs Grant, on Dido? The thought of the secret police or the Gestapo torturing Dido made Persey feel sick and she ran out the back door and bent over, waiting for bile that never came.

'Are you all right?' Stefan's voice came from the end of the garden in the darkness. He'd been sitting on the bench and moved swiftly towards her.

'Yes,' she lied. 'I think I ate something I shouldn't have.'

'You are not worried?' he said.

'Worried?' she said cautiously.

'Yes, about Jack.'

'W-why . . .' she stuttered and then started again. 'Why would I be worried?'

He looked away from her and back towards the rest of the garden, now steeped in moonlight as it emerged from behind a cloud. 'It's a beautiful garden. A beautiful house. You are lucky to live here.'

'Not at the moment we aren't,' she said wondering why he'd changed the subject. What did he mean by his comment about Jack? He knew. He had to know. What did that mean?

He inched ever so slightly closer to her. She felt her heart start a quicker rhythm than usual. 'Is my presence so abhorrent to you?' He tilted his head and searched her eyes.

'No, of course not,' she whispered and this time she meant it. She did feel uncomfortable but for so many other reasons that she daren't admit to herself. The garden, the moonlight, his closeness to her . . . She had to move away from him. 'You were asking about Jack,' she began.

'You are very concerned for him,' Stefan said. 'Why?'

But Persey couldn't answer. Wouldn't answer. She wanted to trust him. Jack and his reasons for being here lay unspoken between them. Stefan knew – of course he knew – but for her to say it out loud to Stefan would be a complete betrayal of Jack who she had known as a brother for so long. She silently begged Stefan not to talk about Jack anymore.

'You'll be pleased to hear they have handed themselves in,' he said suddenly.

'Who have?' she asked in confusion.

'The two British spies.'

'What?' she spluttered.

He simply looked at her and then: 'There have been spies on this island.'

'Yes, I know. But . . .' She gathered her wits together. 'I read it in the newspaper.'

'They had until tomorrow morning to hand themselves in and they have done so tonight. What is that English expression? Just in the nick of time.'

Persey became aware her mouth was open and she closed it, rubbing her finger over her lower lip in contemplation. She looked around, unable to mask the sheer confusion.

'Who are they?' she asked.

'Two British servicemen who have come ashore and been left behind by the navy,' he said kindly.

The navy had a habit of sacrificing men, she thought angrily. 'What will happen to them?' Persey asked. 'Will they be . . .?' But she couldn't bring herself to say the word.

'You were going to ask if they will be shot?' he asked softly.

'Yes,' she said, and then the build-up of the last three days, the last few weeks, overcame her entirely and she clasped her hand over her mouth as she began to cry. 'I'm sorry,' she said. 'I don't know why I'm doing this.'

He pulled her towards him but she remained stiff against the material of his uniform. She couldn't have him that close to her. What if someone saw? But the feeling of enjoying his body pressed against her frightened and thrilled her, and her body slackened slowly. She looked up at him. A line of concern had formed between his eyes. If ever there was a moment of relief, a moment to be kissed, it was now. Damn everything.

Above them came the sound of a window being closed, its latch clicking noisily into place, and Persey snapped back from Stefan's embrace. She came to her senses and the desperate need for tenderness was replaced with fear. She hoped no one had seen Stefan holding her close, but there was no one above and the blackout blind had been slotted into place. Had he felt it too? The thrill? And . . . something unidentifiable that she had never felt before.

'I don't think the spies will be shot,' Stefan said, returning swiftly to their conversation. He stepped back and handed her a handkerchief for her eyes. He appeared to straighten his posture, then added, 'There have been promises that there will be no reprisal, no punishment.'

'I hope that's true,' Persey said into the handkerchief, forcing herself back to the matter in hand.

'I do not know who is trustworthy,' he said. 'But you can trust me.'

Jack had cried with relief when she'd told him. He had raised his head, the weight on his shoulders visibly lifting. Persephone left him in his bedroom, a decidedly different man from the one he had been over the past few days, and went to inform Dido and Mrs Grant of the news. It was Dido who was the most practical, whispering in the kitchen for fear of Stefan hearing, which now seemed most ridiculous. He knew. He'd known all along and was keeping true to his word to protect them, she hoped.

'There will be an announcement in the paper before long, I imagine,' Dido had said.

'I should think so. The poor men,' Persey acknowledged.

'They've given themselves up and my Jack is safe,' was all Mrs Grant could say.

'For now,' Dido suggested. 'But for how long?'

Persey cast her a look.

'What?' Dido exclaimed. 'You said it yourself – Stefan said the situation may change. And then what?'

'And why should the German care?' Mrs Grant said.

'Mrs Grant,' Persey said, 'I do hate to throw stones, but you are rather slow to catch on. He knows.'

And when Mrs Grant protested, Dido cut in, 'But he's not going to do anything. Jack owes him a lot. We all do. Especially you, Persey.'

'I know,' she said. She knew exactly what it was her sister was

202

talking about. The torch. The woods. The soldier who'd sworn he'd seen her and then who'd spotted her in Candie Gardens. Had he remembered her in the end? God, she hoped not.

'What will happen to those who have been hiding those two British officers?' Mrs Grant continued. 'I assume they've been hiding at home. In plain sight.'

'Much like Jack,' Persey said quietly. 'I don't know. Stefan says no reprisals. But even he says he's not sure quite how seriously his superiors are taking that stance. Either way, what they offer them may not be what they offer us.'

'What do you mean?' Dido asked.

'They've been generous,' Persey said. Mrs Grant cut in with a scoff. 'But they may not be for the next set of Islanders who harbour those who shouldn't be here,' Persey continued. 'The Germans won't let this happen twice. The next one found may yet be the example.'

'Jack,' Mrs Grant said obviously.

'Yes, Jack. And us,' Persey said. 'We may be the example they set to everyone else. If they find Jack, that is. If they understand he's not meant to be here and they'll obviously know we've harboured him. I'll talk to Doctor Durand about amending Jack's medical records, backdating them in his files to reflect his heart condition story. Perhaps the doctor can mark the date down prior to Jack's re-emergence here. If there's no record of Jack's re-entry on the island an official medical record might go some way to helping that situation. I need to see Doctor Durand anyway,' Persey said finally and then wished she hadn't.

'Do you? Why?' Dido asked.

'I just do,' Persey said vaguely, realising far too late she had no other plausible reason for visiting the doctor. She could hardly mention Lise's presence there. It would endanger her friend far too much. 'I'm not really sleeping,' she said, which was partially true. 'I wondered if he might recommend something.'

'I told you Stefan wasn't one of them,' Dido said smugly,

reverting to their prior subject. 'He's helping us. We're lucky, really.'

'We shouldn't have to be lucky,' Persey said far louder than she'd intended. Whatever feelings were surfacing after all these years for Stefan, she didn't need a daily reminder how her heart felt. Anger at far too many escalating situations on the island was the overruling force. 'If Jack hadn't come back, none of us would be going through this . . . this . . . unnecessary fear.'

'You can't blame Jack for trying to help his country,' Dido said. 'Trying to help win the war in the only way he knows how.'

'Of course,' Persephone said, noticing Mrs Grant was steeling herself to say something else in defence of her son, and probably very loudly too. 'I'm just annoyed that we've been swept up in this and it's not over yet.'

'If that Nazi thinks—' Mrs Grant began, but Persey rounded on her.

'For heaven's sake, Mrs Grant. He's not a Nazi and he's living in the same house as a British spy, albeit a have-a-go spy but, officially, a spy nonetheless. So do try to go a bit easier on him. Less mustard on his dinner wouldn't go amiss. I'm not asking you to give him the best cuts but, dear God, can't you see it might help in some way if you treated him a bit better?'

'The same could be said of you, actually,' Dido said quietly. 'You're so cold towards him.'

Persey stared at her sister, and in order to stop herself saying anything she might regret, anything that might reveal too much of her heart, Persey walked from the room and went to bed, closing her bedroom door loudly behind her.

'It's happening,' Dido said one morning after breakfast as she read the newspaper. The days were turning colder and while Guernsey's glorious summer had been bountiful, the autumnal winds had begun. Persey stood by the range door, which she'd opened to warm herself.

'What is?' she asked with concern. She no longer took all the news in the paper with a pinch of salt. The paper was rife with German propaganda but now, there was also news of petty sabotage and thefts against the Germans that unsurprisingly the Germans did not like one bit.

'The Jews are being ordered to register and to have red "J"s marked on their identity papers,' Dido read.

Persey was silent for a moment, thinking. 'Nonsense,' she said. 'The Bailiff will never agree to this. The States will never pass this,' she said, referring to Guernsey's own government. 'They have some say in what happens to us still, surely? They'll never let the Germans start harassing the Jews . . . because if they do, whatever next? What kind of people will we have become? What else will happen to them?' But really, she knew what they could expect: the Nuremberg Laws against the Jews had allowed for consistent persecution, forced sales of their businesses, rounding Jewish people up and carrying out horrific violence. How easily could that happen here?

Dido shook her head and looked up at her sister, slowly. 'The States have agreed it,' she said sadly.

'What?' Persey said sharply. 'They can't have done. They can't.'

'They have,' Dido said remorsefully. 'It's here. It's in the newspaper. It's beginning.'

Persey sat at the kitchen table and stared blankly through it.

'Makes me glad I'm not Jewish,' Dido said. 'For everything we have to put up with here, with the Germans breathing down our necks if we dare go outside the front door one minute past curfew, if we dare to own a book that they consider degenerate, imagine being Jewish too. Doesn't bear thinking about. I wonder how many there are,' she said absently. 'Do you think the States knew there were still Jews here when they agreed these measures? Do you think they thought everyone who was Jewish had left for England, maybe?'

'Oh God.' Persey put her head in her hands. 'What an awful,

awful mess.' There was nothing for it now. There was no hope for Lise. This was just the start. Lise had to remain hidden with Doctor Durand. But for how long? It could be months. It could, heaven forbid, be years.

Chapter 20

2016

The museum was cold and so was Lucy now as she stared at the letter on the wall.

'This can't be right,' Lucy repeated.

'Who would do this?' Will asked.

The letter was dated November 1943 and only contained a few lines.

> *There is a Jewish girl still in hiding on this island. The woman hiding her is called Persephone Le Roy. She lives at Deux Tourelles. Search her room.*

It was written in a clumsy attempt to disguise the hand-writing, bold capital letters in a scratchy hand. It was, of course, anonymous.

'We're closing in a few minutes,' a kind voice said from beside them.

Lucy dragged her eyes from the letter and stared at the man. 'Right,' she said blankly. 'Of course.'

They turned, reluctantly, away from the letter accusing Persephone.

Lucy blinked into the light after having spent the afternoon inside a quiet, near-windowless space. Neither she nor Will spoke as they moved towards their cars.

They met back at Deux Tourelles and Lucy pulled a bottle of wine from the dwindling supplies in the fridge while Will strolled out to take a look in the garden. He shook his head in dismay at the state of the vegetable patch.

'Want me to do something about this for you?' he offered.

'No, it's fine,' she said as she led him to the wrought-iron garden bench. 'I quite fancy tackling it myself actually.'

He nodded and they drank in silence, neither quite able to voice their thoughts about the letter.

'What do you think the repercussions were?' Will asked eventually.

'I don't know,' Lucy said. 'But I can't imagine it was good. I keep thinking about that concentration camp notice.'

Will sipped his wine and then said, 'Did the Nazis follow up on all letters sent to them? There were hundreds on that wall. Did they have the time? Did they trust all these uncorroborated, anonymous letters and raid houses, follow people? The Germans had an Occupation to run. Did they really, honestly investigate every petty squabble laid out on paper like that?'

Lucy shrugged and sipped her wine. 'I hope not. I saw something about an archive online that lists people from the Channel Islands who were imprisoned during the war. Hang on.' She ran into the house and grabbed the history book she'd bought from the bookshop and flicked through until she found the name of the archive attributed in the back.

Will looked, pulled out his phone, keyed the information into a web browser and they both waited.

'So what does this website do?' Will asked as it loaded.

'It's resistance archives,' Lucy said, reading the information in the book. 'Papers collected by one man after the war, documenting resistance and those who were punished as a direct result.'

'Punished?' he asked with a shudder.

'Imprisoned, mainly,' Lucy said.

He typed 'Persephone Le Roy' in the search bar and they both waited, Lucy craning eagerly at the phone in Will's hands so that she was almost in his lap.

'Nothing,' Will said a moment later. 'No results.'

'How can there be no results? How can there be nothing at all?' Lucy cried.

'That's good though? Isn't it?' Will asked. 'If someone grassed her up, and she's not listed as having been imprisoned, then maybe the Nazis didn't follow up on it, maybe they didn't hunt her down.'

'Maybe,' Lucy said. 'But what about this Jewish girl the letter mentions. Who was she? What happened to her?'

'Maybe she wasn't anyone,' Will said, pocketing his phone and sitting back. 'Maybe it was a lie to make trouble for Dido's sister, to send a few Germans knocking at the door to frighten her.'

'Why?'

Will gave her an exasperated look. 'I don't know.'

'I wish I'd paid slightly more attention in history classes,' Lucy muttered.

'I wish you had as well,' Will joked. They sat companionably, feeling the gentle sea breeze that was never far away and listened as it rustled the leaves on the trees.

'How do we find out who the Jewish girl was?' Lucy asked.

'We may not have a way to find her,' Will offered.

'They were all told to register,' Lucy reasoned, 'at one point or another. I know that. I think, actually, there were more than one set of rules thrown at remaining Jews. They were weeded out and persecuted until there were none left.'

'So perhaps she didn't register. Would you have done?'

Lucy thought. 'Probably not.' But she was only saying that with the power of hindsight. 'What the Nazis did, what they did to the Jews, did anyone really know quite what was coming? How could anyone have possibly envisaged that? I don't think they could have known in the early days of the Occupation that the Nazis were in the midst of building the extermination camps. We know now. But did they know back then? So what harm could registering have done? That's probably what I'd have thought,' she said.

Will was quiet and then said, 'Somewhat naïve.'

'Well yes, probably,' Lucy bristled, rather offended. She cast him a look. 'Actually, it's very naïve of me considering they built a concentration camp in Alderney during the war.'

'You're kidding,' Will said. 'A concentration camp in the Channel Islands. Really?'

'Yes, it's one of those things that you can't forget when you know. It was only taught as a sidebar to our history lessons, but if you go now, you can see remnants of it.'

'How did they build a concentration camp in the Channel Islands, and no one knew?' His voice was louder than before.

'Alderney was evacuated in its entirety,' Lucy said soothingly. 'The Islanders moved to Guernsey, livestock included. There was no one left there. Population zero. Until the camps were built.'

Will frowned. 'Camps? Plural?'

Lucy took a large glug of wine. 'Some for forced slave workers, some for Jews and—'

'I've heard enough,' Will said.

'I can see how people would hold on to their faith throughout all of that, not relinquish it. And how could they know that's where they might end up as a result? I'm not a churchgoer. Neither were my parents really. Surprises me that Dido was, but maybe it was something she needed. Maybe she needed that faith.'

'Some people do,' Will said.

The conversation reminded her that she and Clara had to choose a headstone for Dido. It had been her father who had initially prompted her to think about this in a text message earlier in the day, and it shocked Lucy to think that she would have easily left Dido in an unmarked grave if her father hadn't suggested a local stonemason. It was all well and good dictating to her and Clara from the sunnier side of the world.

She tried to look at it from her parents' point of view. Dido was their father's cousin, who they'd rarely seen. And her dad – and now she and Clara – were the last of the family. She realised, if they didn't help out then who would? And besides, Dido who she hadn't really remembered all that well had left her a joint share in a house that was going to fetch rather a lot of money. Of course she could do all of this and it wasn't begrudgingly either.

'Listen,' Will said, turning towards her. 'How far do you want to take this?'

'Sorry?' Lucy was confused.

'This search for the Jewish girl and for Persephone Le Roy. They're both dead now, surely,' Will said.

'Yes, probably.'

'Don't you have other things you need to be getting on with? Other things you'd rather be getting on with, instead of museum visits and . . . whatever with me?'

Lucy smiled. She was quite enjoying the 'whatever' with Will. 'Even though it's a serious subject, I'm quite enjoying myself actually. Aren't you?'

Will nodded. 'Yes. But I don't want to push you in a direction you're not happy with. Especially now . . .'

'Especially now?'

'That it's turned in a bit of a sickening direction. Letters grassing your relation up about hidden Jews. I feel we've stumbled into some nasty territory and we might be out of our depth.'

'We might be, yes.'

'So what do you want to do?'

'I don't want to stop, if that's what you're asking?' Lucy said. After all they'd only just got started and Lucy wanted to find out what had happened to Persephone.

'OK. Me neither,' Will said. 'If you still want the help and the company, I'm happy to oblige.'

'Great. So what next?'

'No clue. Is there some kind of local records office we can try?' Will asked with a shrug.

'Yes, I think so.'

'Want to go?'

'Now?'

'No.' He laughed. 'Tomorrow?'

'OK,' Lucy said, knowing she really should be painting rooms in prep for the estate agent's photographer. 'But what are we looking up?'

'Christ, I don't know. What about we look up the history of Deux Tourelles during the war? Do they have files on that kind of thing?'

'I have no idea,' Lucy said.

'And then we can look up Persephone Le Roy,' Will said. 'See if there's some kind of official file on her from the war. If they followed up the letter about the Jewish girl, there must be some kind of note on a Nazi file somewhere. They left records behind when they got kicked off at the end of the war, right? I've seen pictures of them lined up, waiting to be packed off to POW camps with only what they could carry when the British liberated the islands. Doubtful they took all their files with them, too? So maybe that will help. Whatever it was they did to her . . . maybe she just got a bit of a ticking off.'

'A ticking off?' Lucy scoffed. 'From the Gestapo? Not likely.'

Will stretched out his long legs in the last of the evening sun. 'We'll find out tomorrow.'

Chapter 21

The year moved through its seasons. Christmas had been a mute affair, with hardly any presents to gift each other. Stefan had been granted leave and had returned to Berlin to visit his family. On his return – after weeks of Persephone wondering what he was doing and who he was with, whether he was laughing with his family or if they were as mute a household as Deux Tourelles – he'd announced he would be leaving again, this time for longer. Persey's chest had tightened, thinking she might never see him again, but she couldn't admit it to herself, let alone out loud. She cared far more than she should and she wished she didn't.

'I will still be in the Channel Islands,' he'd admitted as they'd stood in the garden in the spring of 1941. 'But not in Guernsey.'

'For how long?' she'd asked, pulling her coat around her and standing up from where she'd been weeding the vegetable patch.

'I do not know. But you will not have another officer here. I have expressed I want this billet on my return. Whenever that may be.'

She nodded, unsure what to make of that. 'I see. Where are you going?'

He'd sighed, looked away. 'Alderney.'

'Alderney?' she'd asked in confusion. 'But I thought there was

213

no one on Alderney. I thought the whole island had been evacuated.'

'It has.'

'Then why are you going there? Who requires the services of a translator on Alderney? By all accounts they've even brought all the livestock over from the farmland so you can't even be translating for the cattle.' It was a poor joke and she'd known it but she couldn't have helped but be curious.

'The population have removed themselves, yes. But there are others who are there now. Germans defending the island and . . . others,' he'd said vaguely. 'I hope I will not be there long.'

'So do I,' she'd said and then wished she'd not said it. 'I didn't mean . . . I'm sorry, I have no idea why I said . . .' She'd looked away, unable to meet his intense gaze.

'Persephone . . .' he'd started and then paused.

He'd always used her full name, never shortening it to Persey. Old habits, she supposed.

'Yes?' she'd prompted.

He'd shaken his head. 'There is always an issue of timing,' he muttered. 'I leave in the morning.'

He had a habit of doing this, toying with her heart, leaving shortly after. Perhaps whatever he was going to say was better left unsaid.

'Will you allow me to take you for dinner tonight?'

Her breath had been short and sharp, the question shocking her, thrilling her. If they'd had dinner out together, where would they have gone? Who would have seen them? 'I can't,' she'd said in a strained voice.

'You do not wish to be seen with me? Or you do not want to have dinner with me?'

'I . . .' She'd collected herself, avoiding answering the question with the truth. 'I'm having dinner with some friends tonight,' she'd said. 'The doctor and his wife. I haven't seen them properly in some weeks and I promised I'd go.'

214

He'd looked away, around the garden, at the orchard, its blossoms falling to the grass like snow, the grass underneath green and lush – what remained of the lawn that hadn't been given over to the now-increased vegetable patch.

'Then I do not know when I will see you next,' he'd replied.

'No.' Why had tears formed in her eyes? She'd looked up at him, longing to ask him to write to her. But he hadn't written when they'd been younger. Why would he do so all these years later? Instead she'd remained silent, unwilling to put her heart on the line by saying anything else.

He'd turned away. 'Then it's goodbye, Persephone.'

'Stefan?' she'd called, although she didn't know what she'd intended to say. Moments passed when neither spoke. 'Good luck,' she'd said eventually. 'With whatever it is you are doing on Alderney. Please stay safe.'

'Thank you. I will be away from the house first thing in the morning.' He'd raised his hand to her and walked away.

He had packed his few belongings, so he had nothing to return to Deux Tourelles for, then he had gone. He had left her a note, slipping it silently under her bedroom door. When she'd woken and seen it she'd stopped breathing and then had rushed towards it, wanting to both rip it open at once and read his words within and also to delay opening it entirely.

But the note had contained only fact and nothing extraneous:

I hope to return to Deux Tourelles soon. Please stay safe, Persephone.
   Your friend, Stefan

She had not expected his departure to hurt so much more than before. After all, this time there had been no kiss. Only words. Before, there had been no words and only a kiss. This was harder. Was it because she was older now, more in tune with her own desires? She'd waited five whole days after he'd left until she'd

215

entered his room and she'd only done that when she'd been confident that no one else was in the house. She couldn't risk anyone seeing her.

It had been excruciating, waiting that long. But by then Mrs Grant had changed his sheets for laundry day on Monday as usual and there was nothing left of him there, no part of him for her to feel close to. Before it had been her mother's room, but already she thought of it as Stefan's. Now it was empty. Like her.

The fact they had not had another German billeted with them throughout his absence gave Persey hope that the room was marked as Stefan's and that he would be returning soon. But every week that passed without him present at Deux Tourelles had hurt Persey just that little bit more.

As 1941 gave way to 1942, she suspected it was no longer true that it was a temporary posting. It felt as if he had inadvertently wrenched her heart out a second time by leaving again for so long. A part of her hated him for doing it. But mostly she hated herself for feeling this way. She wondered if he had returned to Guernsey at all during that time. Had he been staying elsewhere without making his return known to her? Or was he still on Alderney? And what on earth was he doing there? What was there for a translator to do on an island with no one but Germans. It made no sense.

Persephone read the note that Stefan had left a year earlier, folded it up and placed it inside the novel she was currently reading. She told herself it was a useful bookmark, but she opened the note and read it far too many times to know it was not simply serving a function. She read it more than she read the pages of her novel these days.

Two lines of text and then, 'Your friend, Stefan'. She traced the final flourish of his name.

'What's that?' Dido asked from the doorway, making Persey jump.

'Nothing,' she replied, hastily folding Stefan's note and inserting it into her book. 'Edgar Allan Poe,' Persey replied, referring to the novel. 'One of Father's. I'm not enjoying it.'

Dido made a face. 'I'm not surprised. You've missed a telephone call. Doctor Durand. Asked you for supper tomorrow evening. Was very keen to make it clear it was just you invited, which I thought was rude considering he's known us both the same amount of time.'

'Did he? Sorry,' Persey said. 'I suppose you're normally singing most evenings and so I've got to know him quite well these past few years.' It wasn't strictly untrue. She wished sorely she could tell Dido about Lise. But the risk to Lise wasn't worth it. The risk to Dido wasn't worth it either, knowing something she shouldn't. No, it was better this way. The fewer people who knew, the safer it was all round.

It had been weeks since Persey had been able to visit Lise at Doctor Durand's. She didn't wish to raise suspicions by being a frequent visitor and so had opted for sporadic calls as much as possible. She couldn't speak to her friend on the telephone for fear of the Germans listening in, but on prior occasions when she had visited, Lise's spirit had been undiminished, grateful she had been promised a home with the Durands until the eradication of the Nazis from Guernsey. But even Persey couldn't have imagined it would go on this long.

'Would you like to see Doctor and Mrs Durand? If so . . . we could invite them here?'

'Not really,' Dido replied, looking at her fingernails. 'They're not really my cup of tea, despite being old friends of father's. Bit old before their time if you ask me.'

'Which they probably know and which is why you probably weren't invited, I assume,' Persey pointed out.

But Dido ignored her remark. 'Besides, I'm singing tomorrow.'

'Dido?' Persey started. 'Do you think it might be time to stop singing publicly? Just for a while I mean? It's not as if we need the money and—'

217

'No,' Dido responded immediately. 'No, I'm not going to stop. I love it. It's the only thing I have. I know Mother never really approved, but I didn't think you'd go the same way.'

'It's not the singing I object to,' Persey tried to rationalise. 'It's the fact that it's to so many Germans now. If it wasn't for the fact the locals no longer come to listen to you.'

'Only because they don't want to be around the Germans,' Dido countered.

'Yes, quite,' Persey replied. 'Once it used to be singing to the crowds in the hotel ballrooms while tourists danced or the club but now it's just German officers. I'm deeply uncomfortable with it. I have been for some time. Won't you consider stopping?'

'No,' Dido snapped. 'Life has to go on, Persey. The world keeps spinning. I enjoy it. I'm good at it. It's the only thing I am good at. Don't take it away from me.'

Persey blew out a puff of air from her cheeks. 'That's not true. You're good at many things, but please be careful.'

'Oh, Persey,' Dido said. 'Don't be boring. I was going to try out that new Vera Lynn number, see if the Germans can recognise it given all our radios have now been confiscated and we aren't supposed to know any of the new tunes.'

'Don't,' Persey reprimanded immediately. 'It's not worth it. Trust me. Don't give them any reason to suspect we've kept hold of our spare wireless, for God's sake.'

'I was teasing,' Dido said, throwing her hands up in surrender.

Persey rolled her eyes. 'Dido, honestly, don't do that to me. Do you know they've raided Ida Sayle's farmhouse three times so far? First suspecting her mother and father of having a radio, then of having an old weapon from the first war stashed away, and then alleging they were hiding one of those foreign workers. They only just put the contents of the house back in place and another lot of soldiers turn up and turn the house over again. We're taking such a risk with our wireless set. I only allowed you to keep it because you begged and begged me. We need to find a better hiding place than in the back of the pantry.'

'I know,' Dido said, 'but if I didn't have my music I think I'd go mad. And Jack's forever listening to all those coded messages the BBC put out, imagining there might be an instruction in it for him. Not that he'd know what to listen out for even if there was one.'

Jack still considered his role here to be that of a spy, although he had kept true to his word and had found employment in town at a photographic shop. His old job as a clerk had been reassigned upon Jack's departure, and so now Jack really was hiding in plain sight at the front of a shop. He spent most of his days serving German soldiers, much to Mrs Grant's worry. But as her son pointed out, they were the only ones on the island allowed to purchase such fripperies as cameras and films, and he had no choice but to take whatever job he could, given the employment situation wasn't exactly bountiful if he didn't want to work directly for the Germans.

Even Jack wasn't that brave. He'd laughed at how many Germans had been photographing the island, each other and the beaches, posing with the newly constructed fortifications built should the Allies mount an invasion campaign. Jack revealed he'd been studying their photographs as he'd developed them, recognising locations where new gun emplacements could be seen in shot; soldiers photographing each other lounging around and smoking cigarettes as if they hadn't a care in the world. The Germans were providing the evidence Jack needed without him having to lift a finger. He was just waiting for his time to come. Waiting for that moment when he could use his precious information.

He had even confessed that the camera shop's elderly owner had gifted him a broken Kodak Box Brownie, flouting every kind of occupying order. It had been at the back of the shop for years and if Jack could fix it, it was his.

Persey shook her head. 'Yes, I did rather think it was specific codes for specific people. I'll admit it's nice to have the comfort of the news still while others don't, but don't mess it all up by singing a new song you shouldn't know. Please.'

'All right. I'd love to see the looks on their faces though, the Germans I mean, if I did. Especially now they aren't allowed theirs either. And we all know it's so they can't hear about the disasters befalling their army all over the world. As if hiding the news from them keeps up their morale! What would be more surprising is if they'd all secretly kept hold of their wireless sets and sang along with me.'

'Did I just hear you correctly? You've kept your wireless?' the doctor asked Persey.

Persey was helping Mrs Durand set the table in her kitchen and had just relayed yesterday evening's news to her and explained the precarious position with the radio set.

Lise was filling a jug with water and listened, open-mouthed. On the occasions Persey had been invited to join them all for supper, they had always eaten in the kitchen rather than in the dining room at the front of the doctor's cottage. Any knock at the front door would enable Lise to get to her emergency hiding place in the cellar, the entrance to which was concealed in the cold store.

'Yes,' Persey groaned. 'We had two radios, you see. They don't know that and so we've handed one in so as to not look suspicious. They registered which set belongs to which family the first time they confiscated them, and Mrs Grant only handed one in then, so now they only think we have one.'

'If it's anything like last time they'll give them all back again soon enough,' Lise suggested.

'I'm not so sure, actually,' Doctor Durand said. 'They've had them for a couple of months now. I think it might be a bit different this time. Sherry?'

'Yes, please,' Persey enthused. 'How do you still have sherry? All our supplies are long gone.'

220

'A grateful patient, unable to pay in Reichsmarks, gave me the benefit of his black market hoard today.'

'And you cycled home with it in your bag? Are you mad?' Mrs Durand asked. 'What if you'd been stopped?'

Doctor Durand gave Persey and Lise a guilty look as he fetched glasses.

'Thank you for coming,' he said, handing a glass to Persey. She sniffed it with delight as if she'd never smelt sherry before. 'Gosh, heaven,' she said, taking a sip. 'Thank you for inviting me. I know how hard it is, making food stretch without having an extra mouth at the dinner table.'

'Charming,' Lise said good-naturedly, nudging Persey in the ribs as she put the jug of water on the table.

'I didn't mean you. I meant me! Speaking of which, I brought some money with me. It's so difficult to get a substantial amount from the bank these days without someone wagging their finger at you in suspicion so I've brought what I could for now and I'll try to get a bit more in a few weeks.'

She handed the Reichsmarks to Doctor Durand who looked confused. 'What's this for?'

'For Lise. Don't argue,' Persey said as he started to protest. 'It's to help with the little extras and I've brought more fruit from our kitchen garden for you. While I can get away with smuggling it out, I thought I would.'

Mrs Durand took the net bag of food. 'That's most kind. And it will certainly help.'

Lise clutched Persey's hand. 'Thank you,' she said.

'It's the very least I can do. I also brought you some books to help pass the time. Not sure if you've run dry here. I'll swap them over in a few weeks if you like. And if there's anything else you need, you know you just have to ask.'

Lise looked as if she was going to cry and Percy squeezed her friend's hand in return.

Mrs Durand opened the range door and brought out a pie.

'Vegetables only I'm afraid but I've managed to get a bit of suet so we've a pudding for after.'

'Smells delicious,' Persey enthused.

'I've evaporated a bit of sea salt so that should go some way into making the pie digestible,' Mrs Durand admitted, placing a little dish on the table. 'Help yourself.'

'Have you seen any of those poor foreign workers yet?' Lise asked. 'Mrs Durand heard they've been sent from all over the mainland.'

'Most are being treated appallingly, I think,' Persey said as Doctor Durand served the pie. 'Starving, some of them, from the tattle I hear in town. Mrs Grant thinks it's only a matter of time before our vegetable patch gets raided in the night. We were thinking about trying to get a laying hen if we could, but there may not be any point. It may get stolen and eaten. The state the island's in now,' Persey mused.

'It's not better on Jersey, either,' the doctor said.

'You must hear a lot more than we do, in your line of work.' Persey reached for the salt and cast an apologetic glance at Mrs Durand for having to use it. 'You get out and about all over.'

'You're the one with the radio,' the doctor pointed out.

'Yes, but I don't hear anything about what's happening here. What do you know, that I might not? If you know about Jersey do you know about Alderney?' she asked, avoiding eye contact with any of them. She so desperately wanted to know what Stefan might be doing; wanted to be able to picture him on the island, if he was still there.

'I do actually. I treat a few fishermen on the odd occasion. Pay me in fish mostly, now. Sadly not this week,' he said, prodding his vegetable pie. 'They've heard things down at the harbour, not sure how true it all is,' he said.

'Such as?' Persey prompted.

'Alderney's turning into a fortress. Much like here.'

'Oh, is that all?' Persey reached for a glass of water and took a sip.

222

'A huge foreign workforce there now.'

'Foreign workforce?' If those on Alderney looked as sad as those on Guernsey, it didn't bear thinking about. So that's why Stefan and his translation skills were required.

'None of our islands are going to look the same after all this,' Mrs Durand said. 'The amount of concrete . . . I've never seen anything like it. And there's no sign of it all stopping. The coastline is turning grey with concrete. And the RAF must know what's going on here and yet . . . nothing.'

'Why must they know?' Persey asked, curious as to how they could possibly know anything that happened here. Spies perhaps?

It was Lise's turn to guess. 'You've seen the Allied bombers going over, surely? They aren't that high as they leave the British coast. They must be looking down here, seeing it all change.'

'A few of the more daring fighter pilots have been dropping newspapers down to us,' Mrs Durand chimed in. 'Mrs Hubert out in Torteval had a copy of *The Times* land in her garden. On it was scrawled "Not to be removed from the Officers' Mess". I had a chuckle at that.'

Persey smiled, enchanted by the idea that reckless RAF pilots were risking getting shot from the sky simply to drop the news in. 'Perhaps they've heard we've not got our radios anymore.'

'Yes, I wondered about that,' Mrs Durand said as she stood to clear the table. Persey and Lise started to help.

'Speaking of the news,' Doctor Durand said, reaching for his cigarettes. 'You asked if there was anything you could do to help.'

Persey looked at him keenly. 'Anything. Within reason,' she added carefully.

'If I wanted to know the news, a bit more regularly, would you be able to tell me what's going on out there in the theatre of war?'

'Of course.'

'Would you tell anyone who asked?'

Persey stilled. 'No,' she said eventually. 'I wouldn't know who to trust.'

223

The doctor looked thoughtful.

'Why do you ask me that?' Persey narrowed her eyes.

'You aren't the only one who kept a wireless back.'

'I'd imagine not, no. I'd guess there's a fair few and they can't arrest us all.'

'They can, actually. They will. If they find out.'

'And then what?' Lise chimed in.

'I dread to think,' Mrs Durand said. 'It is a huge risk you're taking.'

'Well, it's only because we had two,' Persey said quieter now. 'I'm only hiding a radio. It's not such a great risk as hiding a person as you're doing,' she said.

The doctor smoked his cigarette thoughtfully and then said, 'Fancy writing some of the news reports down?'

'Why?' Persey asked in horror.

'To pass around a bit. I've a patient who told me he's going to help distribute a clandestine news sheet. "Burn after reading" and all that. Now it looks as if radios really are disappearing for the duration. You wouldn't have to do anything risky.'

'Of course she would,' Mrs Durand cut in, horror-struck. 'You're asking her to do something terribly dangerous. Her parents will be spinning in their graves if they'd just heard you ask that of their daughter.'

'I'm not asking her to write the flaming newspaper,' he justified. 'Nor am I asking her to distribute it. Just write down what you listen to, pass it to me. It means others would know what you know,' the doctor said, glancing from his wife to Persephone. 'For a lot of people, the news represents the only beacon of hope they have. Not knowing where their sons are out in the world, but knowing how bad the German losses are slowly becoming, the wins the Allies are getting, whenever they are, would give hope where there is, currently, none.'

Persey looked at Lise for help, but Lise's face was uncertain. Lise was hidden here. Had been stuck inside this house with only

224

the small garden for a breath of fresh air for two long years and might be for so much longer than any of them had originally thought possible. Persey had asked Doctor Durand to hide her friend. He had agreed without question. What he was asking of her was the very least she could do.

Chapter 22

Persey wheeled her bicycle out from the side of the Durands' shed. It was where she kept it when she visited, for fear of theft. No longer could she leave it lying around in plain sight. If the poor foreign workers didn't steal it to aid their nocturnal travels round the island in search of food, then the Germans might take it. Even, she wondered, Guernsey's own civilians, one whose bicycle tyres had worn too thin to repair and couldn't be replaced, or whose own bicycles had already been stolen.

Persey felt so incredibly sorry for the foreign workers, who were slaves mostly, forced into the Channel Islands to help build an impregnable fortress; herded from nations Germany had conquered, stamped on and rounded up. Doctor Durand had revealed even Spaniards who had fled to France after the Spanish Civil War were now slave workers in Guernsey, alongside the Poles and Russians.

'Persey,' Doctor Durand called as she mounted. He glanced behind him into the kitchen and pulled the wooden door closed.

'I have some news I need to share with you. I've told Lise. I hadn't dared tell her thus far, but eventually . . . I had to. She made noises about wanting to leave the house for a few hours – just to get out, I suppose. She said she would be discreet but . . . well . . . It's because of that really that I had no choice but to tell her what I knew.'

'And that is?' Persey asked with concern.

'I didn't like to say over dinner, but they've started deporting Jews from the island.'

'What?' Persey said, a sense of cold descending on the otherwise warm evening. She climbed off her bicycle, unable to steady herself.

The doctor nodded. 'Awful. In a way, we knew this day would come. Part of me wonders what took them so long.'

Persey was propelled into speechlessness and she rubbed her hand over her mouth until she eventually asked, 'When?'

'A few months ago. I only found out recently. I didn't know whether to tell Lise or not. Didn't want to worry her. But when she started on about wanting to leave the house, I just had to tell her, to illustrate how very real the threat was if she was discovered.'

Persey nodded, a cold finger of fear running up the length of her spine. Jews were being forced from the island. Good God. 'How did she take it?'

'As well as could be expected. There were tears. But then she said she was grateful you and I had stepped in to help when we did and, well, we haven't spoken about it since. I daren't open the subject back up again.'

'There'll be more, you know,' Persey offered, echoing the words of Lise's landlady Mrs Renouf from so long ago.

'Yes, I believe there will. They'll take the ones that are out in the open. Then they'll find the ones in hiding. Somehow.'

They were silent for a moment, each contemplating the horror, each wondering how long it would be before they began hunting for Lise. All paperwork on the island must point to the fact that Lise never left.

'How's Jack getting along?' he asked, changing the subject.

'Not well at all. Feels useless. Hates himself.'

'What's he doing for work these days?'

'Taken a job in a camera shop. You were very good to amend his medical records, you know. I'm sure you've saved him.'

'It was a clever idea of yours.'

'Not my idea, not really. Discrepancies were pointed out to me by . . . a friend.'

'A friend you can trust, I hope,' Doctor Durand said, looking concerned.

She thought of how long it had been since she'd last seen Stefan. The strange way it had all ended between them. Again. 'Yes, I think so,' Persey said, hoping wherever Stefan was that he was safe. 'Yes.'

'You'll give some thought to what I asked?' He continued, 'About the newspaper?'

'Yes,' she said with absolute certainty; anything that helped the people of Guernsey and went directly against the orders of the Third Reich. 'Of course I'll help.'

Persey cycled through the lanes, allowing the fresh summer breeze to whip her hair, her Victory rolls bouncing loosely. Ironic, because there was nothing to feel victorious about today. The edges of her cardigan flapped behind her as she picked up speed. With hardly any cars on the road now, all commandeered for use by the occupying force, there was very little chance of crashing into anyone, and now she remembered she had to cycle on the other side of the road to keep with German rules.

And so she pushed the pedals harder and harder, racing through the uneven lanes, becoming breathless as stones chipped around her. She was sure she was becoming more and more unfit as the Occupation wore on. She was getting thinner, certainly. Rations had been lessening and the desire to exercise had, sadly, dwindled. Puddings were almost a thing of the past. The carrageen moss Mrs Grant had been using to make blancmange was losing its novelty value, and she'd much rather do without. If the kitchen garden did get ransacked by the newly imported workers, then they were going to struggle, but what could she do? Stand guard? Those poor men needed the food more than the household at Deux Tourelles did. She'd seen them: filthy, thin, prodded and

228

pushed at every opportunity by guards. Jack heard soldiers in the camera shop boasting Poles and Russians were among the slaves.

'And we know how Herr Hitler feels about the Russians, don't we?' he'd said with a shudder. 'Think he hates them more than he hates British spies.'

In truth, Persey had no true idea how Hitler felt about the Russians, but it had soon become clear as she'd witnessed them herself.

She had passed their camp near Rue Sauvage one day when delivering documents from work to a customer – the field surrounded with barbed wire. The sight of the huts and the men had shocked her so much she had paused and before she'd known it, she'd been accidentally gawping at the men in rags that could hardly be called clothes, scruffily lined up, forced to march toward the beginnings of the concrete bunkers now littering the island. They had marched past her, their eyes barely bothering to look into hers. Perhaps they hadn't had the energy to lift their gaze. How would they lift their limbs and tools to forge on with the fortifications they were being forced to build?

What had these men been doing before being imprisoned? They must have had families, lives, homes, jobs, and now their existence was rudimentary, savage as they'd been scooped up by Hitler's war machine, removed from their lives, brought here to build walls, bunkers, continue a madman's aggression. Now they lived a life of starvation, and beatings from the Organisation Todt guards, who Persey thought looked as if they were enjoying themselves far too much, making free with their fists on poor men who looked to have done nothing wrong and clearly giving them next to no food. There were hundreds here and she was sure there would be hundreds more.

Perhaps she should leave a discreet bundle of food at the entrance to the drive when she could. She was still wondering if that would encourage foraging in their garden or discourage it as she rounded the lane into the driveway at such a pace that her wheels screeched when she pulled on her brakes. Parked in front of the house was a German military vehicle. Persey gasped. Standing at the open front door was a man in German uniform. Her first thought was that it was Stefan, returned after all this time. She was seeing him everywhere, just for split seconds, before she realised it was not him. This man was in the standard uniform of a foot soldier and his rounded helmet gave him away as such.

He turned and gave her a hard stare. It was the man who had chased them through the woodland all those months ago. The man she had seen in Candie Gardens, who looked as if he'd recognised her, but not quite placed where he'd seen her. His eyes widened in amazement and then something resembling a slow smile spread over his face when it became clear he did. She was here, at the house where he had chased her. She had watched him from the window as he'd emphatically gesticulated to Stefan that he'd seen her out after curfew. She had seen him then and he had been adamant he had seen her.

She held his gaze. 'Hello,' she said more confidently than she felt as she dismounted her cycle. 'Can I help you?' Oh God, the radio. Had they all been listening to it while she'd been out? Had they put it away in its special hiding place? Were the Germans raiding them? Had they heard the distinctive tones of the news being broadcast from inside the house? The chime of Big Ben? Her mind tumbled and whirled with panic and she felt her fingers shake. She gripped the handlebars tighter to prevent her hands from visibly trembling.

'No, you cannot help me,' the man said in stilted English. 'I have achieved everything that I came for.'

'And what is that?' Persey asked, hating his clipped tone, wondering if what he had come for was indeed confirmation it was she who lived there.

'I have delivered a message. Your housekeeper has it. Goodnight,' he said and moved towards his vehicle.

The front door to Deux Tourelles was open and just inside the threshold Mrs Grant stood, holding a piece of paper.

'Mrs Grant, what's happened?' Persey asked.

'It's a deportation order,' Mrs Grant whispered, her hands emulating those of Persey's only a moment before and shaking wildly. Without preamble, Persey took it from Mrs Grant's hands.

'Who is being deported?' Persey demanded. 'And why?'

'Me,' Mrs Grant said simply.

Was it because of the wireless? In which case, why only Mrs Grant? Why weren't all of them being arrested and deported? Where was Jack?

Persey read, her eyes scanning quickly:

By Order of the High Authorities the following British subjects will be evacuated and transferred to Germany . . .

'But . . . I don't understand. Why are you taking her?' Persey cried, looking back at the soldier as he climbed into the car.

'I am not taking her. She is to report to the Weighbridge in St Peter Port tomorrow afternoon with only what she can carry.'

'Why? Where is she going? You can't do this.'

He ignored her.

'They can't do this,' Persey shouted. 'They can't do this.'

She pulled Mrs Grant towards her, holding the shaking woman.

'We can,' the soldier said as he climbed into the vehicle. 'We have.' He slammed the door and the noise of the engine momentarily drowned out Mrs Grant's crying.

'Why is this happening?' Persey pulled Mrs Grant inside the house and closed the door. They entered the sitting room and the housekeeper slumped into a settee. Persey knelt on the floor in front of her.

'They're deporting all those not born in the Channel Islands,' Mrs Grant sniffed.

'I can see the words on the deportation order, but they make no sense. Why would they do this? It's so unnecessary. So . . . malicious. You've lived here your whole life.'

'Yes. But I wasn't born here. I was born on the mainland and so . . .' She pointed to the order in her hand.

'Where are you going? Did he tell you?'

'Yes,' she said. 'I'm going to a camp in Germany.'

'A camp?' Persey cried in horror.

'I don't know what kind. That soldier said it was a good one.'

Of course he did. It was clear Mrs Grant suspected lies also and looked frightened and as if she had aged by at least a decade in the last few minutes.

'I'm sure it will be fine,' Persey soothed. 'What about Jack?'

'Perhaps because technically he left and never officially re-entered he's escaped notice somehow.'

'Where is he now?' Persey asked.

'I don't know. I've not seen him. He didn't come home after he finished at work today. I need to pack,' Mrs Grant said pragmatically, standing.

'I'll help. I'll wait up for him. He'll be out past curfew. So will Dido if she doesn't get home soon.'

'He's out past curfew a lot these days,' Mrs Grant admitted.

'I know,' Persey said sadly. But she couldn't think about Jack at the moment.

'You pack. I'll brew some bramble leaf tea up for us and then I'll come and help. Then we'll sit up and wait for Jack together.'

Mrs Grant nodded, a blank expression filtering across her face. Germany. A camp.

'If I could take your place I would,' Persey said. 'You know that, don't you?' She meant it. A camp was no place for a woman in her sixties. How would Mrs Grant survive it? It didn't bear thinking about.

'How long are you going for? Did that soldier say?' Persey asked but she knew the answer to the question before she'd finished asking it.

Mrs Grant shook her head uncertainly. 'I think until the end.'

* * *

232

'You've got your thick winter coat, haven't you?' Dido asked Mrs Grant as they entered St Peter Port the next day, Dido on one side of the housekeeper and Persephone on the other, each carrying a small suitcase for her. They headed towards the Weighbridge where the clock tower loomed, indicating it was nearly time for people to board. 'Because I know it's summer now, but you must be prepared for winter.'

'Yes,' Mrs Grant said.

'And those thermal socks I gave you. Both pairs?' Persey added.

'Yes,' Mrs Grant said.

'I can't believe this is happening,' Dido said. She had arrived home yesterday full of the joys of an evening singing, to be confronted with her sister and Mrs Grant solemnly folding things into suitcases.

'Where is Jack?' Mrs Grant mumbled after realising her son had not returned home to sleep. She'd asked the question almost twenty times an hour since she'd got up that morning. So much so that Persey had gone to the camera shop the moment it opened to find that Jack wasn't due in today. She left a message for Jack to telephone Deux Tourelles if he did make an appearance at the shop, but knew it was fruitless. Who went in to work if it was their day off?

'He'll be all right. I'll find him. I'll make sure he's fine,' Persey said as they rounded the corner to find hundreds of Islanders, queuing and clutching suitcases by the harbour side.

'Bloody hell,' Dido cried on seeing them all.

Mrs Grant didn't issue a call to Dido to watch her language, instead saying, 'So many of us . . .?'

Persey's mouth dropped open. She'd expected only about fifty people at most. But there were hundreds and hundreds of Islanders of all ages, some elderly, some young with small children.

The noise was incredible and the island's St John Ambulance service had put up a makeshift area serving what passed for tea and soup to anyone who needed it. The camaraderie brought tears to Persey's eyes.

Germans stood on patrol in full kit, rifles ready, but instead of civilians rioting, someone somewhere began singing and those surrounding them soon took it up. To all intents and purposes, patriotism had been banned in Guernsey since the beginning of the war. British flags had been ordered down from flagpoles. And in homes, flags were forced to be packed up and put away. The national anthem was banned and 'God Save the King' never said in church anymore. But now, British songs were being sung with gusto. Persey wondered if the Germans would put a stop to it. But how do you stop hundreds of people singing 'There'll Always Be An England'? It was clear the Germans didn't know how.

Persey clutched Mrs Grant's hand as she began singing and on the other side, Dido did the same. Persey looked over the crowds towards one of the taller soldiers, a smile pulling at the sides of his mouth. If it had been almost any other occasion, it could have been joyous. But as the crowd shuffled towards the boats, Persey and Dido were forced to let go of Mrs Grant's hands and watch as the soldiers took the housekeeper's papers, checked her name from a list and ushered her through the barricade. They'd barely had time to hug her and wish her well.

'Look after my Jack,' Mrs Grant called as Dido and Persey were pushed away from the barricade to let more people through to the waiting boats.

'We will,' Persey called desperately, as she tried to stay strong and hold back tears. Dido pulled her sister away from the crush of people. 'We will.'

'What do we do now?' Dido asked as she herself wiped tears from her cheeks. Mrs Grant became enclosed by the crowd and disappeared from view.

'Let's wait for the boats to leave. If she looks back, I want her to see us. I want her to know we stayed here,' Persey said emphatically as they moved through the people to find a higher place to stand and wave.

It took hours to load everyone onto the waiting boats and Dido and Persey found space on a low wall along with so many other people, waiting to wave to their loved ones.

When the boats finally left, the people on board held hands in solidarity, waving goodbye to those remaining on the island, held back behind the barriers the Germans had put in place. The sisters could not see the housekeeper in amongst those on deck, but they waved towards the boats regardless.

'Goodbye, Mrs Grant,' Persey whispered as their friend headed towards the European mainland and out of sight.

Chapter 23

Persey and Dido sat on the wall long after everyone else had dispersed, staring out across the azure blue sea and into the distance towards the islands of Jethou and Herm. Persey wondered what life was like for the residents who had stayed on Herm, the larger island. Had they also just had to say goodbye to their non-island-born community? She looked to the skies, at the deepening blue and the soft, white clouds as they passed aimlessly. How the world kept spinning throughout all of this mania was beyond Persey. So many people being separated by this war, by one man's burning desire for power. None of it made sense.

How would Mrs Grant fare in a camp? Persey wished she knew which kind of camp it might be. Would it be like the internment ones she'd read about in Britain where Austrian and German residents had been held as enemy aliens? Stefan's aunt and uncle would be in one, surely. Stefan. What was he doing? Where was he now? She cared far more than she wanted to. She cared far more than she told herself she should. But the fact was undeniable: she cared.

It was Dido who brought Persey to her senses. 'I may as well get a wriggle on to the club,' Dido said emotionlessly as she stood. 'I'm practising some different songs with the band before tonight. Might as well be early for once. I can't believe she's gone.'

Persey took her hand. 'I can't believe they've all gone. I don't understand why they've ordered so many to leave.'

'Because they can,' Dido said bitterly.

'Does Jack ever come and watch you sing?' Persey asked, trying to fathom what kept Jack out all hours. How he'd missed all this – his mother's sudden departure.

'No. He won't come. Won't be anywhere near the Germans who come along. He'll be distraught he's missed his mother leaving and who knows how long for?'

Persey nodded. She knew the enormity of what had just happened would strike her soon. 'Do you know where Jack goes?'

'I have my suspicions.'

'Do you?' Persey asked.

Dido nodded, wrapping her cardigan tighter around her.

'Are you going to tell me?'

Dido looked around to see how many soldiers were nearby and sat back down again. 'I think he surveys the coastline. Watches the timing of the patrols.'

'What for?' Persey asked.

Dido was obviously choosing her words carefully and she said, 'Has he spoken to you about escaping?'

'Escaping?' Persey said far too loudly and then glanced around in fear.

Dido said, 'Shh, keep your voice down. He hasn't said as much, but he comes back stinking of the beach. You know, that salty smell that lingers on clothes. Waits 'til it's dark, mostly. He's taking such a risk.'

'Yes,' Persey said darkly. 'Yes, he is. He can't be serious.'

'I'm guessing,' Dido added, 'but on the occasions I've seen him traipse back in with ankles wet with seawater he's never got anything useful. Never got any limpets to eat or driftwood for the range. I did actually point that out to him,' Dido said. 'It would be a better cover should he get caught, if he had an armload of driftwood.'

'Oh, Jack,' Persey moaned, closing her eyes for a moment. 'How do we tell him what's happened? How do we tell him his mother is gone?'

Dido's arm came out and she placed her hand on her sister's. 'It'll all be all right, you know.'

'Will it?' Persey asked hopelessly. 'Mrs Grant's just been carted off to God knows where. Jack's nowhere to be seen and probably planning some sort of escape. He's completely missed his mother's departure. The Jews are being taken away too, or didn't you know about that?'

'I did, yes,' Dido said sadly. 'One of the officers was talking about it to me in the club.'

'Really?' Persey asked in shock. 'That was indiscreet of him.'

'Do you know,' Dido started, 'I'm not sure there are that many officers who completely agree with Hitler's ideology. I'm not saying that none of them agree. But a few of them, with a drink inside them, do rather spill the beans about their lack of love for their Führer. Shame I'm not a spy actually, I'd have plenty to take back to tell Churchill.'

Persey thought of the soldier who smiled while the deportees and their friends and families sang earlier that day. And then she remembered the thinly veiled excitement yesterday from that awful soldier who had chased her through the woods, the one who had delivered the deportation notice. The one who knew who she was. 'I think it's only the odd few, Dido. Do be careful, won't you.'

'I'm not falling in love with him or anything like that,' Dido said quickly.

'With who?' Persey said dumbly and then: 'Not a German. Tell me, Dido. Not a German, please.'

'Of course not. Well, he's German but we aren't . . . we aren't doing anything inappropriate. I'm not a Jerrybag.'

Persey's breath caught in her throat. 'Dido, no. You can't.'

'I know,' Dido said forcefully. 'Don't tell me what to do, Persey. You know I don't need to be told what to do.'

Now it was Persey's turn to tell her sister to keep her voice down. 'People will hear.'

'Do you know, I don't care if they do, actually. I'm not doing

238

anything wrong. He's bought me a couple of drinks and supper once or twice. He talks to me. Actually talks to me. Asks me questions about myself. He's kind. I like him. And he likes me.'

'He's German,' Persey whispered.

'So what?' Dido said angrily. 'Why does it matter?'

Persey swallowed, her chest tightening. 'At a time of war, you just can't. You just can't be seen with him,' she said. 'Because of that.' She pointed out to sea where the boats had just carted off hundreds of Islanders. 'Because of what people here will think if you take up with one. And do you know for sure if you can trust him?'

'It's not his fault,' Dido said, standing up. 'None of this is his fault. The same as Stefan.'

'What do you mean?' Persey snapped defensively. She too stood as the row between the sisters escalated.

'I know how you feel about him,' Dido said.

'Don't talk rot. You can't possibly.'

Dido was quiet and then: 'And if I didn't know already, that just confirmed it. I went into your room to borrow a hat. You left your book on your bed and I went to put it back on your bedside table. I don't know why. I just did. I opened it at the page you were on. Just to see how horrid Poe really was. Turns out very horrid. But that bookmark.'

'Shut up,' Persey said, knowing what her sister was going to say.

'It's the note from Stefan.'

'I told you to shut up,' Persey said forcefully.

'It's not even a love note. Not even anything remotely close to a love note. But the way you were looking at it the other day.'

'If you don't shut up I am going to slap you,' Persey said, fighting back tears and then regretting her words immediately.

Dido moved away. 'I understand why you didn't pursue it back then. Although I knew you liked him. I knew he liked you. I wondered back then if it was because he was German. Mrs Grant's

239

husband had been gassed in the first war. Father had returned from the trenches a different man. And I thought that was the reason why. So I understood why you kept your distance from Stefan then, even though no one else seemed to care he was German. That last summer, he made his intentions towards you very plain indeed, I thought. Or did you think I hadn't seen him kiss you on the cliffs?'

'A first crush,' Persey said. 'We were too young. He went away and I didn't know how I felt.'

'Yes, you did. And you did nothing. And now look at you.'

'What do you mean?' Persey asked.

'When was the last time you let a man take you out for supper?'

Persey looked away.

'When did you last let a man take you dancing or to see a film? And instead, you pine for a man you won't let yourself have. I don't want to die alone, Persey. I don't want you to either.'

'Don't be so melodramatic. I've only just turned twenty-seven. Wait for all the men to return from war and you'll see. They'll take you dancing. And I'll let one of the returning British heroes take me dancing, if it pleases you. If we win the war, of course.'

'And if we don't win the war? How long after will you ignore how you feel about Stefan?' Dido demanded. 'A month? A year? Another ten years? I don't want to wait that long,' she cut back in. 'And you shouldn't either. I'm sorry. I'm not like you. In some things,' Dido said meaningfully, 'you can be very brave. In others, you're a complete coward.'

Persey opened her mouth to reply, but Dido had already turned and was walking away in the direction of the club.

Persey sat alone for what felt like hours. She closed her eyes, put her head in her hands and let the tears flow. There were only so many things a woman could take, she thought. But then she looked out to sea and remembered that she wasn't the one who had just been deported. Evacuated, that's what the Germans had called it in their deportation notice. Evacuated. How dare they? Evacuated from what to what?

And now she'd had an almighty row with Dido.

She wiped her eyes. She'd already elicited attention by fighting in the street like a common alley cat. She couldn't have the whole of St Peter Port find her crying after the event as well. What had Dido meant? She'd said she wouldn't be a Jerrybag, but in the same breath had said that she didn't think she was doing anything wrong. What did that mean? Was she stepping out with this man, whoever he was, or wasn't she?

Persey hated the ugly term, Jerrybag, that had sprung up. It was a horrific name, berating island women, although the other terms that had been bandied about far more often than they should were perhaps even worse: horizontal collaborator; and troop carrier, for women on the island carrying the babies of German soldiers. Dido wasn't going to be any of these things. Persey had known it would be inevitable that some women would fall for enemy soldiers, but not her own sister, surely? And not Persey either. What would people think? It was bad enough that Stefan had been living at Deux Tourelles with them, but they had no control over that. She did have control over her emotions. She would not, could not open her heart to him. Not when it could lead to such horrors.

As much as she didn't want to, Persey understood that Dido was frustrated, wasting her years away in Guernsey. And other women, too. Dido needed love. She always had done. Whereas Persey considered herself different, more . . . sturdy. She hadn't really needed love. Had survived without it. Dido had flitted from man to man over the past few years quite happily, without taking any of it too seriously. Persey only hoped she didn't take this man too seriously either. It would end in heartbreak.

Across the harbour, a small German navy boat was making its way into port. Next to her, a car drew up and a Guernsey policeman stepped out of the driver's side. She nodded a hello and he did the same.

'Been crying, miss?'

'No,' she fibbed and then when he looked at her kindly, she forced a smile in return and nodded. 'A little.'

'Hard day,' he said, casting his eyes out towards the sea where the boats had since left the view. 'Did you see them go?'

'I did. Did you have loved ones on board?'

'No, my lot are Guernsey born and bred. Thank the Lord. Still a rum day though. There really will be more of them than there are of us soon if it carries on,' he said and Persey knew he meant the Germans.

'It must be hard for you,' she said. What role did the police really have now? What crimes were they reporting to the Germans? Or maybe they weren't. She assumed most of them were not working quite as hard as they once had when most of the crimes now were petty vandalism, theft and sabotage against the occupying force.

'Could be worse,' he said. 'Don't know why I wear this uniform now though. I should swap it for that of a chauffeur.'

'It'll return to normal, one day,' she said.

He nodded and blew air out of his cheeks. 'Let's hope so. Don't know how much more of this I can take, running officers and their Guernsey fancy pieces around town.'

'Good luck,' she said as he made to move off.

'You too, miss.'

The policeman adjusted his hat, walked away towards the car and waited for his next charge.

The navy boat had docked and she watched as a German officer climbed off, head bent low under his peaked hat, carrying his bag over his shoulder. She lifted her head to look closer at the man, whose expression was hidden. As if sensing he was being watched he raised his head and looked at her before stopping. His mouth parted in surprise before he began smiling. She stopped breathing and stared back. He looked so different to the man who had left over a year ago. Haggard. Awful. She exhaled slowly but her eyes, wide, betrayed her shock. He walked towards her and the policeman

242

opened the car door for him, after checking he was the right person to collect.

Stefan handed over his bag and walked past him, slowly, towards Persephone.

Persey stood up, unsure what to do, what to say, unsure she could even speak.

'Oh, been waiting for him, have you?' she heard the policeman mutter.

Stefan spoke. 'What are you doing here?' he asked her softly, his eyes searching hers.

Her whole body felt rigid. 'I've been here all day.' She wasn't sure if she'd said it out loud, her voice sounded small, lost.

'How did you know I would be here?' Stefan asked.

'I didn't,' Persey said trying not to let her face move into a sudden, shocked smile – burying it all deep down. 'You know they've deported hundreds of civilians to Germany today?'

'Yes,' he said sadly. 'I have heard. You were here for that?'

'Yes, I came to say goodbye. They took Mrs Grant.'

'Oh,' he said, wiping his hand over his tired eyes. 'Because she is English?'

'Only technically,' Persey said.

Stefan and Persey looked at each other as if they didn't know what to say.

He gestured to the car. 'Are you . . . do you want . . .?'

Persey looked at the policeman in horror and then back to Stefan. 'In which direction are you heading?'

'Back to Deux Tourelles. I still have my billet there. Unless I am misinformed. It has been a year.'

'It has,' Persey said, looking at how much he'd changed in that time. Had she changed too? 'And no, your room wasn't reassigned.'

'Well then. Shall we?'

'I can't ride in that car with you,' she retorted.

'Why on earth not?' Stefan asked. 'I am going to your home. You are going to your home. Why not get in the car?'

'Because . . .'

The policeman looked at her with undisguised disgust.

She thought of his words from only a few moments ago. She was no fancy piece and she didn't want the driver to think she was. 'I just can't.'

'Persey, I am too tired for this,' he said pleadingly. 'Get in the car.' He climbed inside, the door still being held open by the policeman.

'I . . .' She looked around in panic.

'I'm sorry,' she said to the man. Persey walked around to the side not occupied by Stefan. The policeman made to walk round and open the door for her. She assumed he would be told off if he didn't treat every passenger with respect, but she shook her head. 'You don't have to open the door for me,' she mumbled in embarrassment as she opened it and climbed in, the door slamming loudly after her.

'You look thinner,' Stefan said, looking at her as they drove away from the harbour and up through the lanes towards Deux Tourelles.

Persey nodded, wishing she wasn't in the car. 'Probably,' she muttered. 'We've got this funny little thing called rationing.'

'You have been well?' he asked. 'Other than the funny little rationing?'

'Yes, quite well, thank you,' Persey said stiffly, wishing she didn't want to smile at his comment.

He laughed and the noise startled her. It didn't suit their surroundings. 'You do not wish to talk to me,' he said. 'After all this time, you still do not want me near you?'

'Mrs Grant has just been deported,' Persey said suddenly. 'Jack wasn't there. He has no idea what's just happened. I now have to break it to him. And I don't know how.'

Stefan nodded. 'I am sorry for it. For Mrs Grant. And for Jack. But it is really not the worst thing happening in this war at the moment. You must trust me on that.'

She shook her head, refusing to reply. She looked at the back of the policeman's head as he drove. Every part of her burned with embarrassment.

'Fine,' Stefan said and went silent for the duration of the journey.

When they reached the house, they climbed out of the car, Persey mumbling a 'thank you,' to the bemused policeman.

Persey let them in to the house. Gone were the days when it was possible to leave the door unlocked. The looting, the ransacking of properties that were now empty, their occupants deported to Germany; and the foreign workers who had taken to breaking in, only for food, had forced the Islanders into keeping the doors and windows locked at all times, even when inside the house.

He walked into the sitting room without even asking her if he might, which he would once have done. Sitting down on the settee, he pulled out three bottles of French brandy from his kit bag, opened one, paused and then drank from it.

Persey didn't know what to say. She sat, gingerly, next to him – keeping a suitable distance and watched his throat as he drank, and as he lowered the bottle she had to force herself to look away. She noticed his body language.

'Why is your hand shaking?' she whispered. What had he seen? What had happened?

He held the bottle in his lap, put his head back against the antimacassar of the settee and closed his eyes, ignoring her question. She looked at the bottles. 'Where did you get these?' she asked. Spirits in general were utterly unobtainable in the Channel Islands now.

'From home.'

'Home?' she asked dumbly.

'Yes. Berlin.'

'Berlin?' She wished she'd stop repeating everything he said. 'You went home to Berlin? I thought you were in Alderney.'

His expression darkened. 'I was there too. And then I went home.'

245

'Really? How long for?' she asked. Somehow, all this time, she'd pictured him in Alderney. It confused her that he had returned home to Berlin and she'd not known, but of course she wouldn't have known. 'You didn't send any word.'

He swallowed and looked at her. 'Why would I?'

His words stung. 'I don't know,' she snapped, reaching out and taking the brandy he offered.

'Why did you go home? Did you get leave?'

'You could say that. I was allowed to leave that godforsaken island, to return home and organise my parents' funeral.'

Persey coughed on the brandy. 'Funeral?' She wasn't sure she'd heard him correctly. 'Which parent?'

'Both of them,' he said.

'Both of them?' she echoed, horror threaded into her words. 'Both of them have died?'

'Yes.'

She collected herself. 'Oh, Stefan, I'm so sorry,' she said softly. And then even quieter: 'What happened?'

'An Allied bombing raid.'

'My God,' she said as he gently reached over and took the bottle back from her, drinking a mouthful. 'I'm so sorry,' she repeated. 'Christ, this war. Stefan, I'm so—'

'Do you want any more?' he asked, indicating the bottle.

She shook her head. 'No, thank you.'

'I am going to bed,' he said, standing.

The front door opened and closed and before Stefan had a chance to leave Jack made his way into the sitting room with a smile on his face. The moment he saw Stefan, the smile departed. 'Oh God, not you,' Jack said. 'What the hell are you doing back? Thought we'd got rid of you for good this time.' And then: 'Bloody hell, is that brandy?'

Stefan looked at Jack and sighed. 'Hello, Jack.'

'Yes, hello,' Jack said without conviction. 'How long are you back for this time?'

'I do not know. I hope for a while.'

'Yes, well let's not hope too hard shall we?' Jack said, his eyes still on the bottle of brandy.

Stefan walked forward and handed it to him. 'You may have some,' he said as he made towards his bedroom. He turned at the door, put his hand on Jack's shoulder in a gesture of kindness, which was immediately shrugged off. 'I think you might need it. Goodnight, Jack. Goodnight, Persephone.'

Persey listened as he ascended the stairs, slowly, pulling himself and his bag along. His bedroom door closed softly and she thought how the tide had turned so dramatically in such a short space of time. He looked awful. He sounded awful. There was no way out of this mess until one side won this war.

'What's he talking about?' Jack said carelessly, opening the bottle. 'Why do I need this?'

'Oh Jack,' Persey said. 'Your mother—'

'What about Mum?' Jack started, looking around quickly as if he'd find her there. 'Where is she? What's happened?'

After she told him, she held him tightly as he sobbed into her shoulder. She had never seen him cry before. Not once. Not even when he'd fallen from a tree in the park when he was twelve and broken his arm.

'Why wasn't I there?' he cried. 'I could have stopped it.'

'You couldn't, Jack. You couldn't.'

'I could!' he shouted. 'Of course I could.'

She held him until he slumped into her. All the fight gone. He drank more brandy than he should and she waited, knowing there was nothing she could say. And after, she went upstairs with him, ushering him into the bathroom so he could be sick before she washed him and pushed him towards his bedroom so he could sleep it off. She watched Jack as he slept, face down on his bed, her heart going out to him as she closed the door.

She felt more determined than ever to do something useful for the islands, so she went downstairs, pulled the wireless from its

247

hiding place in the pantry, waited until Big Ben struck the hour for the news to start and began writing what she heard in shorthand as quickly as possible. Tomorrow morning she would ride over to Doctor Durand's with her notes and, alongside helping keep Lise safe, Persey felt truly rallied by the knowledge she was going to play as much of a role as possible in driving the Nazis from the Channel Islands.

It might take a long time, and her part might be small, but she had to do it. After all, they were all being held prisoner now. It was just that for some, you couldn't see the bars.

Chapter 24

October 1943

Over the course of a few months the residents of Deux Tourelles fell into step alongside each other once again. It was a strange exchange: the loss of Mrs Grant for the return of Stefan, but Persey tried to squash the array of emotions she had felt at his return. She hated herself when she felt remorse when he left for work, and loathed herself even more when she caught herself smiling when the front door sounded as he returned. Why did she have to feel this unidentified emotion whenever she thought of him?

The house was so quiet without the constant thrum of Mrs Grant in the kitchen or around the house, cleaning and laundering. Jack was only marginally buoyed on hearing the deported Islanders were being held together so his mother would be with people from home. And there were no longer the comforting smells of something delicious being created from scraps and uneventful rations. The very fabric of the house had changed. Dido and Persey had been cleaning and attempting to cook, laundering, folding, taking turns queuing dutifully at the grocer's, baker's and the butcher's, not that there was ever much of excitement available. And rations seemed to be getting worse, with only milk rations having increased marginally.

Stefan managed to get hold of slightly more food than they

normally had access to and every now and again he would word-lessly place a precious, small piece of meat on the cold stone in the larder for Persey to find. Autumn was drawing in and the blackout times were changing. Try as she might she still couldn't get her head around German time on the island and its strange habit of bringing the darkness too early or too late depending on the time of year.

Dido was singing tonight. Since their row, their relationship had been strained. There was still sisterly love between them, but it appeared to be stretched very thinly now from Dido's side. As far as Persey knew, Dido was still seeing her German man but now Dido kept her cards very close to her chest about it all.

After a muted dinner one evening, Dido stood to leave.

'I will accompany you if you do not mind,' Stefan said. 'I am in sore need of an evening of gaiety.'

Persey had long since given up offering to accompany her sister. For one thing, she couldn't face sitting in a room full of what Islanders affectionately described as 'greenfly' due to the colour of the uniforms. And for another thing, she had 'work' to do, listening to the wireless, the act of which had long been rendered complicated by Stefan's return. She had promised Doctor Durand she would try to listen as often as possible, and she'd managed to, very discreetly, listen to as many broadcasts as she could over the past months, writing down what she heard and delivering it to him. She suspected it was a newspaper contact who was writing up her shorthand into English and then printing the resistance newspaper. Either way, she didn't want to know. She had chosen moments to listen at night when both the news was being broad-cast and when Stefan was out – the two of which hardly ever seemed to coincide.

She hoped that the risk she was taking had helped Islanders in some small way, knowing what was happening miles from Guernsey . . . knowing that slowly, so slowly there were gains being made by the Allies. If only it would progress faster though.

She'd seen a copy of the illicit news sheet at Doctor Durand's house one evening as he'd proudly brandished it, and explained that he intended to let patients read it as they came and went from his surgery. She glowed with pride. She had helped do this. She had helped offer hope to Islanders who had no idea what was happening in the theatre of war. People knew snippets of detail and it was, in part, because of her.

She'd listened intently when the BBC, who knew of the radio confiscations throughout other occupied countries, had listed detailed instructions how to go about making a crystal radio set, which often involved the use of headsets that hardly anyone on the island owned. It was little surprise that there had been a spate of theft of receivers from telephone boxes across Guernsey.

Persey was now grateful that they still had their wireless. But that was only half the battle as she'd had to confess to Jack and Dido what she was doing as they too avidly listened to the news broadcasts when Stefan was out. She could hardly sit and scribble notes for half an hour without them catching on. She'd expected to be berated for her dangerous activity, but on telling them what she was planning, Jack had simply said, 'Good girl. Another one in the eye for the Germans.'

Dido had looked at her sister and had simply said, 'There's now two of you in this house engaging in clandestine activity. Please be careful where it leads.'

Before she went to work, Persey delivered the news she'd written to Doctor Durand, if she'd managed to listen without Stefan present. Doctor Durand, in turn, delivered it to his newspaper contact. She didn't want to know who the contact was or who the other Islanders were who were listening to the broadcasts. The fewer people who knew about the others in the chain the better, in her opinion.

She knew she ran the risk of being discovered with sheets of news on her person and so she'd pulled on her clerical skills, writing it in shorthand on carbon copy pads she had liberated from the office. She reasoned that if she came across a sudden German checkpoint en route to Doctor Durand's she could dispense with the sheets by ripping them into tiny pieces and scattering them to the wind and – if need be – she could fall back on the carbon copy and deliver it later in the day without the need to listen to the wireless again later that night or rack her memory for the specific details of the news reports, the exact number of Allied wins and Axis losses – for that was surely the way round it should be.

Then, to be sure to evade detection that little bit further, she folded the sheets up and lined her brassiere with them. It made for a most uncomfortable bicycle ride, the paper scraping against her bust as she cycled. But it was nothing to the horrors rumoured to be being carried out across Europe, and so she put up with it.

That evening, Persey pulled the wireless out of its hiding place in the pantry. Was it her imagination or did it get heavier each time? Usually Jack lifted it in and out if he was home. His frenetic comings and goings had decreased over the past month, but he was still openly flouting curfew, even with Stefan in the house, especially with Stefan in the house – taunting him, she imagined. But Stefan had, so far, not noticed the baiting or if he had, he just didn't care enough to comment.

She checked that the front and back doors were locked and she left the hiding place open, ready to lift the wireless back into place and cover it over should the Germans knock at the door. It was still nerve-racking, and she went to the cabinet to help herself to a drop of Stefan's last bottle of brandy. She needed to calm her nerves, but she knew others on the island were engaging in far more frightening activities. Doctor Durand was hiding Lise, and had been for the greater part of three years. The least she could do was hide a wireless.

She looked through the bundle of shorthand notes she'd made. She really should burn them now they'd served their purpose. Dido had told her as much, absolutely horrified to find out Persephone had kept hold of them for the time being. But every time she pulled them out to burn them she found herself rereading them, filling her with something almost like joy – knowing that what she'd been doing had helped in some small way. It was all she had.

She tuned in and listened as the comforting chimes of Big Ben announced the news at nine o'clock in Britain.

'This is the BBC . . . and now for another piece of good news.'

She sipped her brandy and began writing, then paused, not quite able to believe what she'd just heard. *'Italy has today declared war against Nazi Germany.'*

Her pencil hovered over the paper and she opened her mouth and exclaimed, 'Oh my word.' This was it. This had to be it. The end had to be soon if even Germany's closest friends in war were now turning against them. Remembering too late she was supposed to be writing she quickly continued her shorthand. She'd missed a bit, but the thrust of the matter was still there. When the news finished, she sat back as the announcer told listeners to stay on for the BBC Orchestra. She'd have dearly loved to listen to that, but it wasn't worth the risk. As it was, Stefan could walk in at any minute and she still had to lift the—

'I did not know you still had your wireless,' a voice came from the kitchen doorway. 'Have you had it all this time?'

Persey leapt. In her haste to switch the offending article off, she knocked the glass of brandy over, the remnants of its sticky contents spilling across the table.

She stood and then leant quickly forward and switched the radio off as if by doing so she could somehow spirit it away. Like a child playing hide-and-seek and simply covering their eyes. She stood and stared at Stefan and he stared back at her. He looked at the sheets of paper on the table. It was too late to hide them. The front door had been locked. She had been sure of it. She had bolted it herself. She'd intended to unlock it after she'd finished listening.

'How did you get in?' she asked in horror.

'I didn't get in. I was already in. I have been reading in my room.'

She could have screamed. How had she been so stupid? She

had been so convinced he had been out as usual that it didn't occur to her to check inside his room.

'I could have sworn, through the floorboards, that I heard the chime of Big Ben. And then . . .'

'And then?' Persey prompted warily as she glanced at the wireless and the sheets of paper, wishing it would all disappear.

'And then I thought I was going mad.'

Wordlessly he moved to the kitchen cupboards and retrieved a cut-glass tumbler, lifting the bottle and pouring himself a measure. He put it back on the kitchen table and looked at her before laughing to himself. He eyed her glass. 'I did not know you drank alone these days.'

'I do all kinds of things I shouldn't do these days,' she dared.

Stefan laughed. 'I can see that,' he said before sitting down at the table and glancing at the wireless. The creases surrounding his eyes when he smiled vanished. 'So do I,' he said darkly, looking into his glass.

'How long were you standing there?' she asked.

'Long enough to hear Italy change sides,' he replied. He raised his glass. 'What is it Dido says? Down the hatch?' He took a sip.

'It's good for us,' Persey said. 'The Allies, I mean.'

'It's good for all of us,' he said, holding her gaze.

'The war might end quicker. You might get to go home.'

He nodded, looked at her and then away. 'Home. Yes.' He drank from his glass, leant over and topped up hers with a finger of brandy. He exhaled.

Too late she remembered his home had been destroyed, his parents killed. She could have kicked herself. Instead, she picked up her glass, sticky around the side where she'd knocked it over. She wiped her fingers on her dress but it did no good. 'Shouldn't you arrest me?' she probed, knowing he wouldn't but wanting to know his thoughts regardless.

He looked up from his glass and blinked. 'Arrest you? Because of the wireless?'

She nodded.

'Or because of the notes you are making?'

'Both,' she said, knowing there was no possible excuse for them.

He shook his head. 'What is this?' he asked, indicating the writing.

'Shorthand.'

He looked interested. 'I can't read this.'

'That's rather the point.'

'I can't arrest you,' he said, his blue eyes trained on hers. 'Even if I wanted to. I am only a translator, although I cannot translate this,' he said with a hint of laughter.

'But you're not going to tell me to stop?'

His tone changed. 'Do what you like, Persephone. You always do.'

'What does that mean?' she asked indignantly.

'I am not going to tell a soul you have a wireless. I would not do that. Keep listening to the BBC. I will listen with you. Keep writing your notes. I will not even ask what they are for.'

She swallowed. 'You don't want to know?'

'I have my suspicions. But, the less I know, the better, don't you agree?'

She looked at him, accepting his challenge. 'All right,' she said.

He leant forward and stretched out his hand. She reached out towards it and then recoiled, embarrassed, when it was clear his intention wasn't to hold her hand at all but to switch the wireless back on.

Embarrassed, she pulled back swiftly and took a large drink of her brandy.

In the morning, Persephone met Stefan as she was coming out of the bathroom. He smiled at her, stood aside to let her pass and she looked away as she passed him, unsure quite where they stood now. There was so much that had been spoken about between them, and so much that still remained to be said.

255

She had to tell Dido that Stefan knew about the wireless. And that he knew about the notes she was making for the news sheet. And she wondered when she told Jack, what his reaction would be. Jack needed to know that Stefan was categorically on their side. No matter how many times Dido and Persey had tried to reassure Jack that their friend of old was not a Nazi, Jack simply couldn't believe them. Even after Stefan had kept his suspicions about Jack secret, still Jack distrusted him. That distrust was ingrained. But now Stefan knew about the radio, surely that was different. Surely Jack would now see?

If she didn't tell Jack and Dido tonight, it would come as a shock to all of them when they sat down to listen to the wireless to find Stefan joining them. Perhaps she shouldn't tell them. She could do with a bit of light amusement amid all the darkness they were subject to. She laughed just thinking about it as she climbed onto her bicycle.

Jack, Dido and Persey set off at the same time. Jack to his job at the camera shop, Dido to goodness knew where. She felt Dido was being uncharacteristically discreet about her whereabouts, but she daren't ask if she was off to meet her young man in case Dido leapt down her throat about it all again. Persey didn't want to set the cat amongst the pigeons that morning. Now she'd given it more thought she wanted Dido to be happy, she did. In this time of war when happiness was hard to come by, she felt her sister should take the rare opportunity. It was just such a shame the young man in question was German. There could be no happiness in the long term, no future for Dido and her German. Surely Dido saw that? Perhaps Dido didn't think in the long term. Perhaps she was happy for now and that was enough, regardless of the shame it brought with it. Persey wasn't like that. She just couldn't be like that.

She said goodbye to them as they set off towards town and she took the lanes towards Doctor Durand's house, intending to deliver her little bundle of shorthand papers.

She smiled watching Dido and Jack cycle away, Jack lifting

himself from his seat and cycling harder, glancing at Dido, challenging her to keep up as they cycled out of sight. Jack, always hurtling towards an unseen finishing line.

Some things never change, Persey thought with a laugh as she turned in the direction of La Rue des Fontenelles, the road that hugged the coast. If what Dido had said was true and Jack was intending to escape and return to England to rejoin the army, then Mrs Grant's deportation would have only added fuel to that particular fire. Persey glanced at her watch, then looked out over the patch of road that ran into the cliff path down towards Les Sommeilleuses, letting the wind whip her hair as she breathed in the fresh sea air.

She slowed, coming to a stop. The path was rocky at points, narrow, winding but provided the most perfectly rugged of seascapes. While the Nazis had tried to destroy the beauty of the island through the concrete fortifications, there was one thing the Nazis couldn't take from them, the view out to sea, out to freedom that felt as if it lay just that little bit closer with each passing month and now, with each passing news announcement.

'Papers, please,' a voice came from behind her.

Persey turned to find a German on a bicycle. It was the soldier who had delivered Mrs Grant's deportation notice, the soldier who had seen her that night in the woods, running, after Jack's boat never came for him; the soldier who recognised her. Of all the soldiers on the island, why him?

'Papers, please,' he repeated.

She obliged and pulled her identity papers from her little satchel handbag, not daring to remind him they had met before so he shouldn't need to see her papers, in case he pointed out the fact that of course he had seen her running.

He looked at her papers far too thoroughly as Persey glanced around. It was only the two of them on this stretch of road. How had he appeared behind her so suddenly? Had he been following her? How long for?

'Did I just pass you on the road without noticing you?' she asked knowing that couldn't have been the case.

He glanced from her papers to her, chose not to reply and then glanced back down.

'These are in order.' He handed them back to her. 'Where are you going?' he demanded.

It was on the tip of her tongue to reply with none of your business but instead she chose, 'To work.'

'You work in St Peter Port. At an insurance company.'

Persey's mouth dropped open. 'How do you know that?' It wasn't shown on her identity card. More importantly, why did he know that? Her papers only said that her job was as a secretary.

He looked past her. 'You are going the wrong way to St Peter Port.'

'I thought to call in on a friend first.'

'It is early for a house call,' he suggested.

'Got to get them in before curfew,' she said challengingly.

'Your bag please.'

'What?' Persey demanded.

'I would like to search your bag.'

'Whatever for?'

'Bag please.'

'Good God, this is ridiculous. Don't you have anything better to do?' She took the bag off her handlebars and handed it over to him.

He looked inside and opened her little stub of red lipstick, worn down so she now had to scoop out some of the inner tube with her finger to apply it. He looked inside her purse and her heart raced as she imagined he might steal from her. He opened it and raised his eyebrows. 'You have a large number of Reichsmarks here.'

'Not so as you'd notice,' she said.

'I have noticed,' he said simply. 'What are you doing with the money?'

'Nothing. I withdrew it from the bank and it's ready if I should need it.' In truth it was for Doctor Durand to help pay for Lise's ongoing presence.

'For black market purchases?' the soldier asked.

'No, of course not,' Persey said sharply. The money she had in her purse was nowhere near enough to purchase anything of use on the black market; she knew that much. What she'd have given for the chance to buy a bag of sugar on the sly. But even that had gone up to an eye-watering sum now, when it could be found. 'What kind of person do you think I am?' she said primly.

He inched closer. 'You are the kind of person who runs through the woods in the middle of the night when you should not.'

Persey stiffened, waited for what was sure to follow.

'I was reprimanded for that.' He let the sentence hang in mid-air.

'Reprimanded for what?' Persey asked cautiously, but wished she'd not let the conversation continue.

'For insisting it was you.'

'It wasn't me,' she said quickly.

'This is what your . . . what shall we call him . . . boyfriend? This is what your boyfriend said at the time. Assured me you would not do such a thing.'

'He's not my boyfriend,' she said, hoping to push the conversation off course, hoping he wasn't about to arrest her, or take her to the Gestapo. But if he did, and they searched her . . . She had not been quick enough to remove the papers from her brassiere, had not even heard the soldier behind her.

He looked past her, dismissively.

'You had better continue on your way, Miss Persephone Le Roy of Deux Tourelles.'

He watched as she climbed back onto her bicycle, and slowly set off. She would not turn and look at him, would not make eye contact again with him if she could help it. She prayed that he wasn't following her. Minutes later, when she reached the edge of the Durand property, she paused and only then did she allow herself the luxury of turning. She climbed from her bicycle, propped it against the fence and bent to tie her shoelace so that, should he pass her, he would hopefully not think she was stopping there. Mrs Durand opened the front door and raised her hand to wave. Persey shook her head at her sternly and Mrs Durand immediately closed the door understanding something was amiss.

Persephone waited, listening closely. There was more than her life at stake here. There was the doctor and his wife. There was Lise. Persey changed her mind. It was not worth the risk to any of their lives, delivering this bundle. They had others who were listening to the wireless, surely. It wasn't just her. And delivering the news of Italy turning their backs on the Germans and joining the Allies was not worth such risk to any of them. No, she wouldn't do it. Not now. She could try again later.

She could see Mrs Durand watching from the kitchen window and Persey smiled weakly, gave a small shake of her head for the second time, hoping it relayed everything she needed it to, turned her bicycle round and went back the way she'd come. It was only as she saw him, up ahead where the coast path snake-lined the cliff that she realised her mistake. She should not have gone back the way she'd come. Of course he would know she could not have visited anyone in such a short space of time. She should have carried on, gone a very indirect route towards town.

The soldier looked at her with an expression that told her she was right to have feared him. She chastised herself for her stupidity and nodded to him in recognition as she attempted to pass him.

'You have chosen not to make your visit?' he said, barring her way. She came to a stop.

Why was he still here? On his own? What was he doing? Was he waiting for her?

'No, I'm afraid you stopping me like that has now made me late. I don't have time,' she said tersely.

'Perhaps you will visit your friend later. Just down there is it?'

She made to start pedalling, choosing not to reply.

'I am talking to you,' he said.

'What do you want?' she snapped. 'Why are you following me?'

'It is you behaving erratically.'

'Leave me alone,' she demanded.

Within seconds he had moved towards her. She put her foot on her pedal and tried to cycle away, but his hand came out and took hold of one of her wrists. 'Get off your bicycle,' he said.

'No.'

'I admire your courage.' He tightened his grip and spoke slowly. 'I told you to get off your bicycle.'

Her courage failed now, but she held his gaze and repeated, 'No.'

'If you want me to forget I ever saw you in the woods that night, you will get off your bicycle and come with me. If you want me to forget that man of yours has been defying the Führer and lying for you, you will come with me.'

'What do you mean?' she said through dry lips. Her voice caught in her throat.

'Do not play coy,' he said.

No. He couldn't possibly mean what she thought he did.

'What are you going to do?' she asked. But she knew.

'The Islanders have a word for women like you,' he said. 'You are a Jerrybag? No?'

'No,' she spat. 'I am not a Jerrybag.'

'Come with me,' he said, pulling her from her bicycle. It clattered to the ground and she hopped awkwardly from it, catching her foot in the frame as his hands went round her waist and he pulled her further away from her means of escape.

'What are you doing?' she demanded in horror. This isn't happening. This can't be happening.

'Are Nazis better than English men in bed?' he said. 'Is that why some of you girls sleep with my fellow soldiers so willingly?'

'Oh my God,' she cried and began lashing out. 'Get off me,' she cried. 'Get off me.'

'Do not struggle,' he demanded. 'Or it will take longer.'

'No,' she screamed, begging silently for anyone to hear her. 'No,' she repeated over and over as he pulled her towards where the cliff jutted up, a large rock pointing skyward, just big enough to hide them. Is that why he had waited? He had known she would come back this way. Is that why he had chosen this exact point? He started to pull at her dress, his hands over her breasts. She felt the rustle of the paper against her skin. Oh God, the news she had written down.

Whatever happened next, she could not let him find it. That would be proof enough to condemn her. She lashed out with even more violent force than before, scratching him, kicking him in the shin. He bent over in pain, loosening his grip enough for her to break free, but he was upon her too quickly, dragging her back. She screamed as he pushed her into the rock, slamming her body against it and in agony she slumped to the ground. He looked down at her, took off his helmet and it was this nod to undressing that forced Persey into action, kicking out at him again, turning over, trying to gain ground as she scrabbled away like a wild animal.

He launched himself onto her, pinning her down and forcing her over onto her back. Persey scrabbled at the rocks, dirt and gravel embedding sharply under her fingernails, grabbing at rocks and anything she could to gain ground, but it was no use. He looked into her eyes with thinly veiled triumph. And with one final, desperate need to stop him, to live, to survive she grabbed a small, stray rock and swung her hand up, smashing it into his skull.

The first blow stunned him. But it was the second time she hit him with the sharpest point of the object that did the most damage, unsettling him from his kneeling position over her. He rolled off her, onto his back, clutching his head. She watched blood trickle down his face and without thinking, rolled towards him as quickly as she could. Fear, anger, hatred gripped her and she knelt over him. His eyes filled with horror as she struck him again, screaming and screaming at him, letting out all the anger she'd been holding, not just against him these past few minutes, but against the Nazis, for what they were forcing upon Islanders, upon Europe. The bloodshed they had caused, the hatred towards the Jews, that innocents such as Lise had been forced into hiding – or worse, scooped up and taken away, that good men like Stefan had been swept up, however unwillingly as part of their cause, that Dido was now falling for a man she couldn't be with, that Persey and Stefan could never be, not now, not like this. She let all the anger and hatred flow out of her as she slammed the rock into him over and over and over, screaming and screaming, drowning out his shouts that died away with the wind until he lay motionless.

Her breath came thick and fast and she stared at him, waiting for him to move, to justify her hitting him again. She didn't dare take her eyes off him, didn't dare close them for a fraction of a second to blink. She waited until the watering pain of keeping her eyes open forced her to, expecting him to take his chance to move the very moment she did. If he moved again, she would hit him. She gripped the rock tighter. But he didn't stir. She watched him for a minute or two, losing track of time. But the blood was everywhere, over him, over her and her hands, over the ground. As her vision cleared and she saw the scene around them, eventually she knew he wasn't going to move; his chest no longer rising and falling in time to his breath. He had no breath left to give. He wasn't going to move ever again.

She got up off her knees and slumped back into a sitting position. Gravel had embedded into her legs, her stockings were ripped and the rock in her hands was so bloody she could barely see what it was she was holding. She sat for far too long, not knowing what she could do. If she went to Doctor Durand's she would involve him, all of them, in something so horrific. Everyone in that cottage was already in the most precarious position. She stood up, slowly, her legs wobbling and looked down at the dead soldier, his head caved in on one side, blood spattered down his uniform, his face no longer recognisable due to the volume of blood coating it.

And suddenly she sobbed, great heaving sobs. She had killed a man. She had taken a life. She shook uncontrollably and slumped against the rocks, crying into her bloodstained hands, the rock that had become a weapon scraped her face, but she could not let go.

And then another thought struck her. They would kill her. When the Germans found her and found out what she'd done, they would kill her. And she would deserve it. A life for a life. They would execute her. She closed her eyes, resigning herself to it. Persey stood straighter and looked at the man she had killed. He was dead and soon she would follow him there. In trying to survive, she had just secured her own death.

Slowly she unfurled her fingers from the rock and let it drop to the ground. She picked up her bicycle, wheeled it a few paces before climbing on and looking back one final time.

The dead soldier was behind the rock, his legs sticking out, but she made no move to hide him. It was too late to pretend it had not happened. Solemnly she cycled towards home. She would wipe the blood off herself, write a letter to Dido telling her she was sorry for everything, sorry for the argument so long ago, sorry for not being a better sister, sorry for having killed someone, sorry for leaving her on her own. She would write a letter to Jack asking him to take care of Dido. And then, so no one else on the island could be blamed for the death of this man, she would hand herself in to the Gestapo, knowing that very soon she would be made an example of and would stand in front of a German firing squad.

Chapter 25

2016

Spread over three floors, the Island Archives was housed in the deconsecrated St Barnabas Church in Cornet Street. Thousands of documents, files, books and images tracing Guernsey's history from the fourteenth century until present day were contained within the space and when Will and Lucy checked with the receptionist what they were able to look at, they were overwhelmed.

'There's a lot here,' Will said, gulping.

Lucy scanned the walls as files and leather books littered the interior. In truth, she'd had enough staring at walls today. At Deux Tourelles she'd been painting all morning, shifting furniture into the centre of rooms, laying down dust sheets and familiarising herself with which paint colours she'd chosen for each room as she'd totally forgotten since the trip to the DIY shop. Once she'd started with the roller, she had become unstoppable and had put the first coats of a beautiful 'drawing room blue' in the main sitting room and a pale 'estate green,' in the dining room. It had made all the difference. She'd just made a start on the hallway with a dove grey, deciding to pick out the skirting boards in a variation of the grey tone for a subtle pop of difference when a reminder had sounded on her phone and she'd forced herself to down tools, shower off all the paint she'd somehow flicked into her hair and make her way into St Peter Port to meet Will at the archives.

When the research assistant had shown them where the visitor desks were Will had taken hold of Lucy's hand and held it up. The sudden move had made her gasp, but he'd just looked at the streak of dark blue paint she'd failed to scrub off, smiled and let go of her hand gently.

'Drawing room blue,' she muttered, still reeling, not unhappily, from the shock of Will's touch.

He smiled knowingly. 'Swanky. How long do you have to paint the entire house?' He made a face indicating the mammoth task ahead of her.

'We've booked the photographer for next week so I'm cracking on with it. I'm quite enjoying it, actually. It's pure therapeutic joy. Apparently, the estate agent has already got someone interested, would you believe? Clara only signed the paperwork this morning. It's not even on the open market yet but there's a family from the mainland been looking for a large home in Guernsey for a while, so the agent says.'

'It might not matter at all if you don't paint it then,' Will suggested. 'If they're already keen.'

She looked at the blue stain on her hand and thought of the hours she'd put in, the hours of painting left to go. 'Don't say that,' she groaned.

'OK,' the woman said, returning. 'Here's the information you requested.'

'Requested?' Lucy asked.

'I called ahead,' Will replied. 'Asked for anything relating to the house in the Germans' files. There's a small research charge, but it's worth it. Look at this place. I wouldn't know where to start.'

Lucy gave him an impressed look.

'I know. Aren't I clever?' he said with a smile.

The woman continued. 'I found only two documents relating

266

to the time you mention. Deux Tourelles crops up in a few of the German military records left behind—'

'Yes,' Will cried triumphantly. 'I knew they didn't take their records with them.'

'We're lucky,' the researcher said. 'They destroyed a lot of them. But we have a good record of the day-to-day running of the Occupation. A few non-essential files are in German, but those we have translated into English show the name of the house only crops up a handful of times, in particular in staff accommodation files, deportation files—'

'Deportation?' It was Lucy's turn to interrupt. 'What kind of deportation?'

The researcher handed them a box and smiled. 'Shall I let you find out?' She pointed them in the direction of the research tables telling them to come to her if they needed anything explaining or wanted to call up any further documents.

They sat and Lucy opened the box, not really sure what to expect in the bundle that the researcher had just outlined.

The deportation orders had been typed into a list and there were a few lines of text relating to a Mrs Matilda Grant, residing at Deux Tourelles in 1942, Occupation: Housekeeper. She was listed among names slated for deportation in September 1942.

'This is the English being sent home?' Will asked.

'No, you mainlander,' Lucy teased. 'This is the English being sent to Germany. To camps.'

He nodded as Lucy continued, 'All non-island-borns were sent to civilian camps for the duration of the war.'

'Why?'

'Some convoluted retaliation against German citizens being taken prisoner by the Allies elsewhere in the crazy realm of war.'

He shook his head. 'OK. That was news to me. What else is in here?'

Lucy turned to the next document: Feldkommandantur files relating to staff passes and staff accommodation. 'The

Feldkommandantur was the division in charge of running the Occupation,' she explained briefly. 'Food supplies, utilities, infrastructure and keeping the civilian population in check.' Will gave a mock-yawn and Lucy nudged him in the ribs. 'This is serious,' she chastised.

They read the complex file listing ranks and serial numbers until she found on the page a Captain Stefan Keller, who had been billeted at Deux Tourelles from near on the beginning of the Occupation until some time in 1943. Further information followed about the size of the house and the availability of suitable accommodation before the following entry showed the next available property and listed another officer being billeted and so on and so forth down the page.

'This can't be it?' she said. 'Where's Persephone? Where's Dido?'

'Perhaps there was no need for the Germans to mention them in their files? I only asked for help looking up the house in relation to the Germans. Or if they did, maybe they're in the German-language files that the researcher mentioned. Hang on,' Will said and leapt up.

He returned a few minutes later. 'She's going to find the Identity Registration Forms for the sisters for us.'

Ten minutes later the researcher returned with copies of two identity cards. The top one was for Dido Le Roy. It listed her name, date of birth, address and employment as a cabaret singer, alongside her black and white photograph glued onto the page.

'Look at her when she was young. What a stunner,' Will said as they took in the fair hair and startling pale eyes. 'It's funny, thinking of Dido when I last saw her. I can see traces of that elderly woman in the photo of this young one. And I can see fragments of the woman she'd grow into in this picture here. But it still feels so odd to look at her this young.'

'I only have fragments of memories really,' Lucy said. 'From those family parties all those years ago.'

Dido was smiling into the camera; her eyes shining where light from the flash must have caught them. It gave her a real star quality. Her lips were painted crimson, which showed as a dark pout in the image. 'Good for her,' Lucy said. 'She was a beauty and must have known it.'

They turned the document on the table and looked at the one underneath, the identity document for Persephone Le Roy. 'And here she is,' Will said, looking at the black and white photograph attached to the document. 'The elusive Persephone.'

Lucy looked for a long time at the dark hair rolled into sweeps, the dark eyes, the unpainted lips, the wool cardigan draped over her shoulders and, more importantly, Lucy thought, the slightly defiant expression on her face, which smacked of a flat-out refusal to smile for the Germans while they were registering her details.

'She looks pissed off,' Will said abruptly and Lucy's raucous laugh broke the silence in the ancient building.

'She really does. Wouldn't you though?' Lucy asked. 'I'm not sure I'd have been too keen to be "registered" by an invading army so they knew where I lived, what I did for a job, my age . . .'

'It's even worse these days,' Will countered.

'Yes, I suppose. But back then, this must have all been so completely terrifying. So . . . alien.'

'If they were the only files available to us relating to the sisters at Deux Tourelles,' Will said, 'then that letter, the one saying she knew where a Jew was, can't have been taken seriously.'

'Or maybe it was,' Lucy replied. 'Maybe they raided the house to find the Jewish girl, didn't find her because she wasn't real, and so there's no record of it. They must have raided hundreds of houses, week in, week out for the entirety of the Occupation. Or maybe you're right. That wall in the museum had so many letters from Islanders informing on other Islanders, and if that was just a smattering of the selection sent, then I wouldn't be surprised to hear if the Germans learnt to weed out the bullshit pretty swiftly and ignored the vast majority or at least some of them.'

Lucy looked again at the photo of Persephone and then of Dido, wanting to remember what these women who had endured life during the Occupation looked like, before she handed the documents back.

'What do you want to do now?' Will asked.

'I'm not sure what else we can do. We still have no idea if Persephone was arrested and deported to an overseas prison. The online resistance site didn't list her and there's nothing here about her. You're probably right. Maybe the Gestapo left her alone.'

Chapter 26

Still shaking, Persephone wheeled her bicycle into the drive of Deux Tourelles. She stared, wide-eyed at the house. It would be one of the last times she would see it, and she drank it in, bathed in autumnal sunlight, the reddening ivy creeping its way gently northward on the wall where it had been allowed to grow unchecked since the start of the Occupation.

The front door swung open and Persephone paused, her heart clanging desperately in her chest. Stefan stood on the front steps, staring at her, blinking. She looked down at her clothes, bloody and torn, and then up at him seeing herself through his eyes. His mouth dropped, but he said nothing and then, coming to his senses he rushed towards her.

'You are hurt,' he cried. 'What has happened?' He stopped only a few feet from her.

She swallowed, hardly daring to say it; hardly daring to tell him the awful truth of what she had done. And then when she didn't he demanded. 'Tell me,' he cried, reaching out to touch her and then finding nowhere suitable to place his hand, he dropped it. 'You are hurt,' he repeated. His eyes darted, taking in the complete picture of her.

'No,' she said and then, looking at her palm, still indented from

271

where she'd clutched the rock so tightly, and her knuckles and back of her hand smeared with her own blood mixed with that of the soldier's. 'Yes, a little but—'

'Persey,' he demanded. 'Tell me. Who did this to you?'

'No one. I did it.'

'I do not under—'

'I've killed someone,' she said dumbly. 'A man. I've killed a man.'

He stared at her, slack-jawed, and whispered, 'What? How?' And then suddenly, he pulled her by the arm, 'Come inside. Now. Quickly.'

He dragged her inside the house, leaving her bicycle lying on the ground outside. She glanced back at it. Someone might take it. She would have no use for it where she was going, but it would serve as a decent spare for Dido or Jack. Strange how such a mundane and practical thought came to her now. Stefan slammed the door behind him and stood in front of her. 'Tell me. Tell me what happened,' he said, his eyes never leaving hers. 'Who have you killed?' He spoke as if he didn't believe her.

'A soldier.'

He gasped. It made no difference if it was a soldier or a civilian in Persey's eyes. A man was still a man. A life was still a life.

'Why?' he asked in horror.

'He tried to . . . He had hold of me . . . He was going to . . .'

He muttered something quietly in German. He had turned white. 'And . . . did he?' Stefan asked. 'Did he hurt you?'

'Yes, but not like that.'

Stefan was still, his teeth clenched together, his jaw firm. 'I must think.'

'Will you take me to hand myself in?' she whispered, her voice failing her. 'I can't have anyone else blamed for this.'

His eyebrows lifted. 'What?' he asked. 'Where do you want me to take you?'

'To the Gestapo. To the Feldkommandantur. I don't know. Somewhere.'

'No,' he almost shouted. 'Absolutely not. I need to think.' He wiped his hand across his eyes as Persey stood still in the hallway looking calmer than she felt.

'Did anyone see you?' Stefan asked.

'No,' she said.

'Are you sure? Where was this?'

'On the cliffs by Les Sommeilleuses. Can you fetch me some paper?' she asked suddenly. 'I don't want to smear the carpet with blood.'

'What?' he asked again. 'Paper? What the hell do you need paper for?'

'I need to write something. I need to say goodbye to Dido. And to Jack. I need him to take care of her for me. She'll be left alone now.' She spoke absently. Her voice blank, flat, devoid of emotion.

'No,' he said. 'I am not going to do that. You are not going to do that. I am going to help you.'

She looked at him and blinked. 'Are you going to bring a man back to life?'

'No,' he said. 'I'm going to move his body. If no one saw you and if he has not been found yet, I still have time. Where is he?'

'Oh, Stefan,' she said. She reached out to touch his face, but her hands were tainted with the soldier's blood and she couldn't stain him with what she'd done.

'Where exactly is he?' Stefan roared, taking her by her shoulders and shaking her quickly, bringing her to her senses.

'He's behind one of the large rocks. I didn't hide him,' she was quick to point out. 'It's where he dragged me to . . .'

'Wait here,' he said. 'No. Don't wait here. Go upstairs. Go to the bathroom. Clean the blood from you. Burn your clothes. They cannot be saved. Do not tell anyone what happened. Do you understand?'

She stared at him, her mouth open, but she couldn't think of anything to say.

'Do it now,' he shouted at her and she blinked, slipped off her

273

shoes, picked them up and carried them upstairs towards the bathroom. Behind her came the sound of the front door being slammed in haste as Stefan left to find the dead soldier.

Persey ran the bath, watching the water absently run far in excess of what was deemed necessary in times of war. There wasn't enough water in the world to clean her of what she had done. But, under orders, she stripped, leaving the bloodstained clothes on the floor. She found the last of the soap nestled in the dish and scrubbed her body until it was red raw from both the heat of the water and from her ferocious scrubbing. She soaked her hair and watched as the water around her took on a red tinge and she could stand being in the discoloured water no longer.

When she was dry and dressed, she let her hair hang wet, dripping water down her back and soaking her clothes as she moved slowly, unseeing, unthinking. She scooped up her bloodstained clothes and the shorthand notes from the bathroom floor and step by step descended the staircase towards the sitting room, lighting a fire and watching as the kindling took, followed by the wood in the grate, branches broken from the garden trees. She dropped her bloodstained stockings in first, watching them spark and singe to nothing, and then dropped each of her garments on to the fire one by one, taking care to feed the fire gently so as not to douse the flames. The smell of burning cloth became repugnant.

She dropped the notes into the fire. She would not take them to Doctor Durand now. She sat on the floor and watched the flames take all evidence of her actions and then when no trace of the fabric or notes remained, she put her head in her hands and cried.

'Wake up,' Jack said as she shook her a while later. Persey opened her eyes. She must have fallen asleep in front of the fire; she had no idea how long she'd been there.

'I thought you were at work?' she said, blinking. Then the horror of what had happened caught up with her sleepiness and she tried not to throw up the remains of her breakfast.

'Oh good, you're all right,' Jack said in a bored voice. 'Thought you'd died you were in the strangest position. I've been to work,' Jack said, answering her question. 'I've come back.'

'What time is it?' Persey asked. Where was Stefan? What had happened to him?

'After twelve. I was only in for the morning. The rest of the day is mine. Anyone else in?'

Persey shook her head.

'Good,' he said conspiratorially. He sat next to her and threw a piece of bracken from the basket onto the fire. And then, from out of nowhere, 'I've got a boat. A proper one.'

Persey looked from the fire to Jack, who looked delighted with his news as he awaited her reaction. 'A boat?' she questioned dumbly. 'What do you mean you've got a boat?' She couldn't possibly have this conversation now. Out there, somewhere, Stefan was risking his life to save hers by hiding the body of a man. A man she had killed.

'Just that. I'm escaping. I've got to get out of here. I can't do this anymore. I can't . . . be here anymore.'

She closed her eyes and put her head in her hands and spoke into them. 'How have you got a boat?'

'The Germans made everyone with a working boat register them, hand them in for the duration, do you remember? Other than fishermen who aren't allowed out without a German onboard.'

Persey nodded.

'I've found one that's been missed.'

'Found?' she asked. 'How?'

'Remember Richard? One of my old school friends?'

Persey shook her head.

'Well anyway, he used to have this boat. More a dinghy really, but he saved up, bought a motor. We used to career about the bays in it for a time. I've got it.'

'How?'

'Saw his mother in St Peter Port. Told her what had happened to my mother; that she'd been deported. Asked after Richard and she said he'd joined the navy and she'd had no word since the Germans arrived. No Red Cross note, nothing. Imagine that. I said, in passing, that if I had a way I'd leave this godforsaken island and join Richard in utterly annihilating the Boche. She hinted I should have joined up before the Germans came. Took every bit of self-control I had not to tell her there and then that was exactly what I had bloody well done.

'Anyway, she told me to come for tea and then when I did, her husband told me they still had Richard's boat. They've been using it for storage in the barn, could you imagine. All this time, it's just been there. Waiting. I offered to take them with me, but they politely declined. Too old to make the journey to England at night. Because it will have to be at night. Said they'd rather remain here, safely, and wait for news of their son, which is fair. So . . .' he said proudly. 'What do you make of that?'

Persey didn't know what to make of it. 'Does the motor work?' she asked.

'Does now. What do you think I've been doing all this time in secret? Didn't want to get your hopes up but now it's all shipshape, so to speak, we can do it. We can leave.'

'We?'

'The three of us. You, me, Dido. It's only a two-seater really but you and Dido are slips of things and I'm not exactly carrying a lot of muscle anymore. So . . . we're off to England. We're off to join up. I've already joined up, but you know what I mean.'

Persey swallowed and said nothing.

'Good God, I thought you'd be pleased,' he said.

'I'm shocked.'

'You are coming, aren't you?' he said despondently.

'I . . . I don't know.' She needed to know what had happened to Stefan. She had to talk to him first before she made any decision.

'It's such a risk,' she said. 'How will you get the boat to the water, unseen?'

'Easy. Don't worry about that. Richard's father is going to trailer it down there. It'll be there after dark. Then on we hop and off we go.'

'It can't be that easy,' Persey said. 'They'll hear the motor. The Germans I mean, they'll hear the motor.'

'We'll row out as far as we can. Got to get past the rocks first anyway and then time it right for the patrols, kick the motor and we're away.'

Persey made a strange noise with her throat. 'It sounds too easy.'

'Does, doesn't it,' Jack replied triumphantly, missing her meaning.

When Persey said nothing more he pressed on. 'Look, I honestly thought you'd be pleased. Do you know . . .' he started. 'That I've never really felt . . .' He looked embarrassed as to what he was going to say, took a deep breath and continued. 'I've never really felt like much of a man. I've never had that chance to be the man of the house. My father was long gone and we came to live here with your family. And until a few years ago when he passed away, your father always made me feel like a son. But of course I never felt as if I had anything to contribute. Not really. I was always aware this house wasn't mine – it was yours. I know you'd never made Mum feel like "the help", or that I was just part and parcel of Mum being here. But then, joining up felt like the first real thing I'd ever done. It made me feel like a man, finally. And being chosen to be sent back here with a real task to complete . . . I can't tell you how lifting that felt.'

Persey reached out and held his hand.

'And then I got jolly well stuck here and I've felt just the worst ever since my mum got taken by the Germans. But now, I've got the chance to actually do something again; something useful. Allow me to do my mum proud. Allow me to do you and Dido

277

proud. Allow me to do your parents proud by getting their daughters the hell off this island.'

Persey smiled, leaned forward and hugged him. 'Oh, Jack,' she cried.

'Steady on, old girl.' He laughed. He looked over her shoulder as she continued holding him. 'I say, are those buttons in the fire?'

Behind them the front door closed and Stefan stood in the hallway looking at Persey and Jack by the fire. His face was one of confusion as he took in the scene in front of him. He ignored Jack and said to Persey, 'Are you all right?'

'Yes,' Persey said, standing up but not daring to go towards him. 'Are you?'

'Yes.'

Jack looked at each of them in turn before saying, 'I feel as if the two of you are having a silent conversation I can't hear. What's going on?'

When no one spoke, Jack stood up and said, 'Oh I see. I see it now. How long has this—' he motioned between Persey and Stefan '—been going on?'

'There is nothing between Persephone and I,' Stefan said, dragging his gaze away from Persey and angling it towards Jack.

'But you want there to be something,' Jack muttered.

'Yes,' Stefan admitted and Persey drew in a sharp breath. 'But that does not mean that there is something.'

'Persey's too sensible for that kind of thing,' Jack said. 'Aren't you, Perse? Wouldn't get involved with a man in that uniform, would you?'

'No,' Persey said quickly, all good feelings towards Jack diminishing rapidly. A look of sadness passed over Stefan's face.

'Besides, the only good Nazi is a dead one,' Jack said pointedly.

Persey watched Stefan for his reaction. The only good Nazi was a dead one. Oh, what awful words to choose to say just then. If only Jack knew.

'Think about what I said.' Jack touched her on the shoulder. 'Don't think about it for too long though.'

The moment Jack left the room, Stefan closed the door gently and looked at Persey. She felt the urgent need to put aside any suspicions he may have. 'Jack was upset,' she said. 'He just needed a friend. I was just holding him as a friend would do. I haven't told him anything.'

He nodded, indicating he believed her, then lifted a finger to his mouth to signal she should remain quiet. He waited, angling his ear towards the door, waiting for Jack to leave the hallway, then he moved towards her, took her hand and gently pulled her to the settee. 'I found the soldier,' he said, still holding her hand. 'Nobody else was there. I think nobody had found him yet.'

She nodded, her eyes darting to and from each of his anxiously, and he continued. 'He was not close to the cliff edge and he was not a light man, but in the end . . . it will look like an accident.'

'What will?' she asked in confusion.

'It will look like he fell.'

'Fell?' she frowned and then understood. 'Oh my God. Did you . . . did you push him over the edge?'

'I had to. I did not see what other choice I had. I could not take him anywhere. I could not hide him. And if a soldier goes missing, that would be more suspicious than if he is found at the bottom of a cliff with his bicycle.'

'But all the blood on the ground at the top?' she said.

'I covered it over with gravel. It was the best I could do.'

She nodded and looked down at his hand as it held hers. 'Thank you,' she said quietly. 'All because of those notes,' she said.

'What notes?' Stefan asked and Persey told him what she'd been delivering to Doctor Durand.

'I suspected as much. It will be all right,' he said, stroking her face.

She nodded, not quite believing it.

A knock sounded at the door and Jack entered without waiting to be told to come in. He saw them on the settee, hands entwined. Persey pulled her hand away far too late.

'I'm going out,' Jack said pointedly. 'I've got things to do.'

He cast Stefan a look and then slammed the sitting room door.

'Is he jealous?' Stefan asked.

'No,' Persey said, sighing. 'It's not like that. He's protective.'

She didn't want to think about Jack right now. This had been the most frightening experience of her life and the death of the soldier only served to illustrate how short life really was, especially if you were in the wrong place at the wrong time. As the soldier had been. As she had been earlier that day.

Is that what had happened to her and Stefan, back then? It had certainly been the wrong time all those years ago. And now it was both the wrong place and the wrong time: Guernsey in the midst of war. Here he was. But in that uniform. It was so difficult for her to get past, even with his emphatic dislike for what the Nazis were doing.

But life was fleeting. Wasn't that what Dido was always saying? She felt emboldened. She looked at his hands and reached over, taking one in hers, wanting to feel the warmth, the comfort emanating from him. He jolted, looking confused as she touched him.

'Thank you,' she said, not daring to lift her gaze to meet his. Her mouth had become dry. 'I owe you everything. I owe you my life.'

'No,' he said, his voice strained. 'You do not. What good are old friends if they will not help you in your hour of greatest need?'

'Friends,' she whispered.

'Yes,' he said. 'Friends.'

'Did you mean it?' she asked. 'After all this time. After your yearlong absence, did you really mean it when you said that you still would like . . .' She didn't know how to phrase it. 'That you would still like there to be something between us?'

His posture became stiff, wary and his tone even more so. 'Yes,' he said slowly.

280

She nodded. Her lips had become dry, the heat from the room suddenly overwhelming. She couldn't bring herself to say it, couldn't even bring herself to fully think the words she wanted to say. She stood up, reluctantly letting go of his hand. She moved away from him, towards the door. She rubbed her head, the pain of a new headache throbbing behind her eyes, her dry mouth begging for a glass of water.

She had to leave the room – had to go to the kitchen for a drink. She just needed a moment to think, alone. Perhaps she needed to sleep, although that couldn't be it as she'd slept while Stefan had been out.

'Excuse me,' she muttered, opening the door and leaving the sitting room.

In the kitchen, she took a glass to the sink and let the water run cold for a moment or two as she looked out of the window towards the garden. She needed to take her mind off him, off what had happened today. Outside she could see weeds springing up. No one had told her gardening was a never-ending task, but the vegetable patch needed tending to and there were so many jobs that—

'Persephone?'

Stefan had followed her into the kitchen. She turned slowly and looked at him.

'Yes?' she asked warily. She could not let her guard down. Not now. Not when she'd been so strong for so long.

'You are all right. It will be all right,' he said.

The words left her mouth before she could stop them: 'I want it too,' she said suddenly and clutched the glass of water so tight she was in danger of crushing it in her fingers. She put it down onto the side of the sink, spilling its contents while doing so.

'You want what?' he asked. On his face was a look of genuine puzzlement.

Everything Dido had said about Persey forcing love away from her had been true. The world had turned upside down, this island

281

had turned upside down, the war had done so much to throw her and Stefan back together, why not let it throw them even closer instead of driving them apart.

'I don't know,' she said, stumbling over the words she still couldn't quite find. 'Something. This. Perhaps. Between you and I. Only I don't know how—'

'Don't,' he said sharply, stepping back although he was already nowhere near her.

'Don't what?' she asked, the shock of rejection stinging more than she had expected.

He rubbed his hand into his blond hair and looked away.

'You do not want this,' he said. 'You do not want me.'

'I—'

'Don't, Persephone. Not like this.'

'What do you mean, not like this?' she asked. 'Like what then?'

'Not out of gratitude,' he said. 'Not because you feel you should. Not because you think I am "owed" anything. I am not a dog to be rewarded by throwing treats.'

She gasped. 'Throwing you treats? Is that what you think I'm doing? How can you say that to me?'

'After this long, you choose to hold my hand, seem to return my affection, tell me now that you want to be with me?' He looked at her, appearing to actually want a reasonable answer to his question.

'Yes?' she queried.

He nodded and then replied in a matter-of-fact tone. 'It is not because you want to. It is because you feel you should.'

'What—?' she tried to cut in.

But Stefan continued on, knocking the wind from her with his words. 'I love you. I have loved you for a long time, but even I will not let you humiliate yourself like that, and humiliate me, simply because you feel you are paying me for a job well done.'

She opened her mouth, but couldn't speak. Her chest felt as if it had caved in. His eyes wide with something resembling anger,

Stefan turned towards the door, placing both his hands on either side of the frame. His back moved up and down as he breathed heavily.

Neither of them spoke. The shock of his words forced tears from her eyes. She put her hand back over her mouth to prevent the noise of her sobs. He turned, sadly towards her.

'Please don't cry,' he said softly. 'I have done you a service by this, really.'

She couldn't reply, the tears flowing down her face, her throat choked with a hard lump.

When he spoke his tone was kind but the words hurt regardless. 'I suspect you will come nowhere near me now. And that is for the best. We both know where we stand. I did what I did because I hope it will save you from an unspeakable punishment. But I would have done the same to save Dido. I would even have done the same to save Jack. He does not view our friendship with the same lasting reminiscence that I do. But nonetheless . . .'

When it was clear he wasn't going to continue, she mustered every piece of courage she had and forced aside every scrap of dignity that remained. 'Stefan,' she said quietly, the lump in her throat threatening to strangle her words. 'Please believe me. I hate so many things about all of this. I hate that you wear that uniform. And I know you hate it too. I hate that we're trapped here like this. I hate what's happened today. I hate what you just did for me. But I love you.' Her words shocked her into silence before three, four seconds later she continued, 'I love you. Today has nothing to do with that. It's because of what we once almost were to each other, what we missed out on and what we could be. I love you. Please believe me.'

He was silent for a few moments, his face betraying nothing. 'I want to believe you. But you must get some rest,' he said. 'I do not expect anything from you for what I have just done.'

'Stefan,' she started again.

He interrupted to silence her. 'Persephone, if you still feel this

283

way in a month from now, two months from now, tell me again. And if not, then I will know and I promise that I will not mention this again. And I swear on all that is holy that I shall never tell a living soul what happened today on the cliff. I want you to know that.' He smiled kindly at her, and she could only stare after him as he left the room.

Chapter 27

Persephone spent the rest of the afternoon in bed crying and hating herself for it; hating herself for killing a man, hating herself for not being able to do more in this war. And hating herself for loving Stefan. For having never stopped. Not really.

When Dido entered the house, Persey washed her red eyes, neatened her hair and went to find her sister. Dido was shocked there was no dinner and set about starting something, cobbling together a few vegetables. 'I thought soup,' Dido stated. 'Mother really should have invested in cookery classes for us at some point or another,' she added. 'Bet she never thought she'd see the day when her two precious girls would have to cook their own suppers. Come back, Mrs Grant, all's forgiven.'

Persey nodded quietly.

'I'm joking, you know?' Dido said, and then when Persey didn't answer she continued. 'What do you think she's doing now? Mrs Grant I mean.'

Persey shrugged. 'I don't know,' she said listlessly. 'Surviving?'

Stefan joined them in the kitchen, organising a pot of what passed for tea, adding bramble leaves and placing the kettle on the range to warm. He stood silently, watching Persey. Persey avoided his gaze, the humiliation rising afresh.

'Do you know a Captain Werner Graf?' Dido asked, turning to Stefan.

'No,' he said. 'Should I know of him?'

'He's in the Feldkommandantur, like you.'

Stefan shook his head, turned back to watching Persey, a look of concern on his face that she tried her best to ignore.

'He's in charge of military . . . something. Not sure.'

'No. Different department. There are a lot of us here. There are too many of us here. Why?' Stefan asked, pulling his gaze towards Dido as she chopped vegetables.

'Just wondered,' Dido said.

'He is special to you?' Stefan asked and Dido reddened.

Persephone looked up at her sister, waiting cautiously.

'Well . . . I mean . . . I like him, certainly. He's kind and . . .' Dido looked away from the vegetables and gave Persey a challenging look. 'He's a good man. Looks after me. Takes me for nice lunches, long walks. Talks to me about music. About life. He owns a farm. Or rather his father does. I like him,' she repeated. 'I trust him.'

'You go out with him in public?' Persey asked.

'Yes, plenty of times,' Dido dared. 'And I know what you're going to say and it's already happened once or twice.'

Persey gasped, 'What has?' she asked in horror.

'People calling me a Jerrybag.'

'Oh, Dido,' Persey said mournfully. 'It was bound to happen.'

'What did you do?' Stefan asked. 'When they called you such an awful name?'

'Ignored them. Kept walking. What else could I do? One of them called me a Jerrybag when I was actually with Werner. It was all I could do to hold him back from shouting at her. I don't think they see it, the love. I don't think they believe a Guernsey girl could actually fall in love with a German. They can't see past the uniform. Much like you, Persey,' Dido said pointedly.

Stefan looked from Dido to Persey and back again, making no comment. But before Persey could spring to her own defence, Dido said, 'Anyway, I wanted you to know. If I'm not at the club and I'm not here, I'm with him. Nothing untoward has happened, before you ask. He's a gentleman. He's kind. But I didn't want to bring him here for fear of you and Jack losing your minds. But I wanted you to know. I don't like secrets.'

'Neither do I,' Persey said, knowing she had plenty of secrets of her own. She loved Stefan, Stefan had helped move the body of a man she had killed, Dido loved an officer, Lise was in hiding, Doctor Durand and she were helping supply a clandestine newsletter, and Jack was planning to escape.

'Enough,' Persey said, standing. 'Enough.'

'Where are you going?' Stefan asked.

'I'm going to get the remainder of your brandy and drink most of it if no one has any objections.'

'Good Lord.' Dido laughed, missing her sister's depressed tone. 'Are we having a party? Are we about to get squiffy?'

Stefan smiled kindly. 'Why not?'

When Persey returned with the brandy, she poured three glasses and kept the bottle far too close to herself. There was no way she could disappear from this island so she may as well disappear inside herself.

'Will you be here this evening,' Dido asked Stefan far too casually.

He narrowed his eyes. 'Yes?'

'Oh.'

'Why?' he asked.

'No reason,' Dido trilled.

'What happens this evening?'

'Nothing,' Dido said.

'He knows about the wireless,' Persey said darkly, draining her glass and pouring herself another. 'He knows I've been transcribing the news. And why.'

Jack stood in the doorway. 'Well now we're all done for, aren't we?' he cried. 'Why did you tell him?'

'Hello, Jack,' Stefan said.

'Hello, German.'

'He caught me in the act and don't be so bloody rude. I'm sick of it. Apologise,' Persey ordered.

'No,' Jack said petulantly. 'It's not offensive to call him a German. He is. I didn't call him a Nazi.'

'Well done,' Stefan said. 'I am very proud of you.'

'Fuck off,' Jack ordered, but Stefan said nothing, poured the water from the hot kettle into the pot and placed it on the side.

'Tea?' Stefan asked Jack.

'Not when you're all drinking the last of the brandy, no,' he said, fetching a glass.

It was Dido who spoke next. 'He knows Persey's been risking her life to deliver the news and he's not said a word to anyone. He's not our enemy, Jack. He's our friend. He always has been.'

'Yes . . . well . . . remains to be seen. Not going to inform?' Jack suggested. 'I hear there's been a lot of that going on of late.'

'No,' Stefan said. 'I'm not.'

'Well in that case, shall we have a listen later. Joining us, Stefan? Want to hear about your mad Führer's latest plans to invade somewhere else? Where does he fancy next, do you think, the moon?'

Stefan laughed suddenly. 'Yes, I do actually want to hear.'

'Want to hear about the imminent downfall?' Jack continued. 'Heard Italy have turned on you, old chap. That's Russia and Italy knowing which side their bread's buttered.'

'They have not turned on me,' Stefan said. 'They have turned on the Nazis. Not all of us are Nazis. Not all of us wanted this war. Not all of us are enjoying it.'

'Oh, shame for you,' Jack said. 'Not having a good war? Sorry about that. Neither are we.'

'Jack,' Persey warned. 'Leave him alone.'

'Oh, I see you've given up the goods already, have you? I've only been gone the afternoon. Knew it was only a matter of time before he turned you, too.'

Before Persey knew what had happened, Stefan launched himself across the kitchen and punched Jack.

Dido screamed and Persey leapt up to halt the men, but Jack was too slow to retaliate, raising his arm too slowly to return the punch. Sensing his moment, Stefan swiftly hit him again, sending him sprawling onto the floor. Jack groaned, blood pouring from his nose and his mouth. He spat blood onto the flagstones.

Stefan watched him, waiting for him to get up.

'Stop it,' Persey shouted. This was too much. There had been too much blood today.

'Jesus Christ, Stefan,' Jack cried. 'Give a man a chance to hit back.'

After a moment, Stefan held out his hand to Jack who eyed it warily, took a deep breath and then clutched it as Stefan pulled him to his feet.

'Why do you hate me so much?' Stefan asked when it was clear Jack was too engrossed with wiping blood off his face to hit Stefan.

Jack shrugged, wiping his bloody hands down his dark trousers. He slumped into a chair at the kitchen table. 'I'm not sure I have the energy to hate,' he said quietly. 'Not today.'

Dido and Stefan sat down. The four had awkwardness and brandy to bind them.

'I want to leave,' Jack said into his glass. He sounded young, like a child.

'We all want to leave, I think,' Stefan suggested quietly.

'I was going to. I am going to.'

'Really?' Stefan said.

'I was planning to find a way to take Dido and Persey with me. But I sense you've scuppered that.'

'Me?' Stefan asked. 'Why me?'

But it was Dido who spoke next, 'You were taking me?'

'Yes, want to come?' Jack asked with a laugh. 'Fancy getting away from the Nazis?'

'I don't know,' Dido replied, the vegetables she was chopping long since forgotten. 'I would have done before,' she said. 'But now it's different. Now . . . I'm in love,' she said with a smile.

'Oh, not you as well. You were desperate to get away before, but now you've met a man,' Jack said, drinking from his glass and wincing as the alcohol stung his cut lip. He put his hand to his face. 'I think my nose is broken.'

'Come with me and I will see if I can clean it up and bandage it for you,' Stefan offered.

Jack thought and then nodded, 'All right.'

'I am sorry I hit you, Jack.'

'Twice,' Jack stated.

'Twice,' Stefan replied.

'It's all right, I probably deserved it.'

'You did. But I am sorry.'

'I'm sorry I hit you, too,' Jack said.

'You did not actually manage to hit me,' Stefan pointed out but before Jack could protest Stefan said, 'None of this can be good for your heart.'

'My heart?' Jack said. And then, 'Oh yes, my heart.'

'Jack,' Stefan said, 'I think the game is perhaps up on that one.'

'Oh, bloody hell,' Jack replied and then changed the subject. 'Will you help me get Persey and Dido off the island? When the time comes?'

'If they want to go, yes but if not, I will help you to leave.'

'Will you? Really? Maybe you're actually not that bad, Stefan. Do you know that?'

'Yes, I know,' Stefan said wearily.

'You fight rather well, too.'

'Thank you,' he said. 'I was taught.'

'So was I but you're better than me,' Jack said as the two men walked down the hall and climbed the stairs, leaving Persey and Dido alone.

'Will you go?' Persey asked her sister.

'No. Not now. Despite all this, I'm the happiest I've ever been.'

'I'm pleased for you,' Persey said smiling. 'Genuinely. I'm happy for you.'

'Thank you,' Dido said shyly. 'Will you?'

Persey looked into her glass. 'I don't know now. I can probably be of use in England . . . do something for the war effort.' The pain of Stefan's rejection still hung around her. Everything had changed. And nothing had changed.

The two girls held hands across the table and Dido looked at her wristwatch. 'Best get a whip on with supper. Shall we get the wireless out? Might be a spot of music or a play on before the news.'

Persey nodded. 'Yes, let's.'

Chapter 28

2016

It was Molly who suggested the painting party. Lucy had winced at the thought of a five-year-old let loose in the house with a range of paints and rollers, but Clara and John had both agreed it was a wonderful way to get the lower parts of the walls sorted without any of the 'grown-ups' bending down too long and hurting their backs.

'How old are you?' Lucy had teased rhetorically. 'Moaning about a bad back?' But after helping Molly paint some of the lower walls upstairs, Lucy had rubbed her sore back and taken to the step-ladder to apply the higher parts with paint.

She and Molly painted the bedrooms, covering ground slowly but surely while John and Clara continued the good work Lucy had begun downstairs.

It was almost comic relief painting with Molly, who was flicking paint everywhere despite protesting that she wasn't. Thank goodness the carpet would be ripped up. She was grateful for the little girl's buoyant attitude. Lucy couldn't have dealt with the serious-ness of being side by side with Clara. Not yet. It was all just too awkward, still.

The house was being transformed with only a lick of paint. Already it looked different, cosier, less stark and far more inviting.

They only had what had been Dido's bedroom to apply the first coat to and as it had been the only room truly lived in upstairs of late, Lucy had been putting it off until last, although she didn't really know why. Perhaps because it felt too personal, too intrusive.

Clara popped her head round the door to the small back bedroom where Lucy and Molly were replacing the faded magnolia with a subtle pale pink.

'You've a visitor,' Clara said with interest. 'It's the famous Will.'

'Great,' Lucy said and then tried to mask her enthusiasm by hastily removing the smile from her face.

Lucy went downstairs and found Will and John talking in the hallway. John had stopped, halfway through painting the bannisters. Clara stood on the stairs and watched.

Lucy, uncomfortable, just said a casual, 'Hey, what are you doing here?' in a bid to look nonchalant.

'I thought I'd come and help. But you look like you've got it covered.'

'No,' Lucy said too quickly. 'Stay. It would be lovely.'

Will agreed and Lucy introduced them all. He glanced at Clara who made a fuss of heading back into the sitting room to continue painting.

John stopped staring and handed Will a paint roller. 'I was going to start on the bathroom next. You'll need this scraper and pot of filler first.'

Lucy watched as Will, already dressed in an old hoody and ripped jeans in preparation for painting, made his way upstairs to the bathroom to get started. She let him pass her and he gave her a smile, which she returned. Aware she was being watched by her sister and brother-in-law, Lucy stiffly said, 'Right, must get on.' But at the top of the stairs she paused to watch Will as he took off his hoody, his old, frayed T-shirt rising to expose a gap of skin that she couldn't take her eyes from. Downstairs, Clara and John began talking excitedly. Lucy tried to ignore them.

Hours later, Molly had given up, bored, and had curled up on the settee, watching Netflix on John's phone while the adults had given up to reward themselves with a glass of wine as they considered what takeaway to order in. They opted for fish and chips and Will suggested Cobo Fish Bar, which he said he was happy to drive out and collect from.

'Come with me?' he suggested to Lucy and she tried to ignore the knowing look Clara threw John.

In Will's car Lucy became suddenly aware of his proximity and the silence, which was deafening. She stared at the radio, willing with her eyes for Will to switch it on but he didn't. As he changed gear he brushed her leg and said a quick, 'Sorry.' Lucy quickly moved her legs to the left of the car and mumbled, 'It's OK.' They weren't like this with each other yesterday so why so strange today?

'That was odd, earlier,' Will said.

'What was?'

'John and Clara. They're nice, by the way. Just a bit odd with me or am I imagining?'

'You're new on the scene, that's all,' Lucy said.

'Am I on the scene?' Will asked as they pulled up to the fish and chip shop, which was a corrugated metal structure on the beach, unimposing but very much a landmark.

'Um . . .' was Lucy's dreadful reply, not at all understanding the question. 'Oh goody, we're here. I'm starving,' she said, opening the door and climbing out. The sun was beginning to set over the beauty spot of Cobo Bay and they looked out across the sea as the orange line developed along the horizon, pulling the sun down towards the crystal water.

They stood in the queue of locals and tourists and Lucy stared intently at the menu even though she'd chosen what she was going to have the moment they entered the line.

'I'll pay,' Lucy said. 'After all, you've spent all day helping. And yesterday, at the archives. You were . . .'

Will narrowed his eyes and waited.

'Lovely,' Lucy said and wished she'd picked a different word but mumbled it again nevertheless. 'You were lovely. You are lovely.' Oh God, Lucy, stop.

It took Will a few seconds to reply. 'Thanks. The feeling's mutual.'

The moment they got back in the car, Lucy switched on Will's car radio, not wanting a repeat of the earlier excruciating car journey.

They ate dinner at the kitchen table with John and Will bonding over rugby chat and Clara listening intently, waiting to get a word in edgeways for so long that when she finally did, a barrage of questions flew from her mouth.

'Where do you normally live? Are you staying here long? Are you married? Have you been married? Do you have kids? When was your last relationship?'

Lucy both desperately wanted Clara to stop and desperately wanted to know the answers, and so rather brutally did not step in to save Will, instead watching as he quickly began to look exhausted.

'Any more wine?' Will asked Lucy.

'Yes,' she said, squeezing his shoulder in solidarity as she moved towards the fridge.

'So . . .' Clara continued. 'Not married. Engaged?'

'I was,' Will said.

Lucy spun round from the fridge.

'Really?' Clara said, picking up a chip and leaning forward. 'Why aren't you now?

'It ended,' Will said simply.

'Mmmm?' Clara nudged. She put the chip in her mouth and chewed. 'Why?'

Lucy was getting cold she'd been standing by the open fridge door for so long and so she pulled the wine out, closed the door and sat still, unable to refresh their glasses until she'd heard Will's answer.

'Um . . .' Will started.

But John stepped in, 'Leave the man alone, Clara.'

Will turned to Lucy and gave her an awkward smile. Realising

295

she was frowning, she straightened out her frown lines, smiled and poured the wine.

The next day the family reconvened to tackle the one room that remained. Will said he'd happily join later, but he had something he needed to do in the morning.

When Clara arrived she jumped straight on the topic of Will. 'Why do you think Will isn't engaged anymore?'

Lucy played devil's advocate. 'People get engaged, people break up.'

'Do you think she broke up with him or he broke up with her? I'll bet she broke it off with him and he's embarrassed. Or perhaps he broke up with her and he doesn't want to look like a bastard.'

Lucy sighed. Why was Clara like a dog with a bone on the subject of Will?

'You like him, don't you?' Clara asked seriously.

'He's nice,' Lucy said dismissively.

'He is nice, yes,' Clara mimicked, 'And very easy on the eye. And from what I can gather, solvent, which is always good. Has he kissed you yet?'

'What?' Lucy spluttered. 'No.'

'Why not?'

'How should I know,' Lucy raised her voice an octave. 'Why don't you add it to your list of questions.'

'I might.' Clara looked thoughtful. 'Shall we make a start on this room?'

'Yes, please,' she said, hoping it would stop Clara from asking her questions she didn't know the answers to, but the questions continued when Clara tried to move the wardrobe. 'Is there stuff in here still?' she asked in horror.

'Yes, Dido's clothes and things are still here,' Lucy admitted.

Clara stared at Lucy and in a horrified tone said, 'Why?'

'I didn't have the heart to bin them. It's her things, her life and to just chuck it felt . . . wrong.'

Clara gave Lucy a stern look. 'It's not binning them. It's sending them to charity. Someone else can benefit from these. I can't understand why you've not done this. It was one of your jobs. I didn't give you that many.'

'I know you didn't,' Lucy said.

'And a good thing too,' Clara went on. 'You had to show the estate agents round and you didn't get that right. You'd practically slept with one by the end of the day.'

'Hold on, that wasn't my—'

'You've not even emptied the wardrobe and the dressers. Have you sorted the headstone?'

'No, I remembered I had to do it though,' Lucy attempted to defend herself.

Clara took a deep breath. 'It's not the same as actually doing it though. But you've managed to buy paint and clear the garden, which wasn't on the list.'

'Not everything in life is on a bloody list, Clara.'

'Don't get clever.'

'Crying out loud,' Lucy said. 'Do you want to ease off? Why are you suddenly so pissed off with me?'

Clara ran a hand over her face. 'I just wish that you would finish something, for once.'

'What does that mean?'

'You've started the garden. But you've not finished it. You've started painting the house but we've come to help finish that.'

'That's because it's too big a job for one person in such a short time and—'

'Yes. We all knew that. You didn't. You've not emptied the cupboards up here and now we're going to have to do that in order to move this hulking great wardrobe only a few inches just to paint behind it. And, by all accounts, you've left Dido's grave without a headstone.'

'I thought headstones couldn't be laid for at least a few months due to ground movement,' Lucy said triumphantly.

'Yes,' Clara said. 'But you have to choose one and commission it. They don't magically appear.'

'I'll go tomorrow,' Lucy said. 'And I'll take the charity items when I go. Kill two birds with one headstone,' Lucy attempted a joke but it was clear Clara wasn't in the mood.

'Come on,' Clara said in quieter tones as she opened the wardrobe doors, started pulling clothes out and folding them up. 'Go and get some black sacks and we'll sort this together.'

Lucy watched with regret as the remains of Dido Le Roy's existence were removed from the room, folded up and placed on the bed ready to be packed for the charity shop.

The huge mahogany wardrobe was far heavier than they'd expected it to be, even once it had been emptied. John, Lucy and Clara were practically sweating.

'Can't we just leave it and paint round it?' Lucy suggested.

John's shoulders shook with mirth as Clara looked aghast. No one responded and they continued to shuffle the wardrobe out in fits and starts until it was far enough away from the wall for someone to fit behind and paint.

John sat on the bed surrounded by piles of bundled recycling sacks and the old Box Brownie camera that John had found sitting on the sideboard downstairs and had brought up to have a fiddle with.

'Christ, I'm unfit. What's all this stuff?' he asked, distracted by the camera.

'Dido's clothes, shoes,' Clara muttered.

'Is this it?' he asked. 'Not much.'

'Old compact powders and combs and things have gone in the bin,' Lucy said mournfully. Why was she so upset by this? It wasn't as if she really knew Dido.

'How does this even work anyway?' John asked, turning the camera over in his hands.

'I've no idea. Will knows. He's a photographer.'

John looked up and smiled. 'I know. He said.'

'He's good. I've seen his stuff,' Lucy admitted.

John nodded. 'Great.'

'He's coming round in a bit, actually.'

'Is he?' John smiled.

'He's going to help paint again.'

'Would you like to talk about Will for a bit?' John teased.

'No,' Lucy said. 'Shut up. I only meant you can ask him to show you how it works because . . .'

'He's a single, handsome photographer . . .?' John volunteered.

'Shut up,' Lucy cried, stifling a laugh.

'Have we worked out why he was engaged, but isn't now?' John probed.

'I'm going to throw something at you.' Lucy laughed, finding her brother-in-law far nicer than her own sister right now.

'Go and make me a cup of tea instead,' John begged.

'Fine. Just don't break the camera,' Lucy insisted as she went to make them all tea and Clara began laying out the floor sheets and prising open the tin of paint.

A few minutes later, a very smug-looking John and Clara entered the kitchen. Clara was still holding the paintbrush and looked as if she'd realised her mistake, and finding nowhere to lay it down, had to hold it aloft.

'Lucy?' Clara asked. 'Have you opened this camera?'

'Opened it?' she asked. 'No. Why?'

'Had it never occurred to you to open it?' she questioned.

'No,' she said uncertainly. 'Why would I?'

But it was John who spoke next. 'Because there's a roll of film inside.'

Chapter 29

'Why didn't I think to open the camera?' Will asked incredulously when he came over to Deux Tourelles later that afternoon and sat at the kitchen table with Lucy, John and Clara – evidence of their day's painting on their clothes.

'I guess we were so wrapped up in . . . everything else,' Lucy explained.

'It would never occur to me that someone would leave film in an old camera. Who opened it?' Will said, frowning. 'I hope no one opened it in broad daylight.'

'I googled,' John said proudly. 'I looked up how to wind the film back and it said go to a dimly lit room to open and check. So I did.'

'Actually,' Clara said gleefully. 'He climbed inside the wardrobe, shut the doors and then opened it up.'

'And hey, presto: film,' John said, smiling.

'What now?' Lucy asked, staring at the camera, now closed with the film inside and on the middle of the kitchen table.

'I can try to develop it,' Will said. 'If it's not been exposed to light and moisture it should still work. I can start it now.'

'Now? You develop your own film?' Lucy asked.

'Of course. What kind of photographer do you think I am?'

'One who takes pictures on a digital camera,' she teased.

'I do that too,' he said. 'But for authenticity, the old ways are the best.'

He stood up and reached for the camera. 'Want to come and watch?' He addressed the room.

Clara looked at her watch. 'I have to get Molly from her play date.'

'I'll come and watch you develop the photos,' John said and then catching a look Clara gave him, changed his mind. 'No. I can't come. Sorry.'

'Just us then,' Will said to Lucy.

'Do you have a proper darkroom?' Lucy asked as they entered Will's cottage.

'Not here,' he said. 'This set-up is more makeshift.'

They entered Will's bathroom and he pulled down the blind and took a box of chemicals and canisters from underneath the sink. The bathroom was clean, which pleased Lucy no end. There was nothing quite like a man who cleaned his own bathroom. Aftershaves and shower gels were lined up neatly on the shelf and she itched to open the fragrances one by one and smell them. He always smelled nice, fresh, she realised that now.

She watched as he lined up what he needed along the edge of the bath and along the sink.

'It really is makeshift,' Lucy said, edging out the way so Will could work.

'Yeah, sorry. Bit tight in here,' he said as they bumped arms in the small space. When he'd lined up everything he needed, he took hold of the Box Brownie, opened it gently, pulled out the film and said, 'You ready?'

Lucy watched as a variety of chemicals and solutions were added one by one. Then Will went to work silently with pipettes and the different solutions. He looked expert, confident, as if he'd done it a hundred times or more, which he probably had. The process intrigued her and she found herself following his hands as he moved between solutions. He set the timer and every now and again swished the solution, set it down and waited.

'Can I ask you a question?' Lucy dared. 'It's not about all this,' she warned him.

'Go on,' he said dubiously.

'Yesterday, when Clara was . . .'

'Interrogating me?' he finished for her. But before Lucy could reply he said, 'I think I know what you're going to ask me.'

Lucy waited.

'You want to know about my engagement.' It wasn't a question.

Lucy nodded. 'I do,' she said brazenly. 'Sorry. You don't have to tell me, obviously,' she said, but wished fervently that he would tell her.

He rubbed his finger across his lip, waiting, choosing his words. 'We broke up, or rather, I broke it off with her. I'm not proud of it. But getting married . . . we should never have got engaged. I should never have proposed. It was my fault, how it all panned out.'

'How?' she asked, far too curious to let him stop there.

'Everyone else around us was getting married – friends we'd had for years, and we were the last. It was either get married or break up and so, stupidly, I just went with the flow. We talked and talked about it for so long that I think we talked the romance out of it. By the time we were a month away from walking down the aisle in the most outrageously extravagant wedding she could plan, I was . . .'

He stopped talking. 'I was . . .' he sighed. 'I wasn't involved in the wedding. She and her mum wouldn't let me. And that was all right because I didn't care what colour the ribbons on the chairs were, or what colour the napkins were. I wasn't interested in the wedding, wasn't interested in any part of it. Then my nan died and my granddad followed shortly after. They'd been so in love

302

their whole lives and I think that's when I knew I wasn't in love and that going ahead with it wasn't the right thing to do.'

Lucy exhaled loudly. 'I'm so sorry. For your loss. For . . . all of it.'

Will nodded. 'Thanks. Calling it off was for the best. The mad thing was, when I told her, I expected her to throw things at me or cry. Instead she just said, "Do you know how much my parents have spent on this? Do you know how many people are coming? Do you know how embarrassing it will be to call it all off now?"'

Lucy could sort of see her point, but on the flipside . . . 'Was she still in love with you?'

Will shrugged. 'She never used it as part of the argument why we should still get married. Even suggested we go through with it to save face and divorce after.'

'Wow,' Lucy said.

'I just couldn't,' Will said, and then quieter: 'I just couldn't.'

'I'm not surprised,' Lucy said.

'I didn't really want to tell Clara and John that. I'd only just met them really. Not a nice first impression to reveal that you jilted someone with a month to go before the big day.'

'It's not really jilting,' Lucy said, springing to his defence. 'I mean, you probably shouldn't have got engaged really, but at least you didn't go through with something that felt so terribly wrong.' And then after a moment, she said, 'Sorry, that was clumsily put.'

'No, it's fine,' he said. 'It's true. And I'm not proud. Of any of it.'

'Do you still speak to her?' Lucy asked, no idea what his ex's name was and not actually really wanting to know. On the upside at least he wasn't the one nursing a broken heart. Neither was she by the sounds of it.

'Yeah,' he said ruefully. 'She's got the dog. I take him out for walks every now and again when I'm there and I have him when she goes on holiday, but he's old now and as she points out, when he passes away we'll never have to see each other again.'

303

'Ouch,' Lucy said, wincing.

'Yeah I know. Brutal. She hates me. So does her new boyfriend. It's fair enough. Even though they're getting married next year.'

Lucy said, 'All's well that ends well. Kind of.'

Will laughed. 'Yeah. Kind of.'

The way he smiled, his easy-going nature . . . it was leading to too much confusion in this tight space. Lucy suddenly felt engulfed. She wished he wouldn't look at her like that.

'Go on then,' he said. 'Your turn.'

'My turn to do what?'

'Reveal all the skeletons in your cupboard. I've just done mine.'

'No real skeletons. Just never really liked anyone enough to stick around with them.' And then she took a deep breath and tried to think about what Clara had said. 'Perhaps it's because I don't see anything through.'

'What?' Will said.

'Clara thinks I don't finish things. She's right. And I'm trying to work out what that means for past relationships, such as they were. I've had boyfriends but I've never really gone anywhere with them. I've never really felt that spark, never allowed relationships to progress because of that and so I found it easier to stop dating. I stopped making room for dating.'

'Do you have room now?' he asked pointedly.

Lucy swallowed. The room felt smaller. He was watching her, waiting. 'I hadn't thought . . .' she said. And then the timer sounded again, breaking the moment. It took Will a full five seconds before he took his eyes from Lucy and gently clicked the timer to silence it.

The atmosphere turned swiftly technical as Will looked with furrowed brows at the canister, shaking it and setting it and making a great show, suddenly, of moving all the chemicals; talking to her about the differences between a proper darkroom and this, makeshift method. Lucy felt her cheeks warm in embarrassment – happiness too, but embarrassment nonetheless that they had bordered once

304

again on an element of flirtation that had turned gently away from them. What would have happened if the timer hadn't sounded? Would he have kissed her? Or was she imagining the atmosphere?

'It's a long process this, isn't it?' she said to soften the silence, but after she said it she realised it could apply to both them and the development of the photos.

'It is, yeah,' Will said. 'Bored?'

'No, no,' she fibbed. She would see this to the end at least.

'Now for the fun part,' Will replied. Gently, slowly he pulled the film out of the canister, emptied the solutions and discarded it on the side. 'The film is obviously old so please don't be too upset if this hasn't worked.'

'Why wouldn't it work?' Lucy asked.

'So many reasons: the way it's been kept over the years, it could be foggy or it might just be too old to have developed properly. Too exposed to light or moisture.' He pulled the roll out, and Lucy was surprised to see the brown images on what looked like a long sheet of negatives.

'Oh,' she said in confusion.

'What were you expecting?'

'Photographs,' she said foolishly.

He laughed but not unkindly. 'That's the next bit.'

'I'd have got bored and probably given up halfway through,' she said, and then felt a chill go through her in realisation. Is this what Clara meant? She saw herself through her sister's eyes. She really did give up on things that easily; really never quite finished anything. Before she'd put her sister's comments to one side but, actually, now she understood. She brushed that thought away, knowing she'd have to analyse this later, fix it somehow. But what if that was just who she was? She forced her mind onto the task in hand.

'You know,' Lucy said, 'I have another photograph, at the house. Taken in 1930, it's a picture of a very young Persephone and Dido, on the beach with two friends. Maybe boyfriends?'

'Do you?' he asked distractedly as he pulled the roll gently, fixing the top of the roll to a set of clips he'd hooked onto the shower curtain. 'I'd like to see that.'

'It's funny,' Lucy said, watching as the images on the roll slowly started appearing. 'There's no personal trinkets really in the house. No jewellery, but there's that one photo that Dido kept hold of this entire time and then there's . . .'

'Eight more,' he said.

'Eight?' She looked closer as eight images slowly started appearing. 'Of what?'

'Can't tell yet. Some people . . . here . . . do you see?' Will said. 'And then it looks like a lot of scenery. Is that an airplane? This one looks like a bloody large gun, but there's a blurry bit in front of it. I can't even tell what this one is.'

'How do you . . .?' Lucy wanted to ask a question, but didn't want to look stupid so she didn't.

'You want to know how they get turned into photographs, don't you?'

She nodded.

'I need to leave them hanging here overnight, let the chemicals dry then—' He stopped and laughed. 'Are your eyes glazing over?'

'No, it's interesting,' she said, although she could understand why digital photography was now so popular. Click. Done.

'In short,' Will said, 'by tomorrow morning I'll have photographs for you.'

If Will had been hinting that she should get back on the dating scene, the offer of a date had not materialised, leaving Lucy to return to an empty but freshly painted Deux Tourelles feeling as if the afternoon had just been one strange anticlimax. They wouldn't even be able to ascertain what was on the roll of film until Will worked some magic by tomorrow morning. As far as keeping her on tenterhooks went, Will was not a beginner.

Lucy decided not to tell Clara she was going to sort the headstone.

Instead, she just got on with it. That was one job she could finish. All she needed to do was choose and pay. She went to the stone-mason's and quickly grew overwhelmed with choice, the stonemason politely suggesting she have a look at the graves that surrounded Dido's to see what was there so anything she chose for Dido would look in keeping with those of her family.

Of course. She could do that. She couldn't remember what the other graves had looked like at the funeral and so Lucy drove Dido's Renault 5 to the churchyard, stopping at a florist on the way and purchasing some flowers to lay on the fresh grave. It felt like the right thing to do.

Lucy laid them down and stood by the mound of soil that was slowly forming itself back into the earth. She admired the church-yard, its bountiful trees framing the low wall dividing it from the country lane. She'd spent a lot of her youth in this churchyard. Some of the taller headstones had been the perfect place to sit and drink bottles of dubious cider with some of her school friends and she smiled at the memory of her misspent days. It was a wonder she'd got any exam results at all – she'd spent far too much time playing truant instead of buckling down and getting on with her work. But then, she reasoned, she'd not been old enough to know better.

She wandered around the graves close to the family's few plots, one simple elegant one made of an expensive-looking material, possibly white marble Lucy thought, said, 'In loving memory of Werner Graf, friend, beloved', along with a birth date and a death date in the 1970s. She made a mental note that when she died she would quite like someone to call her 'beloved'.

She took a picture of the grave that sat alongside Dido's, a joint grave for Margery and Pierre Le Roy. If Dido had been Lucy's first cousin once removed, what did that make these two? She was no good at following the invisible lines of a family tree but she reasoned these were Dido's parents. The father had died in the 1930s and Dido's mother had passed away in 1940. Lucy looked at the date more closely. She couldn't remember the exact date of the start of the German Occupation but this death was certainly around the very early days of it. How ghastly, to lose your mother and gain a German army. Not at all a fair trade. 'How awful,' she muttered.

'Hello,' a man's voice came from beside her and Lucy turned to see the vicar who had conducted Dido's funeral service.

'Hi,' Lucy said.

'I recognised you from the funeral. Didn't have a chance to talk then,' he said.

'No, I was mostly in charge of the food. Not sure my sister trusted me to do anything else.' She'd meant it as a self-deprecating joke but she was more than aware that it had come out a bit snarky.

The vicar nodded kindly and so Lucy waffled on. 'She's let me help sell the house though because it mainly involves showing estate agents round and no actual signing of paperwork or nego-tiating terms.'

'Deux Tourelles,' the vicar said. 'Beautiful house.' And then, suddenly: 'In any set of siblings, there will always be a leader, I have often found.'

She frowned as she thought about that. 'Yes, I suppose so.' It was the roles they'd automatically fallen into. Clara had always been the leader, and Lucy happy to be led. Until she hadn't been and had simply upped and moved away, eager not to fall headlong into her sister's wake. But maybe, in the end, Clara had fallen into hers. She looked at Dido's unmarked grave and wondered how she and Persephone had fared as siblings. Which one had been the leader? Which one the follower?

'How are you bearing up?' the vicar asked, pulling Lucy from her thoughts.

The question instantly made her feel guilty and so she thought it best to plump for honesty. 'I'm bearing up very well given I didn't really know her.'

The vicar chuckled. 'I'm glad to hear it.'

'Did you know her quite well?' Lucy asked. 'I understood Dido was quite a churchgoer?'

'I did yes, in so far as one can know an intensely private person,' he said.

'Perhaps I should ask how you're bearing up in that case?' Lucy offered.

'Also quite well. She's a missed member of our parish. Always very helpful at the church fete and harvest festivals. Loved to sort the flowers for us when it was her turn on the rota and enjoyed helping the children colour in at Sunday school.'

'Oh, that's lovely,' Lucy said, picturing the elderly woman she'd never really known getting involved with colouring in. 'I don't know why but that's just made me cry,' she said, sniffing and wiping her eyes with her sleeve. 'Sorry,' she said.

'No need to apologise,' the vicar said kindly.

'I was just trying to choose a headstone and got a bit over-whelmed. It's been a funny few weeks,' she said.

'Grief is like that,' he said misunderstanding, as she continued to sniff. 'Better out than in.'

'Sorry,' she said again and then changed the subject, eager to stop sniffling. 'What's this headstone made of?' she asked the vicar as she pointed to Dido's parents' grave.

'Granite. Durable and rather pretty.'

Lucy pulled her phone out of her pocket and took a photograph of it, hoping the stonemason could replicate it for Dido, so it would match.

'Would you like to come inside for a cup of tea?' the vicar offered.

Lucy thought. Five minutes' peace inside a church would prob-ably be quite lovely. 'Actually, yes, I would,' she said, regaining her smile.

As the vicar made tea in the little kitchenette to the side of the church Lucy asked, 'Had Dido always been a regular churchgoer?'

The vicar filled the teapot with tea leaves and set out two bone china cups on saucers. Lucy felt soothed already at the old-fashioned method and sank into the chair opposite the vicar's desk as they moved inside his office. The room was warm, probably due to its small size and because the walls were wood-panelled.

'As long as I have known her, yes,' he said. 'I've been vicar of this church for forty years.'

'You must have been a child when you started.' Lucy laughed.

'I was twenty-five,' he said. 'Not my first posting either. I was once a mainlander,' he said, wiggling his eyebrows conspiratorially, which made Lucy laugh.

'I won't tell anyone,' she said, accepting a biscuit with her cup of tea and thanking him.

'But I gather Dido had been a very dedicated member of the congregation directly after the Occupation ended,' he said.

Lucy found the timing interesting.

'I often find people need to believe in something greater than themselves,' the vicar said as if hearing her. 'To take comfort in knowing that God is there when there seems to be nothing else.'

Lucy let the words sink in before asking, 'Do you think she was lonely?'

'She always seemed happy here,' the vicar said, which wasn't really much of an answer. 'Elderly people who live alone sometimes are lonely, sometimes not. We run a very busy schedule of parish events. She attended a lot of them. Church isn't just about attending on a Sunday you know. What makes you ask?'

'I don't know why but I have this feeling she was lonely. The house is . . . sparse. No personal objects really. She had a sister but—'

'Yes,' the vicar said. 'Died before her.'

'Yes, she died long before I was born,' Lucy said.

'We have a stained glass window in memory of the sister. I'll show you in a bit, if you didn't spot it on the day of the funeral.'

'Really? When did that go in?'

'It was before I arrived. Dido paid for it entirely. During the

310

Occupation there had been a German training exercise that resulted in them sending a shower of bullets through the window. They put in a piece of tatty glass that was nowhere near as beautiful as what had once been there. I believe Dido commissioned the new one in memory of her sister.'

When they finished their tea, he led her from his office into the church to look at it. The light streamed through the window. It was more modern than others in the church. It was a small side window in a narrow part of the building. A few chairs sat ready for private prayer and a stand holding tea lights already held a candle burning in memory. But the window was glorious. It was an image of the backs of a man and a woman on a beach, walking towards the sun. The blues of the sky and the yellow of the beach and the sun were captivating.

'I believe it was a local artist who designed it,' the vicar said, breaking Lucy's contemplative silence. 'You're more than welcome to light a candle for Dido. And to take a moment.'

'Thank you,' Lucy said.

'I must be getting on, but come and see us again, if you like. Any other questions, you know where to find me.' He gestured around the church.

'I will.' Lucy sat and reflected quietly while looking at the window. The man and the woman lit up suddenly as the sunlight moved out from behind a cloud, streaming bright colours onto the flagstones. It is a beautiful window, she thought, and then stood up, took the taper and used it to light a candle for Dido. She smiled as she watched the new wick flicker and flame and then without really knowing why, she lit another one for Persephone, the woman she'd never met but in whose life she'd become strangely caught up. She left the two candles burning for the sisters, side by side, gave one last look at the window and turned to leave.

Lucy emailed the photograph of Dido and Persephone's parents' gravestone to the stonemason and he replied with a quote for a

311

replica design for Dido. In the email was a request: What did they want the words on Dido's grave to say?

She thumped her head onto the kitchen table as she read the email. She hadn't thought about what it ought to say. She needed to consult her dad. She'd put that off until tomorrow. For now though, Lucy would, for the first time since she'd arrived, eschew a shower and run a hot bubble bath in the claw-footed tub and take a glass of wine and a book with her. She'd not read a single page of her novel since she arrived, she'd been over halfway through and, thanks to Clara, she now wanted to finish the novel just so she could feel as if she'd achieved something – finished something. Bloody Clara.

As she soaked in the tub in the newly painted bathroom, the overhead light a dim yellow above her as the skies outside darkened, she thought about Dido and Persephone and what life for them must have been like during the Occupation. Lucy discarded the novel and whizzed it across the floor as if it was a Frisbee so it was far enough away from any water she might spill from the bath. There was something bothering her, only she couldn't put her finger on it. It had to do with the church. There had been something niggling at her ever since she'd been there. Far from feeling peaceful, Lucy was now starting to feel antsy. She was missing something. Only, she didn't know what. It was something so startlingly obvious that she knew she'd laugh at herself for missing it. Only . . . no . . . she had no idea what it was. Perhaps if she slept on it, she'd be able to work it all out in the morning.

She slipped down the bath and into the water so she was completely submerged, her breath held tight and her eyes even more so, letting the dull silent chamber of the bathwater surround her. Slowly she released air from her mouth, the bubbles making the water ripple around her face, and then it came to her and she shot upright, sending water spilling round the side of the bath, cascading onto the tiled floor. She knew it would be something so obvious she would laugh at herself. But instead, she wanted to kick herself.

It was the graves. Dido's parents were there, interned together in one grave. And Dido was there. But . . . if she had died long ago – where was Persephone's grave?

Chapter 30

October 1943

Persephone left work, wheeling her bicycle through Candie Gardens on her way home, her jacket in the basket on the warm day. She felt as if she'd only really moved in a haze since that day she'd killed the soldier, when Jack had announced he was leaving, when Stefan had hit him, when she had told Stefan how she felt about him . . . When he had rejected her. Now she lived in a kind of no-man's-land of love and affection for a man who she knew loved her but who refused to act on it; who believed she was only saying it out of some kind of gratitude for what he'd done for her. He had kept her safe. And he didn't believe she truly loved him.

Persey stared at the statue of Queen Victoria, the island's notorious long summers keeping the last of the seasonal flowers just in bloom at her feet, and took time to pause, to breathe in the fresh sea air that rolled from the coast through the gardens. When German soldiers said hello to her as she strolled through, she smiled politely and said hello in return. She'd never managed to bring herself to do that before. They were here. They had been for some time. That wasn't going to change unless the Allies regained even more ground in this war. But she could no longer bring herself to pointedly ignore them. She looked at them anew. Many of them didn't want this war. She understood that. Despite the fact many looked as if they were having a jolly good time in the Channel Islands.

She watched one soldier purchase ice creams for a group of local children, smiling, asking their names and how old they were in stilted but try-hard English.

What would happen to those Germans after the war was over? Would they remain? Marry? Live here? Would they all leave – be forced away?

What would happen to Stefan? And to her? And to them? Would there even be a them? Not at this rate. Not with Stefan doubting her affections.

As the months rolled by it was becoming less and less likely that the Germans could win. At least, that was what Jack was saying. She'd been listening to the wireless and reporting the German losses, delivering her sheets of paper whenever she could. And she, like many other Islanders, were trying not to be too suspiciously happy-looking whenever a piece of good news sounded through the airwaves for fear the Germans would be able to easily weed out those who had likely been listening to illegal wireless sets.

But it was not always good news. Persephone was shocked when Jack had burst through the door one evening to relay the dreadful news that the Germans had torpedoed two Allied vessels off the coast of Brittany. When Stefan returned from work it was clear he already knew. Bodies of British sailors had been washing up on Guernsey's beaches all day. In the end the bodies of twenty-one sailors and marines were washed ashore, out of the hundreds of sailors who had been killed, and the German occupying force agreed to hold a funeral for all of them with full military honours and a sixteen-gun salute. Over five thousand Islanders attended, and lay wreaths in red, white and blue in direct contravention of showing British patriotism. It was a sign of solidarity from the Islanders that Persey and Dido joined willingly, laying wreaths and saying prayers at the mass funeral for the Allied men who'd died fighting for freedom.

The next day, Persephone returned to look at the graves and to admire the near thousand strong wreaths that had been laid. She wasn't alone. People milled, paying their respects. And as Persey rued the day Hitler had ever come to power she felt a tap on her shoulder.

'I've not seen you in quite some time, Miss Le Roy.'

It took Persey a moment or two to even recollect the woman. It had been so long since Persey's only encounter with her nearly three years ago outside her doorstep. And then Persey turned cold as she'd recognised Lise's landlady.

Persey said simply, 'How are you?'

'Very well. I saw your sister today though. Walking bold as brass through town with her German boyfriend. Someone called out Miss Le Roy and I turned, recognising the name and expecting to see you. But no. I didn't know there were two of you. How's your friend?'

'Which one?' Persey asked dumbly at the quick line of frenzied chatter coming from the hateful woman.

'You know which one.'

'What on earth are you talking about?' Persey asked.

'Another group of Jews have gone. In February. You must have heard.'

'Yes, I did,' Persey said with disgust. 'But I don't know what that's got to do with—'

'Yes, you do. Miss Weber's name wasn't on the list of deportees, I noticed. Got her hidden somewhere nice and safe, have you? You and your sister? In it together? People like your sister . . . no morals.'

Persephone's mouth opened and she said quietly, 'What do you mean?'

'Horizontal collaboration. It's morally repugnant. What else does she get up to that's morally repugnant, I wonder? Wouldn't surprise me if she was only too happy to help you hide Miss Weber. I've long suspected you. But now I've seen your sister's behaviour is less than admirable, I think she's got something to do with it, too.'

'What is wrong with you?' Persey said, her mind in despair. 'If my sister has been seen out with a German, what makes you think she'd be hiding a Jew?'

'Because her moral compass clearly spins in all directions. As I suspect yours does. The German might not care. Her boyfriend might be in on it, too,' the woman said, riling herself up. 'Not all of them respond when you tell them to their faces you've seen things you shouldn't. Some of them laugh at you as if it's you who are in the wrong when all the time you're trying to do a good deed.'

'What is it you want?' Persey asked pleadingly.

'Justice,' she said.

'Justice?'

'It's the law. Miss Weber should have registered. She should have been deported. It's the law,' she repeated.

'She's already gone,' Persey said. 'Went years ago.'

'I don't believe you,' she said, but there was a seed of doubt. 'I'm going to tell them. I'm going to tell them I think you've got her hidden. You and your Jerrybag sister.'

Persey was paralysed temporarily by the onslaught of venom.

'Why would you do that?'

'I told you. Justice. I should have done this long ago. Tell me where she is and I won't write the letter to the Gestapo today. How do you think you and your Jerrybag sister will enjoy rotting in a German prison? She'll be surrounded by German uniforms then; she might actually enjoy herself.'

Instinctively, filled with disgust, Persey reached out and slapped the woman. And afterwards there was no remorse, no regret whatsoever. The woman backed away, stunned. Persey's breath rasped thickly in her chest as her anger grew.

'Why would you involve my sister?' Persey cried.

Mrs Renouf clutched her face and turned back. 'I tell you one thing, Miss Le Roy, if you're not hiding Miss Weber, you two have got nothing to worry about, have you?'

There was no avoiding it. Persey had to tell Lise what had happened. She rode to the Durands' house faster than she'd ever ridden before. Looking down the narrow lane to check no one had seen her, she knocked on the door and entered when Mrs Durand opened it.

'It's been years but she still bears a grudge.' Persey's words flew from her mouth as she relayed the bare facts to a stunned Lise.

'Because of the money I owed when I left?' Lise asked.

'Not because of the money. It's purely because you're Jewish. She's evil and full of hate.'

Lise slumped into a chair at the kitchen table. Mrs Durand took one of Lise's hands and Persey took the other.

'You'll have to stop coming here,' Mrs Durand suggested. 'If that old bat has written to the Germans telling them you've got Lise hidden, then it's only a matter of time before they follow you here when they realise she's not actually at your house.'

'I know,' Persey said. 'And with Stef . . . Captain Keller billeted at Deux Tourelles they'll know instantly Lise isn't at ours. No one in their right minds would hide a Jewish girl under the same roof as a German soldier. No search necessary. Although they may still storm in. And she's mentioned Dido. However . . .' Persey said slowly, thoughtfully. 'I do think there might be another way to keep you safe.'

'What is it?' Lise asked.

Persey took a deep breath. 'I think you should leave the island.'

Lise's mouth opened partly. 'How?'

'Jack has a boat.'

It was Mrs Durand's turn to ask, 'How?'

'He just does. Jack has the gift of negotiation. It sometimes works in his favour. Sometimes not. But regardless, he has one, with an engine, which allegedly works. He's planning an escape.'

'Good God,' Mrs Durand said quietly.

'It's a risk,' Persey continued. 'But Mrs Renouf really hates you. And now me and my sister. I don't believe she'll stop. Even if the Germans don't bother looking, she'll push and push until they've no choice but to at least start a tentative search. I don't know how long this war will last. Far longer than any of us thought so far. But I think if you have the chance to escape with Jack, it may be your only way off to safety. It's your choice, of course.'

The three women grew silent and then Lise said, 'But what if we're caught escaping?'

Mrs Durand said solemnly, 'I should imagine it's not too different to being caught sitting at this kitchen table. I should imagine there will be punishment either way.'

Lise nodded and exhaled loudly.

'I can't tell you to go,' Persey said. 'I can't tell you to stay. Both choices come with risks. For everyone. But most of all for you. If it's any consolation, Jack's an excellent yachtsman. Spent his life on the water. Could navigate his way off the island blindfolded.'

Lise looked uncertain.

'He wasn't intending on leaving immediately, but if I explain your situation to him, I think he'll pick up pace. He's a good man. And he's determined to get the hell off the island. If anyone can get you safely to England, it's Jack.'

The time had come to tell Dido.

Dido sat at the piano playing a tune Persey wasn't familiar with.

She looked up, lifted her fingers from the ivory piano keys.

'Hello, you,' she said with a smile. 'I've had the most wonderful day. Werner and I—'

But Persey had no time and there was no way to ease in. 'I have something I need to tell you,' Persey started.

'All right,' Dido said, a nervous smile flitting at the corners of her mouth.

Persey pressed on. 'I've been keeping someone safe, someone

319

who has been in real danger. And I'm sorry to say . . . it now involves you.'

Dido's smile faded and she looked at her sister with a hard, worried expression. 'Tell me,' she said, her voice shaking with worry. 'Tell me everything.'

'Three years?' Dido asked when Persey had outlined everything. 'The Durands have been keeping your friend hidden for that long?'

'Yes,' Persey said. 'It was the only thing we could think to do. Jews left behind, those who registered, they've—'

'Been deported God knows where,' Dido finished for her. 'I can understand why you've done it. But I can't understand why you haven't told me.'

'To keep Lise safe.'

'I wouldn't have told anyone,' Dido said.

'It was to keep you safe, too,' she said.

'How exactly?'

'The fewer people who knew . . . it seemed safer. Then if you were questioned, you'd have nothing to tell. You'd have been freed from questioning faster.'

'Or tortured to death quicker,' Dido said. 'Who else knows?'

'No one. I'm going to tell Jack. And Stefan . . . I've not told him yet.'

'Why now? Why are you telling us all now?'

'Because I'm going to ask Jack to get her off the island. And Stefan because . . .'

'Because you love him?'

Persey looked away. She could not tell her she loved Stefan. She could not tell her what he had done for her. She could not tell Dido she had killed someone. She just couldn't. She didn't want to say any of it out loud ever again.

When Stefan had told her the Nazi authorities had decreed the sentry's death a tragic accident, his footing obviously misplaced on the bicycle pedal or that he was too close to the cliff edge,

Persey had cried. Fresh tears of relief and shame had fallen from her face. The less Dido knew, about everything, about all of that, the better for everyone, especially now that the landlady was writing a letter to inform on both Persey and Dido. They would be called in for questioning. The less Dido knew, the safer she would be.

But there were some things Dido did need to know. 'I'm telling you for a different reason. Lise's old landlady saw you in town with your man. She says she's going to name you in a letter to the Gestapo, alongside myself, in being culpable in Lise having dodged deportation.'

'How does she know about Lise? How does she know you have her?'

'She doesn't. She's guessing.'

'She's guessed correctly,' Dido said. 'What will happen if we're named in a letter?'

'They'll come for us. They'll search the house for her. They'll watch our movements. They'll pull us in for questioning. I don't know what form that will take, but . . .' She thought back to Stefan's revelation that if Jack were to be questioned about his half-thought-out story as to how he'd got back on the island that he would be begging for his mother by the end of it. Would they do that to Dido? They couldn't do it to her if she wasn't here.

'What about the Durands?' Dido asked. 'They'll be safe if no one knows she's there. I take it you aren't going there again now?'

'No I'm not. It's not worth the risk. She's leaving with Jack. I'm to telephone to give her an hour's notice. I'm not to speak. And then I'm to replace the receiver. But, Dido,' Persey continued, 'you're going to be named in the letter, so I need you to leave with Jack and Lise. I need to protect you. I've looked at the tide time-table and at the weather and given Mrs Renouf is writing her letter and could even have hand-delivered it by now . . . I think you should all leave tonight.'

Dido looked horror-struck. 'I'm not leaving.'

'What? Why not? You have the chance to leave. Why not take it?'

'Because I'm happy, for the first time in such a long time, I'm actually happy.'

'Dido,' Persey pleaded. 'You're going to be named in a letter. To the Gestapo! If we don't all move as soon as possible, it's going to be too late!'

'I don't want to go,' Dido said. 'I'll do what I can to help Jack and your friend leave but I'm not leaving Guernsey. I'm not leaving Deux Tourelles. It's my home. Are you leaving?'

'No,' Persey said. 'Of course not.'

'So why are you trying to make me leave?'

'To keep you safe. To keep you away from all of this for what remains of the war. To stop you being questioned. I can't bear the thought of anyone hurting you, Dido. Once they suspect you of one thing they'll never leave you alone. They'll watch you forever!'

'But they'll do the same to you.'

'Yes,' Persey said.

'It's all right for you to be brave but not for me?' Dido asked.

'Oh, Dido . . .' Persey put her head in her hands.

'What if they don't get away safely?' Dido asked eventually, changing the subject.

'I'm going to help them get away. I have to know they've gone.'

'You can't stop them getting caught,' Dido reasoned.

'I might be able to. I have to take Lise to Jack. I have to know she's made it and then after that, it's up to Jack.'

'What if they're caught by a patrol if they do actually make it out to sea? Do we just leave them to rot alone?'

'We won't be able to do anything to help then,' Persey said quietly.

Dido swallowed. 'They're going to arrest you and I anyway by the sounds of it. And the Durands.'

'No one need ever connect Lise's absence on the island with the help of the Durands.'

'They will if Lise talks?'

'She won't and you're talking as if they might not get away,' Persey said.

'They might not,' Dido cried.

Stefan had returned from his work later than expected. Dido and Jack were in the kitchen discussing the now-accelerated plan. Jack had taken it well, which Persey had expected, enjoying the thrill of the adventure. And when she'd told him the woman he was taking to England with him was Jewish he had laughed gleefully at her story of keeping Lise hidden from the Germans for so long. 'Anything to get one over on the greenfly,' he had crowed. 'You've got her this far, Persey; I'll get her the rest of the way.' Secretly Persey was relieved that Jack wore his hero complex for the world to see. His bullishness would provide Lise with the confidence she needed to board the boat.

While they waited for the darkness of night to fall, Stefan returned and she told him her plan. She spoke in a no-nonsense fashion, refusing to even consider repeating her words of affection now. She could not take the sting of refusal one more time.

'What can I do?' he asked after he had got over his initial shock.

'Nothing,' she replied, hating how much she loved him all the more for asking to help instead of telling her she was mad. She had told him she was going to escort Lise down to Jack's waiting boat and keep watch, then she would return when she'd seen them get away.

Stefan frowned. 'It won't be that simple,' he said worryingly. 'Before, you told me you'd tried to get Jack off the island. But that was in the early days. There are more sentries now. And mines on beaches. You have to know where you are going to avoid them. And there may be barbed wire to cut.'

'I know,' Persey had said. 'Jack knows. We'll be careful.'

Stefan looked uncertain. 'I cannot let you go alone.'

'I won't be alone. I'll be with Lise and then—'

'And then, after they have left, you will be alone. No, I will

323

come with you. Then if you are stopped, I will be there. They will leave you alone if you and I are together.'

'But you can't come in your staff car,' she'd replied. 'You can't park your staff car at the top of the cliff. It will draw attention.'

'I will come with you on my bicycle and I will keep watch for you from the edge of the beach.'

Persey wasn't sure.

'Please, let me help you, Persephone. You cannot do everything alone.'

As Persey helped Jack pack a few essentials she wondered if they were alone in doing what they were doing – the household of Deux Tourelles wrapped up in their own version of resistance, retaliation, escape. Were others across the island engaging in frightening escape plans, other ways to disturb the Model Occupation? She hoped so. And for the Islanders' sakes when it came to reprisals if discovered – she hoped not.

'After the war is over,' she whispered to herself, 'will Stefan and I be together? Can we be together?' She had to believe it would happen, although not now. Too much had been unsaid before. And now everything had been said and it still wasn't enough.

She grew maudlin as she started to think about Dido. What would Dido do after the war? If this blasted war ever ended. Was Dido wondering the same sort of thing about her German boyfriend? How serious were they about each other? Would he come back for her? Or would she go to Germany with him? Dido would. She knew that. Dido fell in love hard.

And then there was that letter. The one that would condemn both her, Dido, and Lise. The three of them exposed in one fatal blow, even though it had nothing to do with Dido. She could make no sense of what drove people like Mrs Renouf to do such terrible things, to inform, when doing good things was so easily within grasp.

Chapter 31

The elusive Persephone really was elusive. She didn't even have a grave. Maybe she didn't die in Guernsey, Lucy thought. Maybe she was sent to the camp? They'd been so focused on her during the war it didn't occur to Lucy to question what Persephone had done after, where she had gone, how long Dido had been alone at Deux Tourelles, and where Persephone was buried.

The next afternoon, Lucy stood in the kitchen and made coffee, absent-mindedly pouring in far too much milk. She'd been busy packing up Dido's clothes, as instructed by Clara. She'd put on the record player, listening to old jazz music that she was slowly falling in love with. Its timelessness provided a suitable soundtrack to her sad task, but in the end she'd had to switch off the record player and plunder on upstairs in silence. After she was done, she began bringing the bags downstairs. She felt awful as she looked at the recycling sacks lined up in the hallway. This was someone's life, reduced to sacks.

There was some small level of comfort knowing that a charity shop would make money from these when they sold them. And that the women who shopped in the charity outlet she was dropping these into would find some beautiful treasures to love and to wear.

But still it didn't alleviate the sadness. She looked down at her mug with dismay, the pale coffee looked almost undrinkable, but she was spared drinking it by a fast rap at the front door.

'Hi,' she said to Will as he entered, clutching a file under his arm.

'Hi,' he said, one eyebrow already cocked.

'You look half mysterious, half smug,' Lucy said, lifting her chin. 'What's going on?'

'This. This is what's going on,' he said, tapping the file.

'Are they the photographs you developed?' She'd expected him to come over this morning with them and when he hadn't, she assumed they'd either not worked or there was nothing of interest in them.

He nodded. 'Do I smell coffee?'

She led him through to the kitchen where he put the file on the table and she made him a drink, the kettle still hot.

'I've been . . .' he started. 'OK . . . How do I say this?'

'Spit it out,' Lucy suggested, handing him a fresh mug of coffee.

'I'm going to show you,' he said.

He sat down at the table, opened the file and gestured for Lucy to sit next to him. Slowly he lifted the photos from the file and one by one laid them out.

He spread out the black and white images and Lucy looked at each one intently. The first two showed two large gun emplacements at two different locations on the island, the sort of large fixed weapons that could easily shoot an Allied plane from the sky.

There was one of a large concrete outpost that Lucy immediately recognised as the large cylindrical observation tower at Pleinmont and one of what had become a small part of the Atlantic Wall, a grey concrete stretch of wall running all along the edge of the beach at L'Ancresse Bay. She recognised it. A wall to halt Allied invasion. She'd sat on this wall as a child eating ice cream looking at the rust of the metal as it reached the edges of the concrete.

Age or decay or both had administered their might to the next image and it was faded into a sepia darkness. Another was of the airport, littered with planes. As Lucy looked closer she saw the swastika emblems on the tails, the cross icons in the mid-sections.

'Luftwaffe planes. These were taken in the war. Whoever took these was taking an unbelievable risk. This is spying, surely?' she said in a mix of awe and shock.

'It was. Yes,' Will said, his voice undeniably excited.

In the second-to-last photo, someone, presumably from a first-floor window, had photographed prisoners walking in a line. But not ordinary prisoners or men in uniform who may have been prisoners of war, but ragged, thin, muddy prisoners wearing what could only be described as fragments of clothing that were hanging off them. The image showed them moving – slight blurs around their arms as they swung limply – and thin legs, bandy through malnutrition.

'This is sobering,' Lucy muttered.

Will laid out the last one. It was of a man, standing inside the front door of Deux Tourelles, the door behind him firmly closed from prying eyes. He wasn't smiling, just staring intently, as if he was waiting for something, waiting to check if the photograph had worked, perhaps? Someone had taken the image for him, risking their lives given that civilian cameras had been confiscated so early on in the war.

'I wonder who this is,' Lucy said, thinking hard. He looked familiar. Where had she seen him before? She had seen him before. But not looking like this, looking younger. The photograph from the beach. The one taken in 1930. The four on the beach – that was it. Dido, Persephone, Stefan and Jack. She had found this camera inside the house. But what was he doing here, like this, in another photograph taken so many years later? Had this man lived here? Or had he just been a willing co-conspirator for one of the sisters? Her mind whirred.

And then Will said something that made Lucy's head shoot up from the photographs. 'I know exactly who it is,' he said. 'It's my grandfather.'

Chapter 32

The sky outside Deux Tourelles was dark. It was time. Persey's nerves had been on the brink of shattering ever since her encounter with Mrs Renouf, but it was important to all that she held herself together, that she stayed strong, confident that the plan would work. Now was not the time to appear weak. Persey admired Jack. His ability to brush every possible hitch off as unlikely or conquerable was helping Persey more than she'd thought possible.

Dido was on tenterhooks and the two sisters sat down together in the sitting room.

Stefan knocked gently, opened the sitting room door and peered in. 'Half an hour,' he said. He was still dressed in his uniform, as usual, which would help if they were stopped. 'You have telephoned the Durands to give them the signal?'

'Yes, half an hour ago,' Persey said. 'Telephoned, connected, then rung off as planned. Lise knows what to do.'

Stefan nodded and left the sisters alone.

'Has Jack already left to get the boat?' Dido asked.

Persey nodded. 'He should be there by now. The owners were taking it round to Le Jaonnet beach and anchoring it at the rocks for him.'

'Poor Lise,' Dido mused. 'Just for being born Jewish.'

Persey held her sister, looked at her. 'Is there any way I can convince you to get on the boat with them?'

Dido shook her head. 'No. I'll stay here. Everything will be fine. In the end. I have to believe that. We have to hope. Or what else is there?'

Stefan and Persey bicycled in silence, neither willing to show fear or false bravado to the other. They looked around constantly for a German staff car or a sudden checkpoint. If they encountered one, they knew they had to jump from their bicycles in the darkness and throw both themselves and their transport over the hedge, to look as if they were lovers in a tryst. An idea that once would have shocked Persey into a blush but now, what she wouldn't give for Stefan to have kissed her again. Just once more, after all this time. There might still be time . . . once all of this was over. Once the war was over.

When the hedgerows gave way to the cliff path they were wide open to attack. Lise was already waiting at the lower part of the cliff steps, crouching low where the large jagged rocks led down towards the sea. Her eyes widened in fear as she took in Stefan in his uniform.

'It's all right,' Persey cried as Lise, clutching her small suitcase, backed away. 'He's a friend.'

Stefan raised his hand in an uncertain greeting. 'I am here to help.'

Lise nodded warily as Persey rushed to embrace her. 'I've been waiting a few minutes because I worried I would be late and then I worried I would be too early and—'

'You're perfectly on time,' Persey said, hugging her friend.

Stefan took Persey's bike and wheeled both cycles towards the rocks to hide them. The sound of the waves crashing filled Persey's ears. It was choppy down there but she daren't say it to Lise for fear of worrying her about the boat's stability. They had to get all the way to the English mainland. In the dark.

'Are you ready?' she asked Lise.

Her friend nodded. 'Scared. But ready. Where's your friend Jack?'

'He should be out there – let's move.'

'Gently,' Stefan said, taking Lise's suitcase from her.

They moved towards the small beach. Stefan went first, leading them down the dangerous cliffs, followed by Lise with Persey coming last, turning to look at every opportunity to see if they'd been seen. In front of them, out to sea, all was quiet.

The rocks rounded down and they moved gently along the coastal path. Ahead of them, Jack had already cut the barbed wire. When they were past it, near the bottom, Persey heard a slight scuffle in front of her and watched with horror as Lise stumbled. Persey was too late to help. She reached out to grab her but the woman was a few feet in front of her and Persey's hands grabbed at Lise's coat but caught nothing but air. She fell a few feet, cried out and tumbled into Stefan who slid down the path, dropping to his knees.

'Lise!' Persey called as her friend went over the edge and onto the sand below.

'I'm all right,' Lise was quick to call. The drop had been only twenty or so feet but Lise's cry that she was fine was swiftly followed by a groan of pain.

Persey began scrambling down the rock face towards her friend.

'Stop!' Stefan called to both Lise and Persey. 'Stop moving. There may be mines on the beach.'

Lise lay on the ground. 'I need to stand up,' she cried desperately. 'I need to get to the boat.'

'I know,' Stefan called in a softer voice. 'I will come and help you.'

He climbed down carefully and Persey carried on moving over the jagged rocks, picking up Lise's case, until she reached the end. She could see Jack some way in the distance, waiting patiently. She raised her hand to him and he raised his in return.

Persey turned back to see Stefan reach Lise's side. He was still on the rocks; she on the beach. He bent, ordering her to lift her hands, which he took in his to pull her up.

Lise cried out. 'I think I've sprained my ankle. I'm so sorry.'

'It's all right,' Stefan said. 'I will come down all the way.'

Persey watched, her teeth clenched together in cold and fear as Stefan carefully made his way onto the beach, placing his feet slowly in the darkness. She glanced up at the rocks above them, prepared to see a patrol but without the slightest idea what to do if she did. If that happened it was over for all four of them.

Persey moved gingerly down the rock path and Jack joined her where the rocks met the sea. 'What's keeping them?' he asked. 'I need to move. Is she coming or not?'

'Yes. She's hurt. Stefan's gone to get her. She fell.'

'Can she climb into the boat? If not . . .'

'She'll be fine,' Persey snapped. 'We've come this far. She's going with you. Just wait.'

Jack watched. 'What are they doing?'

'They're being careful,' Persey insisted as she stood on the rock. She held the handle of the suitcase tighter in frustration at not being able to go onto the sand, not being able to help, for fear of treading on a mine.

Stefan finally lifted Lise clean into the air and placed her on the rock. 'Go,' he said. 'Be safe away from here.'

'Thank you,' Lise said and held out her hand for Stefan to hoist himself up with when she was safely on the rock. She winced in pain but said, 'I'll help you up.'

'No,' Stefan said. 'I will go and watch out for a patrol. I will move to the rocks in a moment. Just go. Quickly. Good luck,' he said to Lise. He called towards Jack. 'Good luck, Jack.'

'And to you,' Jack called to Stefan. 'Look after Persey and Dido. I'll see you when it's all over. If we make it.'

'You will make it,' Stefan called. 'You have to.' He raised his hand in farewell.

331

Persey moved toward Lise as she inched along the wet rocks. She let her friend pass, helping her as she limped with her twisted ankle. As Stefan called to her, Persey turned back to him and Lise continued on alone.

'Persephone,' Stefan said. 'I want you to get on the boat too. There is room. I want to know you are far away from here.'

Persey looked at him as if he was mad. 'No. I'm not going.'

'You must,' he said simply.

'Why must I?'

'Because I must know you are safe.'

'What makes you think I'm not?'

'Everything. Everything makes me think you are not.'

'I can't do this,' she said. 'I can't have this conversation. I must say goodbye to Lise.' She turned to watch her friend in the dark almost reach Jack.

'No,' Stefan called. 'You must not. You must get on the boat so I know you will spend the rest of your life safe and away from here.'

'I'm going to be safe with you . . . for as long as you are billeted here. Now for God's sake—'

'I will not be there to protect you,' he said.

'What? Why?' she said, her body half turned to him, half towards Jack and Lise waiting at the end of the rocks for her to make her decision.

'Because,' he said, 'I am standing on a mine.'

Chapter 33

Will looked at the image of the man standing inside the front door at Deux Tourelles and then he looked at Lucy. 'This man is my grandfather.'

'What?' Lucy asked in disbelief.

'I knew that my grandfather lived in Guernsey,' Will said. 'Not in his final years. Actually, not for a very long time. But he'd never told me what he did during the war. Never spoke about it. He spoke about his love for Guernsey though. He'd wanted to return, but never wanted to, all at the same time. He said it was the geographical equivalent of the phrase "never meet your heroes". He'd loved it here so much so long ago that he'd not wanted to come back and see how modern it looked now, how different. But he'd loved it here and so that's why I came after he died. To see what he saw. To love what he had loved.

'I didn't twig when we looked up about the deportations,' he continued. 'I knew my grandfather was here during the war. But he'd made a new life with my grandmother and they never thought of moving back. They were happy. Their life was in England.'

'Deportations?' Lucy asked, finally able to interject.

'I never knew who my great-grandparents were. My interest lay in my grandfather, who was living and seemed far more interesting

333

than any long-dead relative I'd never known. He'd always been cagey about the war, though. Said he'd never been proud of some of the things he'd done in his early life, but that he'd been proud of being able to do one great thing. He met my gran here, which wasn't particularly interesting to me, I'm ashamed to say, so I didn't think to question further.

'But then here's my grandfather.' He tapped the photograph. 'In an image taken on a camera inside Dido's house. So I went to the archive this morning and asked to see my grandfather's papers. It hadn't occurred to me to do that when we went before, because as far as I was concerned there was no mystery around him to solve. But there is. Because I asked for his identity papers and the papers say he lived here.'

'He lived here?' Lucy asked.

'Yes, during the war.'

'And then the deportation orders made sense because Matilda Grant was deported.'

'Yes . . .?' Lucy said, failing to quite catch on.

'She was my great-grandmother. I didn't know that until I worked out that Jack was her son.' He tapped the photo of the young man. 'This is Jack Grant – my grandfather.'

Lucy sat back in the chair, not quite knowing what to say. She was trying and failing to piece together the relationship between them all. Dido and Persephone, sisters . . . and now Jack.

'He's in two photographs,' Lucy said. 'Hang on.' She ran to fetch the photograph of the four on the beach in 1930.

He took it from her, smiling. 'Oh wow, look how young he is. And look at them – the girls I mean. You can tell which is which now we've seen their pictures on the identity cards in the archives.'

Lucy smiled. 'You can.'

'And who's this other chap?' Will asked and then turned the photograph over. 'Stefan.' He narrowed his eyes. 'You don't suppose this is Stefan as in . . . Stefan Keller, Captain Stefan Keller, who was listed as being billeted with them in the war? All those years later?'

Lucy looked at the image again as Will turned it over. 'Possibly. Maybe.'

'Funny to think my grandfather was living here in the middle of the war and so was a German soldier. Most odd. They left in the middle of the war.'

'Who?' Lucy asked, looking up.

'My grandfather – Jack. And my grandmother, before they got married obviously.'

'They left Guernsey?' Lucy clarified. 'In the middle of the war?'

'Yes.' Will nodded.

'Are you sure about that?'

Will nodded.

'Impossible,' Lucy said, almost triumphantly. 'They can't have done.'

'Why not?'

'Were they sent to a camp or a prison?' she asked.

'No. They went to England in the middle of the war. They went together.'

Lucy looked at him as if he was mad. 'Will . . . do you think the English were running a passenger ferry to and from Guernsey in a time of war?'

He frowned. 'Um . . .?'

'Or even funnier, that the Germans were running one?'

Will smiled, understanding what she was driving at. 'Do you think they . . . escaped?' Will almost whispered the last word.

'Possibly . . . Yes, it sounds that way.'

Will looked at the photograph of Jack in wartime, and the younger Jack on the beach, filled with the confidence of youth. 'Well done, Granddad,' he said to the photographs.

They sat in an awed silence, Lucy uncomprehending how anyone could be so brave as to escape an island under Nazi Occupation. The alternative must have been far worse.

Chapter 34

1943

Persey stood on the rock and looked down at Stefan. 'What?' she cried in horror; unable to believe Stefan, unable to understand what he'd said although his words had been clear.

His voice housed despair. 'I think I am standing on a mine.'

'No.' She shook her head, refusing to believe it. 'No. How can you be?'

'I heard it click. I am sure I heard it click when I helped Lise up from the sand.'

Persey stared at him and then looked down at his feet in the dark. 'How can you be sure?'

'I cannot be sure.'

'Wh . . . What can we do? What can I do?'

'Nothing,' he said.

'Of course something can be done. What can be done?'

'Persey, please. Nothing can be done.'

'No,' she cried. 'No. We must do something. Can I put something on top of it and you . . . get off it?'

'I do not think so. I am not an expert in mines but I think it should have exploded by now.'

'How?' she asked. 'Why hasn't it?'

'I do not know. But they are meant to explode a few seconds after they are stepped on. This one hasn't . . .'

'Is it broken?' she cried, digging her fingernails into her palms, so helplessly.

'I do not know.'

'What if you aren't standing on one?'

'What if I am?'

Jack shouted from the boat. 'Persey, what the hell is going on. We need to leave.'

'You must go with them,' Stefan told her.

'Don't move,' she said. 'Let me think. Just . . . don't move.'

'Please,' he said. 'It is the last thing I will ever ask from you. I must know you are safe.'

'Stefan,' she said weakly.

'Go.'

Persey looked at Stefan, turned and climbed across the rocks towards the boat.

Lise had already reached the edge of the rock, waiting for Persey.

'What is happening?' Lise asked.

'Nothing,' Persey lied. She could not tell them Stefan had stepped on a mine; couldn't have Jack suddenly risk displaying heroics and stalling their escape by offering to help. There was nothing they could do for Stefan that she could not do herself. She just had to work out what that was. 'Come on, let's get you both gone.'

She helped Lise down towards the boat where Jack had tied a rope around a jagged rock. He pulled the oars in front of him and stretched one hand to assist her.

Lise took his hand, climbed in, winced in pain at her ankle and when she was sitting at the back near the motor, Persey handed her the small suitcase, which she held tightly in front of her. 'This is it,' Lise said. 'It's happening. Thank you, Persey.'

'Look after her, Jack,' Persey said.

'I will protect her with my life,' Jack said chivalrously and then gave a mischievous grin at the woman sitting behind him who he had never met, before looking at his watch with concern. 'We've only a few minutes until another patrol boat comes past. We have to go now. Sure I can't convince you to come?' he asked Persey. 'Now or never.'

'No. I have to stay,' she said, eager to return to Stefan. 'Thank you for helping her, Jack.'

'Yes, thank you,' Lise said to Jack meaningfully.

'Don't thank me until we reach England. And it's nice to meet you by the way, even if it is under the most dangerous conditions.'

Lise smiled and Jack looked at her a fraction longer than necessary before turning back.

Persey crouched down on the rock so she was almost eye level with the two of them. Recollecting what she'd read in the newspapers she said, 'Jack, when you reach England, they might try to take Lise as an enemy alien. Will you try to help—'

But there was no need for Persey to continue. 'I know. Of course I will,' he said.

He took her hand. 'Goodbye, Persey.'

Persey touched his arm. 'Goodbye, Jack. Good luck, both.'

She watched as the boat moved with the tide, Jack rowing deftly over the waves and out towards open sea, waiting for the opportune time to kick the motor and cross the Channel to England.

Persey returned to Stefan and manoeuvred herself around the rocks so she was level with him without being on the sand. In the darkness she could barely see and she wanted to be close to him. She looked down at the wet sand. How would she know where there might be a mine if she were to step down? He was looking up at the cliffs and then he looked sharply towards her when he heard her feet scuffle over the rocks.

'You came back,' he said in despair. 'Why? Why didn't you leave? That was your only chance.'

'I was never going to leave,' she said. 'And did you honestly think after you told me you'd stepped on a mine that I would get in a boat and leave you? Now,' she said with more confidence than she felt. 'I need time to think. We need to work out how to get you off safely.'

'I have been thinking this entire time and I have concluded there is no getting off safely,' Stefan said, looking her in the eye and taking a deep breath.

Persey would not let panic grip her. She would not. She looked around in the dark, waiting for inspiration to come to her.

If she could find a rock heavy enough, perhaps she could wrestle it on top and he could lift his foot? But she couldn't see anything loose, just the solid rocks that had formed the island and remained very much a part of its fibre.

'Persephone,' he said calmly. 'I have decided I am going to step off, but first I need to watch you go along the cliff, and be far away from me.'

'No,' she said defiantly. 'No, I'm not going to do that.'

'You must.'

'No,' she said. 'I won't do that. Don't ask me again.'

'It could explode at any moment,' he said. 'Please do not be here when it does. Please go now.'

Her throat hurt with the lump that formed and tears filled her eyes, blinding her. She rubbed them away with the sleeve of her coat.

'Don't cry,' he said. 'Please don't cry.'

She climbed off the rock and went to him.

'What are you doing?' he shouted, holding his hand out in front of him. 'Persey, stop! Stop now!'

She stood in front of him, carefully, her feet a little away from his. There were tears in his eyes, she could see that now. 'I love you,' she whispered. She meant it. She'd meant it for so long, only he hadn't believed her.

'Persey . . .' He closed his eyes. 'I love you,' he said. He opened them and looked at her. 'I've always loved you. You know that.'

'Yes,' she whispered. 'Do you believe me, do you believe that I truly do love you? That I loved you back then – I just didn't know I did? But that I love you now, more than anything.'

He smiled. 'Yes,' he said. 'I believe you.' He inhaled deeply. 'But now you must go.'

'No,' she repeated, standing her ground. 'I'm staying with you. Or . . . or perhaps I can fetch someone?' she said suddenly, resigned that this was not the end.

He laughed but it was bitter. 'Who?'

'One of the military? Can I fetch someone who can help you?'

'And what do you tell them?'

'The truth,' Persey said. 'That you've stepped on a mine.'

'You will be arrested,' he said simply. 'And so will I.'

She looked at him uncertainly. 'Why would you be arrested?'

'When they eventually find out that Jack – who lived in your house – has left the island, and the missing Jewish girl they have been told about is nowhere to be found . . . they will associate that escape with you and I, being on this beach tonight for no good reason. If you go and tell them I am here and they find a way to save me from this mine, I will die anyway for helping an escape. So will you. They will not let us live. And I would rather take my fate with this mine than with the Gestapo. This death will be quicker.'

'This isn't it,' Persey cried. 'This isn't the end. I refuse to let this happen,' she pleaded.

'Shh,' he said, pulling her close, careful that her feet should not touch his. She could not help it. She cried. Great, heaving sobs into Stefan's chest, into the fabric of his hated uniform.

He sighed and placed his chin on top of her hair. 'I am sorry,' he said.

'What for?'

'For stepping on the mine.'

'I don't know what to do, what to say,' she cried.

'You know what to do. You know you have to leave. If I could

340

not get you in that boat then I must get you to your sister. She will need you.'

'She won't,' Persey said. 'She'll be quite fine. I've seen to that.'

'What do you mean?'

'I've done something,' Persey said. 'I've done something to save Dido.'

'What?' Stefan asked. 'What have you done?'

Chapter 35

Lucy and Will moved into the sitting room, clutching their mugs of coffee. Will put the wartime photo of Jack on the coffee table and, next to it, Lucy laid the photograph of the four on the beach in 1930. She thought about what the passing of a decade had done to these four young people, plunging them headlong into war. She turned her photograph over, looked at the looped, swirled writing of all of their names with a smile. And then the smile fell from her face while she thought. She traced her finger absent-mindedly over the lines of the writing and looked towards the window – towards the ivy that was in danger of covering the glass.

'What?' Will asked.

'Hang on.' Lucy fetched the Perspex box, opened the lid and looked through all the detritus of Dido's life until she found what she was looking for: the newspaper from 1940 announcing the Germans' arrival. The one with the official announcement from the Germans on the front page, littering the paper with the new rules to abide by. There it was. The curfew notice and Persephone's annotation next to it:

> *Dido, how will you get to and from the club now? We need to talk about you not singing there anymore. Persey. x*

Lucy looked at it thoughtfully. 'This isn't it. This isn't the only place I've seen it.'

Will put down his coffee mug and joined her on the floor, looking over at the newspaper. 'What are you looking at?'

'The handwriting.'

Lucy sat back, cross-legged and thought. 'I know where I've seen the same handwriting,' she said. She pulled out her mobile and began scrolling through the photographs she'd taken since her return to Guernsey.

She found the photograph she'd been looking for, looked at it hard, wanting so desperately to be wrong. But she wasn't wrong. She'd not seen it then. Or maybe she'd not wanted to see it. But now it was unavoidable.

She showed the phone to Will who looked at it hard, looked at the writing on the photograph and the newspaper annotation and then, when he realised what he was looking at, swore loudly.

It was the anonymous letter informing on Persephone.

They zoomed in on the name of the house.

Lucy looked at the D of Deux Tourelles and the D of Dido's name, written with a flourish on the newspaper and on the anonymous informant letter.

'They're the same,' Lucy said, her eyes wide with something resembling horrified excitement. 'The loop and swirl on the D's are exactly the same. The handwriting is exactly the same.'

There is a Jewish girl still in hiding on this island. The woman hiding her is called Persephone Le Roy. She lives at Deux Tourelles. Search her room.

The last time Lucy had read it had been with disgust. But now, it was with cold horror. It was Persephone's handwriting. Persephone had written this letter. Persephone had informed on herself.

Chapter 36

1943

'I wrote a letter to the Gestapo,' Persey said. 'I told them quite clearly that it was I who had been responsible for hiding a missing Jewish girl.'

'Why?' he asked in horror.

'Because Mrs Renouf said she was going to implicate Dido alongside me. And I couldn't have that. So regardless as to whether she names Dido or just myself, I have named myself. I have taken the blame. I have protected my little sister. Because of Mrs Renouf's letter, they will talk to Dido. But because of mine, they will look extra hard at me. They'll search my room because I have told them to and in it they'll find my shorthand notes. It might take them a while to work out what they all say but I'm sure there's a shorthand clerk on the island willing to transcribe them for a few Reichsmarks or an extra meat ration. And Dido will be safe. They were coming for me anyway,' she finished. 'This way they leave Dido alone.'

He stared at her, his mouth open, horror in his eyes. 'Do you know what they will do to you?'

'They can't do anything to me if I'm here,' she said. 'With you.'

He looked down. 'If this explodes . . .' he said quietly.

'Then it explodes,' she said. 'I'm not scared.'

'You should be. Persephone, I'm begging you.'

'Please, Stefan, don't dismiss me. Not now. Please let me stay with you.'

'This is needless,' he shouted. 'You do not need to be here.'

'Let me stay,' she cried. 'Let me stay. For a while. I'll go soon. I'll climb the cliffs and go home and I'll wait for them to come for me. If that's what you really want. But they'll arrest me. I always knew they would. I had accepted it. Because Lise would be safe. Jack would be safe. And so would Dido. And that was all I wanted.'

'Persephone,' he cried but he had no further words. There was nothing else to say.

She slipped her arms around his waist, nestling into him. He put his arms around her and held her tightly. Persey felt the most comforted she had ever felt, despite this being the most awful of circumstances. 'I love you,' she repeated.

'I love you.'

She would not leave him. She loved him and he would not die alone. He had risked his life to help her, to help Jack, to help Lise. After everything they had almost been to each other, she couldn't let him die alone, scared. Dido was strong. Dido would be all right. Dido was in love and there was not a scrap of evidence she had been involved in any of this.

She tightened her grip around him. 'I'm not leaving you. Hold me tight,' she asked. 'I love you. Tell me you love me one more time. Before it's too late.'

'I love you,' he said quickly. 'I will love you forever.' He placed his lips on hers and she tasted the salt from his tears as they ran into hers.

'It was not our time before,' Stefan said mournfully.

And with a hint of gallows humour, Persey replied, 'I'm not sure this is it now either.'

That Persey would not get to say goodbye to her sister was the thing that pained her most. That she would not get to see her little sister's face ever again. She had intended to go home and wait for the Germans to arrive. To question her, search her room, find the shorthand evidence and leave her little sister alone.

She was not scared of death. Not like this. Not with Stefan. But how would Dido find out about this? What would it do to her? Stefan was looking at her. There wasn't enough time. There was never enough time.

'What might have happened?' she asked him. 'To us, after the war, if none of this had ever happened?'

He kissed her on her head and spoke softly. 'We would have found each other again, after the war. And we would have been together.'

She was silent . . . holding him tighter than before as he held her.

'The only thing that made me happy when I was on Alderney, was you,' he said. 'I thought of you whenever I could. I pictured your face, wondered what you were doing, wondered if you were happy, if you were all right. I fell asleep thinking about you . . . every single night for a whole year.'

'Oh, Stefan,' she cried. The fabric of his uniform was now wet with her tears.

'I am not sure how long we have left,' he said, pulling her back to the present. But she didn't want to hear it, refused to hear it. 'I wanted to marry you,' he said.

She smiled sadly, kissed him the way she'd never been brave enough to kiss him before. He kissed her in return and she wanted to fall into him, have him hold her forever but she daren't move. She wanted this to last as long as possible. It was all they would have.

'I would have liked to have been married to you,' he said again after they broke from the kiss.

'You have to ask me,' she replied as a smile played on her mouth. She touched his face, stroking his cheek with her fingertips, wishing they were anywhere but here.

Stefan gave the smallest of laughs and then: 'Persephone Le

Roy,' he started and she closed her eyes, placing her forehead against his chest, 'will you marry me?'

The pain of this hurt too much. She looked up, willing herself to stop the tears from flowing. She nodded. 'Yes.'

Above them the sound of vehicles arrived at the cliff top. Shouting began and Persey looked up to see soldiers' searchlights beaming down towards them. A flash of fear was swiftly replaced by calm.

'It's over,' Persey said, looking into his eyes one last time. She put her lips on his while above them soldiers shouted and began their descent along the cliff path towards them.

Stefan pulled back a fraction. 'What do we do?' he whispered.

'Hold me tight. Know I love you. And then lift your foot off the mine.'

Chapter 37

2016

Lucy thought back to the stained glass window in the church. That image. The girl on the beach. The vicar had told Lucy that Dido had commissioned it after the war. And now it made sense. Almost.

Will looked at Lucy. 'I don't often say this, but I think I need a drink.'

'Me too,' Lucy replied. 'But first I want to go to the church.' She got up from the floor suddenly. 'Come on.'

Will stood up, confusion all over his face. 'Why?'

'I want to look at the window again,' she said, hurriedly looking for the keys to Dido's Renault. 'I'd seen it before,' Lucy continued. 'But as with the informing letter, there was no way I could connect the dots until now. I just need to look at it,' she said hurriedly. 'One more time.'

They arrived at the church where Dido had recently been buried. In the intensity of the sun, the door to the church had been propped wide open and inside was cool, the breeze ricocheting gently off the cold stone walls.

'Come here,' she said to Will and took him towards the small enclave that made up the Lady Chapel. 'What do you think of that?'

He looked up at the window as the light streamed through. The stained glass window in its array of glorious colours looked brighter today than it had before. Inside this church she still felt as calm as she had the other day.

'It's not very religious, is it?' Will asked.

'No, it's not. I think it's Persephone.'

'Why?' he asked, shocked.

'Because Dido installed it after the war. Long after the war.' She explained the story the vicar had told her about Dido paying for it and having it designed.

'And I don't know who that man is but . . .' She trailed off as Will walked up to the window and stood, neck strained to look up at it.

'Do you think it might be—'

But he was cut off as the vicar arrived. 'Hello, thought I heard voices.'

They greeted him in return and Lucy introduced Will. 'We came to look at Dido's window,' she explained.

'Did you indeed? It is captivating. When the afternoon sun catches it, just like this, it's pure delight.'

'I've been curious about the image,' Lucy admitted. 'Why it's a woman and a man on a beach, walking towards the sun. It's to commemorate Persephone – you told me that much. So is this figure supposed to be Persephone?' Lucy asked pointing to the image of the woman in the window.

The vicar nodded. 'Yes, I thought you knew that.'

'No,' Lucy said. 'I was guessing. It just made sense.'

'So who is this man?' Will asked.

The vicar looked at them individually. 'You didn't ask about her death so I assumed you knew.'

'Knew?'

'About Persephone and her—' he looked around the church making sure there were no parishioners in hearing '—her German boyfriend.'

349

Will gave Lucy a look.

'It took Dido a very long time to explain to me the story behind the window she'd chosen,' the vicar started. 'When she returned, she knew that people could be so very judgmental – not everyone – but . . . some. And she didn't tell everyone about it. Preferred to keep quiet, which of course just lets people come to their own conclusions, which can often work against one,' he said ruefully.

'The man . . .' Will said. 'Is it Captain Stefan Keller?'

'Yes,' the vicar said.

Lucy stared at the window as if seeing it for the very first time.

Will nodded. 'But he's not in a German uniform,' he pointed out.

'Well no, that might have been taking the biscuit a bit don't you think?' the vicar suggested. 'Can't imagine the parishioners would have loved that stark reminder of the Occupation every time they came in for a service, which of course was why Dido kept very quiet.'

'So it's in tribute to both of them,' Lucy said thoughtfully.

'Very much to both of them. Stefan Keller had been Dido's friend as well as the man who loved her sister. And of course they died so tragically. A mine exploded. It took Dido a long time to find out the truth. By the time she'd returned, the Germans were long gone, but she found out in the end. They died doing something truly good, in helping two other friends escape the island, one a Jewish woman whose life was in considerable peril staying here and the other, a spy.'

'A what?' Will asked.

'An island man who got stuck here on a failed spying mission. And a Jewish girl who would have suffered in the gas chambers, most likely. Although they couldn't have known that at the time. No one knew exactly what was going on in Germany just then. But they knew it was right to get her to safety. Hindsight is a wonderful thing, but thankfully not necessary in this case.'

Will could barely speak. He was staring past the vicar, out towards the door but his eyebrows were knitted together.

'Thank you,' Lucy said to the vicar.

'My pleasure. I'm locking up in a moment but you're welcome to stay here until I've tidied a few things up first.'

'Thanks,' Lucy said as they said goodbye to the vicar. Will was still unable to speak.

The vicar left and she moved over to the remembrance candle stand, took the taper and closed her eyes, issuing a silent and not very coherent prayer for Dido, Persephone and Stefan. She lit three candles, in a row, watched as the wick took on each and the flames glowed brightly. She replaced the long candle that she'd used to light the three and glanced back at the window one final time at Persephone and Stefan walking along the beach towards the sea and the warmth of the sun.

Lucy and Will said goodbye to the vicar on their way out of the church. Will's forehead creased in the middle where his frown had deepened. Lucy led a stupefied Will towards the small collection of family graves, the mound on Dido's fresh burial flattening into the earth so very slowly.

'Was he talking about my grandfather? Was he saying he was here as an actual spy? I mean . . . a real one?' Will asked incredulously.

Lucy smiled broadly. 'I think so, yes,' she said and then laughed in shock. She couldn't help it.

'A failed spy, the vicar said,' Will pointed out when he'd come to his senses.

'A failed mission,' Lucy suggested. 'There's a difference.'

'And the woman he left the island with. I already knew they'd left together. But . . . my grandmother, Lise, was Jewish. I had no idea.'

'Didn't you?' Lucy asked.

'She never said,' was Will's simple reply.

Lucy sat down on the grass and Will joined her. It was warm and hardened through the summer sun. 'Perhaps she thought that her religion could have cost her life here and so . . .'

351

'Keeping quiet seemed safer,' Will said quietly. 'What an awful time.'

She reached out and put her hand on his knee as they sat cross-legged. What could she say? It was horrifying. Totally, unbelievably horrifying. 'Poor Persephone. Poor Stefan. They did something good. And died as a result.'

'But they saved two lives,' Will said.

Lucy nodded. 'Without them, Jack and your grandmother wouldn't have got off the island.'

'And they'd not have fallen in love, got married and had my dad.'

'And then you wouldn't be here,' Lucy said.

'Yeah . . .' Will said thoughtfully. He looked at her with a new intensity. Was he looking through her or at her as he processed it all?

Lucy flushed and slowly removed her hand from his knee, aware too late as to what she'd been doing. 'It's got really hot all of a sudden,' she said. 'Is it just me?'

'It's just you,' he said.

Lucy looked at the graves in front of them. 'So there's not a body, I mean . . . for Persephone and I suppose the same goes for poor Stefan.'

'And so no grave,' Will said. 'Hence the memorial window, I guess.'

But there was something else bothering Lucy. It would come to her in a second; she knew it. The clang of the church door sounded across the churchyard and the vicar issued them both a wave that they returned. They watched him go to his car, start the engine, drive away.

Will had become quiet, had found her hand in the grass and taken it in his own. 'Oh,' Lucy said without meaning to as she looked down. But her mind was processing a random assortment of facts and she couldn't think about what it meant to have Will's warm hand holding hers, as much as she knew she liked it.

Lucy had never really known Dido, had never even known Persephone had existed, let alone that she'd died in such tragic but heroic circumstances.

Persephone had died getting Will's grandfather and grandmother off the island and to safety. And in doing so, whether intentionally or not, had sacrificed herself as part of it.

But there was something else nagging at her. Something the vicar had said . . . Dido had paid for the window to be installed to memorialise her sister and the man she'd loved. She had done it after the war. She had done it when she'd returned.

'When she'd returned . . .' Lucy muttered.

'Pardon?' Will asked, his gaze lifting from their hands, one on top of the other, to her.

'The vicar said Dido organised to have the window installed when she returned. When she returned from where?'

Chapter 38

The knock at the door was louder than usual, more forceful. Dido braced herself. So it was going to be tonight. That hateful old woman had sent the letter and the Germans were here for Lise and Persey. Well, Dido rallied, they wouldn't find either of them here. Not tonight.

She put down her book. She'd not been able to focus on it at all this evening; she'd read the same page at least three times such was her worry for her sister. Dido opened the door. Two officers stood on the other side. They removed their hats.

'Good evening,' Dido said politely, offering them her winning smile.

'Good evening,' one said.

She recognised him from the club. 'Oh, it's you,' she said. 'How charming to see you here. What can I help you with?'

He smiled, a thin smile that didn't quite reach his eyes, which did not exactly put Dido at ease. 'Is your sister here?'

'My sister? No.'

'But it is past curfew,' he said.

'She's with our friend, Captain Keller.' Dido made sure to enunciate the name clearly, inferring the importance of his rank.

'I see,' he said, standing at the threshold. 'May we come in?'

354

Dido knew full well that if she said no, they would enter regardless. 'Of course. Such a pleasant surprise. What did you want my sister for? A girl could get a bit jealous you know; after all it's you and I who know each other. I don't think you've met Persey, have you?' She was rambling.

'I have not. But I have heard . . . things and so that is why we are here.'

'Heard what?' Dido said in too high a voice.

'You do not mind if we search the house?' he continued. His colleague remained mute, clearly not in charge.

'What are you looking for?' she asked with confidence.

'A woman.'

'My sister? She's not here.'

'A different woman.'

'A different woman?' Dido repeated dumbly. 'What kind of different woman? Blonde? Redhead?' she teased. 'I'm afraid there's only me. Will I do?'

The second man smiled, enjoying Dido's playful nature. If only she could get the first one onside. He turned and spoke to his colleague. Dido couldn't understand what it was about, but she suspected.

'You are not hiding a woman? Your sister is not hiding a woman?'

'No,' Dido said, her smile fading. 'I am not hiding a woman. Neither is Persey. What kind of woman?'

'A Jewish one.'

Dido crossed her arms. 'With Captain Keller living under our roof. Wouldn't that be a rather silly thing to do?'

He smiled. 'Yes, it would.' He stood his ground, watching Dido for any hint of a lie.

When the silence grew uncomfortable Dido said, 'We don't know anything about a woman. Jewish or otherwise. I'm afraid you're wasting your time.'

She led them into the kitchen, wishing to look hospitable. 'Tea? Only bramble leaf I'm afraid, these days.'

355

'Thank you,' he said as he looked into the sitting room as they went past. He paused, stepped in, glanced around before resuming his tread in the hallway. There was clearly no space in which a woman could hide in the sitting room.

'Beautiful piano,' he said in passing. 'Do you play?'

'I do, yes. But Tommy Riley plays for me in the cabaret act. I just sing.'

'We received a letter,' the officer said suddenly.

Mrs Renouf had wasted no time. Dido stiffened. She hadn't expected the Germans to come so soon. She'd thought they might have another day's grace at least before a big search.

'We received two to be precise,' the officer said as they entered the kitchen. He turned to his colleague and indicated the back door. His colleague exited, presumably to search the grounds.

'Two letters?' Dido said, looking out the door and then turning her attention to the officer. She remembered to give him a charming smile.

'The first stated you and your sister were complicit in hiding a Jewish woman who failed to register at the First Order in 1940. It was clear. It went into a great deal of detail. The woman in question used to work with your older sister. It stated you knew her too and would most likely know of her whereabouts. The anonymous letter was very uncomplimentary about you and your . . . behaviour.'

'Two letters?' Dido asked in confusion. 'Are you sure?' She absent-mindedly stirred dried bramble leaves into the teapot and put the kettle on the range to boil.

'The second, short, to the point said specifically that we were to ask Persephone Le Roy the whereabouts of a missing Jewish woman. This house was mentioned. And in particular, so was she.'

Dido looked away. 'Two letters?' she repeated. She couldn't work it out. Why two? Why one mentioning her and then one not?

'So of course, we come to talk to you. But we come to talk to Persephone Le Roy in particular.'

'There's no woman. What a malicious letter.'

'Two malicious letters,' he pointed out.

'You don't believe it, do you?' she asked.

'We must look into everything that sounds plausible and not in line with the Reich. Regardless, I will need to speak with your sister soon. And we will search the house. We will search your room. I assume you have no objections to us searching your room.'

'No,' Dido said. 'None. Just don't break anything please.'

It wasn't her room that worried her. It was Persey's. What had Persey done with the carbon copies of her shorthand notes? Had she destroyed them? All of them? Why oh why had she sat down-stairs waiting for Persey and Stefan to return instead of going upstairs and checking that everything was as it should be?

The soldier returned from the garden and shook his head. He had found nothing outside.

She had to think quickly. What could she do to stop them? What could she do to prevent them from searching upstairs? Nothing. There was nothing. They would look. And what if they found the notes. That was Persey done for, arrested and . . . then what? Good God, what would happen to her older sister? It didn't bear thinking about.

'You do know Captain Keller lives here, don't you?' she repeated, grasping at anything that might deter them.

'We do, yes,' the officer said.

She turned to lift the kettle from the range as it began singing and while she poured the water into the pot she began humming a tune, hoping to win them round in some way. She continued her song distractedly, her back to the officer as she stirred the leaves around the pot, thinking . . . thinking of anything she could do to stop them looking upstairs.

'What is that lovely tune?' the officer asked. 'I have heard you sing many times before. You have not sung that I do not believe. Will you sing a little more for me now?' Dido felt her chest tighten in panic. Oh good Lord, she wasn't supposed to know any new songs. She wasn't supposed to own a wireless in order to hear any.

'I just made it up. It doesn't have words to it yet,' she brushed him off.

'Hum it again.'

'I . . .'

'Again please,' he demanded.

She'd been singing a few bars of her latest favourite 'Love is a Song'. She'd heard it only a few weeks earlier and the radio announcer had spoken about it being from Walt Disney's newest film, *Bambi*. Dido couldn't wait for American films to be released again. She and Werner were sick to death of all this German propaganda they'd been sitting through at the Gaumont cinema and she wondered how many musical films she'd have to catch up with. That would be a treat worth waiting for. She hummed a little of the song for the officer now, forgetting on purpose the next bar and as for the rest she purposefully sang a little off key. She stopped suddenly, cleared her throat. 'Excuse me,' she said as she coughed.

'I know that tune,' the officer said.

'How can you?' Dido gave a tinkle of a laugh. 'I've just made it up,' she lied.

'No. You have not. I have heard it. It is a new tune.' He stood up. 'Where are you keeping it?' he asked quickly, rising from his position at the kitchen table and splaying his fingers out on the surface of the wood.

'Where am I keeping what?' she asked.

'Your wireless.'

There had been no need to worry about the wireless set. It was hidden. It was well hidden. There had been no need for the Germans to suspect they had one. And now she'd been so stupid.

'Nowhere. I don't have one. We handed it in.'

He looked at her. His voice was cold, hard, deadly. 'Tell me where it is.'

Inside the pantry. It was inside the pantry, hidden far back, so

358

far out of sight that you had to move all the tins and jars in order to find it and even then it was in a recessed area of the wall. But she would be damned if she gave it to him. It was her lifeline to the outside world, her only way to hear the latest music, to feed her soul with pure joy.

'If you don't tell me where it is, I will destroy everything in this house looking for it,' he warned.

'We don't have one,' Dido insisted.

'You are lying,' he said simply. 'You have a beautiful piano in the sitting room. I will start with that.'

'No,' she shouted. 'Not the piano. It was my mother's. Don't touch it. I thought you were looking for a person,' Dido wailed.

'I was. Now I am looking for a wireless. And I will work my way through this house inch by inch until I find it. I will destroy your room to find it. I will destroy your sister's. I will turn over every stick of furniture, I will pull up all the carpets, all the floor-boards until I find it. By the time I have finished with this house, it will be a shell. Unless you give it to me.'

Dido closed her eyes, unknowing how to accept this new horror. She couldn't let them find Persephone's notes, regardless as to whether they could read them. What would happen to Persey? She couldn't let them find them.

'And so we begin,' he said, adjusting his hat and setting off to search the house.

'No, stop,' she called to them. She had to save Persey. 'Stop. I'll give you the wireless.'

Chapter 39

2016

At the graves, Lucy pulled out her phone and opened her web browser. The empty search bar waited for an instruction she wasn't ready to give.

'There's too much that still doesn't make sense,' she said. 'There's more – I can feel it. Dido went somewhere. The vicar said it. I want to know where she went. And why. And when . . .'

Will leant forward.

The search bar taunted her, waiting for an instruction she wasn't ready to give.

'We could ask the vicar tomorrow,' Will suggested.

'I can't wait until tomorrow,' Lucy said.

'What is it you want to know?' he prompted.

She made a noise from the back of her throat. 'Ugh, I don't know.' She put her phone on the grass. It held all the answers. She just didn't know what the question was.

'You do know,' Will said. 'You just don't want to admit it.'

She wanted to make a cheap joke about not realising he was a therapist as well as a photographer. But instead, she said, 'Just because Dido was here at the end doesn't mean she was here all along. We never thought to search for her. The quiet sister. The one who didn't intrigue me. The one who lived here her whole life. The one who never married, never had children, the one who left Clara and I her house.'

Lucy knew now exactly what she was looking for. She opened the resistance archive online. The one they'd used to search for Persephone. She typed Dido Le Roy into the search bar on the website and waited. One result. A wave of cold and dread filled her. Over seventy years since it all happened and Lucy felt that if she didn't click that link . . . what she suspected wouldn't be true. That she could avoid finding out.

'I overlooked her. I cheated her out of her history.' Lucy took a deep breath, looked at the one single result that would tell her what had happened to the younger Le Roy sister in the middle of the Occupation. She hesitated and then when she could hesitate no longer, clicked on the result and waited for the page to open.

There she was, Dido Le Roy, arrested for illegal possession of a wireless in November 1943. Punishment: deportation and imprisonment to Ravensbrück concentration camp.

They were silent, Lucy put her hand over her mouth although she didn't realise she'd done it until it came time for her to speak. Lucy couldn't imagine that fate. She sighed. 'Of course she went to a concentration camp.'

It took Will a few seconds to answer. 'Why, of course?' he said, standing up next to her. He thrust his hands in his pockets and looked out across the churchyard, the late spring flowers in bloom, the breeze ruffling the trees that lined the grounds. 'She never said,' he whispered before exhaling deeply.

'Because of the poster,' Lucy said to his back. 'The poster asking victims of imprisonment in Nazi concentration camps to come forward to seek compensation. I thought it must have referred to Persephone. All this time, in the back of my mind I've been assuming it was Persephone who went. But it was Dido.'

Will didn't speak. He had known Dido. Not for long, but long enough to have struck up a sort of friendship, to have been welcomed into her home for tea and biscuits, to have helped around the property, to have been trusted. If Lucy reached up, touched his hand in comfort, would he want that? She had no idea so she chose not to.

They sat in the churchyard and as the evening grew cold Will looked down at Lucy. 'Come on,' he said sadly. 'We can't stay here all night. I think it's time for that drink.'

Chapter 40

A week later Lucy sat on the bench in the far end of the garden as the estate agent, thankfully not the one she'd had the awful date with, showed round the family of five that he'd mentioned were on his books and had been requesting a house this size for a long time. She'd intended to be gone from the house for the appointment, but was still putting the finishing touches to the rooms, fresh flowers in vases, Classic FM in the kitchen because it was playing lovely songs from old movies that felt quite atmospheric. She'd watched a video on how to dress a house for sale and had styled it with a smattering of home wares that wouldn't have looked out of place in a glossy homes magazine. As such, she'd missed her chance to leave and so had greeted the family and excused herself to let them have a better look around without her breathing down their necks.

She'd watched the husband hold hands with his wife and the three children run past their parents, almost pushing them over, laughing, teasing each other.

'I'm going to choose my room. You can't have the biggest. That will be Mummy and Daddy's. I get the second biggest because I'm older than you and . . .'

Lucy laughed as she heard them, two girls and a boy, breathing immediate, much-needed new life into Deux Tourelles.

The father half-scolded, 'We've not made an offer yet and they've

363

chosen their rooms already,' he said as the estate agent opened the back door and let the couple go out first. Lucy looked away, not wishing to embarrass.

Please buy the house, Lucy pleaded silently. *Please buy the house. You're just what this house needs.*

The woman looked around the garden. Lucy hadn't quite done everything she'd wanted to out here, but she'd pruned, taken all the cuttings away to compost and it was presentable enough. It would take someone more capable than her to bring it fully back to life. She caught the woman mouth to her husband, 'I love it.'

Lucy gave herself a silent pat on the back.

'So tell me the history of the house,' the husband asked the estate agent.

'First time it's come up for sale in three generations,' the estate agent said, launching into a spiel. 'Bought by the family in 1911 from the larger estate house nearby. This used to be the Dower House and . . .' They went out of earshot. That wasn't the real human history behind the house, but Lucy thought there were parts of this house's past even she would never know. And for those she did, it wasn't her story to tell.

Chapter 41

Clara, John and Molly arrived early with a bottle of Champagne the next day. As Lucy greeted them, John led Molly through the kitchen and into the walled garden at the back. It felt suspiciously as if John was keeping Molly out of earshot, leaving the sisters alone.

'So . . .' Clara started.

'So . . .' Lucy echoed, her shoulders slumping. She knew she was in for another earful but dutifully followed her older sister into the kitchen. She could sense something coming. And then, instead of waiting for it, Lucy steeled herself, looked Clara in the eye and asked, 'On the pier, that day, that argument. Why did you slap me? I couldn't believe it.'

'You hit a nerve,' Clara said simply.

'I got that.' Lucy folded her arms and waited but Clara was an expert at playing Lucy's game of stay silent and the other person will speak. Actually, Lucy was sure it had been Clara's game originally.

When the silence grew uncomfortable, Lucy asked, 'Is it because I mentioned you'd stayed behind and given up on life too soon?'

'No. It's not because of that. Can't you read between the lines?'

Lucy was lost. Already.

Clara continued. 'You said that from what you could see I didn't even like John and that I didn't need to marry him. You said other

365

awful things and you were right that I didn't need to marry him but I wanted to marry him because we were in love. We are in love. But not only that, we were also pregnant. And I was angry with you for so many things. Your words stung far too much and I just wanted you to stop bloody talking.' Clara looked at Lucy hard.

Throughout Clara's speech Lucy had turned cold. 'You were pregnant?' she whispered.

Clara nodded. 'And then I lost the baby.'

'Oh my God,' Lucy cried. Her hand flew to her mouth and she almost fell into a chair as she tried to sit down. 'I'm so sorry. How far along were you?' Lucy didn't know what was appropriate to ask and what wasn't.

'I wasn't at three months.'

Lucy couldn't speak at first and then: 'How awful.'

'Yes.'

'Why didn't you tell me?' Lucy repeated.

Clara lifted her eyebrows. 'It's not always about you, you know.'

'I know that. But I would have thought you'd have wanted to share that or to talk about it at some point. But you've never said anything. Ever.'

'I didn't want to talk about it. I wasn't ready to tell the world I was pregnant. It was too early. We hadn't had the scan. And then there was nothing to tell.'

Lucy shook her head in wonder. 'Clara, I'm so sorry.'

'Me too. I thought about the baby all the time. Whether it was a boy or a girl. What it might have looked like. And then I couldn't get pregnant for ages until Molly came along years later, bouncing and healthy and beautiful. We'd been trying for another recently and it hadn't been working out. We're so grateful for Molly but . . . anyway that's why John and I have been rowing a lot. Debating if we need IVF. Wondering if we could afford it. Wondering if it was worth the strain it would inevitably put on our marriage. That's why I've been snapping a bit more than usual. And it all built up. And then you said what you said and, well, I'm sorry,' Clara finished.

Lucy nodded. 'I don't really know what to say. I've never been through it so whatever I say won't be right, but I am sorry,' Lucy said. Why did her sister suddenly feel like a complete stranger? How did she not know one of the most awful things that had happened to her? In Lucy's eagerness to get away, to leave the island and her life behind, she had shed her family far too easily, stopped paying attention when it mattered, stopped being a sisterly shoulder to lean on. And look where it had got her. She and her sister had been so adrift from each other that Clara hadn't been able to share something so awful as being pregnant and miscarrying. Lucy hated herself. But it wasn't too late. They could fix this bond.

'I should never have slapped you. It was awful of me. Just awful. I just saw red,' Clara explained.

'It's all right.' Lucy leant forward and reached out to hold her sister's hand. Clara took it in hers and the two connected from opposing sides.

'It's not all right,' Clara said.

Lucy looked at the dining table, at the grooves marked into the fabric of the wood from God knew how many years of use.

'John and I are very much in love you know,' Clara volunteered. 'I didn't settle by marrying him and staying here. It was actually what I wanted. I know that was never the kind of thing you wanted and so you couldn't see what was right for me and how it differed to what was right for you. But I did.'

Lucy looked up. 'I know.'

'And John and I loved each other back then too. We got pregnant. We didn't need to get married. And then we weren't pregnant anymore but we still wanted to be together, to get married. We still do. So don't feel sorry for me, will you.'

Lucy stared at Clara. 'I don't feel sorry for you. I've never felt sorry for you. I admire you. You built a good life for yourself with someone you love. You have an amazing child. And you did it all right here. You haven't had to go in search of happiness. Happiness found you. I've never had that.' Lucy stopped suddenly.

'You've always chased the idea of a dream and then when you got it, you never quite liked it,' Clara said far too perceptively for Lucy's liking.

'Probably, yes. The things you said to me weren't exactly untrue. I realised that. But since I've been here, I've got better at not giving up on things, not taking the easy way out. I promise.'

'Good,' Clara said, 'because you are worth so much more and you can do so much more than you give yourself credit for.' Clara squeezed her sister's hand warmly for a moment and Lucy squeezed it back.

'Thank you,' Lucy said.

Clara looked at the stack of files. 'What's all this?'

Lucy had left the documents on the kitchen table, the photographs that Will had developed, the notice about the concentration camp, the shorthand documents and the transcriptions she and Will had worked on together that glorious night at his cottage, and the photograph of the four at the beach in 1930 before war brought them all together and then tore them apart.

'It's the story of what happened to Dido and Persephone in the war. Will and I have filled in most of the blanks,' Lucy started and then filled her sister in on what they'd discovered. 'There are some things I don't think we'll ever know . . . such as what happened to Dido after she returned from the camp . . . if she ever found happiness. I hope so but I'm not sure we'll ever know. But we do know what happened to Persephone.'

Outside, John and Molly played football and inside, Clara and Lucy held the photograph of the four on the beach taken before war changed their lives and wrenched them apart. 'It makes sense we never even knew about Persephone's existence, because she was gone so much earlier.'

'Persephone died together with the man she loved, doing an incredible thing,' Lucy said. 'Saving people.'

Clara sighed. 'I'd have done the same for you.'

Lucy nodded. 'I know you would. And so would I. In a heartbeat.'

'We're so lucky we don't have to face things like this,' Clara said. 'We're so lucky our daily challenges are nothing compared to this.' She reached out and held her sister's hand again and the two girls smiled at each other.

'I do love you, you know,' Clara said.

'I know. And I love you too,' Lucy replied.

They were interrupted by the sound of the knocker on the door being lifted and dropped. Lucy went to open it and was confronted with Will, clutching a bottle of Champagne.

He kissed her on the cheek. Something he'd never done before. His face being against hers, the slight brush of his evening stubble on her cheek felt so alien and so entirely, wonderfully normal.

'Congratulations on the house sale,' he said, pulling away and handing her the chilled bottle, beads of condensation running down it.

She could only nod as they walked towards the kitchen.

Clara greeted Will. 'That's two bottles of Champagne now. It's officially a party.'

Will kissed Clara on the cheek and then waved at John and Molly through the kitchen window. The two came in from outside.

'Are we opening this Champagne or what?' John asked. 'Fancy them getting an offer so soon,' he said as he shook hands with Will.

'Some things are just meant to be,' Lucy said, fetching flutes from the cupboard as Will eased the cork from a bottle and began pouring for everyone. 'I really liked the buyers,' she said. 'They're the perfect family for this house – I'm sure of it.'

They clinked glasses, Molly joining in with a Champagne flute full of lemonade but Clara didn't take a sip of hers, instead putting her glass down. Lucy didn't miss that.

'So what will you do now?' Clara asked. 'Deux Tourelles is sold. The antiques dealer is booked to appraise the furniture. It's a case of packing up things like this now,' she said, pointing to the Champagne glasses, 'and sending them to the charity shop.'

'Won't take five minutes,' Lucy said. 'And then I'm surplus to requirements.'

'Not to me,' Clara said, kissing her sister on the cheek.

'Nor me,' Will said. John and Clara gave each other a wide-eyed knowing look as Lucy looked into her glass, avoiding everyone's gaze.

They sipped their Champagne, talking about property prices on the island that could see a family of five laying down millions for a house like Deux Tourelles.

'I'm in the wrong job,' Will said, shaking his head.

'And me,' John agreed.

'I don't really have one at all now,' Lucy admitted.

'What?' Clara asked.

'I'm not taking on any more work.'

'Why?' Clara asked in horror.

'Because I need that push; that fear to do something else, something I actually care about, something I'm actually interested in, instead of . . .'

'Coasting?' Clara finished Lucy's sentence for her.

Lucy smiled. 'Yes, thank you. Coasting.'

'What are you going to do now?' Clara asked. 'Although actually it's not as if you're going to struggle for cash when this place sells.'

'I know,' Lucy said. 'Although I do actually have a plan.' She pulled out the leaflet about gardening courses that she'd found when it had fallen out of her new gardening book. 'Don't laugh, but I really enjoyed doing this house up, but not as much as I enjoyed every single minute I spent out in the garden. I want to learn how to do it properly. I'm not sure where that will lead in the long run but for now . . . there's this,' she said, tapping the leaflet. 'And I know I'll enjoy learning new things, applying it practically.'

'Here?' Clara said.

Lucy looked at Will quickly but his face was unreadable. She looked back at Clara, 'Well, it's online mainly, distance learning, so I'm not sure where yet,' she flustered. 'But I'll have to find somewhere to do some practical work. Perhaps Guernsey for a while. I'll be around a bit more for Molly until the house sells anyway and then who knows. Maybe a little flat here with a sea view?' Lucy suggested.

'Maybe a large flat here with a sea view,' John suggested wagging his eyebrows. 'Thanks to Dido.'

'Perhaps,' Lucy said with a laugh. She sipped her Champagne and looked over at Will who was smiling at her. He raised his glass and she raised hers.

'To Persephone and Dido,' Lucy said, and the others echoed it.

A moment's silence descended and Lucy glanced over at the picture of the two sisters on the beach, flanked by the two boys.

John looked at his watch. 'Agh, Molly's swimming lesson,' he said.

'Right, come on, let's go. Sorry to be short and sweet,' Clara said.

As John ushered Molly out the door to protests that she didn't want to go swimming tonight, Lucy hugged Clara by the front door.

'Anything else you want to tell me?' Lucy whispered into her sister's ear, referring to Clara's untouched Champagne.

'No,' Clara said, pulling back from the hug and looking at her sister with a smile. 'Not yet, I don't. I only took a pregnancy test yesterday. Actually, I did three tests, just to be sure. It's amazing but it's incredibly early days. Whatever happens, I promise to keep you informed.'

'OK,' Lucy said and a huge smile spread across her face as her family climbed in the car and left the gates of Deux Tourelles.

That decided it. She wanted to be here to support Clara, which meant she'd definitely be here for the foreseeable future. And then . . . well, she'd take it all as it came. Her friends could always come and visit her in Guernsey. It wasn't that far.

Will was in the kitchen, washing out John and Molly's glasses and putting them on the drainer.

'You're well trained,' Lucy teased.

'That one's full,' he said pointing to Clara's. 'If you want it? Seemed a shame to chuck it down the sink.'

Lucy took Clara's glass and held it. It was now or never. 'I really like having you around . . . as a friend,' she said tentatively. 'Thank you for being with me, closing the chapter on Dido and Persephone. And this house. It's meant so much to me that you've come round to help paint and fix it up a bit and, well, even though the outcome wasn't what we intended, I'm glad we found out what had happened to them all.'

'It was a complicated time. They were good people who did great things,' Will said.

'They were,' Lucy replied, sipping Clara's Champagne.

'You said before that you hoped Dido had found some happiness and I do think she did,' Will offered. 'She was intensely private for those last months I knew her but she struck me as someone who had lived, who had seen the whole spectrum of life. Not just the bad. Does that make sense?'

Lucy nodded. 'It does. I hope so anyway. I think I'll pop back one day soon and talk to the vicar about Dido in the years immediately after the war, see if he knows a bit more than he's letting on.'

Will nodded. 'There was such a long time from the end of the war until her passing. A full life, lived – that's what I feel she had.'

'I like to think that's true,' Lucy said, smiling. 'I didn't know her but I like to think there was some moment of happiness available to her and no matter the consequences that she reached out and snapped it up.'

Will took his glass from the table and raised it before sipping and looking thoughtfully at Lucy.

A silent moment descended.

'Is that what you think everyone should do, grab that moment of happiness when it presents itself?' Will asked.

'I do. Yes.'

He looked thoughtful, as if steeling himself for something. 'OK,' he started and then coughed nervously. 'You mentioned about us being friends.'

'Yes?' Lucy asked warily and then sipped her Champagne only to mask her face.

'I don't want to be friends with you.'

'What?' Lucy coughed Champagne.

'My intentions towards you are not friendly,' he said and then looked up to the ceiling as if he'd realised that sounded strange.

'That is either the creepiest thing anyone has ever said to me, or by far the sexiest,' Lucy said.

Will laughed. 'That came out wrong. I mean, I don't want to just be friends. I would like to date you. Oh God, why do I sound like this? What's happening?'

She suppressed a smile, deciding to save him. 'Will—'

But he leapt back into the conversation. 'OK,' he said, cutting her off. 'This has gone wrong. I'm just going to do what I should have done the night we had dinner at my house. I don't know why I didn't do it then and I don't know why I didn't do it at your front door when I walked you home. And now, we're here, weeks later, having this weird conversation, And I've still not done it. This is my fault, I admit that, I missed the opportunity.'

And then before she knew it, he walked towards her, took the Champagne glass from her hands, placed it on the table and kissed her.

'I'm happier right now than I've been in such a long time,' Lucy admitted as they walked into the garden to the bench that Lucy had painted a glorious shade of racing green. 'I just think it took until now for me to realise it.'

'Me too,' Will said.

Both Dido and Persephone had lost so much during the Occupation. Their freedom had been taken, Dido had been imprisoned, but Persephone's sacrifice had ultimately been her life, dying when others had lived. And by helping two people escape, it had eventually resulted in Will being born, in Will being here, in Guernsey. He threaded his fingers through hers, lifted her hand to his lips and kissed it gently.

They looked back at Deux Tourelles bathed in the last of the evening sunlight. It would be a happy house again, filled with children and a family. Deprived of her sister for so long, Dido's legacy had been to bring Lucy back to Guernsey, to bridge the divide that had formed between Lucy and Clara and bequeathing them this house. The house deserved a new start, to be lived in loudly, joyously and to once again be a family home.

Lucy rested her head against Will, moving calmly with the rise and fall of his breathing. She thought of Dido and prayed that she had not always been alone. That at some point she had found love. She thought of Persephone and Stefan, their relationship cut so tragically short, here on this island, a love that had ended too soon, lives that had ended too young.

Lucy looked up at Will, lifted her head and kissed him. A new start. As they watched the sun dip behind the house Lucy knew that if there was a chance of happiness to be had, no matter how fleeting it may be, she had to reach out and take it.

Epilogue

To my darling Dido,

*I do not know if this letter will reach you. I am guessing
your address from what you mentioned to me six years ago.
There cannot be more than one house on your beautiful
island with a name such as Deux Tourelles. Do you like the
description I added for your postman on the envelope? 'It is
a large house with two turrets, surrounded by trees, near
the airport.' I remembered how you described it to me. With
a note like that, this letter cannot fail to reach you. I think.
I hope.*

*Will you excuse my bad English the way you used to? It
has been a long time since I have written in English.*

*I write to you now because after you were sent away
from me I did not immediately know what had happened
to you or where you had gone. When you did not meet me
as usual I admit I took it personally and believed it was
something I had done wrong. Even though the previous
week I had told you I loved you and you had told me you
loved me. I worried. Did you perhaps regret saying it afterwards? Long after, I found out that you had been sent to*

*the continent to a prison for hiding a wireless and I hated
myself for sulking when I should have been fighting for you.
I was too late.*

*I too have been in a prison. The last time I saw
Guernsey I was standing in line, boarding a boat to take
me to a POW camp. The British soldiers were very kind.
Would you believe me if I told you that was the first time I
had seen an enemy soldier? I had been in a lucky war
where I had not fired a single bullet and no one had fired
one at me, but in the end, like the rest of the population of
Guernsey, we Germans were dying of malnutrition and
starvation. To be taken prisoner and to be fed was a relief.
But through it all I thought of you.*

*I was released in 1947 and I had the choice to stay in
England or to return to Germany. I confess to you that I
did not like England as much I liked being in the Channel
Islands, but knowing a German would not be welcome back
so soon on the island that we had just occupied, instead of
coming to find you and risk endangering you to the same
kind of treatment you received when we were seen out
together before, I returned home to Germany to help my
father on the farm. He was alone and it was too much for
him to do by himself. He was distraught. My older brother
who I spoke to you about did not return home. He died on
the Eastern front.*

*My sister and her husband lost their home during a raid
and now they live with us. They help on the farm and so I
am able to leave for a time. Although it has been so long
and you may not want to see me again. You may not love
me anymore. It has been so long and war changes
everything, but so does peacetime. So I ask, may I visit you
for a short while? Has it been too long? I will post this now
with a smile on my face and my fingers crossed that it
reaches you and that you forgive me for taking until now to*

376

*write. I have thought of nothing but you and you may not
feel the same but I must take the risk.*

　　Yours now as I was then,
　　Werner xx

Letter from Dido to Werner Graf's parents, summer 1950

Dear Mr and Mrs Graf,

　　*Werner says I should call you mother and father in this
letter, but I'm sure you'll appreciate that might be a little
strange as we have, as yet, not met. Although he's spoken to
me about you so often I feel I know you so well.*

　　*I hope to meet you, and Werner's sister Marta, this
summer when we visit you as part of our honeymoon.*

　　*I think he has already written to you to tell you that we
are now engaged. We cannot tell anyone here we intend to
marry for what I hope are obvious reasons. (Werner has
been pretending he's Swiss the entire time he's been here. I'm
not entirely sure people believe him.) So we may go over to
the English mainland to marry in secret so no one here will
know. And no one here can judge. I believe they think he's
just the gardener! A fib that we may keep up with much
longer than originally intended to keep us both out of reach
of prying enquiries.*

　　*While we are in England we intend to visit my friends
Jack and Lise for a time. Our housekeeper, Jack's mother, is
overjoyed at the thought of seeing Jack again. She no longer
likes boats and has already switched allegiance from me
and asked Werner if he'll hold her hand on the crossing this
time. Werner has also suggested the idea of marrying in
Germany. I'm not sure when or where we'll marry. For now
we are very happy just as we are. I'm not very good at
sorting paperwork. Neither is he, by all accounts. But we
are very good at being in love and I think, for us, that's*

enough. War here has changed everything and while it's not the done thing to live with a man and be unmarried, it's also not the done thing to be in love with a German so soon after the Occupation. I feel the rest of the world may have to modernise around us.

I cannot tell you how much I love your kind, considerate, caring son. He has been a balm in my world, which has been turned upside down even more so since his surprise arrival at my front door last summer. He professed he had written a letter to ask me if he could visit and when I did not reply to confirm that I wanted to see him, he waited for a while and then came anyway.

In a way, I'm glad I never received the letter. When he turned up at my door it was the best surprise I'd ever had and I cried. (I'd just been weeding the hateful vegetable patch and am sure I looked a fright although Werner says not.) But also it's a shame his letter went astray as he says he's not one for letters so I might not get another from him.

Never mind, I have something better, I have him. And for that I feel I must apologise to you because I don't think you intended for your son to disappear for such a long period of time with a girl from an island so far away. But I promise, as long as we are together we will look after each other and love each other and try to visit you as often as we can. I don't have any family left, you see, so I'm looking forward to meeting you and Werner's sister.

Werner is hovering over my shoulder and says he's going to have to write my letter out in German for you, which is prompting me to pop into St Peter Port tomorrow to buy a German phrase book. The next time I write to you, I shall attempt it in your native tongue.

He's trying, unsuccessfully, to teach me and I have hours of fun teasing him by getting my Der, Die and Das completely the wrong way round until we fall into fits of giggles. If we are all to meet one day soon I had better brush up, hadn't I?

That's it from me for now. Werner sends his love but he can write that much more eloquently when he translates this for you in a moment.

While he gets to work, I'm going off to make supper for us all. It's such a beautiful evening here in Guernsey and tonight I think Werner, Mrs Grant and I will eat with the doors thrown open and the last of the day's sun streaming into the kitchen to warm us.

With love, until we meet,
Dido
x

Author Note

It was in the summer holidays after I had just completed my GCSE exams that I found out the Channel Islands had been occupied by the Nazis during World War Two. In amongst my dad's books, that summer I found a battered early copy of Charles Cruickshank's *The German Occupation of the Channel Islands*. I opened it and read it there and then, cross-legged on the floor in front of the bookshelves.

I remember that feeling of utter confusion at having 'discovered' this strange history. I was getting ready to study A-Level History, amongst other subjects, but I had never once heard about this before, let alone studied it. It was a subject never once touched on in any history syllabus I encountered and that's a crying shame.

The Nazi Occupation of the Channel Islands was, and still is, one of those pieces of history that struck me as being so incredibly otherworldly, so utterly unlikely that it has stuck with me ever since. Hitler's army marched into British soil and stayed there for five long years. The Nazis were so close to mainland Britain, and yet as it turned out, thankfully, so far.

All of the historical events I wove into *The Girl from the Island* happened. I took real history and threaded it into my characters' lives. Spies were sent from mainland Britain to carry out reconnaissance missions. Some of them were successful, some of them not. The two Islanders who were sent back to occupied Guernsey in the opening months of the war in the novel and who handed themselves in when realising they had been stranded . . . did do just that in real life. Second Lieutenants Philip Martel and Desmond Mulholland were sent as a forward party in advance of a planned commando raid but instead of being picked up, they became prisoners of war.

Thousands of Brits across the Channel Islands who were not island-born were indeed deported and saw out the rest of their war in internment camps such as Laufen and Biberach in Germany.

An underground newsletter was developed for covert circulation around the island after radios were confiscated in 1942 and it is to this that I had Persey contribute. *Guernsey Underground News Service* was passed secretly to Islanders in desperate need of real news. Ernest Legg, Joseph Gillingham, Charles Machon, Cecil Duquemin and Frank Falla were the orchestrators of this alongside Gillingham's wife Henrietta who listened to the news, wrote it in carbon copy and handed copies to the men to print. The men were betrayed, caught and sent to prisons across occupied Europe where Joseph Gillingham and Charles Machon died.

Frank Falla went on to spearhead the right to gain compensation from the West German government for Channel Islanders who had been imprisoned in concentration camps by the Nazi regime and for those who had died there, their families were given the right to claim on behalf of deceased loved ones.

Horrifically, thousands of men and boys from around conquered, occupied Europe were sent as slave workers to reinforce Hitler's island fortresses across the Channel Islands as part of the Atlantic Wall. Even more sobering, Alderney was used as a concentration camp. Remnants of it can still be seen on this otherwise peaceful patch of British soil.

Jewish civilians did indeed find themselves caught in the Channel Islands – unable to evacuate to mainland Britain because some were nationals from countries with which Britain was at war. And sadly, some were eventually rounded up and transported to places such as Auschwitz where they were murdered.

Some Islanders did inform on people they knew and more often than not it was anonymous and self-righteous, rather than for any personal gain with the occupying force. One such instance of informing that had horrific consequences and on which, in part, I based Dido's fate was that of a Jersey civilian, Louisa Gould, who sheltered an escaped Soviet slave worker and who kept her wireless set. After having been informed upon, Louisa Gould was arrested just before the D-Day invasion in 1944, and then, when the Allies were on their way to begin liberating the camps – was transferred to Ravensbrück and executed. Although I could not give Dido that ending.

One of the parts of this history that really struck me, and which I decided not to cover in the novel for various timeline issues, was that in June 1944 Channel Islanders who looked to the skies would have seen thousands of Allied Bombers overhead, making their way to mainland Europe to begin the long hoped-for liberating invasion. But the Channel Islands were not deemed a strategic Allied gain and were left until last to be liberated. The Allies passed over them by plane, and round them by boat. During this time the islands were, simply, cut off and the Islanders had to continue co-existing with an occupying force that knew the game was up.

No food was transported in from mainland Europe because the Germans had been forced back. Likewise, mainland Britain sent nothing in a bid to starve the Nazis out. It was only the arrival of the Red Cross ship the SS *Vega*, bringing much-needed supplies that stopped the Channel Islanders from suffering total starvation. And then, almost an entire year after the D-Day landings, the Channel Islands were finally liberated in May 1945.

Until 2015, unbelievably, there was no memorial in Guernsey to civilians who had carried out acts of resistance against the Nazis and who had perished in concentration camps. Prior to this, memorials had been unveiled to the near thousand deported from Guernsey and Sark as part of the deportation order, to the evacuees who left before the war started and, among other memorials, one was unveiled to the three Jewish women who were taken from Guernsey and who perished in Auschwitz.

This book is, in part, dedicated to all the Channel Islanders who suffered and died at the hands of the Nazis. It is also dedicated to the twenty-one Jersey residents and the nine from Guernsey who defied the Nazis through acts of incredible resistance during the Occupation and who were arrested, deported to prisons and concentration camps and who never returned home.

A note about research

I started researching *The Girl from the Island* in 2018 when I visited Guernsey. Although back then I didn't know that the notes and photos I'd taken of the landscape and the museums as an avid tourist would help inform a novel a few years later. I knew one day, maybe, I'd write about the Nazi Occupation of the Channel Islands. But at that time I was too busy finishing *The Forgotten Village* and planning *The Forbidden Promise,* and couldn't clone myself to plan another novel at the same time.

And so in 2019 I went to Jersey on a family holiday and it filled the creative well even more. Tentatively, I started writing a book that would eventually become *The Girl from the Island.* But I knew that as wonderful and historically rich as Jersey was, it was Guernsey that I needed to set the novel. I needed to go back. I needed to immerse myself fully in the island now the novel was taking shape in my mind.

I booked flights and a hotel for a week, prepared to palm my children off onto their grandparents. And then the world became a very strange place to live. Britain and the Channel Islands entered lockdown. At the time of writing this note, at the end of September 2020, I've had to admit a trip to Guernsey, after six months of hoping, isn't going to happen any time soon. Guernsey was one of the first locations to beat Covid 19 and to protect its people closed its borders to any country that hadn't managed to do the

384

same. When Guernsey eventually reopened, a complicated period of quarantine meant I couldn't leave my family for the two weeks required to quarantine on the island before starting my few days of touring.

While my historical research was conducted both on location in 2018 and through a wide range of resources since then, geographically-speaking I've spent a lot of time researching on Google maps, clicking and dragging my way through the streets and country lanes I couldn't quite remember from years ago, reacquainting myself with the glorious landscape through the medium of the Internet. So because of this, and because of the events of 2020, I hope you can forgive any inaccuracies you may find.

Acknowledgements

Once again I am the luckiest of authors in that I have two wonderful editors to thank for this novel. For the help and the shaping of my initial ideas for *The Girl from the Island* and for the first (always necessarily brutal and well-honed) structural edits I must thank the wonderful Tilda McDonald. She helped grow the seed for the novel with me, invested so much of her knowledge into that first round of edits and then handed it over to the magnificent Rachel Faulkner-Willcocks who took it so meticulously towards the finishing line. Both of you, in the midst of that global event that I don't think anyone ever wants to mention ever again, were wonderful.

The whole team at my publishers Avon do know how to make a gal feel looked after and appreciated and to everyone in every department who has to think about my books, look at them, design them, promote them, sell them and all the background technical stuff I don't know about . . . thank you. Also big hugs and thanks to Ellie Pilcher, Sabah Khan and copy editor extraordinaire Helena Newton.

Mega thanks to my fabulous super-agent Becky Ritchie. You are proof that not all superheroes wear capes. Just the most wonderful sounding board; always cool, calm, collected and an ace dispenser of wisdom, especially when I send a regular and recurring email usually containing the words, 'So, I've had this idea . . .' Huge thanks to you and the wonderful foreign rights team at A.M. Heath who fight the good fight around the world.

Away from 'the day job', I must thank my gorgeous husband Steve and my two girls Emily and Alice. You deserve unending praise for surviving those non-stop months when I disappear inside my laptop and it must feel like you're practically a single-parent family for a good portion of that time. I am at my most useless at almost every stage of getting a book out into the world but you are all so encouraging and supportive and tell me so often how proud you are of me that I hope I am forgiven. Likewise to Mum and Dad, Rosemary and Colin . . . all the kid-sitting is invaluable. Thank you.

The Romantic Novelists' Association always holds a special place in my heart and to the association as a whole and the many friends I've found there including those in our breakaway faction Write Club . . . thanks for everything. A ginormous thanks especially to my talented writer friend Sue Lovett, the most amazing first reader, whose ideas on the manuscript were invaluable and pinpoint accurate.

And finally the biggest thanks of all goes to you, the reader. Thank you for buying or listening to *The Girl from the Island* or borrowing it from your library. I cannot tell you how much it means to know readers are out there, across the world reading something I wrote. This feeling will never grow old. And so I send you a huge thank you. If you enjoyed it, it would be so wonderful if you could leave an Amazon and/or Goodreads review for *The Girl from the Island*. It helps new readers find our work, keeps me smiling and spurs me on when writing has come to a grinding halt.

I absolutely love hearing from readers and there's no happier procrastination for me than chatting about forgotten pieces of history and about writing, or giving and receiving book recommendations and sharing on social media pictures of our bookshelves, gardens, views from our windows . . . oh, the list is endless. Find me online and say hi!

www.lornacookauthor.com
Facebook: /LornaCookWriter
Instagram: /LornaCookAuthor
Twitter: /LornaCookAuthor

Further Reading

No work of fiction that harnesses fact can be written without research and for further reading I happily recommend these resources and thank the authors for providing me with hours of wonderful research time through their brilliant works:

www.frankfallaarchive.org – a true treasure trove of information spearheaded by Dr Gilly Carr and using original resources provided by the *Guernsey Underground News Service* writer Frank Falla

Life in Occupied Guernsey, The Diaries of Ruth Ozanne 1940–1945, edited by William Parker, Amberley, 2011

When the Germans Came, by Duncan Barrett, Simon & Schuster, 2018

The German Occupation of the Channel Islands, Charles Cruickshank, The Guernsey Press, 1975

Jersey Occupation Diary, Nan Le Ruez, Seaflower Books, 1994

Protest, Defiance and Resistance in the Channel Islands, by Gilly Carr, Paul Sanders and Louise Willmot, Bloomsbury, 2014

I also want to put a special shout-out to one of the best museums I've ever been to: The German Occupation Museum at Les Houards, Forest, Guernsey. It's a real treasure trove of Occupation history complete with a mock-up Guernsey street during WW2. If you visit Guernsey, I encourage you to spend a few hours at this fantastic, independently run museum. It's about five minutes' walk from the airport. You won't regret it.

Don't miss Lorna Cook's #1 bestselling debut

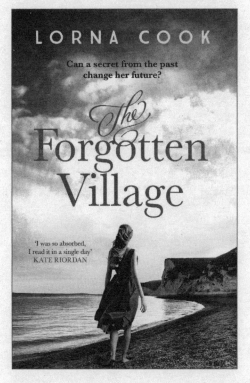

1943. The world is at war, and the villagers of Tyneham must leave their homes behind.

2018. A wartime photograph prompts a visitor to Tyneham to unravel the terrible truth behind one woman's disappearance . . .

Can one promise change the fate of two women decades apart?

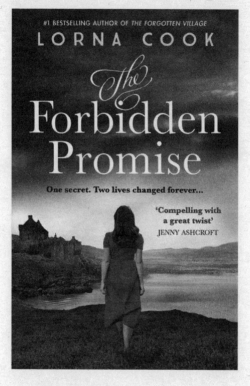

1940. When Constance sees a Spitfire crash into her family's loch, she makes a vow that could cost her everything.

2020. Kate discovers Invermoray House has a dark secret, and she can't leave until Constance's mystery is solved.

Available now